"You," the earl said evenly, "need to be locked up again."

Glenys seized the hand he extended and lurched to her feet. He pulled her close, and despite that mist, she could see his eyes flaming with reproof.

"What the devil are you doing here, Miss Shea? Men have lost their way on these moors and paid for their carelessness with their lives."

"I don't doubt it," she said with genuine penitence. "But there wasn't a hint of fog when I set out. And I thought I saw you, so I followed because—"

"Never mind that. A storm is blowing in. We need to get off the high ground." Turning, he pulled his shirt from his breeches. "Take hold of this and hang on. Try to step where I do. You've wandered into the deadliest of bogs."

She grabbed a handful of soft linen, put one foot in front of the other as Ash led the way, and marveled that he knew where to go. Although she was clinging to his shirt, the earl was no more than a vague shadow in front of her.

Books by Lynn Kerstan:

Raven's Bride
Lady In Blue

Published by HarperPaperbacks

Harper
Monogram

Raven's Bride

⚜ LYNN KERSTAN ⚜

HarperPaperbacks
A Division of HarperCollinsPublishers

For St. Joseph

HarperPaperbacks   *A Division of* HarperCollins*Publishers*
10 East 53rd Street, New York, N.Y. 10022

Cover illustration by Bob Berran

First printing: May 1996

Printed in the United States of America

HarperPaperbacks, HarperMonogram, and colophon are
trademarks of HarperCollins*Publishers*

❖ 10 9 8 7 6 5 4 3 2 1

1

England, 1822

Mist lapped at the foot of the crags, eerie in the dim light of the swaying lanterns as the coach rumbled into the High Peaks. Menace lurked within each copse of scraggly oak, from behind every lurching outcrop of black rock.

Ashton Cordell, Earl of Ravensby, checked, again, the small pistol concealed in a sling above his wrist. Oiled, primed, ready to fire. His eyes burned and his neck ached from the strain of watching the road.

With a sigh, he leaned against the padded leather squabs and told himself to relax. But caution had become habitual. Or compulsive, he thought with a humorless smile.

For years, he had never traveled without at least four armed outriders. Now, he was protected only by the coachman and Big Charlie, whose wits were uncertain at best. And stealth, he reminded himself. No one knew he would be on this road tonight, and Ravenrook was less than two hours away.

Ravenrook. Home in the clifftop aerie, he would be safe. His eyes drifted shut. Perhaps he could sleep for a while.

He was dreaming about Ellen when the coach shuddered to a halt.

"Stand and deliver," yelled a rough voice. A spate of coughing followed the pronouncement.

Groggy, Ash fumbled under the seat for the primed set of pistols concealed there. Before he could reach them, a face appeared at the window.

"Outside, your lordship," said the highwayman in a raspy voice. "Hands in the air. I got you in my sights, so don't make any move I don't like or I'll plug you."

Ash stepped to the ground, hands slightly raised. The shifting light revealed only a tall thin man holding two guns. One was leveled at his chest. The other pointed toward the driver's seat where John Fletcher and Charlie poised, arms uplifted. The highwayman was careful to hold back, all targets in his sights.

Then Ash saw a smaller man some distance away, holding a pistol between both hands. He waved it back and forth, between the two men atop the carriage and the man he had come to kill.

Nervous, Ash decided. The weak link. But why didn't they just shoot? One bullet for him, two in reserve for the driver and Charlie. They must be amateurs. Trained assassins would have finished the job and been gone by now.

"Your money, milord," said the rough-voiced man. When he bent his head and coughed, the smaller man moved forward as if to protect him. "Toss everything you got on the ground, including rings and watch and whatnots. But no sudden moves or I'll pull the trigger."

Ash stared at him, dumbfounded. Could this be a robbery after all? But no highwayman with a jot of intelligence would be waiting on this desolate byway for a victim.

And the man had said "your lordship." Without question, they were expecting the Earl of Ravensby.

"Don't try my patience," the highwayman warned. Again, more coughing and another move forward by his accomplice.

Suddenly Charlie bent over. The robber swung toward him, both pistols raised.

Without conscious thought Ash dropped his right arm and flicked his wrist. The concealed gun fell into his hand and he fired at the same moment the highwayman did.

The robber groped at his chest and the other pistol went off, sending a bullet harmlessly into the air. He pitched over, hands and feet quivering.

Ash dove for the ground just as the second man fired. A bullet whizzed by his head.

For a moment there was silence. Then Charlie, with a war whoop, swung down from the coach, his gun pointed toward the man who stood frozen with the pistol between both hands, aimed at where Ash had been.

A few yards away, the other man lay still.

"Papa!" cried the accomplice in a high thin voice. Dropping his pistol, he rushed to the limp body and huddled over it. "Oh, Papa."

Ash came to his feet and moved forward, pausing a short distance from the astonishing tableau.

Two eyes, golden in the dim light, lifted to his. "You k-killed my father."

Ash felt ice at his fingertips.

"Damn you to hell! You had no right. He never meant to hurt anyone."

By now Ash was sure it was a boy, not a man. He

was smooth-cheeked and painfully slim in ill-fitting trousers and shirt, with a woolen cape over his shoulders and a floppy hat on his head.

Ash glanced briefly at the dead man and at the pistols clutched in his gaunt hands, forefingers still pressing the triggers.

Blood pounded at Ash's temples. He had been careless. Charlie and the driver might be dead by now, and the bullet from the boy's gun had nearly cut him down.

Charlie moved toward the boy, but Ash heard sobs and gestured him away. A son should be allowed to mourn his father, even if the man deserved to die.

"Were you hit?" he asked, relieved when Charlie shook his head. "Then stay here, and make sure that one"—he pointed to the boy—"doesn't get away. We'll send a wagon to pick you up. Bring him to me when you get to Ravenrook."

Golden eyes fixed on him. "Killer!" The boy spat in his direction. "Bloody killer!"

Ash turned away. Why should he be held accountable for the death of a man who clearly intended to murder him? But his hands were shaking as he climbed into the coach. He hated violence, although he had lived with it for what seemed like forever.

Whoever was responsible would pay for this night, he vowed to himself. Someone had hired these pathetic highwaymen, and the boy would know his identity.

When he arrived at Ravenrook, Ash went immediately to the library and poured himself a hefty shot of brandy. He drank it and then another, sensing the onset of a crippling headache.

Now and again drinking helped him to sleep, if he swallowed enough, in time. Since a bullet creased his scalp in Hyde Park five years ago, the headache came often and with little warning, bringing nausea and agony beyond endurance.

But he always recovered, with only the vague memory of time lost and excruciating pain. Once in a while the brandy was stronger than the headache, and he badly hoped it worked tonight. He needed answers, and at last he had found someone who could supply them.

In spite of the brandy, pain swept over him in waves. Two hours later he could barely see the door when he responded to a thunderous knock.

Big Charlie stepped inside, intelligence shining in his eyes. His wits came and went since Waterloo, when shrapnel had pierced his skull. "There was two horses tethered near to where we was attacked. They're in the stables now. Sad beasties, in need of a good feeding. We put the body in the icehouse. Will you be wanting to send word to the constable?"

Ash rubbed his temples. "Yes, but not until I've questioned the boy. And I can't do that tonight. Lock him in the cellar."

"He ain't what he looks like, milord." Charlie shuffled uneasily. "Fact is, he's a girl."

There was a long silence, and then Ash swore long and loud. "Are you sure?"

"Got tits." Charlie's voiced cracked. "Came upon 'em when I searched for weapons."

A girl! Ash regathered his concentration. "In that case, we can't use the cellars. Lock her in a room upstairs, make sure a footman is posted outside, and see that she's fed. I'll deal with her tomorrow."

"As you say, milord." Charlie shambled to the door and turned again, a despondent look on his face. "Mighty upset, she was. He was her father. The man you killed."

Ash winced. "Yes. I thought he was about to fire at you."

"So he did." Charlie stared gloomily at the floor. "I shouldn't have made a move. It was stupid of me. Sometimes I'm so bloody stupid."

Ash crossed the room and took his hand. "You were trying to protect me, and chances are they'd have shot us all if we hadn't fought back. This is a damnable mess, but I will take the consequences."

Charlie raised his head. "I didn't mind what happened until I knew it was a girl. She cried all the way here."

"I should have brought her back in the coach instead of leaving you to deal with her. Well, see that she is made comfortable, Charlie. That's all we can do for now. And remember, you are not to blame."

"Nor you, milord." With a vague wave of his hand, Charlie withdrew.

Ash made his way to a chair, head throbbing. Devil take it, a girl! It was almost absurd. The assassin had scraped the bottom of the barrel when he hired a sickly highwayman and his daughter to keep watch on the isolated road to Ravenrook.

As the room began to spin, he wondered how he would convince the girl to give up her secrets. Dear God, he had killed her father. How she must hate him.

2

Glenys Shea studied the packed dirt beneath her window, recalculating the distance to the ground.

It had not moved any closer.

The rope she had braided from the bedsheets and blankets wouldn't reach nearly that far. She would have to tear down the curtains. But a servant was apt to notice bare windows, so she could do nothing more until her supper tray was removed.

With luck, the same maid who had served all her meals would come back for the tray. Prudence was young, softhearted, and not terribly bright. When she saw a dejected woman huddled on the bed, begging to be left alone, she'd tell the other servants to keep their distance.

Mad Jack Shea would have been pleased to see his daughter taking action instead of moping, but that didn't stop her from feeling guilty. Poor Papa. Better if he'd been cut down at Salamanca or Vitoria—remembered as a war hero instead of a criminal.

She wiped a tear from her cheek, angry because she'd promised herself not to cry again until she was free. On tiptoe, she crossed the room and pressed her ear against the door. After a while she heard a man clear his throat. The guard, posted in the hall when she was hustled upstairs, still blocked her way. It was out the window or face the hangman.

At the sound of footsteps in the hall, she hurried to the bed and flung herself on the counterpane. There was a light knock at the door before it opened.

"I'll be takin' your tray now, miss. Would you be wantin' anything else?"

Glenys emitted blubbering noises.

Instead of withdrawing, Prudence came to the side of the bed. "It's a sad thing, losin' your da. Would you like me to sit with you for a time?"

Glenys shook her head and heightened the intensity of her sobs.

"Tomorrow, we'll have a better-fittin' dress for you," the maid said after a moment. "That's my old one you are wearin'. Mrs. Beagle, she's the housekeeper, is letting down the hem on one of her ladyship's gowns. I'll bid ye good night, then, and see that no one disturbs you. Well, his lordship might send for you, but he hasn't said."

When the maid was gone, Glenys sat cross-legged on the bed for a few minutes, reviewing her predicament. Why were these people so kind to her? She had nearly killed the Earl of Ravensby, for heaven's sake! Now his wife offered one of her own dresses for the almost-murderess to wear. And last night the man named Charlie had wrapped his arms around her while she wept during the long drive to this secluded house.

He had even apologized for searching her, and seemed astonished to discover a female under the trousers and shirt. Although she was wearing her brother's clothes, it had not occurred to her that she was in disguise. She could hardly wear skirts to help her father hold up a coach, and had not dared let him go out alone, sick as he was.

She'd have followed him anyway, Glenys admitted to herself, if only because she longed for adventure. Riding through the dark night, robbing an elegant crested coach, plucking a diamond stickpin from a rich earl's cravat . . . in her imagination it had appeared vastly exciting and romantic.

The reality was savage and bloody.

A glance at the clock sent her off the bed in a flash. Although dusk came late at this time of year, it was past time to finish her preparations. She retrieved the letter opener she'd found in a drawer of the writing table and set to work on the drapes.

Two hours later the rope was finished. Securely tied at intervals with knots her father had taught her, it looked strong enough to bear her weight. She wouldn't know for sure until she was dangling thirty feet above the ground.

Concealing the rope under the bed, she returned to the window and gazed longingly at the solid branches of an oak tree growing just beyond her reach. Even if she swung like a monkey from the windowsill, she was certain to miss.

A long sweep of grass lay just past the line of oaks that bordered the house. Once she stepped onto the lawn, there was no way to hide herself for at least a hundred yards. In the distance was a thick grove of ash trees, and beyond that she could see nothing.

If she made it to the ash grove undetected, stealth and her own two feet would be her sole assets. With luck, she'd have the whole night to get as far away from this place as she could.

The blue sky darkened to gray, and shadows cast by the trees began to lengthen. Almost time to go. Then she heard voices coming from a point not far from her window.

Ducking, she listened attentively and recognized the earl's deep voice.

" . . . tomorrow, for Derby. I'll give him a letter for the constable after I've questioned the girl."

"Will you do it tonight, milord?" That was Charlie.

"The maid says she's overset, and I'm not likely to get what I need from a weepy female. It can wait until morning, but no longer. Keep the guard posted."

After a few moments of silence, Glenys poked her head above the windowsill and saw the earl striding across the lawn. He wore dark breeches and a white shirt, the full sleeves fluttering in the evening breeze. He was headed directly for the same grove of trees where she intended to go.

She muttered a few of her brother's favorite oaths. Now what?

For half an hour she kept watch by the window, and when it grew dark, he had not returned. Probably he came back to the house from a different direction, she decided, around the front where she couldn't see him. In any case, she had no choice. Tomorrow she would be summoned to judgment unless she made her escape.

Careful to make no sound, she changed into Harry's clothes, which had been laundered and returned to her for no reason she could imagine. A good omen and a blessing, because it would be nearly impossible to shimmy down the rope in skirts.

In her pockets she stored the apple, dinner roll, and wedge of cheese she'd kept back from her meal trays. With no idea where she was or how far she had to go, she knew the food would be of use. She tugged the floppy hat over her short curls, pulled the rope from under the bed, and secured one end of it to the leg of a heavy armoire near the window.

The lawn looked like a field of quicksilver under the pale half-moon. After a quick check to make sure there was no one in sight, she slowly let out the rope.

She had miscalculated the distance, but the end hung only a few feet above the ground. Not a dangerous drop, if she got that far.

This is it, she told herself as she climbed onto the windowsill. Wrapping her legs around the rope, she took a deep, shuddering breath and let go of the sill. Ghastly visions of her body splattering on the hard ground seized her for a moment, but the knotted sheets and curtains held.

Clinging to her uncertain lifeline, she began the long descent. With every move she made, the rope swung crazily, banging her against the side of the house. She ignored the pain and lowered herself hand over fist until her legs reached empty air. Then she let go.

The fall seemed to take forever. When she landed, her left ankle gave way and she hit the packed-earth walkway with a loud *whoof.* Immediately she came to her hands and knees and scrambled to the trunk of the oak. There she huddled, listening for any sign that she'd been discovered.

For a long minute the silence was eerie. Then crickets took up their song. In the distance, an owl hooted.

Using the tree for support, she came erect and moved her foot in circles, wincing as she tested the ankle. Wrenched, she decided, but not badly. She could walk. Hell, she *had* to walk, and even run the first stretch across that lawn.

When she was certain the ankle could bear her

weight, she bent low and made a mad dash for the line of trees.

The lawn stretched for miles, or so it felt until she plunged into the welcome shelter of the ash grove. She paused there, to catch her breath and rub her abused ankle. No hue and cry from the house. Everything was quiet.

She hugged herself in relief. So far, so good, but the worst was yet to come. The earl wanted to question her, and instinct warned he was not a man to give up easily. She must be well beyond his reach before morning.

Favoring her ankle, she made her way deeper into the woodlands. Overhead, stars shone through the open canopy of the slender, graceful trees.

With no idea where she was going, Glenys plowed ahead, hoping to stumble across a road or one of the rivers that crisscrossed Derbyshire. Either would lead her to civilization, and at all costs she must make her way to the cottage before her brother came looking for her. Rash and scatterbrained, Harry never failed to get into trouble.

Not that he could fare worse than his father and sister had, she acknowledged. Right now he was probably stomping around the cottage and swearing as only Harry could swear. He'd be furious that she had taken his horse and his gun and his place by Papa's side.

Lost in thought, she tripped over an outcropping of limestone and landed facedown in the dirt. The fall knocked the breath out of her, and when she struggled to her feet, she was dizzy and uncertain of her direction.

Damn damn damn! Trying to orient herself, she made a slow turn and saw light filtering through the trees. The house? Had she been traveling in a circle, only to wind up where she'd started?

Cautiously, she crept toward the glow. No, she had not passed here before. The trees ended near a small ornamental lake, and on the other side a domed marble building glimmered in the moonlight. Warm light poured from the windows, flickering as if cast by torches from inside.

"Holy hollyhocks," she said aloud. A temple, in the middle of nowhere! And so very beautiful. Tall cypress trees stood at intervals along the sides of the building, and a Corinthian portico graced the front.

Enthralled, she padded a bit closer, unable to stop her feet although they were moving in the wrong direction. Any sensible criminal would be headed the other way, but she'd been a criminal for only one day. And in all her life she'd not been sensible even that long.

How could she leave without investigating the most fascinating thing she'd ever seen? True, she had seen very little in her sheltered existence, but that made her all the more determined to peek inside. With any luck, some mysterious ritual was going on in there. She had always wanted to witness a mysterious ritual.

Since her early schooldays, she had imagined herself the heroine of an ancient legend. As Persephone, Ariadne, or Helen of Troy, she dreamed herself away from the tedium of her own life. In the classroom, she plodded through Latin verb declensions only so she could read about Bacchic revels.

Then one of her classmates revealed that her great-uncle had been a member of the infamous Hell-Fire Club. At midnight gossip sessions Amy had recounted, with a deplorable lack of particulars, Uncle Lester's tales of virgins dressed as nuns and men in masks who did unspeakable things on marble altars.

Glenys had wondered for years exactly what unspeakable things those were. Now the bizarre temple, a perfect spot for heathen rites, drew her like a Siren.

She circled the lake, holding well within the shelter of the trees until they ended a short distance from the building. On tiptoe she crept around the side to a high window and lifted her head.

Inside, torches were spaced at intervals along the walls, and niches between them held blazing candelabrum. Light danced on the walls and ceiling, warm and undulating. After a moment she realized that the enormous room held a pool lined with blue tiles. The effect of torchlight reflected by water against the marble was eerie, and she stood mesmerized for a long time before noticing that someone was in the pool.

A dark form swam toward the other side, just across from her, and lifted itself out.

She stared in amazement at the back of a man's body, his bare buttocks glimmering in the light. When he shook his head, water sprayed in all directions. Then he raised his arms and stretched broadly.

Suddenly aware her mouth was hanging open, Glenys pressed her lips together. She had seen her father and brother shirtless during the months they'd lived together in the small cottage. Neither man looked anything like this one.

Papa had broad shoulders, but they were bony. Harry was slender, just her own height, with none of the interesting muscles that rippled in the man's back and legs and arms.

He looks like the statue of a Greek god, she thought, bedazzled.

Then a pair of hands clamped her shoulders. She let out a squeal of surprise.

"Now, now, missie," Charlie scolded. "What would ye be doing here?"

She struggled in his grip, but he was too strong. In desperation she brought down the heel of her shoe on his toe.

He yelped.

"Let me go, you big ox!" She planted an elbow in his ribs.

He gave a loud *oooomph* and took a step back, but his hands maintained a firm hold on her shoulders.

Then her gaze caught the man in the temple. He had turned and was looking directly at her.

Ravensby.

Although he stared back, she was scarcely aware of his eyes. With a will of its own, her gaze moved lower, to the chest sprinkled with curly dark hair. To the flat stomach, the narrow hips and the . . . rest of him.

Heat flamed in her cheeks. She forced herself to look up to his face. His expression was unreadable.

He gestured to Charlie, who swung her around, seized her by the back of her shirt, and marched her to the front of the building and up the marble steps.

"His lordship wants to speak with you," Charlie said, his voice bleak. "I'll have to search you again."

"Don't fret yourself." She twisted from his grasp and emptied her pockets. "Cheese. Bread. Apple. I am now disarmed."

Charlie watched the apple roll down the steps. "Not good enough, y'see. Mebbe you have a knife."

"I did have a letter opener, but forgot to bring it along." She held out her arms. "Paw away."

Blushing furiously, he ran his hands down her sides, hardly touching her at all.

He looked so miserable when he stepped back that Glenys put her hand on his forearm. "I have no weapon and would not use it if I did. Word of honor."

His smile of gratitude touched her heart. He really

was sweet, even though he had recaptured her and was about to send her into the lion's den. Sparing him that responsibility, she pushed open the heavy oak door.

Despite the warm glow of torches and candles, the pool house was icy cold. The earl gazed at her from shuttered eyes. He had pulled on his breeches, but his shirt hung open, leaving his chest bare.

Taking care not to limp, she sauntered to a marble bench beside the pool. It was like sitting on a glacier. "Congratulations," she said. "You caught me."

"How did you get out of that room?" he countered in a soft voice.

"I flew."

"Or cozened the footman." He began to button his shirt. "I'll turn him off."

"You must not!" She hadn't considered that the guard would be blamed for her escape. "I expect the poor man is certain I am still locked up. It's not his fault."

"Indeed? You have not sprouted wings, young woman, and there is only one door."

"You'll find out anyway," she said in a disgruntled voice. "I braided a rope from the sheets and curtains. It's dangling out the window."

A faint, sardonic smile quirked his lips. "Then I must congratulate *you*. Most enterprising, even for a brigand. How long have you been at your trade?"

"Oh, decades." She waved a hand. "I am the Scourge of the Great North Road, don't you know?"

He shook his head impatiently. "Spare me the theatrics. You can't be above sixteen or seventeen years old. What is your name?"

"I'm one-and-twenty! And my name is Gl—" She bit her tongue. "Gladys. Gladys Knox."

"Your father was . . . ?"

"John Knox."

"Right. And I am Oliver Cromwell." He picked up a towel. "I don't enjoy games, Miss whoever-you-are. Your father carried no papers, but the constable will have both your identities soon enough."

"Perhaps." She hugged her sides. "Wh-Where is Papa?"

"In the icehouse." There was a long silence. "What happened last night is regrettable," he said in a somber voice. "I am sorry for it. But I had no choice."

"I know."

He looked surprised.

"Everything went wrong," she said despondently. "We never meant to hurt anyone, and Papa only wanted the money. You have lots of it. If you'd just handed over your purse, we'd have been on our way. But you didn't, and—"

He made an exasperated noise and applied the towel to his wet hair. "Miss Knox, we both know you are lying, about your name and why you were waiting on a private road for me to come by. Things will go better for you if you give me the truth."

What *truth?* Didn't the man recognize a plain robbery when he saw one? She opened her mouth to ask him and clamped it shut again. So long as he imagined she had a secret worth hiding—some piece of information he wanted—she could buy time for another escape. Another *try,* she reminded herself with an interior sigh. She should have been well away by now.

"What do you care about my name?" she asked instead. "And why do you imagine I'd conceal my identity? As you pointed out, the authorities will find out soon enough. I'm astonished you haven't turned me over to them already."

"So I shall, when you've told me what I want to know."

She came to her feet. "If you are so anxious for information, Lord Ravensby, why the devil did you confine me in a room for nearly twenty-four hours? Stow my father's body in an icehouse when he should have a Christian burial? He was—" She turned away, feeling hot tears blister her eyes.

Maybe highwaymen were not entitled to Christian burial. She wasn't sure.

"It's up to you," Ravensby said from close behind her. "Your employer cannot protect you now. I'm ready to listen, if you are ready to tell me who hired you."

Hired? She swallowed her retort. Sergeant John Shea had been driven to crime only because he couldn't find a job. Damned if she would betray his identity, whatever the consequences to herself. It was the least she could do for the father she'd scarcely known but had always loved.

"Why is it so cold in here?" Crossing to the edge of the pool, she dropped to one knee and dipped a hand in the water. It was like liquid snow. "You actually *swim* in this?"

"The pool is fed by an underground spring. Bathing in cold water is good for the health, or so I'm told."

She grimaced. "Don't believe everything you hear."

"Certainly I don't believe anything I am hearing from you. But since you are chilled, we'll continue this conversation back at the house."

Still on one knee, Glenys watched two large bare feet move past her. Soon she heard the door close behind him.

For just an instant she thought of escape. Even with her aching ankle, she could outrun Charlie. But she wouldn't get far, because Ravensby would track her down. She recognized tenacity when she saw it, although she was generally looking in a mirror at the time.

Once again she put her hand into the pool. So cold, like the Earl of Ravensby. Like her father's body in the icehouse.

For a moment, despair sat on her shoulder. Then she shrugged it away. While she lived, she could hope. And she could love life and what it offered—if only the summer afternoons in the fields near Miss Pipcock's School where she wove circlets of daisies for the little girls. Taught the village boys to tickle trout.

Ah, well. Best to get on with matters at hand—Ravensby and, quite possibly, the hangman. She stood and smiled at Charlie, who waited at the door with an unhappy look on his face.

"His lordship said as how I was to take you to the library," he said.

Moving to his side, she linked her arm through his. "I am partial to libraries, but take care. I'm a hardened criminal, Charlie. Very like, I'll try to steal a book or two."

3

Ash headed immediately for the room where the girl had been stowed, pleased to find the footman alert. The young man sprang from the chair by the door and bowed.

"The horse is already out of the barn," Ash said, with no censure in his voice. "Unlock the door, please."

Looking confused, the footman obeyed.

The room was dark, but even in the light from the hallway Ash could see a bedsheet tied around the armoire leg, stretching to the open window.

The footman had the presence of mind to bring a lamp, so Ash was able to trace the long rope that reached almost to the ground. Quite a jump from where the rope ended. His respect for the girl went up another notch.

"I never heard a th-thing," the footman stammered. "She—"

Ash cut him off with a wave of his hand. "From now on we'll need a guard outside, under the window. See to it. And since the young lady has vandalized the sheets and blankets, send for a maid to replace them."

"Yes, milord." The boy put the lamp on a side table and hurried away.

Hands on the windowsill, Ash stared into the night for several minutes, considering how to proceed.

For the first time, answers were within his grasp. But the girl seemed determined to withhold them, and her daring escape proved that she was no amateur criminal. Quite the contrary. She was resourceful and fearless.

Her father had trained her, no doubt. A shot of pain went through him as he remembered the awful moment when his bullet struck the man's heart. Should he have aimed for an arm or a leg? It all happened so fast.

Deliberately, he put the matter aside. He had long since made up his mind to do whatever he had to do to survive.

If only Geoffrey Todd had not been stricken with the mumps that felled his entire staff of bodyguards in London. Geoff was the one friend he could speak his mind to, the one man who'd set him straight when he wasn't thinking clearly. And he wasn't thinking clearly now.

His expression hardened. For now he was alone, facing a keen-witted young felon who had nearly killed him once and would undoubtedly try again.

"Milord?"

He turned and saw a maid with an armful of linens. She curtseyed. "Go about your business," he said, gesturing to the bed. Then a glint of silver on the counterpane caught his attention.

Moving past the maid, he found a sharp letter opener half buried under the remnants of shredded damask. He fingered it thoughtfully. An ideal weapon, easy to hide. Why had the girl failed to take it with her?

In the passageway, he handed the blade to the footman and ordered him to strip the room of anything remotely dangerous.

Slowly, Ash made his way to the library, not sure if he was looking forward to the confrontation or dreading it. The chit had been clever, but careless. And occasionally disarming. "Scourge of the Great North Road" indeed.

When Charlie left her alone in the library, Glenys was immediately drawn to a portrait hanging above the mantelpiece. She crossed to the picture and studied it, envy souring her throat.

She had never seen a lovelier woman. Blond and graceful and elegant, the lady gazed back at her from pale blue eyes. A sweet smile hovered at her lips.

The earl's wife. What a perfect life she must have, married to a handsome aristocrat. She looked serene in her beauty and position.

Some people are born lucky, Glenys reflected. But not many. Most poor sods had to make their way as best they could, which was clearly her own destiny. At least she was born relishing a challenge, and a good thing too. As long as she could remember, challenges had been daily fare.

In the next few minutes she would face the greatest of them all.

"Wish me luck," she whispered to the lady in the picture. The countess had a kind face and might prove an ally, although Glenys suspected Ravensby would keep his wife well away from a highway robber.

When she heard the door open, she scurried to a wing-back chair and tugged Harry's droopy hat over her forehead so that the brim hid her eyes.

The earl dismissed Charlie and moved soundlessly past her to the desk. He was still barefoot.

For some reason, that put her more at ease. The tufts of dark hair on his toes made him seem . . . human. She concentrated on those feet, beautifully formed like the rest of him, and felt heat rise in her cheeks at the memory of his naked body.

Concentrate, she told herself. Ravensby can send you to the gallows.

"This will warm you," he said in a voice that permitted no refusal.

He thrust a wineglass at her and she took it automatically. With her other hand she lifted the brim of her hat and watched him plant one hip on the desk, legs stretched in front of him. Her gaze lifted, and for the first time she saw his face in full light. She nearly gasped aloud.

His eyes were green-gray, with a dark rim around the irises. Thick black lashes lined the lids like kohl. He was handsome, she supposed, but it was impossible to look at his face without focusing wholly on those remarkable eyes.

They seemed to pin her to the chair. No, they saw right through her, reaching places inside herself even she had never dared to look at.

All of a sudden, she was truly afraid of him.

"I want you to tell me the truth," he said softly. "Your name, the name of your employer, and the reason you are hiding his identity. Doubtless he has threatened you, but I can protect you if you are honest with me. Or I can hand you over to the courts with whatever recommendation for your sentence I choose. And I have considerable influence. The decision is yours."

Heart pounding in her chest, Glenys took a long drink of wine. Her name she was determined to conceal, but the rest she would gladly tell him—if there were anything to tell.

Had someone employed her father? It was possible, she supposed. Papa had been certain Ravensby would pass by that particular spot, certain enough to return there when his first attempt failed. But who would care if the earl was shorn of his purse?

"Why would anyone hire us to rob you?" she asked. "That seems remarkably foolish."

"*Kill* me," he corrected, his tone glacial. "You were there to kill me."

She blinked. What the devil was he talking about?

"Don't play innocent. I might have believed you were not a party to your father's real intent, but you shot at me. And when I brought you to Ravenrook, you escaped your room and set out to finish the job. Oh, you'd not have got away even if you tried—guards are posted all around the estate. But you didn't make a run for it. Instead you headed directly for the pool house."

She regarded him in confusion. "As if I knew you were in there? Good heavens, I saw the lights through the trees and followed them."

"Incredibly bird-witted for a fugitive who managed to escape from a guarded room."

"Yes. Obviously I was stupid, but I imagined there was an or—" She bit her tongue.

"Out with it, girl. What did you expect to see?"

What a fool she'd made of herself. But so what? "An orgy!" she blurted. "Or a satanic rite of some sort. You must admit, a temple in the middle of nowhere is odd. This whole place is odd. And so are you!"

She felt better saying that. Never mind that he could see to it she was hung for her crimes. All her life she had defied authority, and she might as well go out the same way.

When he didn't reply, she lifted the brim of her hat. He gazed back at her, shaking his head.

"You are wonderfully inventive," he said. "I would be more appreciative, were the stakes not so high. Exactly how did you plan to kill me at the pool house?"

The man was surely demented. "Death by cheese. Or apple, if I missed the first time. Lord Ravensby, we converse to no purpose. I will tell you nothing more, not even if you torture me."

He released a long sigh. "How very melodramatic. Are you aware Ravenrook is so isolated that I could put you to the rack with no one the wiser?"

"Then do it!" She jumped to her feet and stood there glaring at him. "Or just throw me in the ice water at your Roman temple. That would kill any normal human being."

Before he could reply, someone knocked at the door. She sank back onto the chair, grateful for the temporary reprieve. If only she could learn to keep her mouth shut.

"Come," the earl directed.

Glenys peered from under the brim of her hat and saw Charlie step into the library. His face was troubled.

"One of the guards caught an intruder, milord. Robin thinks he came alone, but we've sent a patrol to check the grounds."

The earl jabbed a finger in her direction. "Don't move from that chair."

When the door closed behind him, she reached for the glass of wine she'd set on a side table and swallowed it whole. What kind of place was this? And how was she to hide a secret she didn't have, to buy a chance to get away from this madhouse?

At least the earl was off balance, she thought with satisfaction. He didn't know what to make of her, which had been true of everyone she'd ever met.

In fact, she didn't know what to make of herself. Sometimes she was so smart—wily enough to escape whenever she liked from Miss Pipcock's School, and from this fortress prison. On the other hand, she was also foolish enough to get caught again for no good reason except that she was curious.

At least she'd seen a naked man for once in her life. It was interesting that all the school gossip had failed to capture the reality. Ravensby might be a typical specimen of manhood, but she doubted it. If that one glimpse was all she would ever have, she had seen a truly magnificent male.

And she would have that image to console her as the noose tightened around her neck. Slumping in the chair and cursing herself for her reckless impulses, she was unaware the earl had returned until he stood in front of her.

"Take off your hat," he ordered.

Without thought, she obeyed.

He studied her intently and nodded. "Yes. You could be twins," he said. "Charlie, bring him in."

She looked toward the door. A young man with sandy hair and hazel eyes lurched into the room.

"Oh no," she groaned. "Harry!"

4

"Glennie!"

Harry's rush to embrace his sister was stopped short by a fit of sneezes. He pulled a filthy handkerchief from his pocket and blew his nose.

With a sigh, Ash handed over his own mono-grammed handkerchief and leaned against the door, arms folded, to observe the family reunion.

Gladys, or Glennie, or whatever her real name was, advanced on the boy, clearly furious. "What in blazes are you doing here, Harry? Why didn't you stay in bed where you belong? Holy hollyhocks, you don't have the sense God gave a cauliflower!"

Harry gazed at her, eyes wide above the handker-chief pressed to his nostrils. "Blast it, I'm not the cork-brained idiot went haring off with *my* clothes. That's my best shirt and I want it back!"

"I'll stuff it in your mouth first chance I get," she promised. "For now, just shut up. I mean it. Don't say another word."

"The devil I won't. Been looking for you all day. Had to walk because you took m'damn horse. What kind of trick is that to serve a fellow?"

She stalked to him and shook a finger in his face. "Listen to me, you numskull. We are in serious trouble here. Hold your tongue before you make it worse."

Ash decided to separate them before the girl took control of her brother. "Time for you to go upstairs, young lady." He seized her elbow and propelled her into the hall, closing the door behind them.

Breaking loose, she whirled around and glared at him. "You just want to get Harry alone and pump him for information."

"Exactly. And if you are lucky, he'll tell me what I want to know."

"But he doesn't know anything at all. He was at home, sick in bed. And he's only a little boy. You have no right to punish him for what I did." Her shoulders sagged. "He doesn't even know Papa is dead."

Ash swallowed a lump of ice in his throat. "Would you prefer to tell him yourself? I'll contrive to evade the subject if he brings it up, and will send him upstairs when I'm done questioning him. The news might come easier from you."

She considered for a moment. "He's bound to ask, and if you put him off, he'll just have more time to worry about it. Besides, you killed Papa. Serves you right to tell his son what you did."

After a tense pause, Ash cleared his throat. "Very well. Harry will join you in a few minutes, and I'll have a cold supper sent to the room."

"Prison cell," she corrected.

He gave her a stern look. "You are facing a real one, and perhaps worse, if you continue lying to me. Give thought to that while I'm speaking with your brother."

Ash nodded to Charlie and watched as he led her away. Then he turned to Robin, who stood with a look of indifference on his chubby face. "Good work, young man. You'll get a bonus for catching the intruder. For now, tell Mrs. Beagle to prepare the room adjoining the girl's. I want everything sharp removed, fresh linens on the bed, and a supply of clean handkerchiefs. Better double the guard in the hall."

He ran his fingers through his hair. What was he forgetting?

Robin spoke up. "Am I still to go for the constable tomorrow morning?"

"I'm . . . not sure. Wait here until I've talked to the boy and I'll let you know."

He paused, hand on the door latch, before reentering the library. Should he tell Harry about his father before or after questioning him? And how was he to soften the blow? So far as he knew, the boy was innocent of any wrongdoing. But his sister wouldn't be trying to shut him up if he had no information.

Deciding to play it by ear, he stepped inside to find Harry looking out the window, hands clasped behind his back with a handkerchief dangling from his fingers, and whistling as if he'd not a care in the world.

Instantly suspicious, Ash closed the door. Damn. He knew better than to leave a stranger alone in this room or anywhere in the house. There was a pistol in his desk drawer and any number of potential weapons scattered about.

"Harry," he said in a soft voice, "put your hands against the window, high as you can reach, and then don't move. I have a gun leveled at your back."

"No, you don't," the boy replied without turning. "I can see your reflection in the glass."

Even so, he shrugged and obeyed.

Ash crossed the room and retrieved the pistol from the drawer, stuffing it in the band of his trousers while scanning the top of the desk.

Dear Lord. He almost laughed aloud.

"It's only quartz," he said. "Worth a few shillings at most."

Harry sneezed.

"Oh, turn around and blow your nose, boy. Then put the paperweight back where you found it."

When Harry's face emerged from the handkerchief, he was grinning. "Had to try, guv." With a flourish, he dropped the crystal pyramid on the desk. "This would have bought supper and a pint or two. Didn't think you'd miss it."

Ash had to force a stern look to his face. "Until now you were only guilty of trespassing, but the penalty for theft is a good deal higher."

"I was only keeping it warm in my pocket. Besides, it's not like I got away."

"Nor can you, unless I decide to let you go." When Harry's face brightened, Ash waved a hand. "That's a long shot, but there is a chance. Answer my questions honestly and you might walk out of here."

"Glennie too?"

Ash nodded.

"I don't suppose you got my horse when you picked her up? You can't want to keep that glue bait. And what about—" He pressed his lips together.

Ash was certain he meant to ask about his father but changed his mind. Probably hoping the man had escaped. "What is your name?"

The boy looked surprised. "Harry."

"The rest of it. Your surname."

"Same as Glennie's. She's m'sister."

Ash rubbed his temples. "For God's sake, just

answer the question. I want your name, how old you are, and where you live."

Harry spoke slowly, as if addressing a simpleton. "I'm Harry Shea. Well, it's really Henry, but only a gudgeon answers to that. Eighteen years old. We're living in a cottage near Hathersage, but it don't belong to us. You won't need that gun, y'know. I wouldn't try nothin' with a big cove like you."

"Not so bloodthirsty as your sister?"

"Glennie?" Harry tilted his head. "She wouldn't hurt a fly. Can peel the hide off a fellow with her tongue, though."

"And is remarkably accurate with a pistol. She came within a hair of blowing my brains out."

"By George, did she now?" For a moment Harry looked impressed. Then he frowned. "Must've been an accident. I'd wager she never fired a gun in her life, unless something havey-cavey was goin' on at that Pipcock school. The place looked prim and proper to me, though. Don't know how she stood it all those years."

Confounded, Ash lowered himself on a chair. The pistol pressing into his waist reminded him that for all their glib tongues, the Sheas were deadly.

"Don't mind if I do," Harry said, straddling a spindly chair and folding his arms across the backrest. "Got blisters the size of potatoes from walking all day."

"How did you know where to come?"

Harry gave him a forbearing look. "Road only goes to here, guv. I figured the gaffer took up where we left off, and Glennie jawed him to take her along. Devilish hard to stop when she's caught the scent."

Where we left off got Ash's attention, although he was having considerable difficulty translating Harry's cant. "Then last night was not the first attempt?"

Harry's eyes narrowed. "Just how much do you know?"

"Too much for your own good. I want to make sure of a few details, that's all. And if you don't give over, I'm certain the constable will wring them out of you."

"But you said we could leave if I told you everything!"

"That's one option." Ash regarded him levelly. "Why don't we start from the beginning. How did you know I'd be coming along that particular road last night?"

"The pig man. Except we thought it would be night before last. He didn't say when, guv. Just that you was headed for home."

Ash released a heavy sigh. "Precisely where did you run into this . . . er, pig man?"

"At the Snake Inn."

Out of patience, Ash pulled the gun from his waistband and set it on the desk where the boy could see it. "I want a straight story, Harry Shea. Find a logical place to begin and tell me what happened."

"How the deuce can I, when you keep throwin' questions at me?" When Ash fingered the pistol, Harry threw up his hands. "Don't kick up a dust. We was coming back from Glossop, the gaffer and me. That was—" He paused to count on his fingers. "—two afternoons before last. Went up there lookin' for work, but no luck."

"You, the 'gaffer,' and Glennie?"

"Naw, she stayed at the cottage. We only got two horses. Anyhow, we saw the inn and thought mebbe there would be somethin' for us there. Woulda been nice," he said wistfully, "working close to home."

"Exactly where is the Snake Inn?"

Harry described a section of the high turnpike road north of Kinder Scout, an area Ash knew well.

"There was a wagon outside with a slew of piglets trussed up, and we took a notion to pinch one." Harry chuckled. "But they squealed like the devil so we went inside. Hardly anybody there, 'cept the pig man and a couple of other coves drinking ale and talkin'. The gaffer asked the man in charge if there was a job, and he said no but gave us both a pint for free. Said he'd been told to make everyone welcome so they'd come back."

Harry paused a moment to blow his nose. "While we sat there drinkin', the pig man said he had to be goin' because the Earl of Ravensby was on his way from London and the kitchen would be needin' bacon. I got the feelin' everythin' was hurried up, like you was comin' home sudden-like."

"So I was," Ash muttered. His own servants guarded their tongues, but he'd never considered gossip from the local tradesmen. From now on he would make sure that everything needed to run the house was produced on the estate . . . including pigs.

Not that he believed a word of this trumped-up story. "What happened next?"

Harry propped his chin on his crossed wrists. "Well, the pig man left and the gaffer decided we should follow him. Didn't tell me why. After a couple of hours the wagon turned on the road to here and we went a ways without seein' anything. Then the gaffer said we should watch for a good place to wait. That was the first I knew he meant to hold you up."

"You never robbed anyone before?"

Harry squirmed on the chair. "I'd rather not say, lessen it matters." When Ash made a gesture, he mumbled something about two previous forays. "Didn't get much—only watches and a few guineas. Not many fancy carriages travel in these parts. Anyhow, we waited all night and saw nothin' but the wagon comin' back without the pigs. Then it rained, and I got to feelin' bad, so about dawn the gaffer said we'd go on home."

"But your father decided to make another try?" Ash prompted.

"Must have, but I slept all day and most of the night after. When I woke up, he was gone and so was Glennie, along with my best clothes and my horse and my gun. I waited a few hours, and then I set out lookin' for them."

Harry lifted his hands. "And that's all I know, guv. Followed the road to this place, and then I was jumped and brought to the house."

"I see." Ash rubbed his chin. He had thought himself a good judge of character, but his instincts were failing him now. For all he wanted to believe Harry Shea's story of hardship and coincidence, he knew it wasn't true.

Ash found himself hoping for excuses to spare these two odd youngsters a fate they had brought on themselves, and wondered at it. He ought to be glad that for once he'd captured a pair of conspirators, however low on the scale they ranked.

He'd one trump card to play, but loathed to put it on the table. Still, Harry had to know about his father. If the news propelled the boy to tell the truth, so much the better.

Rising, he went to the window and stared outside. The darkness engulfing his soul was so black that even the half-moon hurt his eyes when he looked at it.

"Harry," he said in a low voice, "your father is dead." Hearing a gasp, he lowered his gaze until he could see Harry's reflection in the window glass. The boy's head was buried against his crossed arms.

"H-How?"

"He stopped my coach and ordered me outside. Your sister held a gun on me, and he had two pistols of his own. It was dark. At one point I thought your father was about to fire at—" Ash sucked in a harsh breath. "It doesn't matter now. Later I'll tell you all of it if you want to know. I shot him in the heart. He died instantly."

After a long minute, Harry raised his head. "Well,

that's a kindness." His voice shook, but he looked genuinely relieved. "The gaffer wanted to die fast, and said more than once that he wished a bullet had caught him when he was a soldier. Always took it back later, because if he'd been killed in the war, he wouldn't have found me and Glennie."

Ash turned, astonished to find an unsettling smile on the boy's freckled face.

"She kept hoping he'd get better," Harry said, "but I knew it wasn't no use. I'd been with him nearly a year before she came away with us, and he got worse every day. Most nights he couldn't sleep from the pain in his lungs. We got scared to leave him, even for a hour or two, for fear he'd die alone. I 'spect that's why Glennie stole m'horse and went along t'other night."

Recalling the man's rasping cough, Ash wasn't surprised to learn he was ill. But he was stunned at Harry's insouciant acceptance of his father's death. He'd expected accusation and had prepared himself to accept blame, not credit.

Harry's eyes shone with tears, but his smile didn't fade. "I loved him, y'know. Took him a long time to find me after he came home from Waterloo, but he never gave up until he did. Then he looked for honest work, but there was none to be had. When he was sure he wouldn't get well again, we went to where Glennie was so he could say goodbye. He never expected she'd follow us, and tried to send her back to the school, but she wouldn't go. He did his best for us, guv."

Unable to speak, Ash nodded.

"I'm glad he went quick." Harry came to his feet. "Dunno how we'd have managed if he died a bit at a time, with no money for food and medicine. The last few weeks, Glennie nursed him when he took to his bed, and I stole chickens and bread. Then he felt better and took me to Glossop, lookin' to find a job for me. You know what happened after that. Anyways, I can't think of nothin' else to tell."

His face grew solemn. "You ought to let m'sister go, guv. It was the gaffer and me set out to rob you. Glennie wouldn't have been there the second try if I hadn't got sick. So hand *me* over to the law. Not her."

Feeling helpless, Ash went to the bellpull and gave it a tug. "We'll talk again tomorrow," he said in a flat voice. "For now, you can spend some time with your sister. A room has been made ready for you to sleep, so let the footman know when you are ready to go there. And Harry, there will be guards in the halls and outside the windows, so don't try to escape."

The boy gave him a weary smile. "Guv, I couldn't walk another ten yards if you opened the front door and sent me packing."

After the footman led Harry away, Ash summoned Robin and told him the trip to Derby would wait another day. He was not yet ready to turn these children over to the constable.

Alone again, he gazed up at the portrait of Ellen. She would have swept Glennie and Harry under her wing in a flash. Ellen thought the best of everyone, and would never have understood why her husband had come to trust no one at all.

Dammit, he wanted to believe Harry's story. He very nearly did.

But he knew every inch of the territory surrounding Ravenrook, including the winding road between Glossop and Sheffield. He had been there only weeks ago, passing the exact spot Harry described. It overlooked Lady Clough, a barren, deserted stretch of moorland.

There was no such place as the Snake Inn.

5

"Well?" Glenys regarded her brother impatiently. "What did you tell him?"

Harry looked up from the dishes spread across the writing table in her room. He had a sandwich in one hand, a chicken leg in the other, and his mouth was full. Unable to reply, he shook his head.

Sighing, Glenys forced herself to wait—never an easy task. When the footman ushered Harry inside, he had aimed straight for the food with scarcely a nod in her direction.

She couldn't blame him for gorging himself. In the six months she'd spent with her father and brother, they generally went to bed hungry. And if there was a bit of money, by silent agreement it was spent on ale for Papa. Near the end, it became a necessity to ease his suffering.

She regarded Harry with affection. To his vast displeasure, he was a slightly built young man with a face almost feminine in its beauty. The other boys in their small Northumberland village had tormented him unceasingly. She suspected he'd endured worse bullying at St. Simon's School, where he was dispatched after their mother died.

At the time, she'd been immersed in her own troubles. A pair of charitable ladies agreed to take in the nine-year-old girl, and they endured her high spirits for as long as they could. But their conviction she was possessed of a devil, often voiced, only inspired her to greater mischief. Finally, they begged the vicar to place her in another home until her father returned.

But as the war continued, there was not so much as a letter from John Shea, let alone money to support his children. Within a year Glenys had been passed to nearly every household in the parish, without ever taking root.

At wit's end, and over her protests, Reverend Hensworthy applied to her mother's family for assistance. She had told him it was no use, and was unsurprised when they refused to have her. They did send money for her schooling, however—on the condition she never contact them again. It was an easy promise to make, and one she fully intended to keep.

Lord and Lady Haversham had disowned their daughter when she ran off to marry the charming, feckless Jack Shea. Glenys longed to thumb her nose at her grandparents, but longed even more for a good education. She consoled herself with the assurance they resented giving her the funds even more than she loathed accepting their charity.

While she was at Miss Pipcock's School, word came that Harry had run away from St. Simon's. After several years without news, she figured her brother must be dead. And Papa too, until they both appeared from nowhere one afternoon. Suddenly, she had a family again.

Papa insisted she remain at the school, safe and decently fed, but when they left, she packed her few belongings and set out after them.

Two weeks on the road, with no money nor any idea where they'd gone, convinced her she could accomplish just about anything if she set her mind to it. Sure enough, she found them in an abandoned crofter's cottage, and her father was too weak from his illness to escort her back to Miss Pipcock's.

Now Papa was gone, and all she had was the irrepressible, impossible Harry—"slickest pickpocket in Liverpool." She hoped he had not confessed as much to the Earl of Ravensby.

"*Will* you stop eating so we can talk?" she demanded, unable to bear the suspense a moment longer.

Harry waved a bare chicken bone in her direction. "Got a wolf in m'stomach. You should eat some before I finish it all. Too skinny by half, sister mine."

She glanced down, past her flat chest to the narrow waist where Harry's pants hung loose. She was sitting cross-legged on the bed, and her bony knees might have belonged to the same chicken Harry was devouring. "Later. I want to hear every word you said to him, and everything he said to you. We have to get our stories straight."

With a sigh, Harry wiped his hands on his shirt and leaned back in the chair. "You won't like it, but I gave him the truth. Could tell right off he wouldn't settle for anything else."

"Oh, blast!"

"He's a downy one, his lordship. Got eyes that look right into a fellow."

Glenys nodded. She knew all about those eyes.

"'Sides, I'm pretty sure he already knew. Said he did, and just wanted me to back up what you told him."

"Which was precisely nothing! And I warned you to keep your mouth shut."

"Couldn't see the point. He's got us dead to rights, but we're small fish for an earl. I figure our best chance is to throw ourselves on his mercy."

"Mercy?" She sprang off the bed. "There is not one sliver of human feeling in that man. He played you for a fish, yes indeed, and reeled you in without a struggle."

"Says you!" Harry made a face at her. "Fact is, the guv promised he'd let us go if I told him everything. So I did, and chances are we'll be outta here tomorrow."

"Bacon-brain!"

"Wigeon!"

Glenys took a long, calming breath. It wasn't Harry's fault. He was streetwise and clever in ways that astonished her, but no match for the Earl of Ravensby. "What's done is done," she said between her teeth. "But tell me what that is, best you remember, so I can make a plan. He'll not let us go, Harry. I'm sure of it."

Frowning, he crossed his arms. "Didn't mean to let you down. Thing is, I kinda trusted him. And he sent a tray of food up here. Nice room, too, even without any curtains. He coulda stored us in the cellars, Glennie."

"Did you consider he might be softening us up?"

"Nah, but I always figured earls and the like was honorable men. They can afford to be. Don't have to steal to stay alive."

No, she thought. From what she'd seen of this house, Ravensby was a wealthy man. But he imagined someone was out to kill him. Even earls had problems.

"Anyway," Harry said, "I'll tell you what happened downstairs if you'll shut your jaw box so's I can concentrate." Leaning back in his chair, he closed his eyes and began to recite like one of her students delivering a poem the class was ordered to memorize.

He's got a retentive mind, Glenys thought while lost in some business about a pig man. Maybe things weren't so bad after all. Even the earl must have had trouble making sense of Harry's story, not to mention his language. She concentrated on Ravensby's questions, trying to figure out exactly what he was after.

Something about an assassin, but she already knew that. He thought someone had hired them, and she had been willing to go along as a delaying tactic. Now, Harry's ingenuous tale made mincemeat of her strategy.

For all his skill at thievery, Harry couldn't lie his way out of a potato sack. Ravensby didn't know that, however. Not yet. From now on, she'd do all the talking.

When he was done, Harry looked at her expectantly. "Did I drop us in the soup?"

She had no idea. Now that Harry had confessed to attempted robbery, Ravensby could see them both hung. "You should have pleaded ignorance," she said. "The earl would have no reason to hold an innocent child."

Harry erupted from his chair. "I'm eighteen years old. A man, Glennie. A *man,* and don't you forget it!"

"I will not," she assured him. Harry bridled at any insult to his masculinity. For her own part, she longed for the day when a man looked at her and saw a desirable woman instead of a plain, gawky girl. Without pleasure she gazed down at her skeletal body. That would not happen soon, if ever.

Suddenly, grief flooded through her in hot waves.

The Sheas, Harry and Glenys, were fodder for the hangman. Papa was dead. Until Charlie bent to close them, his eyes had stared up at her blankly. There was no chance to say anything, not even goodbye.

Had she ever told her father that she loved him? She couldn't remember.

Harry caught her as her knees buckled. With surprisingly strong arms he led her to the bed and sat her down, holding her as she wept. Distantly, she was aware of his own sobs and his tears stinging the side of her neck.

"He was a good man, Papa," he said in a halting whisper.

"Y-Yes."

"Most of the time," Harry added after a beat. "He drank too much."

"Yes."

"Took the easy way out when he could."

"Did he?"

"Always. 'Cept when it came to his children." Harry's arms tightened around her back. "It couldn't have been easy, finding me. When I heard a cove was asking my whereabouts, I took care to make meself scarce. Figured it was the law comin' after me. Papa didn't give up, though. Musta been a year he looked for me in Liverpool. God knows how long before he tracked me that far. He loved us, Glennie, in his way."

She cried all the harder then, clinging to her brother, needing the release of pain she had buried inside for most of her life.

"Not good at words, y'know. But I l-love you, too, Glennie," Harry mumbled when her tears had subsided.

"Oh, Harry." She pulled away and gazed at his sweet face. At his eyes, so like hers she might have been looking in a mirror. "Thank you for saying that. Since Mama, no one has. Did he ever speak of her?"

"Oh, yes. Mostly about how he ought never have married Lady Melanie. Said he wasn't good enough. He was born to be a soldier, and because of the war, they had barely enough time to make a son and daughter. But she'd have run off with the devil, Papa told me, to escape her family. He took her away because even the life he could give her was better than the one she had."

Glenys wiped her face with a corner of the bed-spread. "What a sorry lot we are, Harry. But think of it. Mama was the daughter of a marquess, and so miserable she ran off with a soldier born of a butcher and a housemaid."

"Papa said she loved him, though."

"She told me the same thing, many times. Is this what love leads to, do you suppose? They cannot have spent more than a few months together, whenever Papa was given leave. I've no recollection of seeing him before the pair of you showed up at the school."

"Me neither, until he found me in Liverpool. But at the end, he came for us both. That's what we gotta remember."

She managed a smile. "Harry my lad, you may in fact have a brain somewhere inside that thick skull of yours. And you certainly have a heart. But now we must put our heads together and find some way to outwit the Earl of Ravensby. At the very least, we had better plot our escape."

"You've been here longer than me. Any ideas?"

She looked at the window. "Not at the moment. A chance may arise, but what we need is a way to communicate without anyone else knowing what we say. Do you speak French?"

"Be serious."

"A code, then. Do you know one?"

He grinned. "As it happens, a good'un. Finger signs. Want me to teach you?"

They spent the next hour practicing an intricate code, with Glenys concentrating on the signs for *shut up* and *run like hell*. Harry knew a whole language with his fingers. He taught her signals that said *watch out for that man, she's lying, someone is coming,* and a series of finger words for directions and where to meet.

When her eyelids began to droop, Harry brushed a kiss on her cheek. "That's enough for now, sis. We'll practice again when we get the chance."

"Will we, do you s'pose?" Exhaustion muddied her words. "Get another chance?"

He went to the writing table and began wrapping sandwiches and biscuits in a napkin. "I 'spect Ravensby will turn us loose tomorrow morning. Why not?"

"Because I nearly killed him," she said in a gloomy voice.

"Oh, right." Harry gazed at her with awe. "I'd forgot. Didn't know you could shoot, Glennie."

"I can't. But I had lots of time to aim while he was standing there with his hands up. Then all of a sudden, guns went off and mine did too." She closed her eyes. "I don't know if I meant to pull the trigger. I wish I could say it was an accident, but I'm not sure. Maybe I really wanted to kill him when he shot Papa."

Harry studied the remnants of their dinner and returned several sandwiches from his napkin to the tray. "I'd have fired too, y'know. Instinct. Trust me, sis—it don't help second-guessing yourself. Forget what happened. Wasn't your fault. Well, you were bloody chuckleheaded to be there at all—"

She made the finger sign for *shut up.*

Laughing, Harry went to the door and knocked. "Eat somethin', Glennie. I've left a bit and it oughtn't go to waste. You got to be strong."

A footman opened the door, Big Charlie by his side. Glenys waved at him and watched his round cheeks go red.

Harry noticed, making the sign for *he's a friend* behind his back. "See you tomorrow," he said aloud.

As the door was locked, Glenys sank back against the pillows. She couldn't muster the strength to undress, or eat, or even slip under the covers.

But she had wept for Papa, and thought she might be able to let him go now. His body was in an icehouse, though. Next time she saw Ravensby, she would demand a decent burial. And beg him to let Harry go free.

She was the one who tried to kill him, after all. And despite what she told her brother, she was rather sure she'd meant it at the time.

6

"There it is!"

At Harry's shout, Ash reined to a halt on the high ridge overlooking the turnpike road. Big Charlie and John Fletcher took up positions on either side of him.

Through the morning haze, he could barely make out a coach-and-four pulling away from the square, three-storied building. He glanced over his shoulder at Harry, who bounced excitedly in his saddle.

"See, I told you! The Snake Inn."

Ash drew out his spyglass and focused on the sign hanging over the entrance. From this angle, the inscription was unreadable. He beckoned Harry forward. "Tell me about the place. Why is it called the Snake Inn?"

"How the devil should I know? There's a crest on that sign over the name, and it's got a snake coiled up at the top."

"Ah." Pieces of the puzzle started coming together. The Devonshire crest must have suggested the name of the inn.

The Duke of Devonshire was a major investor in the new road stretching from Manchester to Sheffield. Ash had been shown a prospectus, but declined to join the board. There was too much traffic through the High Peaks as it was, with mills springing up along formerly quiet rivers.

No inn had been mentioned in the plans, although it should have been anticipated. A change of horses would be required after the arduous climb from Glossop, and this establishment was nearly midway along the route.

Yes, he ought to have figured it out sooner. And might have, had he come at the problem logically. But he'd been caught up in a perceived threat to his life and shaken by the death of John Shea. Unwilling to trust the pair of fledgling criminals who fired bullets at his head and tried to steal paperweights.

Ash was beginning to wonder if this was some bizarre dream. But Glenys and Harry were all too real, and he was almost ready to accept the existence of the pig man.

Almost.

During a long, sleepless night, Ash had made up his mind to verify Harry's story. The boy was roused at dawn, sleepy-eyed and grumbling until he saw the horse chosen for him to ride. From then on he became a major irritant, chattering away until even Charlie and John Fletcher wearied of him.

Ash refused to draw conclusions quite yet. The boy obviously knew of the Snake Inn, but that didn't mean he'd been there when he said, or stumbled across a pig man who chanced to be speaking about the Earl of Ravensby's unexpected return from London.

He gestured to John Fletcher and spoke softly to him so that Harry would not hear. "Find out who is down there and report back. Take Charlie with you, and leave him to make sure there are no surprises."

When the two men were gone, he turned to Harry. "Do you recall the name of the proprietor?"

Harry's brow furrowed. "Longly. No, Longston. Hell, guv, I'm no dab hand at names. A preacher type, though. Said he wanted to set up a church."

"A preacher, running an inn and passing out free ale?"

Harry grinned. "Good way to pick up a congregation, 'specially way out here. Folks might travel a mile or two for gospel talk if it comes with beer."

Ash nearly laughed.

"Can I ride this horse after today?" Harry turned imploring hazel eyes in his direction. "I never been on a nag with any heart to it before. What's his name?"

"I don't know if he has a name. And we'll see, later, about you riding him again." Not at all sure what would become of Harry after this excursion, Ash was unready to make any promise he could not keep.

For all Harry's inexperience, he appeared to have a gift for managing horses. The long trek from Ravenrook to this spot, single file once they ascended the boggy moors overlooking the turnpike, was a test for any rider. Ash had expected Harry to wander off the narrow path, but the boy controlled his mount with surprising skill.

Ash lifted his spyglass again and saw John Fletcher picking his way up the steep track. Seemingly aware of the glass trained on him, John beckoned with a wave of his hand.

"Follow me," Ash told Harry. "The descent will be tricky."

"I know what you mean, guv. Nearly got sucked inter a bog a few months ago. The gaffer pulled me out, but it was a near-run thing. I'll keep m'nag dead on behind you."

John, when they met him halfway, gave a succinct report. "Two ostlers for the horses. Five servants in the inn, three of them women. A proprietor named Longden. One guest. He's in a private parlor, drinking steadily. Thing is, he came in a coach from Chatsworth. Got the Devonshire crest on it."

"His name?"

John lowered his head. "Dunno, m'lord. Longden went suspicious when I pushed him. Want me to go back and try again?"

Ash cursed himself. After the attack two nights ago, he'd begun to jump at shadows. One man, alone, could scarcely be a threat. And Hart wouldn't lend his carriage to other than a respectable gentleman.

"Of course not," he said. "We'll go down together. I expect we could all use a drink and something to eat."

The host, a slender man with penetrating eyes and bushy eyebrows, was talking with Charlie when the three men entered the taproom. He looked up with a welcoming smile that widened when he spotted Harry.

"How are you, m'lad? Find any work yet? No more drinks on the house for you, as it's one to a customer, but the other gentlemen are welcome to the libation of their choice."

Ash crossed to the bar and rested one hand on the polished wood. "Give the young man whatever he wants, and the others too. I'll have a glass of your best brandy."

Charlie and John accepted tankards of ale and took up positions on either side of the room, where they could watch the door. At Ash's direction, Harry settled at a table in the corner.

When everyone was in place, Ash tasted the brandy, nodded approval, and glanced at a closed door to the right of the taproom. "Have you a private parlor?" he asked in a deliberately casual voice. "I prefer to drink alone."

Longden had been observing the odd behavior of the four men with a look of confusion on his face. "We do, but at the moment it's occupied. There are bedchambers upstairs, if you care to make use of one."

"Thank you, no. The young man recommended your establishment, and I was surprised to hear of it. The last time I passed this way—"

"It wasn't here," Longden finished cheerfully. "Everyone says that. We opened for business only last week, and the building was constructed in rather a hurry."

"At Devonshire's behest? He is a friend of mine, but I haven't seen him for a year or more. In fact, I had thought him to be in Italy, but his carriage is in your stable now. I don't suppose he is the gentleman in the parlor? If so, he'd want to know I am here."

Longden's eyes narrowed. "And who might you be, if I may ask?"

Ash regarded him coolly. Although he respected discretion, at the moment he'd have preferred a more garrulous host. "Ravensby." There was no flash of recognition in Longden's eyes. "Perhaps you'll assist me in another way, then. I am looking for someone to supply victuals for my estate, specifically pork. We've had no success raising pigs. Can you recommend anyone in the area?"

Looking pleased to be of service, Longden leaned over the bar. "As it happens, one such was in here t'other night. Same time young Mr. Shea and his father stopped by. Name of Piers Piper, as I recall, and he lives in Hope." He laughed. "That's a town, not a state of mind."

"Yes, I know. Thank you for the referral."

As Longden refilled his glass with quite good brandy, Ash glanced over at Harry. The boy was chatting amiably with a pretty serving maid.

His story had checked out in every detail. There was a pig man after all, and the name matched that of the tradesman who made a delivery to Ravenrook the night before his own return.

He should be glad of it, because he liked Harry Shea. Glenys too, in a way, although she was trouble on two thin legs. He had no idea how to deal with a girl who held up coaches and shot with deadly accuracy and went looking for orgies in pool houses.

He was also back where he started, without the link he thought he'd found to the killer.

With an interior sigh, he picked up his glass and strolled to the window, gazing toward the mist-shrouded summit of Kinder Scout. A raw, beautiful, deadly place, Kinder Scout. It haunted his dreams even now.

His father had lived for hunting season, when he invited his cronies to tramp the high plateau in search of red grouse. The earl hosted lavish hunting parties every autumn, filling Ravenrook with guests who talked of nothing but guns and how many birds they'd brought down.

Ash had been expected to join them, but he could never see the sense of killing for the sport of it. Besides, as a youngster he was thin, awkward, and shy. He could scarcely lift the heavy rifle shoved into his hands, or endure the reproaches of those who tried, without success, to teach him to use it.

As much as his father yearned for hunting season, he dreaded it. And his body reacted, with allergies and colds and fevers that elicited disgust from the earl and looks of pity from the houseguests. "Too bad Ravensby has only this milksop," they would whisper among themselves. "He should marry again. Get a son with some bottom to him."

Ash heard, and knew what they meant. The fumbling boy he had been was no fit heir to the title. But he was never sure why slaughtering birds was the test of a man, although it seemed to be the only thing his father wanted from him.

Perhaps he should have tried harder, but in his own way he was more stubborn than his father. And even now, a crack shot with pistol and rifle, he never hunted. He had been fired at often enough, hit twice, and felt more than a little empathy with any creature at the receiving end of a bullet.

Like Jack Shea, he reflected, a leaden feeling at the pit of his stomach. Ash Cordell refused to hunt grouse, but he had killed a man. The irony sickened him.

He thought suddenly of Geoffrey Todd and the bleak look that came to his eyes when there was mention of the war. Geoff knew about killing. After eight years in the army, he was an expert on blood and death.

Ash swallowed the last of his brandy. He would ask Geoff when killing was justifiable. Ask him how a man lived with the regrets and the memories.

But he would not ask, of course. Men didn't talk about such matters, and even the best of friends found it impossible to confide their own weaknesses. Besides, he had no wish to remind Geoff of what he must be trying to forget.

Life would be so much easier if he'd been born with bottom—a hale, hearty, grouse-shooting country gentleman instead of a scholarly and somewhat philosophical man. He always imagined he was meant to be different than he was, but he didn't know how to get there. Or where to go, for that matter.

And the assassin had made the whole point moot,

because now his only concern was survival. For the last six years he'd been very like a harried red grouse, running and hiding and wondering why someone was trying to kill him.

One more brandy and he'd start to feel sorry for himself. Ash put down his glass and turned from the window. Longden was no longer in the taproom.

He looked at the closed door to the private parlor, gestured to John Fletcher, who moved to the left of the door, and crossed the room.

Chances were the individual enjoying his privacy on the other side of that door was as innocent as the pig man. But since he was traveling in Devonshire's carriage, he'd have news of the duke. And if Hart was at Chatsworth, Ash ought to send his regards.

Moreover, he wasn't leaving the Snake Inn without finding out who was in that room. The back of his neck had begun to prickle when John told him about the mysterious guest, and he'd learned to follow his instincts.

Holding to the wall, right arm slightly raised so he could drop the pistol into his hand if need be, he nodded at John. The young man lifted the latch and swung the door ajar.

Through the crack between wall and door Ash could see a man seated at a small table, facing the other direction. One of his hands was wrapped around a glass. His other hand rested on the arm of the chair. There was something familiar about the shape of his head.

The prickling ran from Ash's neck all the way down his spine as he stepped into the room. "Pardon me for intruding," he said softly.

The man lifted his chin at the sound and emitted a chuckle. Then, slowly, he turned his head.

"Well well, cuz," he said in a voice furry with drink. "Fancy meeting you here."

7

Despite her firm intent to be up with the sun, Glenys slept until well past noon.

She woke to find a tray with crusted chocolate and cold toast on the table next to her bed, and recalled dreaming of a conversation with Prudence. Apparently the maid had really been there.

Suddenly ravenous, she devoured the stale slices of bread and washed them down with the bitter chocolate. A good night's sleep, her first in a long time, left her sparking with energy. She could hardly wait to face the earl again, and had a vague notion she'd dreamed of him too, during the long night.

Chewing the last bite of toast, she tried to call back the dream. She could only remember that his arms had been wrapped around her. His fingers had tangled in her hair.

At school she'd had dreams about men, but all of them wore armor. When she tossed a crimson scarf from her window, they affixed it to a lance and rode off to battle dragons.

Lord Ravensby came to her naked and slipped between the sheets. He was damp from his swim and cold, until she warmed him.

What a goosecap, to imagine such a thing even in her sleep! But as she crossed to open the curtains, lines from *The Tempest* came to her mind—

". . . and then, in dreaming, the clouds methought would open up and show riches ready to drop upon me, that, when I waked, I cried to dream again."

The skies had not opened for Caliban, though. And no handsome earls would be dropping into her bed. Dreams rarely came true for monsters and common folk.

Lady Ravensby's blue muslin gown, freshly pressed, hung in the armoire. Glenys dressed quickly, ran a brush through her unruly hair, and put the soft leather shoes aside with a murmur of regret. They were far too small.

She had always been ashamed of her large feet, and her wide mouth, and eyes that tilted upward at her temples as if God had been drinking when he set them in her face. She had big hands too, with ragged fingernails because she chewed at them.

She was not quite interesting enough in appearance to be a freak, nor so ugly that anyone would call her an antidote. But she would always be the last female any man noticed in a crowd.

The fashion, or so the girls at Miss Pipcock's insisted during endless discussions about such matters, was for petite blondes with limpid blue eyes. A brunette might enjoy a rewarding Season if she was exceptionally beautiful, and a redhead without freckles could achieve marginal success. But in the Pantheon of Beauty, there was no allowance for Glenys Shea.

With nary a man in range and no Season in

her future, she hadn't much cared . . . until now. Approaching the mirror, she saw confirmation of what she already knew. A reed-thin girl stared back at her, everything too large except for her breasts. Those were practically nonexistent.

No wonder she'd easily passed for a boy. For that matter, even Harry was prettier than she. And he had smaller feet.

She padded across the room and rapped for the guard's attention. A tall young man opened the door and greeted her with a slight bow. She remembered him from last night. "Robin, I believe?"

He nodded. "Did you want somethin', miss? Prudence is having lunch in the kitchen, but I can send for her."

She tried to look dignified, not easy with bare feet. "Tell Lord Ravensby I wish to speak with him."

"He's not here, miss. Left this morning with your brother. Said he'd be back tonight unless they ran into trouble."

Dear God. Was the earl transporting Harry to the magistrate, as he'd threatened to do? "Left for *where?*"

"Dunno, miss. All I know is you are to stay in your room and—"

"Hello the house!"

At the sound, which came from downstairs, Robin drew a pistol from his coat pocket. "Don't move."

"Ash?" The voice was louder this time. "Where the devil are you?"

Robin turned his head.

While he was distracted, Glenys pushed him aside and ran full speed along the passageway. She was halfway down the sweeping staircase when Robin caught up and grappled her shoulder.

Three men wearing heavy greatcoats gazed at her

from the foyer. The butler and footman turned around to look, and in the stunned silence she saw two of the men, the burly ones, reach inside their coats for weapons.

Soon there were three pistols aimed in her direction, one from behind and two from the black-and-white-checked marble hall. The absurdity struck her forcefully.

Lifting her arms over her head, she grinned. "I surrender, gentlemen."

Flushing, the men in the foyer lowered their guns and Robin let go of her shoulder. She curtseyed, as elaborately as she could on the staircase with her hands over her head, and watched the pistols disappear under the folds of the men's greatcoats.

"My my." The third man, who had observed the proceedings with a wide smile on his handsome face, stepped forward and bowed. "Whatever has Ravensby been up to?" With a wave of his hand, he dismissed the others. "I'll handle this dangerous criminal, gentlemen. Fortescue, see our luggage unloaded, will you? And let the earl know we've arrived."

The butler accepted hat, gloves, and greatcoat as the gentleman stripped them off. "He is not at home, my lord, but we expect him by this evening."

"Ah. Then I'll have the lady all to myself for a while. Go away, Robin. And do put your arms down, miss. I expect they are aching by now."

They were, and she lowered them gratefully as Robin left her alone on the staircase. The gentleman spoke softly to the butler for a few moments, giving her a chance to observe him without the distraction of guns.

He was almost more beautiful than Ravensby, although comparing them was like matching sun against moon. The earl's dark good looks held center stage in her mind because she had seen him in the flesh—all the flesh—and only his haunting eyes were more compelling than his magnificent body.

The stranger was nearly as tall and broad-shouldered, with blond hair that curled around his ears and neck. Even from a distance his eyes were startlingly blue, like a summer sky. His ready smile was pure sunshine.

She liked him immediately, even more so when he moved gracefully up the stairs and held out his hand. "Will you take a dish of tea with me, mysterious lady? Think before you answer, because I daresay you'll be quizzed over cakes about your unexpected but delightful presence at Ravenrook."

"I'm growing accustomed to inquisitions in this house," she replied with a shrug. "But who are you?"

"Geoffrey Todd. Killain to friends and acquaintances, Lord Killain to servants and strangers, and Major Lord Killain when I'm in company with men of the Fifty-second."

"How are you addressed," she inquired mildly, "by a would-be assassin?"

His expression darkened, only for a moment. "This grows more fascinating apace. And clearly I should have told Fortescue to serve up wine instead of tea. Come, my dear. I am afire with curiosity."

Since curiosity was her besetting sin, Glenys was wholly in sympathy with the elegant gentleman as he led her to a sunny parlor. They settled in chairs across from one another at a marquetry table and maintained a discreet silence until the butler and footman had served up tea, sandwiches, and sweets.

When the servants were gone, she picked up a spoon and stirred honey into her cup. "My name is Glenys Shea," she said. "No additional titles."

"*Assassin* did catch my attention."

"I should have said *alleged assassin*. Lord Ravensby is the one thinks I set out to kill him, but I was only after his purse. *Highwayman* would be more accurate."

He took his time choosing a roast beef sandwich. "You set out to rob him all by yourself? Oh, not that you fail to be most intimidating, but Ravensby is ever surrounded by men carrying weapons. Could you not have found easier prey?"

"Certainly. But where, then, would be the challenge?"

His eyes narrowed. "Miss Shea, I should explain that any attack on Ravensby is taken seriously, especially by me. I head up a rather large contingent of bodyguards, all of us devoted to him. We dare not overlook the slightest threat to his safety."

She had figured that out, considering the number of weapons that had been aimed at her, and the guards assigned to keep her in her cage. But no one had explained why. "Have there been a great many? Threats, I mean. And what has he done, to make such dangerous enemies? Lord Ravensby is not precisely congenial, but I cannot think him an evil man."

Killain regarded her as if taking her measure, an enigmatic expression on his face. Then he held out a platter. "You must try these. Mrs. Hilton has a way with berry tarts."

A neat change of subject, she thought, placing three of the small tarts on her dish. What were these people hiding? The earl's aloof manner and this man's open friendliness were equally menacing, so long as she remained in their power. And her brother too. Dear God, where had Ravensby taken him?

Pretending disinterest, she picked up a tart. Sweet juices squirted in her mouth as she bit down on the berries. The crust was flaky and rich. In all her life she had never tasted anything so delicious.

"You see?" Killain smiled at her look of pleasure. "I've not forgot your questions, Miss Shea, but until I've spoken with Ravensby we'll do better to avoid difficult subjects. Except this one. I assure you, he is anything but evil. Quite the contrary."

He killed my father, she wanted to say. But truth was, he'd shot a highwayman. And Papa wasn't wicked either, even though he tried to rob an earl. Good and evil were only opposites in theory, it seemed. Real life mushed them together until it was impossible to know who was on the side of the angels.

She had always thought herself a decent sort, but came a split second when she genuinely wanted to kill a man. Or thought she did.

"You dislike him intensely," Killain said. "Your silence tells me so. But you'll not convince me he has mistreated you."

She lifted a hand. "I was merely air-dreaming. And no, I've not been put to the rack, although being locked up is worse than outright torture. I cannot endure being closed in."

"Nor I."

"His wife is kind, though. She gave me this dress to wear."

He made a low sound in his throat and leaned back in the chair.

"Did I say something wrong?"

He gazed at her through thick blond lashes. "Lady Ellen has been dead these last three years, Miss Shea. She was murdered."

"Oh God. Forgive me. I didn't know."

He reached for his cup and took a long swallow of tea. "Ravensby never speaks of it. Every attack on his own life has failed, so far, but the countess . . . ah . . . we never suspected she was at risk. I hold myself responsible, and can scarcely imagine the guilt he feels. We should have protected her. Been more careful."

Glenys bit her lip. Now she understood, if imperfectly, why Ravensby secluded himself in this remote house. Surrounded himself with armed guards and suspected everyone. The sweet-faced lady in the portrait, the one she'd envied and admired, had been killed because she was Ravensby's wife. He was the intended victim, but Lady Ellen had been in the way.

Or perhaps that was not the reason at all. The story was probably more complicated than mistaken identity or a misfired bullet. Damn. Whenever she thought she had an answer, it only led to more questions. And this was hardly the time to ask for details. At the moment, she remained a suspect.

"My apologies." Killain sat up and plucked a berry tart from the tray. "Mourning is long since over, and Ravenrook is joyless enough without rubbing old wounds. Tell me about yourself, Miss Shea. How is it you decided to rob coaches for a living?"

"Oh, we developed a fondness for eating," she replied in the same falsely cheerful tone. "My father and brother were unable to find honest work, although I suspect they didn't try very hard. I was in it mostly for the adventure."

"There were three of you? Where are the others?"

"Papa is in the icehouse. He was killed during the robbery." With effort, she kept her voice steady. "Ravensby has gone somewhere with my brother, but I woke up after they left. I expect Harry is in the magistrate's hands by now, which isn't at all fair. He was home sick when we held up the coach. I'm the guilty one."

She fixed Killain with a defiant look. "I fired a bullet at Ravensby's head. By his account, I barely missed."

"Bloody hell!"

"Just so." Deliberately, she bit into her second tart.

"By God, I don't know what to think of you," he said, knuckles white as he clutched the arms of his chair. "You look harmless enough, but—"

"I might well be a hired assassin. Or a madwoman." She licked berry juice from her lips. "So long as you and Ravensby keep me guessing, Lord Killain, I shall keep *you* guessing. And while I'm held prisoner, my bad mood will continue to make me obstinate. Do let me know when we can all speak in plain terms. I've nothing to hide, really, but I can't bear to be manipulated."

Raising his hands, he began to laugh. "You've put me down horse, foot, and cannon," he told her when he found his voice again. "And I'm the charming one, skilled at ferreting secrets. I can't begin to imagine what Ravensby makes of you."

"Nothing good, that's for sure." She wiped her lips with a napkin. "I have never been charmed, my lord, and always wondered how it felt. Would you care to try again?"

At that he came to his feet. "Miss Shea, I would indeed. Shall we take a walk together? I've been in the saddle for longer than parts of me are happy about, and I'd like to stretch a bit." He lifted a brow. "You did mention a fondness for unclosed spaces."

"The earl wouldn't like it," she warned. "Aren't you afraid I'll give you the slip?"

"You won't try to escape," he said gently, "until you know what has become of your brother."

So much for underestimating Lord Killain, she thought with annoyance. After wrapping the last of the tarts and a couple of sandwiches in a napkin, she ran upstairs to put on her halfboots.

*   *   *

Two men had followed them, Glenys noted as they left the sweep of lawn behind the house and entered the grove of ash trees. Sunlight filtered through the branches, creating a play of light and dark on the damp undergrowth. It must have rained during the night, while she slept.

They walked in silence for several minutes. Then he let go her arm and began to stretch, waving his arms this way and that, sometimes bending to touch his toes. She took the opportunity to chomp on a sandwich and a tart, reserving the last of her hoard for Killain.

"I've had the mumps," he said between gyrations. "A mild case, thank heavens, but five of our men are still bedridden in London. We usually travel with Ravensby whenever he is away from home, and you'd not have come in range of him under normal circumstances."

"What is normal about requiring an armed guard?" When he cast her a dark look, she threw up her hands. "I might not ask stupid questions if someone explained what was going on."

"Dammit, girl, haven't you figured it out by now?" Killain winced. "Well, *that* was certainly charming. Pardon me. I lose all sense when it comes to this particular subject. Ravensby has been under seige for, what? Six years, I believe. It seems like forever."

"But why? What did he do?"

Killain gave her a half smile. "I don't know how to answer you. Until we find out who is trying to kill him, the motive is unclear."

"If there are a great number of candidates, Ravensby must have offended lots of people."

"Scores. Maybe hundreds. And it was I who set him on the course, which is why I won't leave his side until he's safe, once and for all. Mind you, he has a whole different theory about the attacks, but I am convinced he is wrong."

Thoroughly confused, she frowned at him. "Have you ever sat down with Ravensby and made a list of suspects? Investigated them one by one?"

"Too long a list. But yes, we've spent years tracking every promising lead. Ravensby has spent much of his fortune hiring Bow Street Runners and private investigators." He took her arm. "Come. I'll show you my favorite place on the estate. And on the way, I'll explain what little I can without violating his trust."

8

Ash watched Jervase Cordell rise from his chair with the languid grace of a cat.

"You are just in time to save me, cuz. I'd else have expired from boredom. This outpost has nothing to recommend it, I fear, save a rather decent claret. Shall we broach a bottle and catch up on the news?" He waved toward John Fletcher, who stood with a pistol leveled at his chest. "Your friend is welcome to join us, of course."

Ash turned to John. "See to another bottle, and open it yourself." When the youngster hesitated, Ash pointed a finger to the door.

Frowning, John backed out, never lowering his pistol.

"Dogs still baying at your heels?" Jervase gave Ash a look of exaggerated sympathy. "Must be, or you wouldn't have gone to ground here in Derbyshire. Dismal place. Don't know how you stand it. But then, you were ever a gloomy fellow, even when you rusticated with your poor relations on school holidays."

Ash propped his shoulders against the paneled wall, his arms loose at his sides in case he needed to use the pistol. That wasn't likely, unless he took a fancy to put Jervase out of everyone's misery. The man's acid tongue and patina of bored world-weariness never failed to get on his nerves.

In the family, Jervase was known as the Changeling. While his father and older brother were stocky, brown-eyed, and chubby-cheeked, he grew up tall and lean, with pale hair and ice-blue eyes. His looks and temperament must have been a throwback to some distant and thoroughly disreputable ancestor.

"Ever the scintillating conversationalist," Jervase drawled. "You may as well have left me in company with that stuffed stag's head."

"Oh, we'll talk," Ash assured him. "I'm waiting for John to come back with your wine."

"You intend to interrogate me at gunpoint?"

"Will that be necessary?"

Laughing, Jervase sat and laced his fingers behind his head. "I am an open book, cuz. And as I recall, you prefer books to people."

Ash was spared from replying when Longden came into the room. He carried a tray with two bottles of wine, one empty glass, and a plate of crackers and cheese.

"I checked everything myself," John whispered as the landlord distributed the food and drink on the table in front of Jervase. "You want I should stay here, milord?"

"Outside, I think, beside that window. I'm not expecting trouble, but you may as well keep watch on the road. Let me know if anyone approaches the inn."

John looked worried. "Got a nasty way about him, that one. Maybe Charlie ought to be in here with you."

"It's all right, John. And we won't be long."

With obvious reluctance, John followed the landlord, closing the door as he left.

"I won't try to pour you a glass of wine," Jervase said, holding his hands in the air. "Doubtless you'll even want to unstop the cork."

"Go ahead. I'm not drinking."

"Ever the austere aristocrat." Jervase popped the half-drawn cork and filled his glass. "Ah well, I'll drink alone to your continued good health. Meantime, fire away, cuz. I assume you want to know why I'm travelling in one of Devonshire's carriages. Or has he already reported to you?"

"Not yet, although I'll have him verify whatever story you give me. You've obviously come up in the world. I'd no idea you were acquainted with Hart."

"I daresay. We minor twigs on the Cordell family tree seldom brush against dukes, at least in England. One of many reasons I prefer Italy, which is where I became the friend and houseguest of his stepmother. Duchess Elizabeth is a rather intriguing woman, despite her odd determination to excavate the Forum." He shrugged. "It has made her popular with the Romans, I must admit. We were invited everywhere."

Trust Jervase to attach himself like a parasite to a wealthy woman many years his senior. He could be charming when it suited his purposes, and had always been a favorite with the ladies. But Hart's stepmother? As if there weren't already a surfeit of scandal in the Cavendish family.

Elizabeth had borne the fifth duke two children while she was his mistress, including a son older than his heir. Not that his wife minded in the least. Georgiana and Elizabeth were the best of friends, and all three lived together in a grotesque ménage à trois.

When Georgiana died, Elizabeth replaced her as Duchess of Devonshire.

Ash kept his face expressionless, although disgust burned at his throat. Hart had inherited his mother's gambling debts, more than a hundred thousand pounds, along with three legitimate sisters and two half siblings by his father's mistress. Apparently, Jervase aspired to become another dependent.

When he reflected on his own unhappy childhood, which he seldom did, Ash always remembered that he had lived in paradise compared to Hart. The two lonely, unsettled boys met at Harrow and had remained friends for more than twenty years.

Jervase finished chewing on a cube of cheese. "Devonshire showed up in Italy a few months ago, trolling for antiquities and sculptures. Congenial man, if a jot high in the instep. I dropped your name, naturally. Our cousinly relationship gave me a bit of luster. He spoke highly of you, though rather too often, and I expect you are the reason he employed me to escort his purchases to London."

He chuckled. "You see what I have come to, cuz—a lowly nursemaid to crates of statues. I shepherded them across borders and through customs, distributing bribes to oily-haired officials, and God help me if a marble nymph arrived in London with a chip on her arse. But we came through right and tight. Devonshire is pleased with me, and I've another assignment."

"May I hope it takes you back to Italy?"

"You are in luck. I sail from Liverpool in a fortnight, which leaves me with time to kill." He raised a brow. "Did a bit of gambling in London, and m'pockets are to let. I don't suppose you'd consider inviting me to Ravenrook?"

When pigs fly, Ash thought. "There's nothing to occupy you there."

"True. Sorry to say, cuz, but even that stag's head is better company than you." He poured another glass of claret. "I came north just ahead of the duke, figuring he'd let me stay at Chatsworth until time to catch the boat. But he sent me off. When all is said and done, I'm no more than an exalted hireling. Still, he gave me use of a coach and driver, and free board at his other holdings in the area. Figured I'd sample this place first."

"And then?"

"Well, you know Derbyshire. Play guide and tell me where to go next. I've access to something called the Rookery at Ashford-in-the-Water."

"A comfortable house in a tiny village."

"*Quelle horreur.* Then what of Buxton? He's built a spa there."

"You can bathe with the dowagers," Ash said, lifting his shoulders from the wall. "Perhaps you'll find a wealthy widow on the prowl for a lover."

Laughing, Jervase reached under the lapel of his jacket. Ash immediately raised his right arm, prepared to spring the pistol into his hand. But Jervase only pulled out a handkerchief, which he waved to show there was nothing concealed in its folds before blowing his nose.

"Picked up a cold," he said, "what with all the fog around here. Does the sun never shine in Derbyshire?"

"Now and again." Ash crossed to the table and straddled a small wooden chair. "Tell me about your plans after the ship sails."

Jervase's cold blue eyes regarded him steadily. "You know, cuz, a man could take offense at being treated like a felon when his greatest crimes are gaming and a fondness for wine and women. Why should I give you an account of what I have done or plan to do?"

Ash met his gaze. "You know why. And if you've nothing to hide—"

"Check with Devonshire. With his stepmother. With the money-grubbing officials I've been haggling with the last few months." His eyes narrowed. "Has there been another attack? I assure you, there are witnesses who can vouch I was in Italy more than a year before heading home. . . . "

Jervase put his elbows on the table and templed his hands. "Sorry, Ash. I know you have troubles. And I'm too self-absorbed to pay them any heed. If it eases your mind, you are welcome to my itinerary. I sail on the *Mary Morgan*. She'll call in at Cadiz and one or two other ports before disgorging me at Naples. Devonshire wants me to visit a studio there, to make sure the sculptor is about the business he's getting paid for. From there, I'm on to Rome."

"For how long?"

"I've no idea. The duke will come over in the autumn, approve what he has commissioned, and I'll escort another load of statues to England. Meantime, I'll sponge off the duchess." He grinned. "You know me."

Undeniably, Jervase had found a perfect occupation for himself—a collop of occasional work, and a chance to mingle with the aristocracy he so desperately envied. The second son of a country squire, with ambitions far above his rank and means, he'd done well.

Ash had always tried to like him. He'd usually spent school holidays in Wiltshire at Uncle Matthew's farm, where Jervase was the only other Cordell not obsessed with cows and sheep. But Jervase resented the accident of birth that would make Ash an earl and heir to a fortune. He made no secret of it.

Sometimes, Ash envied him too. Even without the money and title he craved, Jervase had the freedom to go where he wanted and do as he liked. There was a lot to be said for irresponsibility.

Ash rarely saw his cousin, and they had not spoken since his wedding to Ellen four years ago. Jervase had been drunk, he recalled. And mocked him for getting leg-shackled to a woman without the wits to write her own name.

As if he'd had a choice.

Or perhaps he did, and lacked the bottom to stand up for himself.

His father insisted on the marriage. It would make up, he said, for the harm Ash had done to the Ravensby name with those damnable investigations. And what fault could his son find in a beautiful, sweet-natured girl who happened to be the daughter of a longtime family friend? A girl who clearly adored him?

None at all, Ash had finally conceded. He was in company with Ellen three times before the betrothal, never privately, and thought her as shy as he was. They made trivial, stumbling conversation. She gazed at him from serene blue eyes, and stroked his hand once, under the dinner table. He imagined she wanted him, and that he might be falling in love with her.

How could he have guessed? And by the time he found out, it was too late.

Jervase had known, though. He thought the whole situation vastly amusing. Everything amused Jervase, which made him good company for some people and a pain in the backside for others.

"You'll set a spy to watch me," Jervase said amiably into the silence. "Don't bother to deny it. Have you a bodyguard with some conversation? If so, he is welcome to ride in the carriage to keep me company."

Ash ignored the question. "What is your brother up to these days?"

"Evan? Same as always, I expect. I didn't send word to the old homestead that I was back in England.

M'father would expect me to stop by for a tankard of home brew and a tedious chronicle of the lambing season. Squire Matthew is in poor health, from what I heard in London. You must think me a bad son not to visit him, but we never got on well."

When it came to sons not caring to spend time with their fathers, Ash was wholly in accord with Jervase.

"Evan married a proper shrew, did he not?" Jervase took a long drink of wine. "Jane could shred an oak at twenty paces with her tongue. Will any Cordell ever marry well, do you suppose? Must be a family curse. We men choose badly, when we choose at all. I needn't bother, but you must get an heir sooner or later. Please do. Jane is detestable as it is. If Evan comes into the title, she'll be unbearable."

"More likely it will be one of her sons," Ash said. "I've no intention of dying young."

"Dear me, and here I thought you half dead already. What's the point of sticking around when you don't know how to have any fun? Sorry to say it, cuz, but life is wasted on you."

"Possibly. But I am as stubborn as you are profligate, *cuz.*"

Jervase lifted his glass. "In that case, you will live forever. And I hope you do. You were always the best of us, dull dog that you are. One day, if your horde of investigators tracks down the killer and sees him hung, I'll take you to Italy and teach you to laugh."

"A tempting proposition, certainly." Ash stood. "How long will you be here at the inn?"

"Another day or two. Plenty of time for you to send reinforcements. That young chap with the large pistol would be no match, were I bent on mischief."

"Thank you for the advice. By the way, I was in

London too, until a few days ago. Odd that our paths failed to cross."

Jervase shrugged. "Never thought to look you up. And you weren't likely to be found in the hells where I was busy losing my blunt. Anyway, Devonshire soon sent me north with the boxes and crates, except for one god-awful statue of Endymion taking a nap. He wanted to show it to his cronies. Surprised you didn't run into him. He was dragging people off the streets to ogle the damned thing."

Careful not to turn his back, Ash made his way to the door. With most of his bodyguards down with the mumps, he'd confined himself to the London town-house, meeting only with business associates and, two or three times, his mistress. No surprise he was unaware of Hart's presence, or Jervase's. But even in the aftermath, it made him uncomfortable. "I thought you said Hart was at Chatsworth."

"He is, now. Showed up yesterday and kicked me out. Politely, of course. Any more questions? I'm astounded you didn't search me for weapons."

"Next time, I will," Ash promised. "And while it was not exactly a pleasure to see you again, I wish you well."

"And I you." Jervase tugged at his forelock. "*Ciao,* my lord earl, until we meet again."

In the taproom, Ash paused briefly to rub the back of his neck. His muscles were tighter than halyards in a windstorm. A few minutes in company with Jervase always gave him a headache.

Charlie stood at the wall, just beside the door to the private parlor. He had been listening, Ash knew, for any sound that implied trouble.

Harry, a slab of roast beef in his hand, was deep in conversation with the serving maid. Something he said made her giggle.

Young lust, Ash thought with a pang. At Harry's age he'd been too reserved for a flirtation with a barmaid. Eventually, Geoff had seen to his corruption, on a small scale, and kept him from going to his marriage a virgin. Left to his own devices, and always fastidious, he wouldn't otherwise have gained the slightest experience before bedding Ellen. Not that it helped.

Regathering his wits, he crossed to where Longden was polishing glassware with a cloth and requested an accounting.

"On the house, milord. The youngster told me who you are."

"A man who pays his bills." Ash tossed a sovereign on the oak bar. "Two men will need rooms for the night, perhaps longer. Is that a problem?"

"Not at all." Longden smiled. "We can use the business."

After directing Charlie to pry Harry from his meal and the girl, Ash went outside to speak with John Fletcher. "You will stay here," he said, "to keep an eye on Mr. Cordell. If he leaves, you follow. I'll send someone to back you up, and enough money to pay your shot for the next two weeks. My cousin is supposed to sail out of Liverpool in a fortnight. See that he does. And meantime, let me know where he goes and who he speaks with. Anything that catches your attention."

John flushed. "How, milord? If you mean me to use the mails, I can't write."

"Ah. I'll make sure the other man is literate, then. And when you return to Ravenrook, you will have lessons. Get the horses, please."

While he waited, Ash studied the crest of Kinder Scout opposite the turnpike road. It was barely visible, as a heavy mist settled over the High Peaks. They would be lucky to make it home before the fog enveloped the road.

He wondered what Glenys Shea was up to. Chewing nails, he expected—iron ones, not her own. In the hurry to leave that morning, he'd neglected to write her a note of explanation.

At least he was returning with good news, of a sort. She was exonerated of all crimes save highway robbery, and her father had already paid a mortal price for that. He shuddered at the thought.

And wondered if he was the only one mourning Jack Shea's death. Harry, chatting up the barmaid, gave no sign of being in the mopes. And Glenys was too busy trying to escape, or to look in on an orgy, for grieving.

He didn't understand them. Not one bit.

And what the devil was he to do with them now?

9

Glenys followed Lord Killain as he left the ash grove and took a path along the edge of a cliff. At the highest point, he paused and gestured to the landscape below.

A narrow river sparkled in the afternoon sun. Behind it, the deep valley gave way to rolling green hills studded with sheep and ablaze with wildflowers.

"How beautiful," she murmured. "How terribly beautiful."

Nodding, he continued along the cliffside track and she fell into place beside him, chafing at his silence. Despite his promise to account for the attacks on Ravensby and Lady Ellen, he had not spoken for nearly half an hour. She decided he must be reviewing the story, selecting bits and pieces suitable for her to hear.

Her imagination ran riot with possibilities. How could one earl manage to offend scores of people? Inspire any number of them to murder? Well, perhaps only one individual had gone so far, but others had sufficient motivation to keep Ravensby guessing.

She tugged at Killain's sleeve. "You told me you'd explain."

He came to a halt and regarded her somberly. "I am having second thoughts, Miss Shea. The earl is an intensely private man, and while he tolerates most of my failings, he would not easily forgive me for speaking out of turn. Better you apply to him for information."

"B-But—" She snapped her mouth shut. How could she object to his loyalty, a virtue she admired above all others? "I understand, sir. Lord Ravensby is fortunate to have such a devoted friend. I'd not make trouble between you."

"Thank you, my dear. Among my faults is a tendency to leap to conclusions. I have decided you are not, for all your efforts to convince me otherwise, a hardened felon. But that doesn't free me to speak of Ravensby's private life."

He began walking again, rapidly, and she had to sprint to catch up. When she arrived, breathless, he murmured an apology. She waved it off.

"What a glorious afternoon," she said brightly. "Thank you for taking me outside to enjoy it."

He slowed his pace to match hers. "It occurs to me that *you* have a story to tell. I'd like to hear it."

Loath to give information while she was kept in ignorance, she pretended fascination with a peculiar outcropping of limestone. "Look! That's almost in the shape of an elephant."

He chuckled. "By th' mass, 'tis like an elephant indeed."

Casting him a look of surprise, she joined the game. "Methinks it is like a weasel."

"It is backed like a weasel."

"Or like a whale."

"Very like a whale."

Laughing, she took his arm again. "I ought to have started with a camel, but it really does resemble an elephant."

"My dear, a woman who can quote *Hamlet* at me is a treasure indeed. If you are able to converse in Latin and Greek, Ravensby will take you to his heart."

She wrinkled her nose. "I've little Latin and less Greek. Girls are taught a smattering of French, needlepoint, and music. Any education we manage beyond 'female accomplishments,' we secure on our own."

"A pity, that. Half the minds in the nation are wasted, which accounts for the sad state of affairs in England. But you have clearly set yourself to be educated. Tell me how you did it."

A cozener, Lord Killain. And definitely charming, as he'd warned her. But the pleasure of speaking openly to a man who was not threatened by her schooling, as Harry and her papa had been, was too good to pass up.

An hour later Killain knew everything about her there was to tell. That was pathetically little, and she was embarrassed when her narrative wound down. Life in an isolated village, followed by years in a school for young ladies, was dull stuff indeed. Glenys Shea had bored the only man who paid her any attention.

Oh, he'd asked lots of questions and feigned genuine interest, which made her like him all the more. But like him in a sisterly way, which perplexed her. A man that handsome ought to rouse other feelings, the same feelings Ravensby stirred up. Maybe if she saw Lord Killain naked . . .

Horrified at where her thoughts had led, she fumbled for a change of subject. And found herself telling about the night she and Papa lay in wait for the earl's coach, and the shooting, and even her attempted escape, although she omitted the incident at the pool house.

When she was done, they had arrived at another viewpoint, this one overlooking a desolate moor. The river must have gone underground. Only a stretch of damp, boggy earth lay below them. Except for a few patches of bracken sprinkled here and there, the landscape was barren. Forbidding.

To her left, about a quarter mile away, a stone tower perched at cliff's edge. She caught a glimpse of light and realized a spyglass was trained in their direction. Ravensby had advised her of the guards posted on the estate, and she began to realize what an elaborate network he'd established. Looking down the path she and Killain had taken, she saw a man hunkered behind a small bush, waiting for them to move again.

She doubted anyone could scale the cliff that stretched for more than a mile, but the earl left nothing to chance.

"My heavens," she said when Killain failed to respond to her monologue. "Have I put you to sleep?"

"On the contrary. Fact is, I've been having second thoughts again. Or is it third thoughts by now?" He smiled. "Come, Miss Shea. There is a shortcut back from here."

"We are being followed, you know."

"I certainly hope so. Rather dashing to my self-esteem, the notion you might overpower me, but I'd dismiss any of my men who failed to allow for that possibility."

The shortcut led through another grove of ash trees, more dense than the one nearer the house. They were forced to walk single file. Killain went ahead, and they had gone nearly a mile before she remembered about his "third thoughts." She tapped him on the back.

"Did you change your mind about telling me why someone is trying to kill the earl?"

His shoulders hunched. "I'd hoped you would forget about it."

"I am relentless. Although I did forget for a time," she added with uncharacteristic honesty. "Please, Lord Killain. I am terrified for my brother, and how can I help him when I don't know what this is all about?"

He sank in place, cross-legged, and patted the ground beside him. "Very well, Miss Shea. Only the background information, though. For details, you must apply to Ravensby. I'll ease your way with him, best I can, but don't press me now."

She nodded.

"We were schoolfellows," he began softly, "at Harrow and Cambridge. He is brilliant, by the way. I devoted myself to pleasure, and would not have passed my examinations without his help. Then I bought a commission, while Ash stayed on at the university doing research. Don't think him a coward. He'd have bought colors too, but his father wouldn't hear of it."

He rubbed his forehead. "We lost touch for a time, but during my service in the Peninsula I became aware of—well, to put it bluntly, Miss Shea, the materials sent us were defective. I speak of everything from artillery, rifles, and bullets to tents and mess kits. Not all of them, to be sure. But in every battle, men died needlessly because their own guns exploded. Cannons misfired, allowing the enemy to sweep over us."

"Good heavens," she murmured.

"When we were bivouacked, shipments of flour were ridden with weevils. Sacks of corn were weighted with metal so they'd pass cursory inspection, but the rest was mostly straw. Wellington protested, of course—he was always careful of supplies for his troops—and still we were sent inferior equipment and food."

He made a low noise in his throat. "So I wrote to Ash and begged him to investigate. Every war breeds profiteers, men who fatten their pockets at the expense of their country, but no one was doing anything to stop them. Certainly not Parliament."

Glenys squirmed on the hard ground. While she bemoaned her own tedious existence at school, men had been fighting and dying. She'd not given them a thought.

"Ash took my request seriously," he went on in a flat voice, "as only he would. He set himself to track army supplies to their sources, and from there to the investors who were making money. Within a year he'd uncovered any number of flagrant abuses."

Killain smiled. "You have told me you are relentless, Miss Shea, but you've nothing on Ashton Cordell. As heir to the Earl of Ravensby, he was able to make his voice heard. And he made a difference, I assure you. Others joined his crusade, although not a one of them lent his name to the endeavor. They worked behind the scenes, while Ash became the focus of resentment from those exposed by the investigation."

He growled what she suspected was an oath. "Factories were shut down, or their products subjected to intense scrutiny. Investors who had claimed windfall fortunes suddenly found themselves going broke. And every blackguard with a grudge to bear focused on Ash Cordell, because he was the only man brave enough go public."

"And that's why he has hundreds of enemies," she said. "My God. I never imagined."

"How could you?" Killain took her hand. "I've overstated this, in part. When the country geared up for the war effort, most people invested honestly and had no idea what was going on."

Glenys lifted her chin. "So long as the money kept rolling in, I expect they didn't want to know."

He regarded her with appreciation. "They should have suspected something was wrong, those who earned fifteen and twenty percent on their funds. But they turned a blind eye. And many were Ash's peers, or close friends of his father." His gaze lowered. "But that is another story, and one Ravensby must tell. At least you now understand how he gathered so many enemies, and why it's bloody difficult to pin down the one among them who has set out to kill him. Succeeded in killing his wife."

"Yes." She squeezed his hand then, and let it go before the moment became too intimate. "Thank you, Lord Killain. Until now I could not imagine why the earl reacted to our amateur attempt at highway robbery as he did. I have misjudged him."

"And he has misjudged you, of course. What a coil. I'm truly sorry about your father."

"Thank you, again, but Harry and I have come to terms with his death. It was merciful, in an odd sort of way. I only wish he could be buried properly."

"We'll see to it." Killain struggled to his feet. "Lord, I'm sore. Don't let me sit down again. And don't worry about your brother. I know Ravensby. He never acts in haste, and will not call in the law unless convinced of your guilt."

"Where did they go, then?" she inquired sourly.

"Shall we go back and find out?"

She followed him through increasingly heavy foliage, grateful when he stepped aside to hold away branches so she could pass. What a lovely man.

Ravensby had not returned when they reached the

house. Lord Killain left her with Robin, making polite excuses as he went off for a hot bath. When she looked envious, he directed one for her too.

Immersed in steamy, soapy water, Glenys reflected on what she had learned that afternoon. Worry about her brother played like an undertone in her mind, but she kept thrusting it away because something else niggled at her consciousness.

The water was cold before she realized what it was.

According to Lord Killain, Ravensby had a whole different theory about the murderer. Not someone exposed by the war investigations, but some other enemy. As if he didn't have enough of those already.

Who could it be?

And why the devil was she worrying about his problems? She had more than a few of her own.

10

"*You aren't helping.*" Ash refilled his glass from the brandy decanter and moved to the window. Twilight was settling over the grounds. In the distance, fingers of rose and amber stretched from the setting sun into a pale turquoise sky.

Geoff gave a negligent shrug. "How can I, when you've scarcely explained the problem? Not that you ever explain, I might add." He lifted his feet to the low table in front of the couch where he was sitting and crossed his ankles. "Besides, I have troubles of my own."

Ash cast him a worried glance and returned his attention to the sunset. From the droll look on Geoff's face, those troubles were not of serious consequence.

"It's possible I am impotent," Geoff said as if commenting on the weather.

Ash swung around and regarded him with horror.

"Devilish thing, but there it is. Or maybe it isn't. Haven't had a chance to test it out." Geoff assumed a martyred expression. "I was at pains to get back to Ravenrook before you landed in trouble, but apparently I was too late."

"Yes. You were. But what in blazes makes you imagine—"

"Mumps, my friend. The bloody mumps. And who'd have thought it? But the sawbones informs me the illness can be worse than fatal to a grown man. I'd only a mild case, but the others are out of service for a while. Jaws swollen like ascent balloons."

Ash took a long swallow of brandy. "I hope you told them to stay in London, under a doctor's care."

"Naturally. But we'll be shorthanded until they are recovered, so I'd rather you not go haring off to obscure inns and the like. Damned fool thing to do."

Ash gave him a sour look. "Right. I'd expected a lecture. Are you done with it? And what has my excursion to do with your impotence?"

"Please!" Geoff lifted a hand. "*Possible* impotence. And nothing at all, but I wanted to get your attention. It has been sorely lacking this last hour."

"Seriously, man, if you need time off to—" Ash felt heat rise to his ears. "—well, feel free to take leave. I promise to remain here, and even inside the house should you insist."

"Not a chance, m'boy. On your own, you are a magnet for trouble."

Ash turned back to the window, watching the last light fade from the sky. Geoff invariably brought laughter to his throat, even if it never slipped past the rock that had been lodged there for as long as he could remember. "Am I to worry about your manhood or not?" he asked gruffly.

"Not," Geoff assured him after enough time to raise the hairs on the back of his neck. "My fault anyway, taking the men with me when I visited m'sister and her brood of mumpy brats. She might've warned me."

Ash felt guilt nuzzle at his spine. "Since I insist you keep our every move confidential, she had no idea you'd be in London."

Geoff let out an exaggerated sigh. "I was just working myself up to an apology, but you anticipated me as always. Sorry I wasn't with you when your coach was held up, Lord Ravensby. Not my fault, of course, nor yours, but you've a peculiar need to assign responsibility for every chance occurrence."

Ash slammed his glass on the table beside him. "It's been a long day and I'm out of temper. Not of a mood to be baited, Geoff."

"Nor I. But I'm forced to desperate measures when you worry at a problem like a sore tooth. What say you tell me, directly, what has you on edge?"

"I killed a man."

Geoff stood, crossed the room, and put his hand on Ash's shoulder. "You must deal with Jack Shea's death on your own, of course. If I know you, and I think I do, it will take a long time."

"Yes." Ash stared at the carpet. A very long time.

"Meantime, what are we to do about Jervase Cordell? I don't want him within fifty miles of Ravenrook."

"What *can* we do? If he's latched on to Devonshire, there will be no prying him loose. Jervase milks every cow until it's dry."

"You could send a message to Hart, warning him to drop the man. He'd do it on your say-so."

"That's one possibility. But I'd rather not drag yet another friend into this mess. And Jervase has long since been ruled out, however much you'd like to cast him as the villain. He was on the continent through most of the attacks on my life, and in

Scotland when Ellen was killed. He can't be the one."

"Unless he hired others to do his dirty work. He spends most of his nights in gaming hells, and consorts with lowlifes who will do anything if the money is right."

"He has no money to pay them with. And the property he'll acquire if I die without an heir is an arid tract in Yorkshire. He can't farm it, nor sell it for more than a pittance. No motive, Geoff. We've been over this a hundred times."

Sighing, Geoff went back to the sofa. "Even so, I'll be glad when Fletcher reports that he has left Derbyshire. Wilcox is on his way to the inn, although he's nearly as inexperienced as John. You wanted someone who can read and write, which narrowed my choices."

"He'll do fine. Jervase knows I've set men to trail him. He might play games, to torment them, but he won't make serious trouble."

When Geoff failed to respond, Ash resumed his contemplation of the sunset. At the moment, Jervase Cordell was the last thing on his mind. During the long ride home, he'd wrestled with the most immediate problem confronting him, and had yet to find a solution.

The Shea whelps were his responsibility now.

If they had family, other than Jack Shea, surely Harry would not have been living on the streets of Liverpool. Glenys had apparently been teaching at a school for proper young ladies, although that was hard to credit. What school would employ an undisciplined termagant like Glenys Shea?

But Harry had told him as much, on the journey back from the Snake Inn. And while Glenys could lie without batting an eyelash, Harry was painfully honest for a boy who made his living as a thief.

"Worrying your head about the children?" Geoff

inquired mildly. "I've been wondering what you plan for them."

Ash shot him a withering look. "You know damned well I haven't the slightest notion how to handle this. Good Lord, what a pair of miscreants. Harry can't resist pocketing anything he might be able to sell, and his sister nearly blew my head off. She is literate, from what I can tell, with a varnish of good breeding from that school she attended. But at heart they are both wild as wolves."

"Monkeys, perhaps." Geoff ambled to the bell rope and gave it a tug. "Or horses, from good stock, in need of a little discipline. I met Harry only in passing, before you dispatched him upstairs, but spent an hour or two with Miss Shea this afternoon. Rather an engaging young thing."

"Quick-witted," Ash conceded. Glenys Shea made him nervous, and it had nothing to do with the bullet she'd fired at him. "Why did you ring for a servant?"

"If we are to settle their fate, it's only fair to let the youngsters join the deliberations. Have you considered asking them where they want to go, or what they want to do?"

He had not, even for an instant. As if Harry the Pickpocket or Glenys, Scourge of the Great North Road, had anything to say about it. Good God, until last night they were carrying guns and holding up carriages. Wiser heads would make decisions for them.

Moving quickly, he intercepted the butler and dismissed him with an apology. Then he turned to Geoff. "I daresay their own ideas are anything but realistic. We shall do better to figure out exactly what options they have, and present them in a logical manner. If they have a preference for one or another, they can say so."

Geoff shook his head, laughing.

"You find this amusing?"

"Not this. *You.* Now you'll marshal arguments for and against each choice, outlined and subdivided like a rhetorical exercise assigned you by a Trinity don."

"Too rational?" Ash inquired with a touch of ice in his voice.

"Sorry, old man. I doubt the Sheas will appreciate your systematic imperatives, but it will be interesting to observe their reaction. Meantime, I expect you've already considered a number of possibilities. Enlighten me."

Ash picked up the crystal paperweight from his desk and began to pass it from hand to hand. "Truth is, I'm a blank. Or nearly so. What think you of sending them to America?"

For once, Geoff regarded him with wide eyes and no quick retort, which gave Ash a measure of satisfaction. It wasn't often he caught the man off guard, and he couldn't remember the last time Geoff was truly surprised by anything he said or did. Damned uncomfortable, having a friend who could virtually read your mind.

"Not so outlandish as you imagine," he continued. "Lord Heston and his bride plan to emigrate. Boston or Philadelphia, I believe. His family was enraged when he married a cit, and refuse to acknowledge her in spite of her fortune. Heston thinks they'll do better in a country where people are not judged on lineage. When they get settled, I expect they'll do me the favor of welcoming the Sheas and introducing them about. The girl might even find a husband there. Women are scarce in America, from what I hear."

Geoff choked on a swallow of brandy. "At the least, America is so far away you'll never have to give them a second thought."

That sounded like a reproof. Was he wrong to rid himself of Harry and Glenys? It wasn't as if he had anything to offer them in England. They would go mad, confined on this remote estate.

Sometimes he thought he'd go mad himself.

"What can we do for them here?" he asked quietly. "Miss Shea is scarcely fodder for the Marriage Mart, even if we found someone to sponsor her. She could teach, I suppose, but Harry has no skills that won't land him in prison sooner or later. Perhaps we can apprentice him to a blacksmith or a baker or—"

"That won't fadge," Geoff interrupted. "According to Glenys, their mother was the daughter of a marquess. I don't mean to be a snob, but there is good blood in them, and spirit too. They deserve better than to be fobbed off with menial jobs and no propects."

"How in blazes do you figure that?" Ash dropped the paperweight on the desk and watched it bounce to the carpeted floor. "In strictest justice, they should be handed over to the magistrate."

Geoff merely looked at him, and even that was more censure than he required. Ash already knew he would not put them at the mercy of the law, or farm them out somewhere they'd not be happy. He admired Glenys for her courage and resilience. And he respected her for defending Harry, the same way Harry had taken responsibility for a robbery he had no part of, in order to protect his sister.

They were brave and loyal, the both of them—to each other and, he suspected, to anyone else they cared about.

No, he could not wash his hands of Glenys and Harry Shea, even if that meant lying to the magistrate and assuming obligations he was in no way prepared to handle.

He shot a dour look at Geoff's annoyingly bland expression. Why not consign them to his care? Geoff had a way with people, as he'd proven time and again by putting up with Ash Cordell. He would probably think it a relief to be saddled with a pair of youngsters instead of a beleaguered earl.

Not a bad idea. He could send them all to the Sussex estate, the seat of the earls of Ravensby and a place he'd not visited for years. By now the tenants could use a directing hand, and he dared not go there himself because the manor was impossible to secure. Too many roads leading in, too many ways for an assassin to gain entrance. A hundred bodyguards could not protect him at Ravenscourt.

But it was close enough to London for Geoff to scout for a bride and make a life for himself. Geoff would never let go his falsely assumed duty to protect him, Ash knew, unless given another responsibility. One of his greatest fears had always been that his best friend would grow old and curmudgeonly here at Ravenrook, which was likely to be his own fate.

"I don't suppose you'd be interested in my opinion?" Geoff inquired.

Ash shrugged.

"Your enthusiasm is gratifying. Even so, may I suggest we take our time instead of rushing to an unsatisfactory decision? By Miss Shea's account, Master Harry is sorely in need of schooling, and who better to tutor him than Trinity's most brilliant graduate?" When Ash scowled, Geoff held up both hands. "It will do you good, old thing. You are too much in cloud-cuckoo land, and a return to the basics will clear your head."

"I suspect Harry has little interest in scholarship."

"Then you must find a way to inspire him. As for the young lady—"

"She cannot remain here without a chaperone," Ash said firmly. "I have considered keeping them at Ravenrook for a while, although it was my intention to turn Harry over to you. And until Lord Heston is established in his new home, we cannot send the Sheas to America. Perhaps Aunt Nora would agree to spend the summer with us."

"No!" Geoff rose from the sofa. "Wilfred Baslow is another of your father's potential heirs. I won't permit his wife within striking distance."

Ash bent to pick up the crystal paperweight. "Nora hasn't lived with him since shortly after they wed. As for Wilfred— Dammit, Geoff, you take *me* to task for burying my head in books. Wilfred Baslow is positively obsessed with early English kings and Viking invaders. That's why Nora left him, not that she ever cared a bean for the man. The most inconvenient marriage of convenience I ever saw."

"Nevertheless, he is one of the four named in the will."

"Wilfred will inherit a dull stretch of land in Suffolk. What possible use could it be to him? If he could lay hands on my library, it might be a different matter, but I've offered to send him whatever books he requests. I often do, and he faithfully returns them. Wilfred cannot be the villain. He has absolutely nothing to gain, and if I died, he'd lose access to a research source he values. Moreover, he is a sixty-year-old recluse. How dangerous can he be?"

"Nora could be dangerous, if she put her mind to it."

Ash lifted a brow. "I won't deny it. But she is a friend, and I'd bet my life she has nothing to do with this."

"You will be betting your life if you invite her to Ravenrook."

"So be it. Besides, she is the only woman I know who could be persuaded to rusticate here for the summer and take Glenys Shea in hand. Indeed, I expect she has better things to do. But we can ask."

Geoff crossed the room and snatched the paperweight from his hand. "*Will* you stop tossing this about?"

"You needn't worry about Nora," Ash said with conviction. "She isn't the one."

"Which leaves your uncle Matthew, who is all of seventy and houseridden with the gout. He'll have to dispatch you quickly if he hopes to inherit before sticking his own spoon in the wall. Or do you figure he's after the title for his son? He dotes on Evan, which is no surprise since Jervase is somewhat of a black sheep."

"And so, again, we have quarreled about my family. Good Lord, Geoff. Evan was born to be a country squire. He is perfectly content to farm his father's considerable holdings and raise his own sons and daughters."

"He can't be the one," Geoff mocked. "Four men, two with wives, stand to benefit to a greater or lesser degree if you die without an heir. But whenever we discuss them, you insist there is little motive, or less opportunity, or no capacity at all, to carry off the attacks. And yet, Lord Ravensby, it is *you* who thinks the villain is one of these people." He ran his fingers through his hair. "Has the contradiction never occurred to you?"

"Now and again. Reason tells me it isn't Evan, who has the most to gain, or Jervase, who is no stranger to crime. Matthew and Wilfred are too old to care. Reason tells me someone exposed in the investigations is seeking revenge. But my instinct says family, and I can't explain it any better than I've done."

Closing his eyes, he rubbed his temples with both hands. And when he looked up again, Geoff was standing in front of him, holding out a full glass of brandy.

"Another headache coming on?" he asked softly. "Drink this and try to get some sleep."

"We haven't decided what to do about the Sheas," Ash protested.

"That can wait. Meantime, there is something that cannot. Tomorrow, we must bury their father."

11

At the top of a softly rounded hill, the ash-wood coffin holding the body of Sergeant John O'Reardon Shea was lowered into the ground.

The noonday sun warm on her neck, Glenys held her brother's hand as Lord Killain presided over the service. Big Charlie and Robin had helped carry the coffin to this spot, nearly a mile from the house. Fortescue the butler, Mrs. Beagle the housekeeper, Mrs. Hilton the cook, Prudence the maid, and fifty people she did not know by name stood silently as Killain spoke the words of the Twenty-third Psalm.

Only Ravensby was not there.

Perhaps the earl had decided his presence would be awkward, or unwelcome. Or perhaps he didn't care enough to come.

With effort, she wrenched her thoughts to what Killain was saying. He'd begun to speak of Jack Shea, the soldier who spent most of his adult life in the service of England. Around her, people nodded their heads in appreciation as the battles he'd fought were named. Harry must have told Lord Killain the stories that followed—slight, touching anecdotes of a soldier's life, most of which she'd never heard.

Tears gathered in her eyes to think of it. Jack Shea had been given a hero's burial after all, here in this beautiful place, with scores of people gathered to honor him.

"When I was dispatched to the Peninsula," Killain said in a ringing voice, "wearing the insignia of my purchased rank and ignorant as sin, it was a man like Sergeant John Shea who taught me to lead my battalion. It was the experienced men, the career soldiers, who defeated Napoleon. England has not welcomed them home as they deserve. But now God has opened heaven's gate to John Shea, who looks down with pride on his children. They are his legacy to the country he loved. They carry in their hearts his indomitable courage."

Beside her, Harry made a choking sound and she passed him her handkerchief. Then she had to turn away, to wipe her eyes on her sleeve. And as she did, she saw him.

The earl stood on a slight rise behind the crowd, in the shadow of a large tree. His hands were clasped behind his back. The soft breeze lifted his hair as he watched, his face without expression.

Was he thinking of the night her father died? she wondered. Or was he grieving for Lady Ellen, remembering the day he buried his wife? Her heart went out to him even as she turned back to the grave and joined the others in speaking the Lord's Prayer.

After that a hush fell over the crowd. She realized Killain was staring at Harry, gesturing slightly with his hand. Harry stared back, a confused look on his face.

It occurred to her that he'd not been to a funeral since their mother died, and he wouldn't remember that. "You are supposed to toss dirt on the coffin," she whispered.

Hastily, he picked up a handful a damp earth from the mound beside the grave. "Goodbye, Papa," he murmured. "Thanks for coming to find me."

Glenys bent to the mound of dirt and saw, growing beside it, a circle of bright yellow dandelions. She plucked those instead and dropped them one by one into the dark hole. "I hope you've found Mama by now," she said softly. "Watch over Harry, will you? And me too. I wish I'd known you better, Papa. I love you."

Lord Killain spoke a beautiful prayer then, about angels leading Papa's soul into Paradise, and when he was done, the mourners moved slowly down the hill. Not certain what to do, Glenys took Harry's hand and followed them, glancing over her shoulder to the place where Ravensby had stood.

He was gone.

Harry chattered on the long walk back, telling her how Lord Killain had taken breakfast with him and asked about Papa. She barely listened. And when they neared the house, she broke away and headed through the ash grove, hoping to come upon the pool house again. She thought Ravensby might have gone there, and she wanted to speak with him.

In daylight the marble building was not so mysterious as when first she'd seen it, lit from within by torches. Now the classic Palladian temple, reflected in the water of the still lake, looked serene and pure. Not at all a place for orgies, she realized, settling on a large stone to wait.

This time she didn't dare peek in the window, even

to make sure he was there. The earl's opinion of her was low enough already.

Despite the warm sun on her back, she shivered. What was to become of her now? Of Harry? Would Ravensby turn them over to the law, or let them go free? Without tuppence in their pockets, the future would be grim, but even a hardscrabble life on the streets was better than prison.

She tried to plan a speech to give the earl, logical and conciliatory. But all she could think of was how he looked, standing alone under that tree.

Before anything else, she must thank him for giving Papa an honorable burial.

That was kind of him. Unexpected, although after what Lord Killain had told her, she didn't know what to think of Ravensby. At least his suspicions made sense, now that she understood what lay behind them. And from Harry's account of their trip to the Snake Inn, the earl accepted the odd coincidence that led to the fatal meeting on the road to Ravenrook.

He no longer thought them assassins—only robbers. Progress of a sort, she supposed. Perhaps he would let them go, if only to rid himself of a pair of troublemakers.

The trouble was, she wanted to stay.

That revelation surprised her even as it came into her thoughts. Stay? Whatever for?

A score of reasons passed swiftly through her mind. Warm bed. Good food. Security. The list went on and she dismissed each item as it flitted past. Only one came back, again and again, until she was forced to acknowledge it.

She wanted to see him smile.

A mutton-headed notion, but she could not rid herself of it. The Earl of Ravensby was the most joyless creature she had ever encountered. She could not bear the thought of leaving him that way.

It made no sense whatever. As if *she* could change a thing.

And yet, she knew what it was to have nothing to look forward to, day after day, except more of the same drudgery. Ravenrook was ever so much more comfortable than Miss Pipcock's School, of course, and the earl could make his own schedule and do what he liked within the confines of the huge estate. But he was as much a prisoner as she had been.

Looking down at the soft muslin of her lavender dress, a gown that had once belonged to his wife, she felt the walls that encircled him closing around her too.

She thrust them away. Pain, she had learned, was inevitable, and much of what happened in life was beyond one's control. She had been born poor and plain. She had no particular talent she could think of. Her sharp tongue and irrepressible curiosity never failed to land her in trouble.

But for all that, she had a gift for happiness. God, generous in His inscrutable way, had blessed her with optimism, a sense of humor, and the assurance tomorrow would be better if she worked hard to make it so. The fact that most days of her life plodded one after the other, with no discernible change, never dimmed her hopes for the future. And always she took joy in the present.

Not much to offer the somber Earl of Ravensby, but she rather thought a touch of what she did well was exactly what he needed.

He was unlikely to agree.

Still, the challenge tingled at her fingertips and toes, feeling altogether right. And having resolved to see to the earl's happiness, she couldn't wait another moment to begin. Bouncing to her feet, she hurried up the marble steps and opened the door.

The cavernous pool house was as cold as she remembered, and empty. Like blue glass, the water reflected light from the windows onto the marble ceiling. She stood for a moment, watching the play of sunshine on the icy pool. In this place the warm brightness of the sun was transformed into a cold, sterile glare.

She had been so sure Ravensby would come here, to thrash out his bottled-up energy in the arctic water.

Shoulders drooping, she made her way outside and lifted her face to the brilliant afternoon sky. Had she thought it would be easy? Lord, she couldn't even find the man.

With a sigh she headed in the direction of the house, or where she thought it was. But an hour later, thoroughly lost, she found herself emerging from the woods near the rise of a steep hill. With nothing better to do, she followed the curve of the hill for a time until she came to an unmistakable path upward.

From the top, perhaps she would be able to see the house and plot her way back. Lifting her skirt, she began the ascent.

It was only the first of several hills, she quickly discovered. The next was higher yet, and she mounted it too. Even so, she could see nothing but the tops of trees and, more distant than she expected, the marble dome of the pool house.

By the time she reached the summit of the third hill, she was hot and panting with exertion. Although the sky remained bright overhead, the pool house, trees, and landscape below her were lost in a haze. Above her loomed yet another hill, this one enormous and flat at the top.

As she regarded it, considering whether to go up or

down, she saw a man striding briskly along the lip of the escarpment. His shirtsleeves, starkly white against the ruddy moorland and blue sky, fluttered in the wind. He wore a broad-brimmed hat and carried a large walking stick. The wide shoulders, narrow hips, and long legs belonged to the earl, she was certain, although he was dressed like a commoner.

Shading her eyes with her hand, she looked again. But he was gone, and she wondered if she'd really seen him at all.

Tired of holding on to her skirt, she gathered the fabric and tied it in a knot above her knees. At least her scruffy halfboots were suitable for walking. And walk she would, because she'd already made up her mind to follow him.

The path ended at an enormous plateau, barren and featureless except for eroded gullies and jutting gritstone. The sun beat down on her bare head, although the sky had gone gray. She could not see more than a hundred yards in any direction. The man had disappeared. But the path was distinct, and she followed it carefully, not trusting the moist, brown-red earth on either side.

Small footpaths veered off now and again, but she held to the wider track. A thick odor, of acid and stale water, hovered in the air. Warm droplets condensed on her nose and chin. She walked nearly a mile, so busy watching the trail that she failed to notice the mist closing around her. And when she finally looked up, she could see nothing at all.

Within seconds, even the path had vanished from sight. She held out her arm in front of her and could not distinguish her hand. The silence was absolute.

Oh dear God, she thought. What have I done?

Enveloped in the swirling mist, she abandoned her

attempt to follow the earl and began to retrace her steps. Somewhere to her right was the high escarpment, so she held to the left edge of the path. After a while it seemed narrower than before, but she couldn't be sure. Even though she bent over till her back ached, she could scarcely make out her own feet.

The ground on either side of her made a hissing sound, as if foul gasses were spewing from the boggy soil. Once, she stumbled and veered off the track, her boot sinking to the ankle in earth that felt like thick molasses.

After that she crawled on hands and knees, fumbling ahead to make sure the ground in front of her was solid. No question about it now. At some point she had left the wide path. The stench of decaying vegetation had become overwhelming, and she'd only to reach a few inches on either side to encounter mushy quagmires.

"Oh, hell," she swore. The farther she went, the more lost she'd get, so what was the point?

Dropping to her buttocks, she folded her legs, crossed her arms, and settled in to wait for the fog to lift. The invisible sun remained warm, and if the man she'd seen was indeed the earl, his bodyguards could not be far behind. One way or another, she would be rescued.

After what seemed like a very long time, she wasn't so sure. The mist had thickened, sweeping by her as if on its way somewhere in a vast hurry. Alone in the midst of the windblown clouds, she began to reflect on her own mortality.

One day someone would find her bones and wonder who she had been. Perhaps a monument would be erected to the Lost Virgin.

Hugging her knees, she permitted herself a sigh of regret for all the things she had wanted to do with her life. And to pass the time, she began to list them one by one. Travel. Read every good book ever written. Go to the theater and the opera. Look at great paintings. Seek out people needing help and find a way to change their lives for the better. Have babies and nurse them, watch them take their first steps, wipe their runny noses. Talk for hours with someone intelligent about the meaning of life. Make love.

That shot immediately to the top of her list. She did *not* wish to die a virgin, monuments notwithstanding. Surely God hadn't created her with so much passion and longing, only to lead her here and leave her to die in this desolate place.

She chuckled. Poor God, always blamed for everything. She had come here of her own free will and for no good reason. And really, she did not expect to expire on the moorland. Eventually the fog would lift and she'd find her way back to the wide path.

But she filed her list in her heart, promising herself that she would achieve every single one of those goals.

For too many years she'd allowed herself to drift, accepting her fate and making the most of it. She had remained an unpaid servant at Mrs. Pipcock's School only to be sure she had a place to lay her head and a meal to eat.

No more. Never again would she squander another minute of precious life for fear of the consequences, whatever they might be. From now on she would strike out on her own and do exactly what she wanted.

And right now she wanted to scream for help.

Her voice sounded muffled in the ever-thickening mist, but she kept it up even when her throat hurt and she'd long since despaired of anyone hearing her. Only when she was croaking like a frog did she stop.

Tears of frustration burned her eyes. And when a

tall, dark figure emerged from the fog, she was not altogether certain he was real until she heard his voice.

"You," the earl said evenly, "need to be locked up again."

Glenys seized the hand he extended and lurched to her feet. He pulled her close, and despite the mist, she could see his eyes flaming with reproof.

"What the devil are you doing here, Miss Shea? Men have lost their way on these moors and paid for their carelessness with their lives."

"I don't doubt it," she said with genuine penitence. "But there wasn't a hint of fog when I set out. And I thought I saw you, so I followed because—"

"Never mind that. A storm is blowing in. We need to get off the high ground." Turning, he pulled his shirt from his breeches. "Take hold of this and hang on. Try to step where I do. You've wandered into the deadliest of the bogs."

She grabbed a handful of soft linen, put one foot in front of the other as he led the way, and marveled that he knew where to go. Although she was clinging to his shirt, the earl was no more than a vague shadow in front of her.

Once, he came to a sudden halt and she fell against him, her nose at his shoulder and her knuckles pressed against the warm flesh near his waist.

He shook her off, as if he found her touch offensive.

"Would you rather I hold your stick instead of your shirt?" she asked.

There was a long pause.

"I require it to feel the ground in front of me," he said brusquely. "Just try to avoid stepping on my heels, and keep your mouth shut."

She did, for nearly half an hour, and managed to restrain her rebounding spirits when they began to move downward. With each step the mist grew less impenetrable.

He needs a haircut, she decided, studying the damp tendrils that curled slightly against the open collar of his shirt. Despite his name, Ravensby's hair was not raven-wing black. Dark brown, more like, with slight touches of auburn and gold. Multicolored, like his eyes. Like the man himself.

I will find you, she told him silently. *I will unravel you and put you together again, without the sadness.*

Tonight she would make a list of what he needed and all the ways she could give him those things.

Harry always laughed at her bedtime habit of making a list, outlining what she intended to do the next day. And she laughed with him, because her efforts to get organized invariably came to nothing.

She planned meticulously. She acted impulsively.

But from now on her lists would be more than a slate of dreams and good intentions. If the earl was to change, and she had determined that he must, so could she.

"You may let go now," he said.

Looking around her, Glenys saw they had come to the spot where she first began her climb. She stood on green grass again.

With surprising reluctance, she let go her handful of shirt and turned to gaze at the hills behind her. They were shrouded in heavy gray fog.

"Up there," the earl said at her shoulder, "the weather can change in an instant. And when the mist sweeps in, it often lasts for days. Even sheep are wise enough to stay off the highest plateaus."

"I think that was an insult."

"A warning," he corrected. "It borders on a miracle that I heard your cry for help. The fog muffles sound as effectively as it blinds sight."

She whipped around. "If it's so dangerous, what in blazes were *you* doing up there?"

"I've walked the high country since I was a boy. I carry a compass, a flask of water, and some dried venison whenever I set out. I leave a note where I have gone." His lips curved, not quite a smile but as close as she'd ever seen him come. "In truth, I too was caught by surprise. It looked a perfect day for a walk."

"But where are your bodyguards? I thought you never went anywhere without them."

He glanced away, color staining his high cheekbones.

"Slipped the collar, did you?" Frowning, she shook her finger at him. "Unwise and inconsiderate, Lord Ravensby. By now they must be frantic. I expect they are searching the estate at this very moment. And can you imagine how they would feel if you sank into a bog or were accosted by an . . . an *accoster?*" She was practically sputtering near the end. To her horror, she realized she had actually poked him in the chest.

He looked down at her finger, which was pressed just below his collarbone. She jerked it away.

His gaze lifted to her face. "Are you scolding me, Miss Shea?" In spite of his wet hair, limp hat, and the mist-damp shirt that hung loose outside his buckskin breeches, Ravensby was every bit the aristocrat as he waited for her reply.

"Apparently so," she said. "Under the circumstances, I think you require a scolding. Not from me, of course, because I've no right to point out the error of your ways. Is there anyone you will listen to when you misbehave?"

He stared at her, his mouth slightly open.

"I suppose not," she continued thoughtfully. "Who takes precedence over earls? Perhaps there is a duke or a prince with authority to call you to account. Not that you would heed any one of them, and I can't say I blame you. Miss Pipcock read me lessons in proper comportment for years and years before she finally gave up. Hoping I'd listen, that is. She never stopped nagging at me."

"I see you have chosen to emulate her," he observed dryly.

She sighed. "How low I have sunk. A nag. God save me, I am well on my way to becoming everything I loathe. You must do exactly as you wish, of course."

"In fact, I rather wish to throttle you, Miss Shea. Scamper to the house while you can, and reflect on your brush with disaster."

She took off at a run, wondering which brush with disaster he meant.

12

After several failed efforts, Ash managed to produce a satisfactory letter. Aunt Nora liked to read between the lines, and if he told her everything, she would feel cheated.

When the sealing wax had dried, he franked the corner and rang for a footman. Robin would take the letter to Derby, put it aboard the next mail coach for London, and hand-carry another letter to the magistrate. The death of John Shea and his burial on the estate had to be reported, if somewhat inaccurately, for the records.

When the footman was gone, Ash leaned back in his chair and gazed at the ceiling. Nora was almost certain to accept his invitation. When last he saw her—was it only a week ago?—she had complained about the tedious country house parties to be endured at Season's end.

Ravenrook would be no less dull, but where else could she play duenna to the Scourge of the Great North Road? Yes, Nora would come, if only to satisfy her curiosity. And when she arrived, he could draw his first easy breath since Glenys Shea erupted into his life.

Miss Shea was havoc on two legs. All energy and no sense. A disaster in the making. Even a brush with death in the moorlands had failed to dampen her spirits. The chit thought it a great adventure, but only because he chanced to appear and lead her to safety before the adventure soured.

Had she spent a night on the plateau, buffeted by howling winds and icy mist, she might have learned some respect for the mountain. As it was, she'd scramble there again on the slightest whim. Or she would decide to explore one of the caves that riddled the limestone peaks. He must remember to warn her about the caves.

Not that it would do any good. Discipline was noticeably absent from the Shea vocabulary. But he intended to put it there, in capital letters. While he took responsibility for the boy, at least in the schoolroom, his formidable aunt would shape the wild girl into a proper young lady.

And by the end of summer, the plaguey Sheas would be gone. Where, he had no idea, but he would devise a plan that took them far, far away. Even America was too close for his comfort.

Straightening in his chair, Ash began to gather the papers and books he'd been working with before his trip to London. The servants knew better than to touch the piles surrounding his desk or the jumble atop it. What appeared chaotic was perfectly ordered to him. Soon he was able to pick up where he'd left off, with an accounting of Wellington's requests for tents and the contracts offered by the government to suppliers in Lancashire.

Immersed in complex numbers and the convoluted

language of bureaucratic committees, he replied to a knock at the door with a harsh "Go away!"

But the knocking persisted, and he put down his pen with an oath of annoyance. "Come ahead," he called.

He regretted it immediately.

Glenys Shea stepped inside with a suspiciously bright smile on her face. She had changed into a yellow dress, which must have belonged to Ellen, although his wife never wore yellow because of her blond hair. The color was remarkably flattering on Miss Shea, though. It made her tawny eyes appear golden, like new-minted guineas.

More like the eyes of a barn cat he had tried to befriend when he was a child. A rotter, that cat. It sometimes brought him half-chewed mice, nuzzled his ankles one day and hissed at him the next—

"Pardon me for intruding, Lord Ravensby. I wished to thank you for the funeral."

For making it necessary? he couldn't help thinking.

"Well, that *did* come out wrong," she continued, blushing. "But . . . it was lovely, the service and all. Harry and I are ever so grateful."

"Then you must thank Lord Killain. He made the arrangements."

His curt response appeared to suck the air from her. The bright, beautiful smile collapsed and the glow in her eyes dimmed. The whole room seemed to go dark then, as if he had snuffed her light with a few careless words.

"Please sit, Miss Shea," he said more gently. "I meant to have this discussion tomorrow, when you were recovered from your ordeal on the mountain. Or later still, because I know you mourn deeply for your father. But so long as you are here—"

"Oh, *yes!*" She tugged a straight-backed chair directly across from him and sat, propping her elbows on the desk. "In fact, I've been pacing the hallway nearly an hour, gathering my courage to knock on the door. But I did, even though Robin said you were not to be disturbed, because I cannot bear waiting. I've lots of questions, but you start. What did you wish to discuss?"

He rubbed his aching temples with his thumbs. The girl changed moods with the speed of rolling dice. He could not keep pace with her. Logic, he told himself. Ordered sentences and rational discourse, unswayed by this mercurial creature and her odd flights of fancy.

"It was necessary," he said, "to inform the authorities of your father's death." When she gasped, he waved a hand. "In my letter, I told as much of the truth as I could. For the official record, John Shea was sick of a lung disease and expired in the arms of his daughter. I assumed responsibility for his children, both of age but in need of a place to live."

"My heavens." She sat back, regarding him warily. "I cannot believe that *you* told a lie. Several, in fact. That's so out of character."

What the devil did this wigeon know of his character? But her guess was on target, because writing that letter had scraped his conscience raw.

He believed in truth. It was his one anchor during the long years he investigated and exposed war profiteers. Even when his father insisted he cover up information damaging to family friends, he had refused. His father never spoke to him again.

Still, he remained convinced that aristocrats and commoners alike should be held to account for their actions. How else could justice be done? And he held himself to the same standard. A court of law would exonerate him immediately, but he longed to confess that he had killed John Shea.

It would be no more than balm to his conscience, of

course. And for the satisfaction of telling the truth, he'd have embroiled the Sheas in a judicial system that had little pity for criminals without title and wealth.

So he had lied. And if he felt guilty for it, Miss Shea must not think herself a part of the deception. He had, quite deliberately, given her no choice in the matter.

"There is a remote chance," he said, "that the authorities will pursue the circumstances of your father's death. But I expect they'll accept my word, if only because they hesitate to meddle with affairs here at Ravenrook."

"Should they question me, I will tell them whatever you wish. You are protecting us, I know, and I'm sorry for putting you in such a position."

"I'll not lie for you again," he warned. "Your career as a highway robber is at an end."

"And good riddance to it," she said airily. "I was not precisely a success, and felony is rather less glamorous than I'd imagined. In future, I'll leave the Great North Road to the professionals."

"You relieve my mind."

She leaned forward, her expressive face suddenly taut with anxiety. "Does that mean Harry and I are free to go?"

Did she want him to open the door and shoo her out? "Have you a destination in mind?" he temporized. "Family, perhaps, who will take you in?"

"*No!*" She bit her lip. "I mean, there is no one. But you can't want us here. Even on our best behavior, we are certain to disrupt your peace. Harry and I can make our way, somehow and somewhere, if you'll lend us a bit of money to get started. I swear on my life to pay it back."

"You require more than money, Miss Shea. Tomorrow we shall have a meeting to discuss your future, and I suggest you and your brother spend this evening in serious contemplation. Decide what you'd like to do when you leave Ravenrook. England will not be safe with the pair of you haring about, so I wish to hear of serious goals and plans to achieve them."

"Does that mean you'll let us stay here for a time?"

She didn't seem displeased, which surprised him. He had thought Glenys Shea eager to knock the dust of Ravenrook off her halfboots as soon as possible. "You will be my guests for the summer, *if* I am able to secure a chaperone. This is a household of men, except for the female servants. Although no one in my employ would do you harm, you cannot be permitted to run loose. It would be bad for morale."

"I see." Her lips turned down. "I am to be subject to yet another officious female with rules and regulations oozing from every pore of her body. You might as well send me back to Miss Pipcock."

"Would she take you back?" he asked with a surge of optimism. That would solve the greatest of his problems.

"No. Maybe. But I'd run away even if you convinced the headmistress to employ me again. Not that she ever paid me. I was her pupil for seven years and her slave for five years after that." She stood and leaned over the desk, planting her hands amid the stacks of papers. "I'll not die a spinster teacher, Lord Ravensby. I'd rather take my chances on the streets."

He nodded and then gazed past her, to the portrait of some distant ancestor on the opposite wall. Her fierce passion overwhelmed him. There would be no easy escape from Glenys Shea, he realized with guarded pleasure.

"You will choose where you go," he said. "But while you are on this estate, I expect you to obey me."

"I daresay you do." She released a theatrical sigh. "Unfortunately, obedience is not in my nature."

Trailing one finger on the edge of his desk, she moved to his side and peered curiously at what he had been writing. "Good heavens," she said after a moment. "This is *Latin!*"

Her hand rested on the back of his chair, and she leaned over him so closely that her breath tickled at his neck.

Was the child devoid of sense? he wondered. Although underfed, not at all pretty, and definitely annoying, Miss Shea was nevertheless female. Rather terrifyingly female.

To his vast relief, she straightened. "Are you aware, my lord, that almost nobody speaks Latin these days? If you mean to publish whatever this is, it won't have readers queuing up at the bookshops."

He nearly laughed. "An accounting of the economics of the Peninsular War isn't meant to be read. But some-day historians will find the information of use, and the details should be recorded while primary sources are available."

"In English," she said firmly. "Or French, if you must."

"I've every intention of translating to English," he assured her. "The discipline of writing in Latin helps order my thoughts."

"And assures that the book will take twice as long to complete."

He drew in a breath. She had grasped, immediately, that he drafted in Latin mostly to extend the project. When it was done, he'd have nothing to occupy his time or his mind.

"It will take *three* times as long if you don't leave me to work," he said. "Take yourself off, Miss Shea, and try to devise for yourself an honorable profession."

From the door she flashed him a saucy grin. "That rather eliminates all the fun things, doesn't it?"

Glenys leaned against the closed door of the earl's study for several minutes, trying to catch her breath.

In his cold, autocratic way, Ravensby had given her almost everything she wanted. In one single day he buried her father with honor, saved her from her own folly on the moorlands, lied to the magistrate on her behalf, and offered his home to her for the summer.

It had taken every ounce of her strength to keep from hugging him.

There were a few flies in the honey, of course. A chaperone would be a damnable nuisance, but only a desperate old lady was likely to accept a position in this isolated fortress. She'd be no match for Glenys Shea, who had eluded even Miss Pipcock's stern supervision.

And he expected obedience, which was patently absurd. A man who wrote long dull books in Latin was scarcely qualified to make rules for normal people.

But then, the Sheas weren't precisely normal—not by any standard definition. Chuckling softly, she headed downstairs in search of Harry.

"Ah, Miss Shea, I have been looking for you." Lord Killain came into the house just as she arrived in the foyer. "Will you spare me a moment of your time?"

She regarded him apprehensively. "Does this concern my afternoon stroll up the mountain?"

He looked surprised. "Why, no. I assumed Ravensby would ring a peal over you for that bit of foolishness. But if he did not—"

"Believe me, I have been duly reprimanded. The thing is, anyone could have followed him the same way

I did. He was clearly visible, you know, at least until the fog set in. And no one was there to protect him."

"Yes, I do know. The estate is relatively secure, but he is certainly at risk when he takes off without a guard. It is a subject we often discuss, with some heat, to no avail. When all is said and done, Ravensby gives the orders."

"Doesn't he, though." She scuffed the toe of her boot against the carpet. "It seems he is ordering up a chaperone for me. I hope he doesn't succeed."

Killain's expression darkened. "Come into the salon with me, Miss Shea."

He ushered her to a chair and stood directly in front of her, legs slightly apart. "I wish this conversation to be strictly our secret. If you cannot agree to that, please say so now. We'll not be violating the earl's trust, but he wouldn't approve of what I'm about to tell you."

"Oh my." She folded her hands in her lap. Why would Lord Killain confide in her, of all people? "You have my word," she said after a moment.

"Good." He began to pace, aggressively, like the soldier he had been. "The chaperone you mention, if she agrees to come, is Lady Nora Baslow. Ravensby's aunt. I don't trust Lady Nora, nor do I want her here, but he has overruled me. And because you will be in her company more than anyone else, I require your help."

"Y-You think her dangerous?"

"Possibly." He swiped his fingers through his hair. "We've reason to think a family member is behind the attacks on his life, although no motive can be determined for any one of them. And Nora Baslow is the least likely candidate, I must admit. She is in her fifties and has little to do with any of the family. Ravensby is the only one she keeps in touch with, and contact is rare."

"Then I don't understand why you are concerned.

What harm could she do here, with all the servants and guards about?"

"I am overreacting, as always. But some years ago there were several attempts to poison the earl. Two of them nearly succeeded, and poison is a woman's weapon. Not exclusively, of course, but Lady Nora has sufficient intelligence to plot a murder and more than enough cunning to escape detection. *If* she wanted to kill him, which she probably does not." He sighed. "Nevertheless, she will be *here*. And I don't like it."

"I assume you have tried to talk the earl out of inviting her?" When he nodded, she nodded back in perfect understanding. A supremely stubborn man, the Earl of Ravensby.

"If she's up to anything at all," he said, "it would be in the nature of evaluating the security at Ravenrook. Or acquainting herself with Ravensby's habits, like taking long unaccompanied walks. The information could be passed to an accomplice later, when she is no longer in residence. I doubt she'd try anything on her own."

"I believe I understand. You wish me to spy on her, while she spies on us."

"In effect. I sense you to be a good judge of character, Miss Shea, and remarkably observant. If anything she does strikes you as out-of-the-ordinary, let me know immediately."

It was the first praise, of any sort, she'd ever heard from a man. For just a moment she allowed herself to relish it. Then she turned her thoughts to a problem that had occurred to her with his final words. "If Lady Nora proves a strict chaperone, I may not be permitted to speak with you alone."

Without responding, he crossed to the window and gazed outside.

She watched him, puzzled. Was it such a sticking

point, this matter of communication? They could arrange a place to drop notes, or she might teach him some of Harry's hand signals.

Finally he turned, a smile wreathing his face. "Could I persuade you to become infatuated with me, Miss Shea?"

Her mouth dropped.

"A masquerade only," he assured her. "A humbug. But it would serve as a distraction, don't you see? In my experience, infatuated young women behave most peculiarly."

Glenys didn't like the turn of this conversation. "You've a great deal of experience in these matters, I suppose?"

"My share, but that doesn't signify. If Lady Nora sees you trying to get my attention, or stealing away for a private moment with me, she will be concerned only for your virtue. The notion we are in league together for some other purpose will not occur to her."

"Wheels within wheels!" she declared. "As if the whole notion of chaperones weren't silly enough. Should a woman decide to surrender her so-called virtue, no other woman is going to stop her. All Lady Nora can do is make a consummate nuisance of herself, and I fear she will."

"As to that, I am certain you can outwit her. And if she detects anything unusual about your conduct, such as watching her closely, she'll figure you are plotting ways to give her the slip." He frowned. "I do not mean to put you at risk, my dear. On the contrary, this scheme, outlandish as it must appear, is designed to protect you."

"Well, I don't see how it accomplishes anything but making me look like a goosecap," she said frankly. "Take no insult, Lord Killain. I daresay most women find you irresistible."

"But you do not," he said with a laugh. "And just as well. If I thought you might truly develop a *tendre,* this ruse would be a terrible idea instead of a poor one."

That hurt, more than she wanted to admit. Of course a handsome man like Lord Killain would never be attracted to the likes of her, but he needn't have been so blunt. She nearly told him that compared to Ravensby, he came in a very poor second.

He moved to the sofa and sat beside her. "I see you must be told yet another secret, Miss Shea. Two, in fact. If I draw you more deeply into my confidence, will you hold to the promise you already gave me?"

She inclined her head.

"Good girl. The reason Lady Nora may be a threat to Ravensby concerns the will written by his father. Most of the properties are entailed, so the old earl could not prevent Ash from claiming them. But four members of the family stand to inherit parcels of land if he dies without an heir."

"Are they valuable?"

"Not a one of them. In fact, there are several unentailed properties willed to Ravensby without any such entanglement. His father was, in effect, stomping a foot. It was a gesture at most, a way of punishing his son for disobedience. The lands are currently held in trust, by the way, for Ash's firstborn son. Assuming he lives long enough to sire another child."

Killain rested his elbows on his knees. "Ravensby believes his wife was murdered to prevent her from giving birth. Until it became known she was pregnant, she was never the object of an attack."

"Dear God. Lady Ellen was killed to eliminate an innocent baby? And by a member of Ravensby's own family?"

"That is the logical conclusion, if one assumes the

inheritance is involved. But the motive could be revenge, and connected to the war investigations. Always, we are guessing. And for that reason we take every precaution. If you pretend affection for me, no one will imagine a possible alliance between you and the earl."

She twisted her skirt in her hands. "I don't see the point of this deception. It's perfectly obvious Ravensby would never look twice at me. I'm a nobody. I'm not even pretty."

Killain squeezed her hand. "You underestimate yourself, young lady. But the fact is, he'll not permit himself the slightest attraction to any marriageable woman for the reason I've just explained. She might become a target. However, the killer is not so enlightened about his character, so we must make it perfectly clear your affections are otherwise engaged. Do you understand?"

She took a deep breath. "I think so. But I've never been infatuated. How do I go about it?"

"Oh, your female instincts will direct you once you get in the spirit of the thing. One day you'll be truly in love, but in the meantime, you can practice your wiles on me."

"You will be pretending too," she reminded him. "Or will you play the part of a harried male pursued by a bothersome nitwit?"

"Never that!" he protested. "Take no offense because I advised you against developing a genuine interest in me. You *were* offended, I believe."

"A trifle, since the idea of ensnaring you never occurred to me. It's a hard thing, to be rejected before there is reason for it."

"Rejection is not in question here. And so we come to the last of my secrets . . . if you are prepared for yet another shocking revelation."

"I'm beginning to think nothing you say will ever astonish me, Lord Killain. But go ahead."

"Very well." He gazed directly into her eyes. "From the age of nine or ten, I have always known that one day I would enter a religious order. Ah, I see I managed to surprise you after all."

Since her mouth was hanging open, she could only nod.

"Don't think I failed to struggle against my vocation. But there is no escape, if God really wants you. And for reasons I've yet to understand, He seems to be fixed on my poor self. I had thought to enter a monastery after leaving Cambridge, but instead I bought colors and went to fight on the Peninsula. At the time, I'd no idea if I was trying to escape or merely going where I was meant to be. Later, I knew I'd made the right decision."

"Are you Catholic?" she managed to ask.

He laughed. "It's a requirement, for the Franciscans, anyway. If they accept me, I'll become one of them when this business with Ravensby is done. I'll not leave him while he's in danger."

"God doesn't mind? I should think He'd want you in his clutches right away."

"It will come about, in His own good time. And, to be candid, I've never been in a hurry myself. Like St. Augustine, I've prayed, 'God, give me chastity. But not yet.' I'm no saint, Miss Shea, although I'll hold to my vows once they are made."

"Well, I think it's a terrible waste. How can a man with your splendid looks and remarkable talents run away from the world?"

"I wish to embrace the world," he said simply. "All of it, not just the bits and pieces that give me pleasure. Someday we'll speak again of this, if you remain curious. For now, understand that my path is clear to me."

"Holy hollyhocks," she muttered. "You are the last person I'd ever expect to become a monk. Does Ravensby know?"

"He does not. And you mustn't drop the slightest hint. He harbors enough guilt as it is because I stay here at Ravenrook instead of cutting a dash in London or settling down with a wife. If he thought for a moment he stood between me and God—which I assure you he does not—I'd be thrown out of Ravenrook on my ear."

"My heavens," she said, still awestruck. "You a Franciscan. I'm not altogether sure what those are, but they sound awfully dull. For a man like you, anyway."

"Sometimes it scares me too," he said. "Not the dull part—my life with them will be anything but that. I worry that I'll not measure up to my vocation, though, and admit to long nights sweating about what I'll be giving up. Then I think of what God's grace can work in me, for His own ends, and I am at peace again. We must trust, Miss Shea."

She regarded him dubiously. "If God has plans for us, why is Ravensby's life in such a mess? Mine too, and Harry's? Or does He care only about the people He calls to be vicars and nuns and Franciscans?"

"After seven years at war, watching my friends screaming in pain as they died all around me, I ask the same questions over and over again. But I have no answers." He touched her arm. "We do our best, Glenys Shea. We plod along, and teach ourselves to love, and make little puddles of light where we can."

Her eyes watered. "You will make a wonderful Franciscan," she said after a long time. "And it will be very easy to pretend I am in love with you, Lord Killain. I expect I am, in a strange sort of way. I don't know much about love."

"On the contrary. I have an instinct about these matters, you know. You have a loving heart, my dear, and a loyal one. May I count on you to help me protect Ravensby?"

Sniffling, she sat straighter on the chair. "Absolutely. I'll watch Lady Nora like a hawk, report to you, and keep every one of your secrets."

"That's my girl. Just one more thing. Try not to do anything that will give Ravensby an excuse to send you away."

Her heart sank. "Does he wish to?"

"He thinks he does."

13

In a flurry of silver swords, Ravensby and Killain moved with dazzling speed around the large, bare room.

As Glenys watched, the clash of steel resounded in her ears. Like two magnificent, deadly animals, they circled. Attacked. Withdrew. Attacked again.

Beside her, buckled into the fencing jacket Killain insisted he wear for his lessons, Harry practically bounced with excitement. "I can do that!" he whispered loudly. "Lord Killain says a fencer doesn't have to be tall if he's fast."

"You'll be an expert in no time at all," she assured him without taking her eyes from the swordplay. Privately, she thought that height and a long reach were bound to be useful in a real fight.

After a particularly swift engagement, the men separated for a moment, saluted, and began again. Killain fought with flash and daring, nearly always the first to attack. Ravensby's style was more methodical, although no less effective. He watched for openings, seized opportunities, and allowed his opponent to make the mistakes.

No, he elicited those mistakes, she decided after close observation. Sometimes he'd appear slightly off balance, or out of position, only to erupt in a dizzying counterattack when Killain tried to exploit a momentary weakness that didn't exist.

Lady Nora gathered her skirts and stood. "Glenys, dear, I begin to weary of this masculine posturing, and perspiration is not among my favorite odors. Join me in the conservatory when you've had enough, will you?"

"Yes, ma'am," she replied vaguely. Ravensby had driven Killain to the wall, where the blond man threw up one hand in a gesture of surrender.

"Well done, rascal," he approved. "But the next time you'll not be so lucky. I tripped on something."

"Of course you did." Ravensby gestured at the smoothly polished floor. "A wonder we weren't both brought down."

"Oh, leave a man some pride, will you?" Killain touched his blade to his forehead. "I miss the good old days, when you never won a bout."

"Take pride that you taught me so well. And now, young Master Shea grows impatient. I'll leave you to work your magic with him."

Hearing his name, Harry bounded across the room.

"No rest for the wicked," Killain said as he chose a foil from the boxes on the floor. He passed it to Harry and led him to a large mirror on the opposite wall.

Ravensby watched them for a moment before picking up a towel next to the boxes. While his back was turned, Glenys crept behind him.

"It is unwise," he said quietly, "to approach an armed man from the rear."

"Towels at dawn?" she challenged with a laugh.

When he turned, she saw the sword in his hand. He'd been using the towel to wipe the blade and grip.

"Has anyone ever mentioned your tendency to impulsive behavior, Miss Shea?"

She thought he was teasing her, although his tone remained low and calm, as always. "Not a soul," she replied breezily. "Impulsive behavior was forbidden at Miss Pipcock's. We were trained to be models of predictable deportment. Whatever that is," she added after a moment. "Predictable deportment was the unofficial school motto, drummed into our heads at every conceivable opportunity."

"In your case, it must have passed directly out again. Predictable is the last word that comes to mind when I think of you."

Did he really think of her? she wondered with a flutter near her heart. In the two weeks since Lady Nora's arrival, she had scarcely seen him. He dined alone, in his study, and never joined them for games of charades and twenty questions in the evenings.

She knew he went for morning rides with Lord Killain and Harry, though, and longed to go with them. But when she asked permission of her chaperone, it was refused.

"Men require time among themselves," Lady Nora had informed her, "so they can behave like oafish schoolboys. When ladies are not about, they rattle interminably about cockfighting and horse racing and fisticuffs. They use foul language and, I'm sorry to say, emit unpleasant bodily noises."

After six months in a tiny cottage with her father and brother, Glenys knew all about those noises. But since she was a poor rider and would spoil their fun, she had let the subject drop.

"I did not mean to offend you, Miss Shea," the earl said in a tight voice. "That was intended to be a jest, not a reproof." As if regretting the admission, he began to apply the towel to his damp hair. The sword bounced against his chest as he rubbed, and with a muttered oath he looked around for a place to put it.

"May I?" She took the foil from his hand and swooshed it through the air.

He quickly stepped out of the way. "Careful! The tip is buttoned, but the metal has a sharp edge."

Moving to one side, she watched Harry and Lord Killain go through a basic exercise. It looked easy enough.

Placing her heels together at a right angle, legs straight, her body slightly turned, she sent her front foot forward and bent her knees, holding the blade at the eye level of her imaginary opponent and arching her other arm behind her.

This is fun, she decided immediately. And so . . . empowering.

Suddenly both men lunged. The front foot never left the floor, she saw. It glided forward as the back leg extended with a snappy motion. The back arm went parallel to the back leg, and the front arm directed the blade. Such a simple move. Even Harry could do it.

"En garde," she cried, commencing a lunge of her own. Her front slipper glided smoothly, and the foil darted out dramatically, but her rear foot caught in the folds of her skirt. She began to topple backward. Flailing wildly, she pulled her foot loose and staggered forward.

Ravensby dodged just in time.

The tip of her foil hit the wall, sending vibrations down her arm that all but knocked her off her feet. With a yelp she let go of the hilt. The sword landed on the hardwood floor with a resounding clang.

For a moment no one moved. Then Harry's braying laugh cut through the silence.

Glenys whirled and jabbed a finger in his direction. "Shut up, you great looby, or I'll give you what I just gave that wall!"

Killain planted a hand over Harry's mouth before he could take up the challenge and turned him back to the mirror. Soon they were both lunging and retreating with a grace she could only envy.

Cheeks hot with embarrassment, she bent to pick up the sword. *A wonder it's still in one piece,* she thought, not daring to look at Ravensby.

"Do you wish to join them?" he asked. "They've had only a few lessons. Killain will help you catch up."

She turned to him in surprise. "After that display, you think I could learn to fence?"

"Why not?" He wiped his neck with the towel. "You'll require mask and jacket, and a lighter foil, but we can purchase those if nothing here fits you."

"I'd also need to wear trousers," she said. "It was my skirt that tripped me up. Is that acceptable? Do women wear trousers when they fence?"

"I've no idea. In general, females do not fence, nor wish to. Killain must guide you. Meantime, you may as well join your brother and get a feel for the movements."

Bobbing a curtsey of gratitude, she was about to rush across the room when Harry's voice, loud and whiny, held her in place.

"This is *boring,*" he complained. "When do we get to fight?"

Killain spoke to him quietly, Harry looked chagrined, and they resumed the exercise.

Bowing her head, Glenys studied the sword in her hand with regret. Then she went to the padded box near the earl's feet, lowered herself to one knee, and reverently laid the foil in its case. "I cannot," she said. "But thank you for offering me the chance."

"Will you tell me the reason?" he asked from just behind her.

Standing, she turned and gave a tiny shrug. "For Harry's sake. But I cannot explain, because sound carries in this room. He mustn't hear me."

"Outside, then." Dropping his towel, Ravensby led her through the French doors into a tiny rose garden. "Would he be resentful if you claimed a bit of Killain's attention?"

"Not that." She paused, choosing her words carefully. "Harry desperately wants people to regard him as a man. And he's so small and slender that no one ever does. To his way of thinking, fencing and shooting are manly pursuits. If his sister takes them up, his sense of accomplishment will be diminished. Even worse, should I best him at either sport—"

She sank onto a wrought-iron bench. "I would try, you know. Not to beat Harry, but to excel."

"It's possible he will leave you in the dust," Ravensby pointed out. "Killain tells me he shows great promise. I'm teaching him to shoot, and already he gives evidence of a good eye and a steady hand."

"Oh, I hope you have told him so! Harry idolizes you. But I expect you know that."

His brows arched in surprise. "It is Killain he admires. I'm the one forcing him to read Shakespeare, speak the king's English, and rewrite his execrable compositions. Most days he's quite out of charity with me."

"It's true that he despises schoolwork," she said pensively. "But that's to be expected after what he endured at St. Simon's. The other boys called him 'Miss Harry' and beat him up because he was too small to fight back.

Well, he did try, but to no effect. When he ran home, the vicar told him to be a man and sent him back again. Eventually he ran away for good, in the other direction."

The earl propped one stockinged foot on the bench and folded his arms across his knee. "For all that, he absorbed rather a lot in the classrooms. It's returning now, that smattering of education. He will never be a scholar, but he'll be able to write and speak as a gentleman should."

"He'd rather ride and shoot and fence the way you do. I understand he's struck a bargain with you—extra lessons with a pistol in exchange for good essays."

Ravensby grinned, and she was so surprised she nearly slid off the bench in a heap. A grin wasn't precisely a smile, but it was close enough to send butterflies to her stomach.

"Your brother is a born horse trader. And I've yet to break him from pocketing anything he can get his hands on. He can't be selling what he steals because he's not left the estate, but—"

"Everything is stored under his mattress," she advised. "It's a wonder he can sleep atop that pile of booty. I think he must have taken the clock from the parlor, because last night we couldn't locate it when we played charades and needed to mark the time. He's stocking up, you know, against the day we find ourselves without a feather to fly with."

"You'll not be cast out of Ravenrook," the earl said stiffly. "Nor left to fend for yourselves without a legal means of doing so. Can you possibly make him understand that?"

"I've tried. But Harry was on his own for years and kept himself alive by stealing. It will be some time before he breaks the habit. Are you very angry with him?"

"I'm not angry at all. But the thieving cannot go on forever. Perhaps when he's gained a bit of confidence—"

"That's exactly it!" she broke in, delighted that he understood the problem. "Harry lacks confidence. I know you can't imagine what it was like for him, scorned and tormented by bullies. No doubt you were first in your classes and the envy of all your schoolmates."

"Not . . . precisely." Lowering his foot from the bench, he clasped his hands behind his back and moved to examine a rosebush. "My first week at Harrow, I was christened 'Spindle-shanks' in a ceremony that included stripping me to the altogether, painting me with glue, and locking me in the privy overnight."

When she gasped, he cast a brief look at her over his shoulder. "Mind you, I was already tall for my age, and so thin you could read a newspaper through my chest. I played no sports. And I was too naive to conceal my talent for languages and mathematics. While my father lived, I held the courtesy title of Viscount Castleton, which fueled antagonism from those who lacked a title. They took to calling me Lord Spindle and tugged their forelocks every time I came into a room. I thought I'd died and gone to hell."

"I'll wager you didn't run away, though," she said with more confidence than she felt. If he had, she'd just embarrassed him.

"No point in trying. My father was a slice more terrifying than my schoolmates, and he'd have sent me back after a whipping. But I did consider taking ship as a cabin boy."

"Holy hollyhocks." She worried at her skirt with both hands. "And I thought Miss Pipcock's School the vilest place in England. There was snobbery, of course, and backbiting, but I don't remember actual cruelty.

We girls banded together against our common enemy—
the faculty. Even when I became a teacher, I was always
on the side of the students. Are boys so different? Why
do they delight in tormenting one another?"

He turned, an arrested look on his face. "A fascinating question. Ragging is common fare at schools for
young men, and be assured I was not the only object of
persecution. Nor did it last beyond the first few months.
When Lord Killain practically adopted me, he forced
me to take up rowing. That put some flesh on my
bones. He also taught me to fence, the same way he is
teaching Harry now, and to use my fists. After I blood-
ied a few noses, the bullies left me alone."

You really do understand, she thought. But as the
sunlight outlined broad shoulders and muscled arms
under the earl's linen shirt, she realized that Harry
would never be tall and strong and compellingly masculine in the same way as this man. Her brother would
always be short and wiry, with curly ginger-brown hair
and rounded cheeks and a sweetly curved mouth.

All his life Harry would be forced to prove himself,
again and again. Her heart went out to him. And she
cursed the contrary fate that made him beautiful while
she, who longed to be beautiful, was not.

To her astonishment, Ravensby plucked a newly
opened yellow rose and handed it to her. For a moment
she allowed herself to imagine it a gesture of friendship,
or something more than that.

But his face wore the cool, aloof expression that
warned her to keep her distance. "Give that to Lady
Nora," he said, "as a peace offering. By now she must
be wondering where you are."

And with that he wound his way through the garden
and disappeared around the side of the house.

Bemused, Glenys lifted the rose to her face, savoring

the heady fragrance as she stroked the soft petals against her cheek.

Ravensby had grinned. Even tried to make a joke, although his sense of humor was clearly rusted over from lack of use. He had confided to her a story from his childhood.

He had given her a rose.

It was meant for her, she knew, in spite of what he said. And he was probably cursing himself for lowering his guard and permitting a stray bit of himself to escape.

Unless she figured a way to prevent it, he would hunker down again, draw the shutters ever more tightly, and play least in sight for another week or two. No question about it, getting through to this man would not be easy. But if that grin were to be transformed into a real smile, Ravensby had to be pried from his study and that pitiful excuse for a book. How could she force him to rejoin the world of the living?

She plucked another rose, this one for Lady Nora, and went upstairs to her bedchamber.

As she searched for a way to preserve her precious token, which she would cherish all her life, she realized how few things she had to call her own. There wasn't so much as a small cedarwood box to hold the flower, or a book where she could press the leaves and petals.

Shortly after her arrival, Lady Nora had examined the made-over dresses in her charge's wardrobe and mounted a shopping excursion to Matlock. Now the armoire held a number of simple, serviceable gowns, new shoes, a pelisse, and a warm woolen cape. On the dresser were a comb and brush.

She had an umbrella too, and a supply of jasmine-scented soap. A stand of drawers contained an assortment of underthings, six handkerchiefs, and two muslin night rails.

As the footmen carried parcel after parcel to the carriage, she had worried about imposing on the earl's generosity. And when Lady Nora selected a shot-silk evening dress for her to wear at dinner, Glenys protested that no one came to call at Ravenrook. Plain clothing would do well enough, although the simplest of her new frocks was finer than anything she'd ever worn.

Except for the gowns that had once belonged to Lady Ellen, she reflected with a pang of remorse. It must have hurt the earl to see them on the person of a scrawny girl and remember how they had looked on his beautiful wife.

She wanted to ask him if a servant could be sent to retrieve her meager possessions from the cottage, but Harry would not permit her to reveal its location. "We might need to hide there again," he'd insisted. "And I daresay a thief has made off with everything by now."

He was probably right, about the thief, and she had nothing of value stored there anyway, except for a few favorite, dog-eared books.

After some thought, she slipped her rose, the one the earl had given her, between the soft fabric of her night rails. Perhaps the scent would waft into her dreams, which continued to feature a man in the bed beside her.

Although she awoke clutching a pillow to her breast instead of a warm male body, the dreams lingered hazy and indistinct in her mind. She knew they had been infinitely more exciting than anything the day would bring.

And, like Caliban, she cried to dream again.

14

In the conservatory, Lady Nora had arranged a still-life display on a small table, set up her easel, and begun to produce another of her eccentric paintings.

Glenys quite liked her chaperone's slapdash, whimsical artistry. The masterpiece in progress featured a pineapple surrounded by daffodils and tree bark, although one had to examine the array on the table to be sure of that. The bright slashes of color on the canvas bore little resemblance to the model, or to anything else in the known universe.

"Lord Ravensby sent you a rose," she said by way of greeting.

"How nice." Lady Nora pushed her spectacles up her long nose to examine it. "Stick it in that pointy green thingamabob on top of the pineapple, will you? Too bad the rose is yellow, though. With those daffodils, the color is a bit redundant. Perhaps I'd better make the daffodils pink, for balance. What do you think?"

"I'm no artist," Glenys said, lowering herself to a

window bench. Since they were unrecognizable as daffodils anyway, the color was relevant only to her surprisingly amiable chaperone.

After the fit of energy devoted to replenishing Glenys's sparse wardrobe, Lady Nora had all but melted into the background. She seemed perfectly content to paint, embroider, and spice conversations with her droll humor and pungent observations about human nature.

By Lord Killain's account, she had been a veritable lioness in high society for twenty years. That was difficult to imagine. At first look she was singularly unattractive—tall, angular, with narrow eyes and a prominent mole on her chin. She wore drab clothes and no jewelry, not even a wedding band.

But she had lovely hands with manicured nails, her gray hair was cleverly styled by Wilma, her ancient maidservant, and her slate-gray eyes missed nothing. An air of self-confidence trailed her like a fine mist.

Glenys had tried to reserve her judgment, remembering Killain's warning that Lady Nora was shrewd enough to get away with murder. Of that she had no doubt whatsoever. But she could not imagine Lady Nora hiring thugs to kill a pregnant woman. Or trying to poison Ravensby, of whom she seemed genuinely fond.

"Pardon the cliché," Lady Nora said, "but cat got your tongue? I'd hoped for a bit of conversation."

Startled, Glenys cast about in her mind for an unobjectionable topic. Every subject she really wished to discuss was beyond the pale. Ravensby's dead wife, for example. She badly wanted to know more about Lady Ellen.

"I expect Killain has appointed you to spy on me," Lady Nora observed placidly. "Don't trouble to deny it. He wants no outsiders at Ravenrook."

"I'm an outsider too," Glenys pointed out. "And I thought you were meant to keep an eye on *me*."

"Not at all." Lady Nora jabbed her paintbrush on the canvas and swooshed it around. "You would be astonished to know why I am really here. And no, I'll not tell you the reason. It has taken me the better part of two weeks to figure it out, and from now on I intend to enjoy what promises to be a most intriguing summer."

Glenys nearly stamped her foot in frustration. "Lord Ravensby said I required a chaperone. What other reason could there be? Although," she added candidly, "why a female of no account, who isn't known to be here anyway, needs someone to vouch for her reputation escapes me. Especially since my reputation is in the mud already."

Laughing, Lady Nora came to her feet and propped the tree bark higher against the pineapple. "Exactly. And by the way, you needn't pretend to be head over ears in love with Killain any longer, at least for my sake. I've no objection you spending private time with him, even if you meet only to discuss the ways I may be plotting to murder my nephew. He's a good boy, Geoffrey Todd, and he'll not do anything of which I'd not approve."

Tilting her head, she studied the pineapple from several angles before resuming her seat. "That's better. Composition is so important, don't you think? What's your opinion of Ravensby?"

Jolted by the sudden question, Glenys blurted the first thing that came to her mind. "He's dead inside."

Heat rose to her face as she realized what she'd said. It wasn't wholly true, of course, because he'd almost smiled that very afternoon. But it was very nearly true. There was no joy in him.

"That was my impression a few weeks ago, when he came to London," Lady Nora remarked. "It was the first I had seen of him in more than a year, and I'd hoped for some improvement in his disposition. But for the most part he closeted himself with the men he's hired to investigate the attacks, or those he does business with. He spent no time at all in polite company, and little more with his mistress."

When Glenys gulped, Lady Nora waved her paintbrush, spattering red droplets on the nearby plants and tiled walkway. "Unmarried men invariably employ mistresses, young lady. Unless they cannot afford them, in which case they take up with opera dancers or, worse, street fare. You should be aware of this weakness in their natures. In fact, most married men of my acquaintance have a bit of muslin on the side. They claim a physical urgency which requires regular access to female bodies, preferably attractive ones."

Fascinated, Glenys leaned forward and propped her elbows on her knees. Until this moment no one had ever discussed manly needs in such a forthright way with her, although there had been endless speculation at Miss Pipcock's. And she was wildly curious about a certain man's physical urgencies, although she dared not say so.

Casting her a sly look, Lady Nora continued as if Glenys had actually voiced the question burning on her tongue. "Some men do keep to the marriage vow of fidelity. I'm sure Ravensby did so when his wife was alive, and for a good time after her death. He has a strict conscience, my nephew. When he finally chose to take a mistress, I introduced him to a lovely and refined widow. She was in need of funds while the complexities of her late husband's will were settled in court. She remains so, after all this time. Lawyers!"

Lady Nora made a sound of disgust. "They have all but ruined her life. I've a special fondness for her, because she harbors no ambitions and accepts that

Ravensby will not marry again. He has told her to look about for a husband, and I expect she will apply herself to the task now that their relationship has dwindled to almost nothing."

"But what will he do if she marries?" Glenys asked with painful curiosity. "I mean, regarding the . . . urgency?"

"Oh, he'll be stoic. Ravensby wears self-discipline like a hair shirt. Or he'll immerse himself in an obsession the way my own husband has done. Mind you, Wilfred was set on his course long before I made his acquaintance. He cares only for ancient history—Viking invaders and the like. We married because I was too ill-favored to attract any man I might desire, and Wilfred would have wed a barn owl if it came equipped with a sizable fortune."

"How awful," Glenys murmured. "And how sad."

Lady Nora dabbed splotches of blue paint on her increasingly nightmarish pineapple. "Not sad at all, my dear. We each got what we wanted. Our settlement left me in control of half the money, and as a married woman I can go where I like and do as I wish. Wilfred stays in Suffolk, out of my hair, and spends his portion on books and archaeological digs. We never consummated the marriage, nor did either of us wish to. Odd fish, the both of us, but perfectly suited. Have I shocked you?"

The woman's habit of dropping startling questions into her monologues had begun to amuse Glenys. "I am duly shocked," she said, hoping she sounded nonchalant instead of deeply shocked, which she was. "But in all these years, have you never regretted what you gave up for your freedom? Didn't you ever want to fall in love?"

Lady Nora put down her brush and turned to Glenys, a kindly glint in her eyes. "Examine this face, young woman. As I grow older, people expect me to look a hag and pay it no mind. But in my girlhood men gave me a wide berth, even the most desperate of fortune hunters. Although they could douse the lights when they bedded me, they feared I'd produce a babe as ill-favored as its mother. Only Wilfred, longing to uncover a treasure from the past and in need of funds to pursue his dream, could be brought to scratch."

Glenys knew better than to feel sorry for her. In her own way, Lady Nora was perfectly content. But if unbeautiful women could aspire only to neglectful, fortune-seeking spouses, Glenys Shea—who lacked the fortune—would unquestionably live and die a spinster.

"Lord Ravensby wishes me to settle on a profession," Glenys said in a thin, unhappy voice. "But for the life of me, I cannot fix on one. Even teaching, which I loved, means closing myself up in a school like Miss Pipcock's. I'm not sure I could bear it again."

"Women have few choices," Lady Nora agreed. "If all else fails, you are welcome to live with me as my companion. But I'm sure you can do better for yourself." When Glenys began to stammer her gratitude, Lady Nora waved a negligent hand. "Be off with you, child. Of a sudden, my artistic muse calls me to solitude."

From the conservatory door, Glenys gazed for a moment on the straight back and narrow shoulders of Lady Nora Baslow. This woman was no murderess. And the next time she spoke with Lord Killain, she would tell him so.

Ash was just pulling on a clean shirt when Fortescue knocked at the door of his dressing room and stepped inside.

"Fletcher and Wilcox have returned, milord."

"I'll meet them in the study—no, send them here directly."

When the butler was gone, Ash leaned his hands

against the dressing table for a moment. He had given that feckless child a rose, just like a lovesick swain. What had possessed him? He was not an impulsive man. And damned if he was remotely attracted to the chit. How could he be? She was under his protection, after all. Wholly ineligible as a mistress.

Where had *that* idea come from?

God help him, he'd bloody well better get used to living alone and without a woman in his bed. He had long since disciplined himself to ignore the maids at Ravenrook, hiring only married women for his staff. If the mere presence of a female who wasn't a servant set him on fire, life would become unendurable.

Smelling of sweat after a hard ride, John Fletcher and Peter Wilcox appeared at the door.

"He's on the ship, milord," Fletcher said. "It sailed two days ago."

"You are certain Jervase sailed with it?"

"The night before, he stayed at a pub near the docks. Wilcox saw him drink himself sick. I checked with the captain, and a cabin was reserved for Jervase Cordell. Next morning, we both saw him go aboard. Had to be helped, since he could hardly walk. He didn't come off again."

Ash nodded. "Have you anything to add, Wilcox?"

"No, milord. Like I told you in my letters, he went from the Snake Inn directly to the Crescent Spa at Buxton. Talked to a lot of people, mostly women, and took one to his room most every night."

John Fletcher plucked at Wilcox's sleeve. "You forgot the . . . you know."

"What?" Ash demanded.

"He takes opium," Wilcox said. "I was in India, and saw how men act when they've got the habit. Can't say for sure, milord. But he met twice with the kind of bloke who'd be selling opium. And he went to the apothecary shop in Buxton four times. I asked what he bought, but they wouldn't tell me."

All the signs, Ash thought. Wilcox was probably right. No telling if an opium addiction made Jervase more dangerous or less so, assuming he was ever a threat. In any case, he was gone and would not be back until autumn.

"Thank you, gentlemen," he said. "Take a few days off, visit your families, whatever you like. If you think of any small detail I should know about, send word."

"I took notes, milord, about everything he did. Descriptions of the people he talked to. Before I go home to Edale, I'll write up an account."

"Good work, Wilcox. And, John Fletcher, I haven't forgot about lessons for you. When your holiday is over, you'll be put to work at your letters."

John grinned. "I got nowhere to go, your lordship. Can I start right away?"

"Monday next. For now, you both require a bath."

When they were gone, Ash stared at his face in the mirror. He fancied Glenys Shea stood just behind him, a haunting presence wherever he went.

He had no idea why he kept thinking about her. Indeed, he made a point of staying away from any place she might appear. But her energy, her astonishing vitality, reached through the walls and across the empty spaces at Ravenrook until the whole estate was filled with her.

She had been a teacher, he suddenly remembered. Perhaps she'd be willing to instruct John Fletcher. For that matter, she could hold classes for others on his staff who could not read and write. He would ask her.

No, he'd tell Geoff to ask her.

At all costs, he must keep his distance until he regained control of himself.

And in the meantime, he thought wryly, he'd take a great many long swims in his blessedly cold pool.

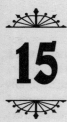

15

Ash put down his pen and swiped a limp handkerchief across his forehead. The early afternoon sun, streaming through the west-facing windows of his study, had begun to creep up the side of his desk. Soon he would be caught in the full heat of an unusually sultry June day.

With an oath, he pushed his chair back, went to the window, and raised the casement. Immediately, a light breeze lifted the damp hair at his collar, carrying with it the sound of laughter.

Just below, on the lawn, a game of croquet was in progress. He nearly closed the window again, to shut out the distracting noise, but then he caught a glimpse of Big Charlie wielding a mallet.

Charlie, playing croquet? Curious, he leaned his shoulder against the window frame and folded his arms to watch.

At the edge of the lawn, under a tree, Nora was perched on a folding chair in front of her easel.

Scattered about were several of Geoff's men and more than a few servants from the house, all chatting among themselves and enjoying the game. Their voices floated to the overheated study, teasing at his ears.

Harry and Geoff stood just below the window, mallets in their hands. Without meaning to, he looked around for Glenys and saw her near the goal stake, wearing a wheat-colored dress, her bright curly hair shining like a torch.

Tall and slender, she leaned casually on her mallet as Charlie lumbered across the lawn to a yellow ball, spread his feet, and swung the mallet back between his legs.

"Wait!" The sound of Glenys's voice carried all the way to the study. Charlie froze, looking confused. She rushed to his side and turned him around, pointing to a hoop in the opposite direction. Nodding, he addressed the ball again, took a powerful swipe, and sent it skittering to his right.

Even from fifty yards away, Ash saw the crestfallen droop of Charlie's massive shoulders. But Glenys patted him on the forearm and said something that brought a wide smile to his face. Then she linked her arm in his and drew him aside while Geoff moved in to take his own shot.

After several minutes, Ash was altogether fascinated by the game. Charlie made little progress, even with Glenys to direct him, but turn by turn he came closer to the hoop. And when he managed to direct the ball through it, cheers broke out from all the observers. Geoff clapped him on the back, Harry shook his hand, and Glenys beamed at him. Ash, caught up in Charlie's success, barely restrained himself from shouting his own approval from the window.

As the match progressed he began to notice how the

players' methods reflected their distinctive personalities. Geoff played with his usual careless ease, enjoying the game without concern for its outcome. By contrast, Harry concentrated fiercely on every shot, as though his life depended on reaching the goal stake ahead of the others.

Competitive little rascal, Ash thought, and a good man to have at your back in a fight.

But his gaze kept returning to Glenys. Graceful as a willow, she hovered near Charlie until it was her turn. Then, clearly bent on mischief, she ignored the hoops and aimed at her brother's ball. Sometimes she missed, but more often she succeeded in knocking it off course, forcing Harry to recover lost ground. She made little progress toward the striped goal stake, but neither did he.

Harry was not amused. After each hit from his unremorseful sister, he stomped around in frustrated circles, shaking his mallet at her and probably swearing a blue streak. The more he squawked, the more she laughed.

Ash glanced at the stack of papers on his desk, took another look out the window, and called it quits. He'd get no more work done in this heat, certainly, and his collar was beginning to strangle him. But he took his coat from the back of the chair where he'd draped it and put it on again, not wanting anyone to get the wrong idea.

He was simply on his way elsewhere, for a breath of fresh air. If he paused to observe the game, well, nearly everyone in his household had found an excuse to stop by. Why shouldn't he?

As he arrived on the edge of the playing field, Glenys was lining up her next shot. And from the wicked glint in her eyes, she was aiming for Harry's ball. It lay inches from the hoop nearest the stake.

Head tilted, Glenys calculated the angle and the lay

of the grass. Ash could almost see the wheels turning in her head as she fired a cheeky grin at her brother, pulled back her mallet, and sent her blue ball on a straight line for the red one.

With a sharp crack, her ball struck Harry's and sent it flying into a cluster of buttercups.

For a brief moment everyone held still. Then, to raucous laughter from the audience, Harry dropped his mallet and launched himself at Glenys, hands outstretched to grapple her throat.

Harry was fast, but with her long legs, Glenys was faster. Lifting her skirts, she fled down the long sweep of grass with her brother hot on her heels, directly toward where Ash was standing.

Before he thought to move away, she had darted behind him.

"Spoilsport," she threw at Harry. "Bad loser!"

Harry, who seemed unaware of the man standing between him and his prey, nearly ran into the earl. "Cheat!" He jumped left and then right, trying to throw Glenys off balance so he could get to her. "You don't play fair!"

Feeling rather like a Maypole, Ash stood immobile while Harry and Glenys circled around him, shouting insults at one another. Then, to his astonishment, Glenys seized his waist from behind and used him as a shield.

"Come ahead, wretch," she dared.

For a moment Ash thought Harry would try to go right through him. But the boy took hold of his senses long enough to pause, feet splayed and arms outstretched, a look of derision on his face. "Cowardly chit!" he accused. His gaze lifted. "Do you mean to protect her, my lord?"

Ash pried Glenys's fingers from his waist and stepped aside. "Not at all."

With a cry she took off again, but Ash grappled Harry's arm as he rushed after her. "Gentlemen do not assault women," he said calmly. "Even when they misbehave."

Panting, Harry struggled in his grasp. "She deserves a good smack! Did you see what she did to me? I was just about to win."

Ash swallowed a laugh. "You must learn to choose your battles," he advised. "A game is worth no more than your best effort to play well, even when you are thwarted by a vexatious sister. And brute force against a female, however irritating she may be, is never acceptable. *Never.*"

When Harry went limp, Ash let go his arm. "I wouldn't have really hurt her," he muttered. "Honest."

"I know. You'd have chased her down, made a great noise, and felt ridiculous because it was all sound and fury, signifying nothing." Ash stepped away. "Remind me to take up *Macbeth* at tomorrow's lesson. Meantime, there are other ways to get your own back . . . if you put your mind to it. Glenys has earned a comeuppance, don't you think?"

"I'll see she gets one," Harry vowed. "It's better to outsmart them, right? Women, I mean."

Better, but not easy, Ash thought as Harry bounded off to plan his revenge. In a battle of wits, his own money was on Glenys.

Two footmen had come out of the house carrying trays with pitchers of lemonade, glasses, and plates filled with small sandwiches and biscuits. Suddenly thirsty, he moved to join the crowd swarming around the refreshments.

Immediately, everyone moved out of his way, leaving him to go first. For some reason, that annoyed him.

Accepting a glass of lemonade, he wandered away, across the lawn. They could not address him informally, he knew, these men and women who worked for him. He was lord of the manor and they were servants, or bodyguards, or dependents in one way or another. Only Geoff, Nora, and the impertinent Sheas spoke their minds in his presence.

He found the shade of a tree and leaned his back against the trunk, sipping the cool lemonade. Nora had abandoned her easel for the moment and was engaged in a lively discussion with Geoff and Harry. Soon Glenys joined them, handing a biscuit to Harry. It was quickly devoured and she passed him another before wrapping her arm around his shoulder.

In a tight, enviable clutch of friendship, the four of them chatted and laughed as he watched, wondering what they found to talk about. Since Ellen's death, he rarely ventured into company. And when he did, all the awkward shyness of his youth flooded back. He listened, nodded, and made polite observations while wishing to hell he were someplace else.

Now Geoff, the one person he felt wholly comfortable with, spent most of his time with Glenys Shea. Nora had remarked on it soon after her arrival and asked, with a sly look on her face, if there was any reason to keep them apart.

Several hundred came to mind, all selfish and, at bottom, unreasonable. He told Nora to use her judgment, and set about resigning himself to a liaison between Geoff and Glenys.

Geoff had a small property of his own, in Devon, and it was past time he settled there to raise a passel of children. After years devoted to the interests of others, first in the war and later by playing nursemaid to his best friend, he richly deserved to cultivate his own happiness. And if he assumed responsibility for Glenys and her brother, so much the better.

None of them belonged at Ravenrook. Geoff should have been gone long before now, and the Sheas could not remain beyond the end of summer. Yes, the marriage was advantageous on all counts. It solved any number of his own problems. He would give his blessing, as if that mattered, when Geoff brought him the news.

And in the meantime, he might as well get on with the troublesome listing of factories that had failed to supply munitions by contractual deadline. Draining the last of the lemonade, he set the glass where a servant would be sure to see it and started back toward the house.

"Lord Ravensby!" Glenys hurried after him, flanked by her brother and Geoff. "We're about to start another game. Will you play?"

"No, thank you," he said politely. "I've work to do."

"Nonsense. It's too nice a day to be shut up indoors. But we needn't play croquet, if you'd rather do something else. Shall we take some boats onto the lake?"

"I'd rather shoot," Harry put in.

"You'll have your next lesson when you've finished the essay on syllogistic reasoning," Ash told him. "It was due yesterday."

"Have some pity on the boy," Geoff said. "Who wants to think about syllogisms on a sunny June afternoon?"

"Not me," Harry affirmed.

Not me either, Ash thought, to his own surprise. "As I recall, Miss Shea, there are a few ancient dinghies stored in the boathouse. But they'll need to be inspected and repaired before we can take them out. I'll put someone to it, and perhaps later in the week—"

"Oh, pooh." Then her face brightened again. "Are there fish in the lake? We could catch our dinner."

"There are fish." Ash looked at Geoff. "Have we any poles and hooks?"

"Charlie would know. He likes fishing, although I can't say I've seen him at it on the estate."

While Geoff went off to consult with Charlie, Glenys, ever optimistic, dispatched Harry to the kitchen for bait. "Ask for bacon," she called after him.

Suddenly alone with her, Ash clasped his hands behind his back and tried to think of something to say. "Are fish partial to bacon?" he finally asked, wanting to kick himself as the ridiculous question left his tongue.

"Who knows?" She gave a light shrug. "They haven't much access to pork, unless a pig happens to drown in the lake. Perhaps it's regarded as a delicacy. Anyway, *I* like bacon, so why shouldn't a fish?"

Lacking an answer to that, he trailed behind as she headed to the center of the lawn and began to gather the croquet balls.

"The servants will clean up here," he advised, noticing that most of them had disappeared shortly after his arrival. They probably expected a rebuke for stealing a few minutes from their duties, but he had no intention of providing one. Until Glenys and Harry showed up, entertainment had been virtually nonexistent at Ravenrook. The staff was more than entitled to an afternoon off.

"Lady Baslow repainted these," she said, holding out the green ball for his inspection. "This one used to be black, but she thought it too funereal for a game, even though a green ball tends to get lost in the grass. Mind you, we were lucky she agreed to solid colors in the end. She had already completed one masterpiece before we knew what she was up to. Come look."

She led him to a box that held a few extra hoops and

one croquet ball. It was striped in green and yellow, and spangled with red stars and blue quarter moons.

"Only a bit less frightening than her pineapple," he said dryly. Nora had showed him the painting and directed his attention to the yellow rose—the crowning touch, in her opinion. Glenys had given her the rose after all.

He'd meant her to, of course. He was disturbed only because Nora painted it with blue leaves and put a red splotch—a bee, she explained—at the center.

"We have fishing poles," Geoff announced, striding across the lawn to Glenys's side. "Charlie's gone to fetch them and will meet us at the lake."

Harry arrived moments later, breathless, a small basket in one hand and a half-eaten sausage in the other. "Cook gave me scraps of bacon and cheese and bread," he said, popping the last of the sausage in his mouth.

"Good heavens, save some bait for the fish!" Glenys snatched the basket away and, as she did, the croquet balls she'd been holding fell to the ground. She immediately set the basket at her feet and began to gather them up again.

Before Ash could remind her about the servants, she tossed him the blue ball. "That one's for you," she said. "Harry, you take the green." She passed the yellow ball to Geoff and kept the red for herself. "There's a game I learned at school, using ribbons, but these will serve as well. I wish to play it."

Harry shook his head. "Rather fish."

"We will," she assured him. "This is for later. What do you say?"

"Fine with me," Geoff agreed, and Harry reluctantly added his approval.

Glenys turned to Ash. "The game requires four players, my lord."

Despite the three pairs of eyes fixed on him, Ash badly wanted to decline. He'd never been good at games, even as a child, and didn't think himself capable of enjoying one now. "What about Charlie?" he suggested. "Won't he feel left out?"

Glenys's eyes clouded. "Oh dear, I hope not. But I don't think he'd feel comfortable playing. This is a game of wits."

"He's *in alt* to be fishing again," Geoff said, "and won't even notice. What say you, Ash? We seem to need a fourth."

"Oh, very well." He looked over at Glenys and felt her smile hit him like a blow to the midsection. For some reason, this game meant more to her than she was saying. "What are the rules?" he asked, suddenly very nervous.

"Pay attention, Harry!" She slapped his hand, which was reaching for something in the bait basket. "The first object of the game is to hide your ball where no one can find it. Ravenrook is enormous, though, so we'll confine ourselves to half a mile in any direction from the house. The ball must be in plain sight, if someone guesses where to look. No fair burying it or anything like that."

"Is the house itself off-limits?" Geoff asked.

"The public rooms are fine, and the same goes for any building where we won't be intruding on anyone's privacy. We'll have until sunrise to choose our spots, and it's against the rules to spy on the others or try to follow them. That means you, Harry."

He looked offended. "Wouldn't cross my mind."

"Right." She grinned at Ash and Geoff. "Watch your backs. Anyway, the second object of the game is to find the balls before sundown tomorrow. If you succeed in locating one, you must retrieve the ball and present it to the owner in order to claim your reward."

"Which is . . . ?" Ash inquired with a raised brow.

She tossed her ball in the air and caught it with the other hand. "Oh, the finder may declare what the forfeit is to be. In honor, it must be paid. Not money, of course, because some of us don't have any. It cannot be extravagant, nor require a great expenditure of time. And should there be a dispute, the other two players will render a verdict. Charlie can break the tie, if there is one. Any more questions?"

What are you up to? Ash thought immediately, but Harry had a question of his own.

"What if nobody finds my ball? Don't I get something for concealing it?"

"Thank you for reminding me. In such a case, the successful hider may demand a forfeit from each of the other players."

"An incentive to join the search," Geoff observed with a meaningful look at Ash.

Since he'd planned to hide his ball and wash his hands of the game thereafter, Ash glowered at his mind-reading friend. He should never have agreed to be part of any cork-brained scheme instigated by Glenys Shea. And he didn't believe for a moment this game had ever been played at Miss Pipcock's School.

Glenys had some devious goal in mind, and the cro- quet balls had suggested a half-baked idea to get her started. She'd almost certainly been making up the rules as she went along. Moreover, there was no reason on God's green earth why a fourth player was required.

She wanted him in the game. He didn't know why. And when he found out, he knew he wasn't going to like the answer.

The Scourge of the Great North Road had taken to the highways again.

16

The next morning, Ash arrived in the breakfast room while Geoff was filling a plate at the sideboard. He took his usual seat at the head of the table, where a dish of sliced melon was already laid out for him.

"Kipper?" Geoff inquired over his shoulder.

Ash gave him a sour look. After three hours in the hot sun, only Charlie had managed to pull in a fish of any size. And in his enormous hand, even that one looked like a minnow. He'd tossed it back. "I should see about restocking the lake, I suppose."

"Good idea." Taking the seat next to him, Geoff dug into a pile of scrambled eggs. "Hide your ball yet?"

"I did."

A footman set a cup of coffee on the table. "Will you have the usual, milord?"

"Yes, please." Ash speared a slice of melon with his fork and looked over at Geoff. "Where are the children?"

"Oh, Harry was off at dawn. He intends to pluck a forfeit from each of us if it means combing Ravenrook inch by inch to find all three balls. I met Glenys on the stairs. She breakfasted with Nora and was on her way to change into trousers before going out. Said she might have to climb a tree or the like."

"Good God."

"Makes sense to me. Skirts must be a bloody nuisance." Geoff cut into a wedge of rare sirloin. "When I've finished here, I'm going for Harry's ball. One of us had better find it, old boy. Otherwise, he'll have us at fencing and shooting lessons from dawn to dusk."

Ash put down his fork. "Does something about this game strike you as odd? It feels like a conspiracy to me, with more at stake than a fencing lesson."

"Can't blame you for seeing a conspiracy everywhere you look, but I think you're wrong this time. Both those rascals will take full advantage of us if they can, but there is no collusion. Fifty-nine minutes of every hour they are at daggers drawn, or hadn't you noticed?"

"They've a private way of communicating with each other, though. With their hands."

Geoff nodded. "I think it's a code Harry used on the streets. He still figures the world is going to cave in on them, and is trying to make sure they have a secret weapon in case they need to make a run for it. It's harmless enough."

"Perhaps."

The footman returned with a rack of toast and a pot of honey, and for a few minutes the two men ate in silence. Ash drank several cups of coffee, trying to shake the lassitude he felt after a sleepless night.

The headache had been milder than usual, but it sufficed to keep him pacing his room until sunrise. Random thoughts had played in his mind, but with the

pain, he could not order them to coherence. And now
he could only remember that some of those thoughts—
too many of them—had been erotic.

Geoff tossed his napkin on the table. "I'm off, and
wish me luck. A green ball will be blasted hard to
locate, what with all the grass and trees. Maybe we
should split up the territory. I trust you intend to join
the hunt?"

Ash slathered honey on a slice of toast. "I've work to
do. If you need me, I'll be in the study."

"The devil you will!"

"Think again. I was coerced into this nonsense. And
I hid the damned ball, which leaves me open to some
preposterous forfeit when it's found. If you want to do
me a favor, find it yourself and spare me a dun from
one of those rackety Sheas."

Geoff threw up his hands. "You didn't used to be
such an ass, Ravensby."

"Things changed. I changed." With effort, Ash
restrained himself from pounding his fist on the table
like a schoolboy. "If you disapprove of my behavior,
take yourself off for good. There's nothing holding you
at Ravenrook, and I sure as hell don't want you here."

From the door, Geoff cast him an amiable smile.
"When you are done with your tantrum, I'll expect to
see you outside. And for Glenys's sake, look around a
bit and pretend to be enjoying yourself."

When he was gone, Ash glanced at the footman. The
youngster stared at the opposite wall with a bland
expression on his face. Damn and blast. Gossip about
the quarrel would flash through the servants' quarters
like a wildfire, and he had only himself to blame.

"That will be all," he said to the footman in his
calmest tone.

Looking startled, the footman snapped to attention.

"I beg your pardon, milord? I must have been air-dreaming. Mr. Fortesque says I never pay attention to what's going on around me. Did you wish something more?"

"Only privacy, and another pot of coffee."

"I'll send it up on the dumbwaiter, milord."

As the slender boy, clad in Ravensby black and silver livery, crossed to the door, Ash let go a deep breath. "Thank you, Joshua," he said.

The boy turned and bowed. "My pleasure, your lordship."

When the door closed, Ash stood and wandered to the window, which looked out on the lawn and the grove of trees just beyond.

Loyalty. Of all the virtues, he valued loyalty the most, if only because it was so rare. And it was no respecter of persons, eluding aristocrats who betrayed friends and country in their mad chase after money and power.

But young Joshua, who would live and die in service, who might rise to underbutler in twenty years or so, was loyal. Loyal to a man who provided his servants with nothing more than good wages in an isolated household where a commonplace game of croquet became a festive event.

The words he'd spoken to Geoff echoed in his head. He had changed. Everything had changed. Since Ellen's death he'd huddled at Ravenrook, making desultory efforts to track the murderer and distracting himself with his book.

Somewhere along the way, without realizing it, he had become a colorless fish at the bottom of a quiet lake, trying to make himself invisible. Mistaking survival for life.

Was there any way to change again? he wondered.

Anything at all he could do for the people who depended on him?

He heard the creak of the dumbwaiter and reached for a clean cup on the side table. As he did, his gaze fell on a mound of fresh fruit in a chased silver bowl. Half buried under the peaches, apricots, cherries, and hothouse pears was a suspiciously round, startlingly red apple.

Glenys had even affixed a stem and a couple of leaves to her croquet ball, he noticed with a mental tip of his hat. The fruit bowl was a clever hiding place.

To her credit, Glenys had given herself the most difficult task. There were any number of places for Harry to conceal his green ball, and Geoff had doubtless found a patch of buttercups to match his yellow one. Perhaps she was playing fair after all.

But he doubted it. Leaving her ball for Harry to find, he poured himself one last cup of coffee. There was no forfeit he wanted of the chit, except good behavior, and he wasn't so stiff-rumped to ask for that in a game. But he'd check the fruit bowl shortly before sundown, just in case Harry failed to sniff out the trophy.

Damned if Glenys would get two shots at him.

She had earmarked one prize for herself by handing him the blue ball, because she knew bloody well there was only one logical place to hide it. At the least, she figured he'd opt for the pool house, if only because searching out another spot would be too much trouble.

But she had tripped herself up with her own rules, which required the finder to *retrieve* the ball. To claim the reward, she had to present him with proof she'd earned it. And to do that, she would have to get wet.

He'd tossed the ball to the very center of the pool, where it was nearly invisible against the blue tiles. She would find it, of course, because she knew exactly where to look. But there was no way to reach it without taking a swim in very cold water. He only wished he could be there when she was forced to take the plunge.

Why not?

Well, he couldn't deliberately spy on her. He was a gentleman, after all. And even though she'd once ogled his naked body through the pool house window, he was certain she had been even more surprised than he.

At the least, he could lurk in the vicinity and enjoy the look on her face when she emerged, dripping wet, from the pool house. Besides, he'd meant to check the condition of the dinghies stored in the boathouse, and from there he would have a clear view of the portico.

After swallowing the last of his coffee, he headed outside and was unsurprised to see footprints in the dewy grass. They led directly to the path that wound around the lake and ended at the pool house. Glenys must have passed this way within the last few minutes, because the flattened grass hadn't sprung back again.

She had rather large feet for a woman, he'd noticed some time ago, although he couldn't remember ever looking at her feet.

Arriving at the edge of the lake, he turned left, toward the squat wooden shed where the boats were stored. A dank smell, of stagnant water and moldy wood, assailed his nostrils as he went inside. He doubted anyone ever came here except the elderly gardener, who stored a few tools in the corner.

The boats had all been pulled from the water and stacked like tortoises against the wall. He rapped his hand against the side of a dinghy and splinters fell away like chaff. One lodged in his knuckle and he bit it out, realizing that he'd do better to scrap these derelicts and buy a vessel that would float.

Abandoning his plan to evaluate the boats for safety,

he returned to the door just in time to see Glenys, clad in trousers and a loose shirt, hurry down the stairs of the pool house. Her bright hair shone in the sunlight, unmistakably dry.

He could not credit that she'd given up so easily. She must have seen the ball at the bottom of the pool. Was she so put off by the cold water that she'd abandon a chance to claim her prize?

Until now it hadn't dawned on him that she might be unable to swim. For some reason, he'd assumed she could. But when had she the chance to learn, at that school where she'd spent most of her life? Swimming was not an accomplishment expected of a young lady, and for that matter, most men of his acquaintance confined themselves to hip baths.

Unaccountably disappointed, he turned away from the pool house and took the narrow path that circled the lake. Within a few minutes his long stride had carried him to the opposite shore. From there he looked across the unruffled water, imagining himself skimming underneath, along the mud and among the waving plants that grew there.

A small, insignificant fish. Charlie would throw him back.

Lifting his eyes, he saw a shape, small in the distance, headed for the pool house. Glenys. She'd come back for another try.

Suddenly breathless, he watched her vanish inside, her arms filled with things he could not identify at this range.

He couldn't help himself. He had to know what she was up to. Bypassing the shed, he moved into the shelter of the ash trees and padded cautiously toward the pool house.

If she'd taken off her clothes, he would turn away immediately. And even as he made the promise, the fantasies that had engulfed him last night returned in stark, vivid color.

He saw himself on white sheets, his body entwined with a woman's. She had long, slender legs. A bright cap of curly hair. She moaned under him, took him inside herself and cradled him there. Sent him out again, in a white heat, back into the light.

He propped one hand against the cool marble wall to gather his senses. It had been only a waking dream, a product of his headache. He'd had them before, although they were usually writhing with monsters and he always died at the end.

Moving to a window, he looked inside and saw Glenys's smoothly rounded rump.

He blinked and looked again.

She was on her knees and elbows beside the pool, directly in front of him, wielding what looked like a fishing pole.

Holding the pole underwater, she leaned out as far as she could, waving her arms backward, forward, and side to side. Was she actually trying to hook a croquet ball, for pity's sake?

Sure enough, among the pile of objects at her side sat the small bait basket from yesterday's fishing excursion. Did she imagine that croquet balls, unlike the carp in the lake, had a partiality for bacon?

Chuckling, he folded his arms on the windowsill to await developments.

The mathematics of the situation had eluded her. Since the ball lay more than ten feet from the pool rim and seven feet down, she couldn't possibly reach it with a six-foot pole. That was bound to occur to her after a while, he thought, but fifteen minutes passed with no change in her tactics.

Now and again she sat back on her heels and heaved

a visible sigh, shaking first one arm and then the other to relieve cramped muscles. Then she set in again, her backside wriggling deliciously as she applied the pole to the water.

Tenacious little devil. But smarter than that, he would have vouched until this moment. Only Big Charlie persisted in a clearly futile task, for hours if left to his own devices, unable to grasp why it wasn't working.

Vaguely disappointed, Ash made his way back to the house. Even army requisitions for soap and tooth powder held more appeal than watching Glenys make a fool of herself. But halfway across the lawn he turned again, and a few minutes later he resumed his position at the window.

In his absence, Glenys had discovered the cupboard where the bath towels were stored. She'd wrapped one towel around her shoulders against the cold and folded another under her knees for comfort. Otherwise, she continued to move the pole in the water, just as before, although she rested more frequently now.

Her arms must be aching, but he was unable to summon an ounce of sympathy for her. Bird-witted ninny. His fingers itched to plant themselves on her delectable little bottom and shove her into the pool. If she couldn't swim, and if she asked nicely, he might fish her out.

Looking closely, he realized that three or four green leaves floated on the water, just over the spot where he knew the ball to be. They had not been there when he left. And as he was considering that mystery, Glenys began, with exquisite care, to draw in the pole.

Hand over hand she pulled it toward her. The handle slipped under her elbow and soon nearly six feet of pole extended behind her. And kept coming, until Ash could have grasped the end had the window been open.

So much for underestimating Glenys Shea. She'd bound two poles together with fishing line, the narrow end of one secured to the handle of the other, creating a rod nearly eleven feet in length. More than long enough to reach the croquet ball.

With a crow of delight she dropped the pole and leaned over the water, looking straight down this time. And then she jumped to her feet, so quickly Ash barely had time to duck.

When he ventured a peek over the sill, she was sitting cross-legged on the marble floor with her back to him. He couldn't make out what she was doing, but she had detached the two poles. One lay beside her, a limp circlet of bent willow twigs and leaves at its tip.

His respect soared to new heights. All this time, she'd been struggling to trap the ball in the center of a wreath and draw it to the pool wall. It remained out of reach, though, under seven feet of water. Her clever rigging, designed to drag the ball, could not lift it out.

By now he was certain she had a plan for the next step. The end of the other pole lay across her lap, and her elbows were moving. Then one hand reached for the bait basket and he understood.

A few minutes later, with the small basket secured to the tip of the pole, Glenys resumed her position on hands and knees. The pole began its descent into the water, but it quickly became obvious the plan had developed a hitch. With a cry of frustration she brought the basket out of the water and fumbled through the pile of odds and ends next to her.

The straw basket wanted to float, he surmised, and she needed to weigh it down. With more fishing line, she attached something to the basket and lowered it once more.

Although he couldn't see what was happening at the bottom of the pool, he could well envision the difficulty of snaring the ball. It would tend to roll away when the basket nudged it. And since Glenys kept moving sideways, as if chasing the recalcitrant ball around the edge of the pool, that was apparently the case.

Soon he was forced to move to an adjacent window, in order to preserve his excellent view of her derriere. She'd not give up, so the outcome held no more interest for him. But her lithe, graceful body, and the energy radiating from it, held him like a grappled fish.

Three weeks of regular meals had filled her out in all the most interesting places. Her brother's trousers, which hung loose and shapeless when first he saw her wearing them, now molded themselves to a pair of well-shaped thighs and trim calves. When she raised her arms to manipulate the pole, he got occasional glimpses of a pert breast outlined against her shirt.

Bloody hell. He was behaving like the worst sort of voyeur! Disgusted, he relocated to the window most distant from where she knelt and forced himself to look at the play of light on the water instead of at her.

Glenys Shea was firmly off-limits, like a sister or a ward. And there was no real danger he'd cross the line. He had long since reined in his sexual desires. Marriage to Ellen taught him what discipline he'd not already acquired, and there were few opportunities for self-indulgence in the years after her death.

He could control his fantasies too, by immersing himself in his book. The waking dreams of last night had roused feelings he'd thought safely buried, but they would vanish again after a good night's sleep. Or a long, arduous hike in the moorlands. As soon as Glenys snagged the ball and claimed her forfeit, he would head for the hills.

With a shout of triumph she leapt to her feet and danced a little jig, the blue ball clearly visible in her hand. Her voice echoed in the pool house and carried outside.

"Got you now, my lord Ravensby. Got you now!"

17

Ash steeled himself to take his punishment.

Not wanting Glenys to imagine he'd been spying, he pulled off his coat and tugged his shirt from the band of his trousers.

As if planning a swim, he entered the pool house with the coat held over his shoulder by his thumb and feigned a look of surprise to see her there. "I beg your pardon, Miss Shea. If you wish to have a dip in the pool, I can return later."

"What a corker!" She gave him a sassy smile. "You know precisely why I am here and what I've been doing!"

Heat slithered up the back of his neck. Had she been aware, all along, of his presence outside the window?

She made a tsking sound with her tongue. "I must say it was poor-spirited of you to plant this"—she lofted the croquet ball—"dead in the center of the pool. You meant me to go in after it, did you not?"

"For an otherwise intrepid young woman," he

responded blandly, "you are remarkably averse to a touch of cool water."

"*Cool!* I only wonder how that pool remains liquid. It's cold enough to be a solid block of ice. But your plan failed, because I figured another way to get at the ball. Want to see how I did it?"

He swallowed a groan of relief and followed her to the fishing poles, strands of catgut line, waterlogged basket, and assorted paraphernalia. She looked vastly pleased with herself, bright-eyed as a robin and gesturing with both hands as she described her strategy.

He listened with half an ear, wholly enchanted with her delight. Some men would enlist for a thousand games like this one, just to see Glenys Shea in full display.

Then she pointed an accusing finger at him. "I outwitted you, my lord, but that does not excuse your beastly attempt to force me into the pool. For future reference, hell will freeze over before I set one toe in that water."

"There is also," he observed, "the matter of your own underhanded deviltry. Need I be more specific?"

To her credit, she didn't pretend to misunderstand. "I set you up by inventing the game. You tried to circumvent my plot. I bettered you." She lifted a brow. "Does that about cover it?"

"Perfectly." He met her gaze. "All but the forfeit, and I shudder to imagine what it is you want from me. Name your prize, Miss Shea, and let us be done with this nonsense."

To his astonishment, flags of color blazed on her cheeks. "You won't like it," she murmured, examining the ball in her hand with sudden fascination.

"I didn't expect to. But gentlemen pay debts of honor, and it seems I have acquired one."

"Here, then." She passed him the ball and took a step back, her chin raised in a gesture of defiance.

When she said nothing more, the hairs at his nape began to prickle. "Well, what is it?" he demanded impatiently.

"I want you to kiss me."

The ball dropped from his hand.

They both watched it roll to the edge of the pool, teeter there for a moment, and disappear under the water with a plopping sound.

She looked back at him, shoulders squared. "You heard me. A kiss. Just one. It involves no money, and no great expenditure of time. Exactly like I said in the rules."

He rubbed the spot between his eyebrows, unable to believe what he was hearing. "Miss Shea, you exceed every boundary of proper conduct. It is out of the question. I am astonished you even suggest such a thing."

"You shouldn't be," she said frankly. "By now it must be obvious I've had absolutely no contact with men who weren't related to me. Not since I was nine years old, anyway, and I don't think we can count Reverend Hensworthy. Well, there was also a gardener at Miss Pipcock's School, but he was positively ancient."

Thoroughly bewildered, Ash could only stare at her.

"The point *is*," she went on, "I require experience. By now I should have been kissed, don't you agree, and most women of my age have some notion of what it feels like. But I have none, which is awfully unfair because I've been curious about it for donkey's years."

"In that case, you can wait a bit longer," he said sternly. "Your husband will teach you everything you've ever wanted to know."

"Pooh." She tossed her head. "I'm more likely to find a buried treasure than a man who wants to marry me.

One I'd accept, at any rate. For all that I'm in no position to be choosy, I've terribly high expectations."

Do I meet them? he wondered briefly. Not that it mattered. He thrust the question from his mind. "You should have gone for Killain," he said between his teeth. "Whatever your *expectations,* I am certain you could do no better. And he'll be more than willing to educate you."

Her peal of laughter rebounded from the marble walls.

What in hell was funny about that? He glared at her, furious because she was willing to betray Geoff, who was obviously smitten with her, for a stolen kiss in a pool house with another man. Was she trying to mount a comparison? Good Lord, Geoff would win hands down. Geoff had kissed ten women for every one Ash Cordell ever held in his arms.

"His ball is affixed to a rosebush," she said. "I saw it this morning. But I'll leave Harry to find it, because my brother wants something from Lord Killain and I do not."

Trying to absorb that startling avowal, Ash ran his fingers through his hair.

"I made my choice," she said when he failed to speak. "I wanted *you* to kiss me. But apparently the idea is repellent to you, so I withdraw the forfeit. You may give Harry three extra shooting lessons instead."

"You continue to misunderstand, Miss Shea." Aware he sounded like a pompous ass, he gentled his voice. "I have taken you and Harry into my charge. As a consequence, it would be a violation of honor to—"

"Words, words, words." Picking up the towel she'd dropped while dancing about, she wrapped it around her shoulders. "And I thought it was cold in here before you came in. Compared to you, Lord Ravensby, that pool is a boiling cauldron."

"I speak of your own good, young lady."

"On the contrary. You quibble with me about honor, which a moment ago required you to pay your debt and now prevents you from doing so. Next we'll be debating how many angels can stand on the point of a hat pin. Pray forget I ever mentioned the subject of kissing, my lord. I'll seek what I need elsewhere."

"The devil you will!" In two quick steps he came up to her, grasped both ends of the towel, and pulled her against his body. "We'll get this over with now."

He meant to press a swift, impersonal kiss on her lips and be done with it. But she melted against his chest, pliant and supple, closing over him like warm water. God save him. Immediately, he was lost in her.

His mouth brushed her cheek, and the smooth line of her jaw, and her throat. He kissed her eyelids, and her thick, furry lashes, and finally her lips.

They were chastely closed, but infinitely soft. Her arms encircled him and her hands moved over his back, and she made a tiny sound when his tongue licked at the corner of her mouth. He nibbled at her full bottom lip, tasted the moist, velvety flesh underneath, and willed her to open for him.

She did, eagerly, rising on her toes to match his height.

His hand tangled in the soft curls at the back of her head as he pulled her closer still and deepened the kiss. Cinnamon and peaches, he thought hazily. And then her tongue met his with naive passion, vibrant with the life that flowed from her in waves. Flowed through him, until he felt as if he were kissing the sun.

After forever, all of him ablaze, her fingers clawing into his back and his hand reaching to cradle her breast, consciousness hit him like a mace.

What in bloody hell was he doing?

Disentangling himself, mouth and arms and the thigh that had pushed between her legs, he set her firmly away.

She gazed up at him, her eyes confused. "Oh my," she whispered, taking a step back. And then another, one finger touching her swollen lips. "Oh my. I had no idea."

And he had no idea what to say. What he'd just experienced was equally new and startling. Stunning.

Frozen in place, he watched her take another step back, shaking her head as if trying to emerge from a dream.

"How splendid you are," she said. A luminous smile curved her mouth. Her eyes shone like stars.

Bedazzled, he saw her take another step back.

Her foot met empty air.

Before he could react, she dropped like a stone into the pool.

Glenys managed one gulp of air before the icy water closed over her. She seemed to sink forever, but her toes met the bottom tiles and she kicked against them, shooting up faster than she'd gone down. She popped out of the water and back again, thrashing and sputtering and colder than she'd ever been in her life.

Paddling furiously with one hand and both feet to stay afloat, she pushed a clump of wet hair from her eyes and looked up at the earl.

He was doubled over. Laughing.

She could hear him, even through the water in her ears. The sound echoed in the marble pool house, bouncing at her from the ceiling and walls.

Suddenly, she felt warm all over. He was *laughing*.

In her joy, she began laughing too. And forgot to paddle. In a flash she was underwater again.

This time, when she emerged, Ravensby knelt by the

edge of the pool, an expression of concern on his face. Her flailings had carried her to the center, almost to where the croquet ball had been. "Can you swim?" he called.

She was tempted to pretend she could not, forcing him to dive in after her. But he had laughed, so she dog-paddled to him and lifted her arms.

He took hold of her, pulled her out in a swift, easy move, and propelled her outside into the sunlight. "Stay here," he ordered. "I'll get some towels."

She watched him disappear into the pool house and hopped about on the lawn to keep herself from icing over. The place around her heart still felt warm, but the rest of her had gone numb.

When she thawed out, she would think about that kiss. Relive it a thousand times, probably. It had been the best thing that ever happened to her . . . except for the moment when she saw him laughing.

And he had liked kissing her too. For just a little while she, Glenys Shea, had made him happy.

There would be no more kisses, though. She understood him well enough to know he would not touch her again. Suddenly, her future looked woesomely drab. What could ever measure up to being kissed by that glorious man?

But he might laugh again, if she was careful to put him at ease with her after what they just shared. Concentrate on the laughter, she told herself. Don't threaten him. He'll come back all righteous and gentlemanly, wearing honor like a suit of armor. Don't let him know how you feel or you'll drive him away.

Ravensby, jaw set and eyes distant, returned with an armload of towels. He took care not to look at her as she dried her face and arms.

Glancing down, she saw that Harry's shirt and trousers were plastered to her body, outlining every dip and curve.

Her nipples, on breasts that had puffed out after a few weeks of good food, were clearly visible. With care, she tied one towel around her waist and draped another over her neck, making sure her breasts were covered.

"Can you make it to the house?" he asked in a flat voice. "You are shivering."

"Truly? I didn't know icicles could shiver." She grinned. "Are you pleased with yourself? You got your way after all."

"I . . . ?" His taut face relaxed slightly. "Ah. Because you wound up in the pool. I confess that was my intention, but it was a damnably stupid idea and you have my apology for even thinking of it. Moreover, I should not have laughed when you—" He waved a hand, clearly lost for words.

Yes, he was reacting just as she had expected. Which failed to make it any easier to deal with him. "Holy hollyhocks!" she exclaimed. "What nonsense. It was fun matching wits with you, and I love a challenge. Nor do I mind a bit when I lose. Actually, I won on all counts except the last, when I went clumsy and stumbled into the water. And that, Lord Ravensby, was funny. Had you *not* laughed, I'd have given up all hope for you."

"It will not be in the least amusing if you come down with a cold, young lady." Briskly, he took her elbow and steered her at a fast pace toward the house. "You will have a hot bath, hotter tea, and a fire in your room."

There's a fire in my heart, she thought, struggling to keep pace with him. You put it there.

So cold you are, my lord earl, but you send me up in flames.

And I burn and burn and burn.

18

As Glenys had expected, Ravensby withdrew even more into himself after the incident at the pool. For the next week, they exchanged only formal greetings when they chanced to meet.

She made lists the first few nights, of ways to entice him from his study and that ridiculous book. But when she wrote *Drape yourself naked across his desk,* she gave it up. Although her figure had improved, she remained the plain female she'd always been—perhaps a jot more alluring than a parsnip.

The days passed slowly, in company with Lord Killain, Lady Nora, and Harry. But often she chose to spend time with Big Charlie, who took her on long walks around the estate. He seldom spoke, except to point out a particular flower or tree. Sometimes he would start a sentence and be unable to finish it. She felt comfortable with him, though.

Lord Killain had told her about Waterloo and the fragment of metal that pierced Charlie's head on the battlefield. There was no telling what he'd been like before the shrapnel hit. Killain found him wandering in a Brussels alley, brought him to England, and nursed him until his body healed.

"I'm one of his strays," Charlie once said. "So is the earl. Lord Killain sweeps up the lost people and takes care of us."

The same way Ravensby took care of the Sheas, she understood. Unlike Killain, he wasn't in the least warm and friendly. He didn't know how to be. But he cared for them nonetheless.

At dinner on Sunday evening, Lady Nora put down her soup spoon and focused her sharp eyes on Harry. "Your table manners are atrocious, young man. They must be mended, along with your conversation, and we must see to your wardrobe immediately. Gentlemen do not dine in buckskin breeches."

"I got nothin' else," he protested.

With a sniff, Lady Nora turned to Glenys. "The both of you require proper dress and more experience with polite discourse. No wonder my nephew refuses to join us at the table. I'll see to it he does, once you are fit company. Killain, day after next I'll take these reprobates into town for some decent clothing. Make the arrangements, please."

"I'll be happy to," he said. "Where would you like to go?"

"Castleton," she said after a moment's thought. "As I recall, there is a ruined fortress overlooking the town. I wish to paint it. We can shop in the morning and have a picnic lunch after."

"Peverel Castle," Killain said, chuckling. "I cannot wait to see your portrayal, Nora."

She lifted her chin. "You, sir, have no appreciation for art. Why should I paint the castle as it is? One may as well look at the thing and be done. I interpret. I transform. I illuminate the essence of inanimate objects."

"And I," he said with a gleam in his eyes, "will see to getting you there."

"Excellent. Invite Ravensby to come along. He's been all but a hermit of late. Not good for him."

Glenys agreed wholeheartedly.

Two days later they set out for Castleton.

Glenys, anxious to improve her skills on horseback, elected to ride. And to please her brother, she asked his advice about controlling the lively gray mare Killain had selected for her.

Harry found fault with every move she made. By the time they arrived at Castleton, the two of them were no longer speaking.

Lord Killain took a sullen Harry off to buy shirts, stockings, and cravats, while Lady Nora and Glenys called at the sole vendor of ladies' clothing.

"I cannot like any of these fabrics," Lady Nora complained when the dressmaker went to the back room for measuring tape and pins.

Glenys held out a length of forest-green crepe. "This will do well enough."

"For a matron, my dear. It would not flatter you."

Glenys doubted any material on the planet was up to that challenge. With effort, she tried to look interested as Lady Nora consulted again with the dressmaker.

Ravensby had not joined the excursion, and his absence leached away her pleasure. She had lain awake most of the night, formulating a list of conversational topics designed to amuse him. With a whole day in his company, she could certainly find a way to make him laugh again.

But when they had all gathered after breakfast, Lady Nora in a carriage with two of the maids and everyone else on horseback, Ravensby failed to appear. Glenys pulled Lord Killain aside, begging him to change the earl's mind. Who could know of their outing, or that it took them to Castleton in particular? Besides, Charlie and half a dozen other bodyguards would be there.

"This is meant to be a holiday for them," Killain explained gently. "They'll bend an elbow in the pubs, chat up the comely lasses, and forget their duties for a few hours. That will not be possible if Ravensby comes with us."

She was disheartened only for a moment. If she remained behind, she would have the whole day alone with the earl! Unfortunately, her story about a sudden headache failed to move Lady Nora, who merely suggested she ride in the carriage instead of on horseback until the headache went away.

All this, Glenys reflected, elbows propped on a bolt of black kerseymere, because of a stupid dress she didn't even want.

Eventually Lady Nora decided on a pale apricot sarcenet, chose a pattern, and rummaged through a box of embroidery thread while the dressmaker took Glenys's measurements.

"Make certain the gown and your bill are delivered to Ravenrook by tomorrow afternoon." Lady Nora pulled a coin from her reticule to pay for the thread. "Dinner is to be a special occasion."

Glenys looked at her curiously.

"Ravensby's birthday," she explained. "Mrs. Hilton is preparing all his favorite dishes, and we shall plan an entertainment for after the feast. I don't suppose you sing?"

"Like a frog. But why didn't you tell me earlier? I want to give him a present."

"How convenient, then, to be in Castleton where you can purchase one instead of nursing your headache at home." Lady Nora gave her a shrewd look. "Is it still troubling you, my dear?"

"Not since the dressmaker stopped poking at me." Glenys followed Lady Nora out of the shop. "I can't buy anything for the earl because I haven't any money. And before you offer, it wouldn't be the same if you paid for the gift."

"I would not dream of it. But there is nothing objectionable about a small loan, at moderate interest. While your pride does battle with your common sense, shall we look in at the jewelers? There is a stone, I am told, which is mined from the caves in this area and found nowhere else on earth."

The stone was called "Blue John," they learned as the talkative jeweler produced trays of rings, earbobs, and pendants. The two large caves where it was mined were open to visitors, and he would be most happy to arrange a private tour.

Glenys shuddered. She could scarcely abide a closed room, let alone the thought of a cold dark hole inside a mountain. But she thought the stone exceptionally beautiful, expecially when held to the light. Each piece was different—some nearly purple, others creamy with blue streaks, and a few with touches of burnt orange.

When Lady Nora asked to see items suitable for a gentleman, the jeweler pulled out a tray of heavy rings and silver snuffboxes with lids of Blue John.

Glenys had never observed the earl taking snuff, nor seen him wear jewelry other than his gold signet ring. She knew instinctively that he would not care for any of these things. Muffling a sigh of disappointment, she tried to catch Lady Nora's attention.

"What think you of this, my dear?" Pushing aside two of the snuffboxes, Lady Nora exposed a simple gold stickpin topped with a polished stone of translucent blue and ivory.

"Oh, it's exquisite." Glenys picked it up, imagining how it would look against a white cravat.

But when the jeweler, in a hushed tone, named the price, she shook her head and returned the stickpin to the tray. Already she was indebted to Ravensby for the very clothes on her back. It was unthinkable to assume another obligation for the momentary pleasure of presenting him with a birthday gift.

"We'll take it," Lady Nora said crisply. "And I'll hear not a word from you, young lady. Ravensby has little enough to give him pleasure these days. Killain bought him a new saddle and will help Harry select handkerchiefs or some other trifle. He tells me Charlie has been working the better part of a year on a sculpture. It's not quite finished, but he'll show the earl what he's done so far. I have sent one of my paintings to be framed, and it will be delivered tomorrow. Do you wish to be the only one without a gift to offer him?"

Put that way, Glenys could not refuse. She accepted the parcel, making a mental note of the price. However long it took, even if it meant flogging oranges in the streets, she'd repay Lady Baslow. And when she was back at Miss Pipcock's, or in America, or wherever Ravensby chose to send her, she would imagine him wearing the stickpin and thinking of her.

When they left the shop, Lord Killain and a very disgruntled Harry were waiting for them beside the carriage. "I have to come back again this afternoon for a fitting," Harry grumbled. "And the bugger wanted to pad me! Damned insulting to a fellow, I can tell you."

Nodding sympathetically, Glenys carefully set her package on the leather squabs of the carriage. "Is it time for the picnic now?"

"The maids have already gone up with the baskets," Lord Killain replied, "and Charlie has the easel, paints, and folding stool. The path starts just over there, beyond the church." He held out his arm to Lady Nora. "May I assist you? The ascent is rather steep."

"I'm not decrepit!" But she tossed her packet of embroidery thread into the coach and linked her arm in his. "Nor so old I cannot enjoy the company of a handsome man."

Laughing, Glenys pointed over Harry's shoulder. "Oh my. Just look at that!"

He spun around, shading his eyes against the bright sunlight. "Look at what? I don't see anything."

While his back was turned, Glenys took off at full speed and shouted at him over her shoulder. "Last one to the castle is a rotten egg!"

It was late afternoon before everyone reassembled for the two-hour journey to Ravenrook. Glenys, rather sore from her morning ride, had hoped to go back in the carriage with Lady Nora. But there was no room for her. Even one of the maids had to ride outside, next to the driver.

"My painting is not dry," Lady Nora insisted as she propped the large canvas on one of the leather squabs. "If we put it on top of the coach, it will attract dust and insects."

Privately, Glenys thought an insect or two could only be an improvement. Lady Baslow's rendition of Peverel Castle, all done in pink, put her forcibly in mind of spun sugar. Turquoise birds—crows, she was told when she imprudently asked—were scattered across the yellow grass and perched in the crimson branches of trees.

Evidently, she shared Lord Killain's lack of appreciation for art. Glenys took a last look at the ruined castle on the hill, its broken walls and weathered stones stark and serene against the clear blue sky. This was the picture she wanted to take with her, along with the memory of a surprisingly happy day.

After lunch she'd had a long talk with Killain about nothing in particular while Harry played tag with Charlie and the maids. For all his size, Charlie moved with surprising speed. The others had to cheat only a little to let him win.

Then Killain escorted a loudly protesting Harry down the hill for his second appointment with the tailor, leaving Charlie to watch over the ladies. As Lady Nora painted and the maids packed the remnants of the picnic lunch, Glenys wove a crown of wildflowers and placed it on Charlie's head.

Despite a few odd looks from the other bodyguards, a bit off their mettle after several hours in the pub, he still wore the wreath when they left Castleton and made their way along the winding road.

Glenys, twisting on the sidesaddle in a vain search for comfort, cast Harry a barbed look when he rode up beside her, laughing. "Care to trade places with me?" she snapped. "You won't think it amusing after a mile or two on this rack."

"Queer contraptions, sidesaddles," he agreed amicably. "Don't see the point of 'em m'self."

"It is perfectly clear they were designed to torture women." She adjusted her knee over the pommel. "I expect the inventor had a shrew for a wife and took his revenge on the lot of us."

"Papa let you ride normal-like. Did Ravensby say you was to use a sidesaddle?"

"Lady Nora. But it's her job to see I conform to standards of proper behavior for females. And *those* are set by men. Arrogant brutes. Sometimes they make me want to scream."

Harry sliced her a grin. "Oh, you like 'em well enough. Better than you ought, I daresay."

"Fat lot you know about it!"

"I sees more'n you think, wigeon. Took me a while to snag your play, though. Figured you'd gone sniffin' after Killain, 'cause you was practically living in his pocket. But it's Ravensby."

She felt a blush creep from her toes right up to her scalp. "F-Fustian. Sniff after a man indeed! As if I would do such a thing."

"I ain't seen nothing you *wouldn't* do," he retorted. "Not if you set your mind on it. Plucky little devil, for a girl." His expression grew serious. "It won't fadge, Glennie. He's an earl, and earls don't marry soldiers' brats. And he's a gentleman, which means he won't do nothin' else either. If you know what I mean."

She knew exactly. Or almost exactly. Ravensby had already done a good deal more than she'd expected, when he kissed her.

She hadn't realized that a man enjoyed putting his tongue in a woman's mouth, or dreamed how good it would feel. And for those few minutes in the pool house, he'd wanted all the rest of the "else" too. She was sure of it.

But as Harry said, he was too honorable to take advantage of her. She'd certainly not have tried to stop him. A man of experience, Ravensby had surely been aware of that. He must think her the veriest strumpet.

Sighing, she took a belated look around, but none of

the other riders were close enough to have overheard the provocative conversation. When the road narrowed, most of the bodyguards had moved in front of the carriage. She and Harry rode behind it, at a distance to avoid the dust and pebbles cast up by the wheels. Killain and Charlie brought up the rear.

"Didn't mean to read you a lecture," Harry said. "Damn fool thing for a brother to do, and bound to make you dig your heels in. But you'll only get hurt, Glennie. Take my word for it."

He meant well, and she gave him a smile to show she wasn't annoyed with him. Although she was. Not with Harry specifically, but with men in general because they took too much upon themselves. Why did males, even striplings like this one, assume the right to make all the decisions?

In the pool house, Ravensby had given her no choice. They both wanted to make love, but *he* decided otherwise. Now Harry cautioned her not to set her sights too high, although she already knew the earl would never marry her.

Was Glenys Shea a jackstraw, with no will of her own? If she chose to toss away her already dubious reputation, or risk heartbreak, what gave any man the right to stop her?

And if all that were not enough, she was forced to bruise her bottom on this scurvy sidesaddle!

The best thing she could say for men was that they weren't women. She had spent most of her life in female company, emerging with no great respect for her own gender. Instead of asserting their wills, women put leashes around their own necks. Their fondest hope was for a man who would lead them down the road *he* wanted to go and spare them the responsibility of thinking for themselves.

Even Lady Nora, the most free-spirited woman Glenys had ever met, expected her to conform. Like Harry, Lady Nora meant well and was only trying to spare her the inevitable hard knocks if she failed to be a good little girl.

But she'd been good, or reasonably so, long enough to see where it got her.

Nowhere.

She cast her brother a sideways look. Since she had made up her mind to rebel against dictators, male and female alike, Harry was a good place to begin. Despite the best efforts of Killain and Ravensby, Harry had not lost his taste for anarchy, nor learned to school his tongue.

"Have you ever done it?" she inquired casually.

He turned redder than one of Lady Nora's painted trees. "Are you dicked in the nob? Can't ask a fellow a thing like that." His voice cracked with embarrassment. "What's the matter with you, Glennie?"

"A mad attack of curiosity. You had plenty of opportunities, I would imagine, living on the streets. Certainly more than I had at Miss Pipcock's. I only wondered what it was like."

"You'll find out when you get married," Harry said firmly.

"I can't wait that long. Better you tell me now, before I decide to experiment."

Harry stared at her, horrified.

"You needn't go into detail," she told him, "nor apologize for indulging your manly needs. Lady Nora has already explained about the urgency."

Choking, Harry kicked at his horse, which was so startled after an hour of steady plodding that it nearly threw him off. When he regained control, he drew even with her again and jabbed a finger in her direction.

"Promise you won't tell anyone. And promise you won't experiment."

"I'll do exactly as I like," she said honestly. "But I'm not altogether a fool, nor a carrier of tales."

He emitted a gusty sigh. "If you must know, then, I never did. It. Wanted to, of course. Lady Nora is right about the . . . urgency. But I never had money to pay the girls who made a living tossing up their skirts, and it wasn't fair to ask them to play for free. They didn't like it much, y'know. Said they always pretended they was someplace else."

Hot-cheeked with regret, Glenys made a gesture to cut him off. She had not intended to rouse painful memories.

Harry, his eyes fixed on something she could not see, continued in a muffled voice. "They was good girls. Showed me the ropes—doorways where I could sleep, shops that tossed bread to the beggars when it was too stale to sell, that sort of thing. And when I got old enough, they let me kiss them sometimes, and see their bubbies. I couldn't take advantage more'n that. Didn't seem right."

She longed to hug him, but only nodded. Harry, sifting through garbage to survive on the streets of Liverpool, had been as much a gentleman as any aristocrat.

"We lived in packs," he said. "Some of the girls, the ones who didn't go professional, slept with the older fellows for protection. But sometimes they got—well, you know—and a baby can't make it out there. We buried three or four, I remember. And one girl bled to death when the babe wouldn't come out. We buried her too."

He looked up at Glenys, his eyes old beyond reckoning. "There were good times, and we watched out for one another. But I was glad when Papa found me."

She held out her hand, and after a moment Harry took it.

With an act of will, she kept silent. Harry would be insulted if she expressed the pride and respect and, yes, the pity she felt for him at this moment. And the gratitude, because he had opened himself to her, letting her glimpse what he kept hidden all those months in the cottage they shared with Papa.

A good man, she thought. My little brother, obnoxious and tactless and sometimes downright beastly, is a good man.

A sound, like the clap of distant thunder, caught her ear just as her mount sprang forward. She grabbed for the pommel, but a hard body swept her off the saddle and threw her to the ground.

She heard Killain's voice shouting orders even as he covered her body with his own. His hand pressed her cheek to the rocky earth. She was dimly aware of Harry scrambling for cover under the carriage. Hooves pounded on both sides of her as riderless horses stumbled around, directionless and frightened.

Killain planted himself over her like a turtle shell and lifted her by the waist. "Crawl toward the carriage," he directed. "Keep your head down and go to the left side."

When they reached the shelter of the coach, he opened the door and tossed her inside. She landed on top of Lady Nora and the maid.

"What happened?" she demanded as Killain shut them inside and disappeared.

"I think someone is shooting at us," Lady Nora said. "Are you hurt? There's blood on your face."

Glenys lifted her hand to her cheek. It was sticky, and her knees and ribs ached from the fall. "I'm fine." Removing her knee from the maid's stomach, she raised herself on the carriage seat and looked out the window.

The bodyguards, pistols drawn, had spread out along the steep hill and were moving steadily upward, wriggling like snakes. She saw Killain to the right and in the lead. He made a gesture and two men rushed forward then dropped again.

At another gesture from Killain, a third man exposed himself to fire for a few seconds before flattening himself.

It seemed to take forever, but as Glenys watched, the men advanced singly and in pairs until they had nearly reached the summit. Then Killain hurtled over the top of the hill and vanished from sight. Moments later the others followed.

With a sinking heart, she realized that Big Charlie was not among them. She wrenched open the carriage door and jumped out.

A hand wrapped around her ankle. "Get back," Harry ordered from under the coach. "I mean it!"

She kicked at the hand, clinging to the open door for balance. "Let me *go!*"

With a yelp of pain, Harry released her. She heard him running behind her as she sprinted toward the large body stretched on the road a hundred yards away.

Long before she reached him, Glenys knew Charlie was dead.

Blood was spattered all around, already drying in the late afternoon sun. Charlie lay facedown, one massive arm stretched out as if to fend off the bullet that had shattered the right side of his head.

The wreath of flowers she'd woven for him, soaked in blood, still circled his brow.

19

Late the following morning, Geoff returned to Ravenrook.

From the window of his study, Ash saw him dismount, slowly and without his usual grace, before slouching toward the house.

Ash immediately rang for the butler. Geoff looked like a man in need of a drink.

When he arrived at the study, moments after Fortescue had delivered the decanter, Geoff dropped onto a chair and accepted a glass of brandy with a nod of thanks.

Ash waited for him, patiently, as Geoff swallowed the liquor in two long, slow draughts. There was no hurry now. His hollow eyes and despondent expression said everything Ash had not wanted to hear.

Finally Geoff looked up and gave a doleful shrug. "Sangford and Blake are still there, poking around, but it's no use. Thought I'd better come back and fill you in." His hand shook and he set the glass on a side table.

"I'm sorry, Ash. We've
could all be over if we'd caug

"Good God, what more could
in any way to blame."

"That's what I'm always telling *you*
won't make me do so again, in this case."

"I don't wish to hear it, certainly." Ash lowere
hips on the edge of the desk. "Did you come up with
anything in the search?"

"From the signs, there were two of them. Only one
shot, though, so it's possible the second man was
reserving his bullet in case we got too close. Or he may
have been along as a guide. They chose the perfect spot
for an ambush—protection for the shooter, clear sight
to the road, and an ideal means of escape."

Ash lifted a brow but didn't interrupt. Geoff was so
weary it was a wonder he could organize his thoughts at
all.

"At the foot of the hill, we found the entrance to a
cave. It was small, concealed by shrubbery, but a man
could make his way in on hands and knees. I took one
of the coach lanterns and went about a hundred yards
until the cave branched into two tunnels, both large
enough to stand upright. My guess is a played-out lead
mine, maybe from the Roman occupation. The narrow
passage was probably a ventilation shaft."

"Then I expect you are right about the second man
being a guide. Only a local would know about that passage."

"I had to send to Castleton for more lamps, and then
we split up to follow each tunnel, and split again when
they branched. There were two or three more ventilation shafts, but after a few hours we found the main
entrance. It was large enough to shelter a pair of horses,
and there were plenty of signs they'd been there. But

All tracks

, understate-

never been closer, and this

ht him." I trust you

you do? You are not

oping to pick up

e of disgust. "Our

e who noticed a

e had some rest, I'll

pubs. But there must

. It will take time."

," Ash pointed out. "I
once .... in the Shire had been employed to watch
the roads for .... me. The general idea still
has merit."

"I agree. And your cousin Jervase passed through
here not a month ago."

"On legitimate business, or as legitimate as he ever
gets. He's well on his way to Italy now. I admit, the
coincidence is striking, but there remains the question
of motive. He has nothing of value to gain by killing
me, and every reason to behave himself while
Devonshire is lining his pockets."

Geoff did not look convinced, but it was his self-
appointed duty to be suspicious of everyone. "I suppose
it's occurred to you that Nora planned the trip to
Castleton. Without advance word of our excursion,
how could the shooter know we'd be on that road yesterday?"

"A carriage and ten or so riders may have attracted
notice," Ash responded with a touch of sarcasm. "You
spent much of the day in Castleton, so there was plenty
of time for the men to take up their position and wait
for you to pass by on the way home. Besides, she knew I
would not be one of the party. Why call out the dogs for
no reason?"

"*Did* she know? Right up to the time we left, Glenys expected you to appear. Nora may have been under the same misapprehension."

Ash levered himself off the desk and filled a glass of brandy for himself. "More for you?"

"Not if you want me to stay awake until we've finished." Geoff rubbed the bridge of his nose. "Do you recall discussing your plans with Nora?"

"I said nothing to her. We are rarely in company together."

"In that case, she is definitely a suspect. Send her away, Ash. Immediately."

"I'll think about it." He crossed to the window and gazed outside. The overnight rain had long since passed, bringing after it a bright, clear day. "Why Charlie?" he said in a shadowed voice. "The shooter could not have mistaken him for me."

"I've been gnawing that bone all day. Charlie and I were at the rear, side by side. When everyone had passed by, with no sign of you, the killer may have picked off a victim out of sheer frustration."

Ash swore profoundly. "Charlie was murdered because I wasn't there?"

"You'd rather have taken the bullet, I suppose. Which is equivalent to me wishing I'd been riding on the right side, where the bullet would have hit me instead of him. For God's sake, Ash, let us discuss this like two rational men. We can't afford to indulge ourselves in *what-ifs* and *might-have-beens*."

"You are right, as usual. Any other ideas why Charlie was the target?"

"Vague notions at best, and not in accord with your own theories. You remain convinced the attacks are linked to your father's will." Geoff sipped at his brandy. "For the moment, let's consider the other possibilities."

Ash shrugged. "Vengeance, from someone exposed by the war investigations. But this has been going on for six years. Who would pursue a vendetta all this time, with nothing to gain but the satisfaction of killing me?" He regarded Geoff somberly. "I should think he'd want me to know his identity before the final stroke. How else could he savor his revenge?"

"Good point. And it fits into my second theory about why Charlie was killed. Ellen too. What if the murderer doesn't care who he brings down, so long as it's someone who matters to you?"

"The early attacks were all directed at me," Ash reminded him.

"Yes." Geoff leaned back in his chair. "But once you'd surrounded yourself with bodyguards, it wasn't easy to get at you. So the killer went for your wife, hoping you would overreact and expose yourself to attack. You very nearly did, before I convinced you to come here to Ravenrook."

"And wait it out," Ash said bitterly. "But he hasn't gone away or given up."

"No. I had begun to hope, since there has been no direct attack in the last three years. But I was wrong, and now I think him more determined than ever. It may be only a soldier's instinct, but I sense time is running out. He took a risk yesterday. Without the rain, we might have tracked him. And even if the trail led only to a hired killer, I swear I'd have beaten the truth out of him."

"We are back to my original question, then. The intended victim didn't show up. Why take that risk to kill Charlie?"

"Because it will make you reckless." Geoff leveled a finger at him. "Ash, I can feel rage building in you. Right now you want to go charging out of here on your own, to draw the fire."

"That may be the only way to put an end to this," he said between his teeth. "I'd bloody well rather be dead than watch anyone else die because of me."

Geoff pulled himself to his feet. "In your place, I'd be tempted to the same folly. It appears the simplest way out, does it not?"

"Dying isn't simple," Ash gritted. "I've no particular taste for it."

"I am relieved to hear it. Sometimes I've wondered. You have been walking the edges of despair, my friend."

Ash acknowledged the truth of that with a nod. There was no use trying to hide anything from Geoff. But for the last few weeks, since Glenys and Harry Shea exploded into his dreary existence, he'd begun to emerge from what John Bunyan had named, so aptly, the Slough of Despond.

In the mornings, he awoke with something to look forward to instead of the boredom and aching solitude that had marked his exile at Ravenrook. There were lessons with Harry, never dull, and occasional encounters with Glenys. Scapegraces, the both of them, but they'd brought laughter to this house and back into his life.

Until yesterday, when Charlie was murdered.

He felt a hand on his shoulder.

"Ash, you must not lose sight of one thing. Unless you see to it, we'll never catch the man, or the woman, responsible for killing Ellen and Charlie. I haven't the funds or the resources to carry on. Without the goal of keeping you alive, I'm not certain I even have the will. If there is to be justice, only you can bring it about."

"But how? Dear God, Geoff, *how?* What in blazes can we do that we haven't tried already?" He looked directly into bloodshot, cloudy blue eyes and swore under his breath. Geoff was beyond answering even a question that had an answer. This one did not.

"Get some sleep," Ash said. "This evening, just before sunset, we'll bury Charlie. I thought to place him next to John Shea."

"He'd like that," Geoff said in a ragged voice. "They were both soldiers. Call me in time, will you?"

20

The next morning, Ash rose shortly after dawn, amazed that he'd slept at all. To be sure, half a decanter of brandy probably had something to do with it.

He'd drunk enough to fend off the headache that began as Charlie was lowered into the grave. After tossing the first handful of earth onto the coffin, he had left the others to finish the service and withdrew to his bedchamber for a raw, sleepless night.

The pain hovered still, just beyond the edges of a mild hangover. He shaved, swallowed several glasses of water, and decided to clear his head with fresh air and a long walk.

Wearing leather breeches, a cotton shirt, and his dilapidated straw hat, he located his walking stick and set out for the kitchen. At his request, Mrs. Hilton tied slabs of bread and cheese in a napkin. He thanked her, attached the napkin to his belt, and headed outside.

The early morning mist had only just lifted, and the grass was wet under his boots. He started to make his way for the path leading into the moorlands, but turned instead toward the hill where Charlie lay in his wide, silent grave.

Yesterday evening he had not been able to pray with the others. He didn't think he could pray now. But he would at least stand there for a moment, in tribute to Charlie and with gratitude for his loyalty and courage.

As he mounted the long slope, Ash saw that someone was there ahead of him.

Glenys, her arms filled with wildflowers, came over the other side of the hill and knelt beside the mound of brown earth, already half covered with blossoms. She dropped the flowers beside her and began, with care, to place them one by one on the grave.

Unwilling to disturb her, he started to back away. But she looked up and caught his eye. "Good morning, my lord." Her smile drew him, against his every intention, to her side.

She gathered a bunch of daisies and put them in his hands.

Silently, he dropped to one knee and began to strew the flowers over Charlie's grave. Like Glenys, he took care, watching her and making sure every inch of brown dirt was covered.

"He carved the stone marker for my father," she said, picking up the last daisy. "I wanted to give him something in return." Placing the flower, she closed her eyes for a moment. "Goodbye, Charlie."

And then she jumped to her feet, brushed off her hands, and regarded the grave with satisfaction. "It looks much better now, don't you think?"

"Yes." Standing, Ash watched moodily as she began to name the blossoms, directing his attention with her finger.

"Those are rockroses. The white ones that look like stars are ramsons. There are the lilac primroses, and mountain pansies, yellow iris, lily-of-the-valley, and wild thyme. Lots of heather, because it's easiest to find. Charlie showed me where the flowers bloom on the estate, and told me what they are called. This was his favorite." She plucked a flower from the grave and held it up. "Cloudberry. Isn't that a wonderful name?"

"Yes," Ash said again. He could think of nothing else to say.

Glenys bent to replace the cloudberry, and then picked up the walking stick he'd left on the ground. She gave him a stinging look. "My lord, surely you cannot mean to go on the moorlands today. Anyone might see you, or be waiting there already."

He reached for the stick and she snatched it away, holding it behind her back.

"But of course you were not," she said. "Forgive me. I know you would never be so foolish. You will confine yourself to the estate, which is large enough for a good long walk without any need to go farther afield."

That sounded, he thought, very much like an order.

She handed him the walking stick. "Will you permit me to come along?"

With effort, he located a few words and managed to string them together. "I'd not be good company, Miss Shea." A poor excuse, he knew the moment it came out of his mouth. When was he *ever* good company?

"We needn't talk," she said.

"I prefer to be alone." There. That was clear enough.

With a telling look, she directed his attention to the graves of Charlie and her father. "There will be time enough for solitude, Lord Ravensby."

A sick feeling churned in his stomach. If, one day, he fell to a bullet or died of poisoning, would it matter so much? The transition from his solitary life to a lonely grave would be all but imperceptible.

"Very well." He set out across the grass. "Join me, if you wish."

She fell into step beside him and they walked in silence for nearly an hour. Now and again he stole a glance at her face. It was uncharacteristically serene, and he wondered what she was thinking.

Pleasant thoughts, he decided after a while. Rather like his own. Instead of brooding, which he'd planned to do on the moorlands, he watched the breeze ruffle her curly hair and considered the lovely shape of her cheek and slender neck. A faint, tranquil smile curved her lips.

Until now he'd not imagined her a restful sort of woman. She usually seethed with barely constrained energy. He couldn't remember Glenys holding her tongue for more than a few seconds at a stretch.

But she seemed perfectly content to walk beside him companionably, making no demands for his attention. Or perhaps she knew it was focused on her, the way women had of knowing such things.

They came over a rise, to the path that ran along the cliff at the north edge of Ravenrook. Below, the River Derwent sparkled in the sunlight.

"Have you been here before?" he heard himself ask.

"Yes." She smiled up at him. "With Lord Killain, the first day we met. There's a guard tower about a mile to the left, is there not? Could we climb it and borrow the spyglass? I've wondered how far one could see."

At the mention of Killain's name, his mood soured. "Another day perhaps."

"That's a promise, and be sure that I'll remind you of it."

Had she failed to hear the word *perhaps?* "You should wear a bonnet outdoors, Miss Shea. We'll go back now, through the woods, before you are sunburned."

"Oh, I rarely burn," she said cheerfully. "Besides, the brim of a hat cuts off the view, and I always wish to see everything."

"Nevertheless, young woman, you will wear this until we arrive at the house." Removing his wide-brimmed straw sun hat, he placed it firmly on her head. Her face, right down to her pert chin, vanished from sight.

"If you insist," she said in a muffled voice. "But I'll need to hold on to your shirt again, like I did when you found me in the mist."

He regarded her for a moment, all hat and chin, and broke out laughing. "My mistake," he said when he caught his breath. "Obviously you've an uncommonly small head."

"Or you an excessively swelled one!"

He lifted the hat away and plucked a bit of straw from her hair. "Point to you, Miss Shea. I'll say no more on the subject of bonnets."

For some reason her smile, always glorious, was almost preternaturally radiant as she gazed at him. He could not think why, unless it was because she'd bested him on the matter of headgear.

"Lady Nora reads me daily lectures about hats," she said as they began to walk along the trail that led to the woods. "Mind you, she never wears them herself, but she says young women must be concerned about their complexions. And it's true that I run to freckles every summer, although I prefer freckles to hats."

She made a grumbling sound. "According to Lady Nora, I must aspire to skin like peaches and cream because that is what gentlemen prefer. As if I cared. And a good ripe peach is nearly orange, for heaven's sake."

Swallowing a laugh, he drew her to a halt and considered her well-shaped nose with its faint sprinkle of incipient freckles. "It is only my opinion, of course, but I think them rather attractive. The freckles, I mean."

"Oh my." Her eyes widened. "Until now I have never, *ever*, received a compliment on my appearance. Not from anyone, let alone a man." Then she chuckled. "Not to quibble, but couldn't you have said *exceedingly* instead of *rather*? And *splendid* instead of *attractive?*"

His lips twitched. "You have exceedingly splendid freckles, Miss Shea."

"La, sir." She curtseyed deeply. "You quite take my breath away. Dare I feed you a whole series of lavish compliments, so that you can give them back to me by rote?"

He laughed out loud. "Enough, minx. I've no talent for the social graces, as you have already discerned. The most I can offer you is bread and cheese, if you are hungry."

"As it happens, I'm ravenous." At her direction, he lifted his arm while she worked at the knot holding the napkin to his belt. "Who tied this thing? And where is Alexander the Great when we need him?"

Stepping back, Ash reached into his pocket for a small folding knife. "It's hardly the Gordian Knot, Miss Shea. I expect this will do the trick."

"My hero," she said dramatically as he sliced through the napkin and handed her a wedge of crusty bread topped with a slab of cheddar.

Hero. The word reverberated in his head as they made their way through the woods, munching on their makeshift breakfast. Glenys went ahead of him on the narrow path, slim and graceful in a pale green muslin dress. Her lithe body, outlined by the sunlight that streamed through the branches of the tall ash trees, conjured memories of how she had felt in his arms when he kissed her.

Dangerous memories.

He could reach out now and seize her. Turn her around and pull her against him and kiss her again. Lay her down on a bed of soft ferns and make love to her.

She wouldn't resist. She'd have lain with him on the cold marble tiles of the pool house had he not thrust her away. And she would take him now, inside her, if he touched her shoulder.

It would take no more than that, to tell her what he wanted. But he kept one hand firmly wrapped around his walking stick and the other tightly clenched at his side.

He was no hero, not by any definition he could imagine. Heroes rode out, alone, to face their dragons. Ash Cordell holed up on his estate, never venturing beyond the gates without a circle of bodyguards to protect him.

Only once had he been strong. He left Glenys Shea with her virginity. And that was an act of courage he was forced to repeat every time he was alone with her.

He scarcely noticed that they'd emerged from the woods until Glenys took up a position beside him and linked her arm in his. Then he felt his body go on fire.

Every good intention fled, along with the shreds of his control. One gesture from her, one word or one of her seductive glances, and he'd throw her down in plain sight of the house and lose himself in her. Find himself again in the brilliant light that always hovered about her, as if she held life itself within her soft flesh.

God help me, he begged silently.

"Ash!"

He looked up to see Geoff waving at him from the low building near the stable where the bodyguards had their rooms. Glenys let go his arm and sped across the grass as he followed, half grateful for the interruption even as he wondered how it would have been to throw honor to the winds, just once.

Geoff met him with a melancholy expression on his face. "I've been going through Charlie's things. He hadn't much of value, except for a few weapons. I thought to distribute them among the men who knew him best."

"Deal with the matter as you see fit," Ash told him as he watched Glenys step into Charlie's room.

"Come inside," Geoff said. "He was preparing a birthday gift for you. It's not finished, but he'd want you to have it."

The room was plain, with whitewashed walls and two small windows on either side of the door. A faded picture of the Madonna and Child hung over the bed.

Glenys stood beside the night table, which held a chipped vase overflowing with slightly wilted bluebells. "I gave him these," she said, lifting one flower from the vase. "He won't mind if I take one, as a keepsake."

Geoff studied the picture of the Madonna in its warped frame. "And I'll reserve this for myself. Ash, have a look over there."

A thick slab of wood, raised waist-high on cinder blocks, stood in the corner, along with a three-legged workman's stool. Ash crossed the small room and saw, amid a scatter of tools, an object draped with a stained white cloth. It was about a foot high. His birthday gift.

He'd altogether forgot that he was born on the sixth of July. Except for a hunting party staged by his father when he turned one-and-twenty, his birthdays had passed without notice. Ellen could not remember dates, and he had no reason to celebrate.

Heart racing, he lifted the cloth.

His own face stared back at him, roughly carved in black granite. The eyes, fierce and inky, seemed to gaze through him to a place he only visited in his nightmares.

"Dear God," Glenys whispered. "He caught you exactly."

Charlie had hacked him out of a solid block of stone, face and neck and hair, to a point just beyond his ears. The rest, a square of polished black, held the image in eternal ambiguity. He might have been imprisoned in the rock, or on the brink of escaping it.

"Charlie began this more than a year ago," Geoff said quietly. "But he could only work on it a few minutes at a time, for fear of losing his concentration and ruining the stone. When Nora suggested a birthday party, he decided to give it to you even though it wasn't finished."

Ash replaced the cloth, lifted the heavy sculpture to his chest, and made for the door before anyone noticed how his hands were shaking.

"It's perfect just as it is."

21

That evening, in the salon, Glenys looked from one grim face to the next. "Shall we take a vote, then? Lady Nora?"

"I have been with you from the beginning, my dear." She sucked the end of a length of embroidery thread and lifted her needle to the light.

"Harry?"

He wriggled on his chair. "Can't see what I have to do with it, but count me in."

She turned to Lord Killain, who sat on the sofa with one arm draped across the back. After many hours of discussion, first in private and then in company with Lady Nora and Harry, he remained unconvinced. And without his support, there was no hope of persuading the earl to go along with her plan.

He met her gaze steadily. "Even if I make the vote unanimous, which I'm by no means ready to do, what is the point? I promise you, Ravensby will have no part of this scheme."

"He might, if you backed it with a semblance of conviction. He trusts your judgment. Can you not stand with us until he makes up his own mind? Right now, you are doing that for him."

"I expect that's true," he said after a moment. "Perhaps I've been trying to spare you disappointment."

"Please don't. I'm well aware Ravensby will dig in his heels, and still I come back to the question I've been asking you all day. Have you a better idea? Any *other* idea? Are we at least agreed that things cannot go on as they are?"

"You are a remarkably determined young woman, Glenys Shea." Killain sat forward, resting his elbows on his knees. "The inescapable fact is, I have failed. Always I advised caution, figuring the most important thing was to keep Ash alive while we tracked the hellhound set on killing him. Considering the money paid out, and the number of men we hired to investigate, I frankly thought—"

"You did everything you could," she said impatiently. "Without you, the earl would not have survived this long. But Charlie is dead. Lady Ellen is dead. I add their voices to my own and say it is five votes in favor of setting a trap for the murderer."

"Only one vote counts," Killain reminded her.

"We shall deal with Lord Ravensby once you come over to our side. Otherwise, we've no chance at all to make this work, and a grudging assent will be no help. You have to *believe* in this, and help me persuade him. *Can* you believe? Will you help?"

Killain released a long sigh. "In fact, yes. Mind you, that is only because I fear what Ravensby will do on his own if we offer him no alternative. Your idea has merit because it includes time to make plans. Have you any, by the way?"

"None. Only the general concept. Ravensby is the one to work out the particulars."

"Indeed. I expect he can figure some way to bring this off, if he puts his mind to it. Not that he will."

"Because of me," she said unhappily. "I am the sticking point."

"He was bred to protect women. How you, or all of us together, will prevail on him to put you in danger is beyond my reckoning."

"Say you'll try." Glenys met his gaze earnestly, pleading with him to stand by her. "That is all I ask."

He closed his eyes for a moment. Then he nodded. "Very well, Miss Shea. I shall be your greatest advocate, not that it will signify. Once he hears what you have in mind, he'll dismiss it out of hand and be gone."

"Would you consider tying him to a chair?" she asked with a faint smile.

"I doubt I could. You will need to be most persuasive, my dear, to hold him in this room."

"Me?" She made a strangled noise. "But I assumed *you* would tell him. Good heavens, this requires orderly discourse, like—what does he call it, Harry?—syllogistic reasoning. Logic is not my strong suit, and he already thinks me a scatterbrained ninny."

"You devised the strategy, General Shea, and you will explain it." Killain went to the bellpull. "Shall we send for him?"

Ash was sitting at his desk, contemplating Charlie's sculpture, when Fortescue arrived with a note from Geoff.

The summons, brief and without explanation, sent a chill down his spine. He glanced at the clock on the mantel shelf. What could be so urgent at ten o'clock?

Dismissing the butler, he linked his hands behind his neck and gazed at the plasterwork ceiling, dimly aware of the stony eyes fixed on him from the top of the desk. His own eyes, haunted and angry, stared in silent accusation, demanding something from him. He didn't know what it was.

He wondered if Charlie, in his simple wisdom, had known.

Pulse drumming in his ears, he stood and lifted his coat from the back of the chair. Charlie had only sculpted what he saw. The accusation and the anger emanated from Ashton Cordell, not that chiseled bit of rock.

He stuffed his arms into the sleeves, retied his neckcloth, and took a swift glance in the mirror over the fireplace. He had a sudden urge to smash the glass with his fist.

Geoff had been right about the fury building inside him. He burned to seize control of his life again, to strike back at the nameless, faceless enemy who had rendered him helpless for so many years.

And still, it was all he could do to force himself out the door of his own study at the request of a friend. He took one last look at the sculpture, draped the cloth over it, and made his way to the salon.

The minute he stepped inside, Ash felt again the vague threat he'd perceived when Fortescue handed him the note.

Nora glanced in his direction and immediately returned her attention to her embroidery. Harry, perched on a spindly chair, stuffed both hands under his thighs and rocked back and forth.

Geoff lounged on a sofa, sipping from a glass of wine. He looked up, grinned, and nodded toward the heavy oak sideboard.

Ash followed his gesture and saw Glenys perched there, her feet inches off the floor, ankles crossed. One slipper had come loose from her heel. Her hands were folded in her lap, concealed by the folds of her blue dress.

With a growing sense of dread, he raised his eyes to her face. She met his gaze steadily, her mouth set in a thin line.

"Will you be seated, Lord Ravensby?"

"I think not." He propped his shoulders on the closed door and folded his arms across his chest. "Presumably you have some reason for inviting me to join you?"

Her nose twitched at the sarcasm, but she mustered a jittery smile. "This is not the Spanish Inquisition, you know. I—that is, *we*—have a proposition to offer, and it would be a great deal easier if you relaxed just a bit."

If she meant to disarm him, it hadn't worked. More than ever on his guard, he merely lifted a brow, waiting for her to throw down whatever gauntlet she was hiding behind that smile. It occurred to him that despite the presence of Geoff, Harry, and Nora, he felt very much alone in the room with Glenys Shea.

"If you are determined to be difficult, so be it," she said. "And in case you are wondering, this is not easy for me either. But it's terribly important, my lord earl. I beg you to hear me out to the very end. Please."

Beg? Repressing a sigh, he nodded. "Have at it, then, and I will listen so long as you speak plainly. I'm not in the mood for another of your games."

"Fair enough." Her chin lifted at a stubborn angle. "So far, whoever is trying to kill you has had things all his own way. He chooses when and where to strike. He selects victims he can reach when he can't get at you. The strategy of defense and prolonged investigation has not worked." She gestured broadly to the others in the room. "We believe, and I expect you do too, that it is past time to go on the attack."

Dear God. Glenys Shea thought to meddle in affairs that were none of her business. Life and death affairs. He fired a look at Geoff, who gave him back a rueful shrug.

"I— *We* have a plan," she continued doggedly. "It's designed to force the killer's hand. If we draw him out, compel him to make a move when we expect it and are prepared, there is a better than even chance he'll be caught before anyone else is hurt."

"Only *better than even,* Miss Shea?"

"If you require a sure thing, Lord Ravensby, you will be entrenched in your study writing an excessively dull book for the next fifty years!"

He stifled a laugh. This was the girl he could deal with, the one who spoke before she thought. Doubtless Geoff also realized she could not be stopped until she'd had her say, however preposterous her scheme for trapping the murderer. As Geoff must have done earlier, he would listen tolerantly and thank her for her concern. Then he would bid her good night.

"Ash, I suggest you pay attention," Geoff said in a low voice. "At the first, you won't like her idea any more than I did. But I changed my mind. If nothing else, neither you nor I have come up with anything better."

Astonished, Ash regarded Glenys with mingled curiosity and apprehension. A good idea he wouldn't like. One that Geoff supported, with some reluctance. "Are you able to summarize this plan coherently?" he asked with a touch of impatience. In his experience, females had a tendency to dither.

"I'll do my best."

She jumped off the table and planted her feet on the carpet in a stance that reminded him of . . . himself. At his most arrogant moments, except that she carried it off better than he did.

"You have fallen madly in love," she informed him. "In the throes of uncontrollable passion, you have proposed marriage to an altogether unsuitable woman, and nothing—not even the danger of exposing yourself to attack—will prevent you from celebrating your happiness with a lavish wedding."

She took a step forward. "All your family will be invited. Lord Killain tells me you suspect one of them to be the villain, and they will be gathered in one place, under close scrutiny. You also believe the inheritance to be a factor. One of the people named in your father's will, should your marriage produce a son, will be cut out of something he badly wants. Hence, the villain won't like the idea of you marrying again. Have I got that part right?"

Stunned by what he was hearing, and not sure how it made enough sense for Geoff to lend his support, he could only nod.

"So." Her chin went up a notch. "I expect we should do this in London, in case you are wrong about your family. If the killer is someone after revenge because you exposed him as a profiteer, he'll have access to you there. I admit freely that if we are dealing with a madman, this will not work. Only family, and aristocrats who might have it in for you, will be invited to the festivities."

"Festivities?" The concept felt wholly alien.

"Oh yes. We must have parties, rather a lot of them. Your trusted friends can come too, but anyone who is remotely under suspicion should be present at least once or twice. I expect the suspect will be suspicious—" She frowned. "That made no sense. Sorry. I *am* trying to be logical."

He gazed at her blankly.

"The point is," she went on, "we must give all possible villains a chance at you, under controlled circumstances. And a deadline. That's most important. He must think this the last opportunity to mount an attack. We'll put it out that after the wedding, you plan a quiet life here at Ravenrook under heavy guard. More than ever before, because of what happened to Lady Ellen."

Her voice broke at the end and she lowered her head. "I am making a muddle of this. It's all so clear in my head, and so hard to put into words."

Ash looked at Geoff, who was staring into his glass of wine, a pained expression on his face. Nora plied her needle with fierce concentration. Only Harry met his eyes, daring him to embarrass Glenys with a snide comment.

Ash swallowed the first four things he had been about to say. "I am truly lost," he confessed.

Harry relaxed on his chair.

"No wonder," Glenys said. "But let me try again. We stage a wedding, with a week or two of parties beforehand. We invite everyone remotely under suspicion. We make it clear you will all but vanish after the ceremony. And we mount guards everywhere, from the kitchens where food is prepared to . . . well, everywhere. Lord Killain assures me we can bring in any number of men he served with in the army. Many were officers, some with titles, and they can mingle freely among the guests."

She took another step in his direction. "The villain will not be surprised that you protect yourself, my lord. He will expect it. He will also know this is likely his last chance, and will set himself to outwit you." She held out her arms. "Anyway, that's my theory. And I am certain you are smart enough to outwit *him,* if we plan with care."

Ash levered himself from the door, fighting the temptation to be caught up in her enthusiasm. She had left unsaid what made this otherwise intriguing plan out of the question. "Do you cast yourself in the role of bride, Miss Shea?"

She made a nonchalant gesture. "Who else? I understand that no one would believe you in love with me, under normal circumstances. But you don't meet very many women these days, Lord Ravensby. And after your first wife was murdered, legitimate potential brides can't be blamed for shying away. On the other hand, a no-account female willing to spend the rest of her life in confinement has some credibility. I'm already known to be here at Ravenrook, because the man who shot Charlie must have seen me."

Her last step brought Glenys face-to-face with him. "The villain will think I'm the best you can do," she said. "If you contrive to look happy about it, so much the better. A besotted bridegroom will appear an easy target. The urgency will have made you careless."

Urgency? He mopped his forehead with his hand. "What made you think, for the barest moment, I would agree to this? The man who killed Ellen wouldn't hesitate to kill you too. And if he's someone after the inheritance, you would be the first target."

"Not the first. You might wed again, after me. How many wives can he kill before getting caught? He will go for you, Lord Ravensby."

"We're not sure of that."

"We're not sure of anything."

She was right, for the first time. There were too many suspects. And if the killer would be satisfied to punish him by hurting someone he cared for, setting Glenys at risk was unthinkable.

"No," he said flatly. When she opened her mouth to object, he lifted a hand. "Thank you for wanting to help, Miss Shea. I admire your courage, more than I can say. But no." He felt for the door latch near his hip. "The subject is closed."

To his relief, he escaped into the passageway before anyone stopped him. Immediately he headed for the foyer and the door that led outside. He fled, that was the only word for it, into the cool night.

Mist hovered near the ground, but overhead the black sky was crowded with stars. A thin moon hung above the horizon. He didn't know if it was on the ascent or about to sink into the void.

Bent over, hands on his knees, he breathed deeply. At the back of his head a too-familiar pain began to claw its way over his scalp, digging deeper as it moved toward his eyes.

I need to get upstairs, he thought lethargically. By one of the side doors, though. He stumbled along the gravel path that led around the house.

And was unsurprised when Glenys stepped out of the French doors that opened from the salon onto the grounds. He had known she would not surrender easily.

Cursing himself for taking a route that led directly to her, he straightened and clasped his hands behind his back. "Go away," he said, rather certain she would not obey.

"You didn't let me finish," she said calmly. "And I will chase you all over Ravenrook until you hear me out."

Not doubting that for a minute, he braced himself. "Finish. And then get out of my sight before I do something we'll both regret."

He wasn't sure what he meant by that, but hoped it sounded like a threat. She had offered to risk her life for him. He wanted to slap her, if only to prove he wasn't worth it. He wanted to carry her onto the dewy grass and make love to her because—because he wanted to.

"You are being noble," she said. "I expected that. So did Lord Killain. He didn't think you would stay past the first minute or two."

"I'd not have done, but I couldn't figure out what you were talking about."

"I did a lamentable job of explaining," she acknowledged. "But you'd have reacted the same way if I had been perfectly coherent. Only sooner."

"Yes. And I've said I'll hear no more. Was *that* clear enough?"

Her slanted eyes, witchy in the starlight, held him in place. "You can protect me," she said. "I am sure of it. I am willing to bet my life on it."

This is madness, he told himself. A hollow roar thundered in his ears. She must go away—be *sent* away—before he yielded to every temptation she offered. She was in more danger than she knew.

Who would protect her from him?

He stared beyond her, to the branches of a tree. "In the morning, I shall begin arrangements for you to leave Ravenrook."

She made a raw noise of protest that caught at his heart, but he continued purposefully. "It has been my intention for some time to put you in the care of friends who emigrated to America. I'd hoped to wait until they were settled, but that is no longer possible. Although the necessary communications will take a few weeks, I am confident of their welcome and will book passage for you to Boston."

"I won't go!"

"I beg your pardon? You will do as you are told, Miss Shea."

"Don't count on it. You can certainly toss me out of Ravenrook on my rump, because I have no right to be here. But you cannot tell me where to go, or what to do when I am gone. If I choose to take up residence in a tree, so long as it's not a Ravensby tree, you haven't the power to stop me."

"You are mistaken, young woman."

"Oh, spare me the threats about the magistrate. You won't turn us over to the law."

"Nor will I permit you to wander the streets, or remain in England now that the killer knows about you. If you haven't the sense to protect yourself, I shall do it for you—by whatever means. That includes tying you up and locking you in the hold of the ship."

He heard what sounded like a sniffle and wrenched his gaze to her face.

"Why do you wish to be rid of me?" she asked in a hurt voice. "What have I done to make you so angry?"

All her defiance had melted. She looked bereft. And he dared not console her, as he longed to do. He shook his head, unable to respond. Whatever he said, it would be the wrong thing.

"Was it the plan?" She clutched at her skirt with both hands. "I expected resistance, but never guessed it would cause you to drive me away."

"You misunderstand." He took a deep breath, searching for a way to express the impossible. He had thought his feelings safely buried, but they were breaking loose, wild as tigers, and she was the reason. Glenys herself, and her plan, and her blind faith in a man who had lost faith in himself.

"And you cannot explain," she said gently. "That much I do understand. I wish you would try, though." The corners of her mouth lifted. "Would it help to write it out in Latin first?"

As always, her unpredictable shift of mood staggered him. In only the last few minutes, he had seen her obstinate, furious, dejected, sympathetic, and amused. No wonder he could not order his thoughts. In her presence, he was invariably bewildered.

"Perhaps I should explain to you what you are thinking," she suggested. "At the least, I've a fairly good idea why you object to my plan."

Back on solid ground, he found his tongue again. "That requires no explanation, Miss Shea. No gentleman would put a woman in danger to save his own life."

"But who says I am doing this for you?"

He looked at her in surprise.

"Charlie was my friend. I want to catch his murderer. Lord Killain is my friend too. Until the murderer is stopped, Killain will not leave here to make the life he wants for himself. I want to repay you for your kindness to me, and to Harry. I don't want anyone else to be hurt. I want to see justice done."

Not meaning to, he put his hand against her cheek. "I too want all those things, save one. You owe me nothing, Miss Shea."

He felt her jaw move and her warm breath tickle at his wrist when she finally spoke.

"There is another reason, my lord—a selfish one. You imagine I am offering myself as a sacrifice, and I probably would. The reasons are good enough, and I've little to lose. But primarily, I need to do this for myself. Just once, I want to be of some importance. I want to matter, and do something of value."

He pressed his thumb against her lips before she could go on. "You *are* of value, child. You are a shaft of light in a dark world. We who live in the shadows would gladly die to keep that light glowing. I cannot put you at risk. I will not."

Covering his hand with her own, she lifted it from her face and held on, tightly, when he tried to pull away. "And I cannot give up, my lord. Isn't it strange, though?

One month ago we had never met. Now we wrestle with each other, me for your life and you for mine."

What use is my life? he thought wearily. And how could I go on living, if you died for me?

"It will astonish you to hear this," she said, "but I am the tiniest bit stubborn. And so far, you have not convinced me we cannot make this work if we put our heads together."

He looked down, to her fingers threaded through his, to her thumb pressed against his palm. She would come to his bed now, if he led her there. Reckless, heedless woman. She lived, always, for the moment, with no thought to the future or the consequences.

And he lived—nowhere. Suspended like a puppet, he rarely touched ground.

He cleared his throat. "I will have a promise from you, Miss Shea. Let me alone for a time, and say no more about your impractical scheme. In return, I agree to consider it privately."

"With an open mind?"

"With a deranged mind." He let go her hand. "Only a madman would even tinker with the idea."

"In that case, Lord Ravensby, it's just as well you are all but Bedlam bait. Tinker away. Meantime, I'll start making lists of things to do. Oh. Does that mean you won't be sending me to America on the next boat?"

"I fully intend dispatching a letter to my friends, asking them to receive you. But I'll not specify a time. Eventually you will set sail, because you and your brother have a better chance of doing well for yourselves in America. England is calcified with rank and tradition, I'm sorry to say, and there are few opportunities for a young man with Harry's peculiar skills. I think you'll both be happier in Boston. Mind you, while you remain at Ravenrook, you will not leave the estate again."

"Fine with me." She gave him a toe-curling smile. "I like it here."

He realized that he was smiling back. "Take yourself to bed, Miss Shea."

With a curtsey, she headed toward the house. But something that had niggled at his mind from the beginning took shape. He called her back.

She regarded him with troubled eyes. "You haven't considered long enough, sir. Ten seconds is not nearly long enough."

"Don't worry, my dear. As you know, I have to put everything in Latin before it makes sense to me. One question, though. Killain does not trust Lady Nora. I fail to understand why he supports your scheme, knowing that she is aware of—"

Glenys cut him off with a laugh. "As it happens, I spent most of the afternoon arguing with him about that very thing. He seems to have a blind spot where Lady Nora is concerned."

"Because she is related to me."

"That dratted inheritance. Was your father altogether demented when he made out his will? Anyway, if you die without an heir, Lady Nora's husband controls the parcel of land. She doesn't give a fig for him, and would not swat a fly on his behalf. Besides, we need her. I don't know how to go on in society, and she can groom me to be a proper lady. No one will credit that you are madly in love with me as I am."

Except me, he thought. He liked Glenys Shea pretty much as she was. He also liked his aunt, and trusted her in spite of Geoff's excessive caution.

"That answers my question," he said. "Thank you. And good night."

She tilted her head. "Don't worry over the problems, Lord Ravensby. Pretend you have already agreed to our plan and concentrate on what needs to be done. Make lists."

He watched her go, with a slight bounce as she moved. Ellen had always glided, like a swan on a lake. Glenys bounced. As if the earth was not where she belonged, he decided. As if she was always on the verge of taking flight.

Glancing at the crescent moon, he saw that it hung higher in the sky. It was rising, after all.

He must be moon-mad to see that as an omen of good fortune. But his spirits lifted, and his headache had vanished, and he wondered if there might be hope for the future if he let himself dream Glenys's dream.

22

For the next two weeks, Ravensby took care to avoid her. If they chanced to pass in the hall, he bowed politely and moved quickly on.

But Glenys kept track of him every minute of the day. Mornings were devoted to Harry's schooling, where, from her brother's account, he was a "bloody slave driver." Harry, pouting because his shooting and fencing lessons had all but ceased, grumbled about the extra compositions he was forced to write.

She helped him, during the afternoons when the earl and Lord Killain closed themselves in the study. They were making plans, she knew, her confidence growing with each tray of correspondence handed by the butler to a footman for mailing.

At night she often saw him from the window as he crossed the lawn on his way to the pool house. Sometimes she thought to follow him, but always thought better of it.

Instead, she made lists of the female accomplishments she needed to master before appearing in London as Lord Ravensby's bride. They were, to her chagrin, extremely long lists.

Under Lady Baslow's supervision, she molded herself into a right proper lady. Forgotten skills, taught her at Miss Pipcock's School, reemerged as she practiced sitting, standing, and wielding a fan. She walked miles, or so it seemed, circling the drawing room with a book on her head to improve her posture and smooth her unfeminine stride.

One by one she crossed a few items from her list.

Tea-pouring went first, because she'd always been rather good at it. When parents came to visit the school, Miss Pipcock frequently enlisted her to serve refreshments.

She had stopped biting her nails. Her curtsies were perfect. She had nearly eliminated objectionable words from her vocabulary, but they resurfaced when Harry got on her nerves, so she put "Mind your language" back on the list.

She memorized correct forms of address, for dukes and footmen alike, along with a number of innocuous observations about the weather to fill silences in a conversation. She learned how to conduct herself in a receiving line, and which implement to use for what at a formal dinner table, and how to smile without showing all her teeth.

Finally, on a Thursday night, the earl called a meeting.

He was late to arrive, having taken his meal, as usual, alone. The others were gathered in the salon, Lady Nora plying her needle, Harry squirming on a chair, Lord Killain calmly pouring wine from a decanter.

Glenys prowled restlessly, unable to sit in the ladylike manner she'd been practicing. Ravensby would surely have told her privately if he'd rejected the scheme, so she had no fear of bad news. But she could hardly wait to hear the plans he'd made during those sessions with Lord Killain.

"You are wearing down an expensive carpet," Killain said as he handed her a glass of sherry. "Relax, my dear."

"How can I?" She flopped on a wing-back chair, pulling her knees together when Lady Nora cast her a look of reproof. "This is the most important night of my life."

He smiled. "You will think that many times before you reach my advanced age."

The door opened and Ravensby, carrying a sheaf of papers, strode commandingly into the room. His neck-cloth was tied in an elaborate knot over a bottle-green coat and tan breeches. His thick hair was neatly brushed. Usually careless about his appearance, he had dressed for this occasion.

Glenys watched him with a surge of unabashed desire as he took up a position near the sideboard—at almost the exact spot she'd sat two weeks ago. His beautiful eyes held a light she had never seen before. He moved with energy and purpose.

She willed him to smile, but he did not.

Leaning his hips against the sideboard, he planted his hands on the polished wood and looked at each of them in turn. His gaze lingered on Harry, and a muscle jumped in his cheek.

The silence became intolerable. "Well?" she demanded. "What have you decided?"

Then he did smile, so briefly she wasn't sure she'd seen it. "Nothing final, Miss Shea. But while I continue to evaluate your plan, we may as well proceed as if I have agreed to it. Otherwise, lack of preparation will make the decision for me."

He patted the stack of papers. "As you suggested, I

have made lists. There is one for each of you. Tonight, I will give you a general idea of where we are headed, and what we must do to get there. Later, you must study your individual instructions and decide for yourselves if you wish to continue."

Once again he looked at Harry. "Mind you, not a single item can be rejected. We are in this together, all the way or not at all."

"I don't care what's on my list," Glenys told him. "Count me in."

The others nodded, but Ravensby lifted a hand. "Don't speak too soon. I may call this off tomorrow, or at any point. Unless I am convinced that Miss Shea will be safe, you may all find that your hard work has been in vain."

Lady Nora set her embroidery aside. "Get on with it, young man. What are we to do?"

He turned to Killain. "Geoff, why don't you start? Explain the general security."

Killain sat forward on his chair. "In the next few weeks, a great number of men and women will arrive here, one by one to avoid the appearance we are gathering an army. Empty carriages, shutters drawn, will leave, empty luggage stored on top. For all we know, Ravenrook is being watched. We want to give the impression of visitors come and gone."

He smiled. "Actually, they *will* go, again one by one, after a few weeks of training. By the time we arrive in London, a staff of armed servants, ranging from tweeny to butler, will be in place. Most are men I served with in Spain, and their wives. They'll not be the most experienced maids and footmen in the world, but I can vouch for their loyalty."

Ravensby took up the story. "As of Monday last, our greatest difficulty was solved. My townhouse in London isn't large enough to handle the family members who will be staying with us, let alone the balls and dinner parties we require if"—he nodded at Glenys—"all the *suspects* are to be gathered. But the Duke of Devonshire has given me the loan of Devonshire House, which has the added advantage of a high wall surrounding the property. With a patrol of armed guards, we can be sure no one comes in except through the front door."

He shifted his gaze to Lady Nora. "You are responsible for seeing to Miss Shea's wardrobe. She mustn't leave the estate, nor can you bring in seamstresses and a mantua maker, so this will not be an easy task. You will also groom her to conduct herself in polite society, which will involve dancing lessons. Killain can help with those. Or do you dance already, Miss Shea?"

"No."

"Concentrate on the waltz, then. I'll be expected to lead you out, but otherwise you needn't join country dances and the like. I anticipate one ball, to celebrate our alleged betrothal, and perhaps another to gather the . . . er, minor suspects."

He looked back at Lady Nora. "Your list is somewhat longer than you might imagine, but we'll return to the difficult items. Meantime, let us deal with the bride. Miss Shea, you will be the center of attention. Do you know what that means?"

"Oh, aye," she drawled. "I must be a model of predictable deportment."

Another fleeting smile curved his lips. "I cannot begin to imagine that, nor do I expect it. Be yourself, young lady. My aunt will teach you the rudiments of how to deal with bores and toplofty aristocrats, but you already have good manners when you think to use them. My concern is for your safety."

His expression grew stern. "You are never to be alone in a room, except your bedchamber. Come to think of it, a maid ought to sleep there in a truckle bed. Guards will be posted outside your door. You are never to be in company with any man or woman without an armed servant to protect you. You will not eat or drink anything unless it is handed to you by someone on the list I will give you. Above all, you will not leave Devonshire House without my express permission. I doubt that it will be given."

"Yes, sir!" She saluted. "Exactly how long will we be in London?"

"Twelve days," he replied. "The first banns will be posted at St. George's Hanover Square before we leave Ravenrook. It will all be called off, of course, but we must schedule an actual wedding."

"When do we start?"

"Patience, Miss Shea. It will take several months to get ready. I am aiming for early November, when—"

"November?" She jumped from her chair. "We could mount a campaign to take back the American colonies before November!"

"—when," he continued implacably, "the Little Season is in full swing. If you wish to assemble everyone who has a grudge against me, we do it then or wait until next spring."

"November it is," she said immediately, subsiding onto the chair again.

"What about me?" Harry asked. "I want to help."

With obvious reluctance, the earl turned his attention to her brother. Glenys sensed trouble.

"You have a crucial role to play," Ravensby said. "I hope you are up to it."

Harry slid forward until he was barely perched on the edge of his chair. "You bet I am!"

"Reserve your decision, young man. As you know, we cannot proceed until I am certain your sister will be guarded at every moment, by someone able to handle a weapon and alert enough to use it if necessary. But there are times when a woman finds herself alone with other women."

Glenys saw, with surprise, that the earl's cheeks had gone pink.

"To an extent, we'll rely on the maids Killain will tutor. But only someone expert with knife and gun can protect her in such places as"—his cheekbones were scarlet by this time—"the retiring room."

"So?" Harry shrugged. "I can't go in there. Do you want me to stand outside the door or somethin'?"

Ravensby took a deep breath. "Harry, I want you in there with her. And that requires you to disguise yourself as a female."

"Oh no!" Harry was on his feet in an instant. "Not a chance. Forget it."

"As you will," the earl said peaceably. "I didn't expect you to agree." He gathered the lists from the sideboard and stood. "That's an end to it, then. Really, I ought to have begun with Master Harry. It would have saved time."

"Wait!" Harry shouted as Ravensby made for the door. "Wait a minute!"

"What for?" The earl glanced over his shoulder. "Don't feel guilty, young man. In your place, I'd have had the same reaction."

"Well, how *could* you be in my place?" Harry demanded. "You couldn't never pass for a girl."

"I'm too tall, certainly. If your sister had only me to rely on, this plan could not go forward. I'd look a perfect ass, wearing a dress."

"So would I!"

"You would only *feel* a perfect ass," Glenys said hotly. Her whole scheme, all of Ravensby's plans, *everything* was going up in smoke. "But if you were terribly clever, you could carry it off. Holy hollyhocks! If *I* can learn to be a lady, so can you."

"Damned if I will, though."

"And I'll wring your neck if you don't at least try." She stalked to him and poked her finger against his narrow chest. "It is only for twelve days, gudgeon! Twelve short, desperate days. We need you." She turned to Ravensby. "Do we? Is this essential?"

"Absolutely." He leaned against the wall. "From the first, there were two linchpins to this stratagem. We required a house in London we could make secure, and Devonshire has provided it. We also required a companion, altogether reliable, to be with you at all times. I had counted on Harry to be a man where men cannot, as a rule, be present. But if he will not, that is that."

With an oath from the Liverpool streets, Harry bolted.

Glenys made a graceful curtsey. "Excuse me for a moment, please."

Then she tore after her brother, shrieking his name.

Ash shut the door behind them and went to the wine decanter. "A neck, I fear, is about to be wrung."

Killain laughed. "Oh, they'll be back. It was only the shock made Harry scarper. Didn't we agree you would speak to him in private?"

"I changed my mind. Or lost my nerve." Ash poured himself a glass of sherry. "He is so damnably set on proving his manhood. Every time I looked into those earnest eyes, I put off telling him for another day, and another. Should have made you do it, Geoff."

"As I recall, you tried. And I was no less chicken-hearted." Killain studied the toes of his boots. "A fine pair we are, Lord Ravensby."

"Just so." He glanced at Nora. "Nothing to say?"

"Only my shopworn observations about the general uselessness of men, which you have heard before. The young lady will bring her brother to heel. In the meantime, shall we continue our discussion? If you plan to invite Wilfred to this party, I wish it clear he is to be ensconced at the opposite end of Devonshire House. We'll not share a bedchamber."

"Will he come, do you think?"

"Oh, yes. For access to the duke's library, he'd crawl to London on hands and knees. Can't imagine why you'd want him, though. Useless old sod, Wilfred Baslow."

Ash grinned at her. "Miss Shea insists that all suspects, however unlikely, make an appearance. Which reminds me, Geoff. I had a letter from Hart this afternoon. He is planning a trip to Italy in September, and when he arrives, he'll dispatch my least-favorite cousin back to England with another load of statues."

"To be delivered to Devonshire House, I presume, right about the time we take up residence." Killain chuckled. "Good for Hart. How much have you told him, by the way?"

"As little as possible. To my astonishment, he's rather fond of the scoundrel. And he had a letter from him, posted at Cadiz when the ship called in, so we know Jervase is really out of the country. He can't be the one who shot Charlie."

"Might have hired someone before he left, though."

"Perhaps." Ash took a sip of wine and set the glass aside. Thinking about relatives trying to do him in always put a bitter taste in his mouth.

Nora selected a length of scarlet thread from her basket. "Jane will make sure Evan abandons his precious farm long enough to join us. Encroaching woman. When she learns you intend to marry again, she will tear her hair out."

"I'm more worried that she'll dig her claws into my prospective bride."

"Glenys can handle Jane. But it's as well if we avoid a catfight."

"That takes care of Evan and Jane, Jervase, and Wilfred." Killain counted dramatically on his fingers. "What about the last member of the annoying Cordell clan? No insult, Nora."

"I am as bothersome as the others," she said. "And I'm fully aware you do not trust me, boy. Let's not shilly-shally."

Killain flushed. "I was referring to Evan's father."

"That gouty idiot? We should not expect Matthew to make an appearance. Unless I miss my guess, he'll not live to see November."

"Will you leave the squabbling to Harry and Miss Shea?" Ash put in wearily. In his judgment, Matthew lacked the intelligence to mount a campaign that had lasted all of six years, even if he were determined to see his son inherit the title.

In fact, the more he thought on it, the more sure he became that this entire scheme was a great waste of time. It focused on his relatives, and the ones smart enough to plot a murder lacked a credible motive.

His heir, Matthew, had one foot in the grave. And when the rest of him settled there, Evan would be next in line. For all his wife's ambitions to call herself a countess, Evan was happiest planning crop rotations. If he came into the title, he'd probably try to give it back.

Dear God. What was the point? Fired by Glenys's

optimism, he'd devised a plan. Made lists. Closed loopholes and accounted for every contingency. But at the end, all the wrong people were invited to step into the trap.

"Sooner or later, you must come to a final decision," Nora said.

"Yes. And I have a deadline of sorts. Devonshire thinks the wedding is really to take place. He has a fondness for entertaining guests at Chatsworth, and wishes to announce the betrothal at a grand ball."

Ash took another drink of wine. "Before he leaves for Italy, Hart will give his servants a holiday so that we can replace them with our staff. The houseparty will take place the second week of September. It will be a trial run, and if I'm content with the security, we can set our sights for London."

"No turning back from then on?"

"No promises. And we've yet to see if Master Harry will agree to be Miss Harriet. Should he decline—"

The salon door hit the wall with a bang.

Looking up, Ash saw Harry shuffle into the room, propelled by his sister. Glenys had both hands on Harry's shoulders and a satisfied smile on her face.

"He'll do it," she announced.

Harry nodded, looking thoroughly miserable. "I said I'd try. But I don't see the use of setting *me* to protect Glennie. I'd just as soon kill her myself."

Glenys punched him. "Shut up, Harry. You promised to behave."

Wondering what weapon she'd used to glean that promise, Ash crossed to Harry and extended his hand. "Thank you."

Harry gave him back a surprisingly firm handshake. "I'll do m'best, guv . . . er, Lord Ravensby. But I'll make a devilish ugly female."

"Nonsense!" Glenys chuckled. "Everyone will wonder why the earl is marrying me instead of my beautiful sister."

Before Harry could fire a countershot, Ash steered him to Nora. "What do you think? Can you make a passable female of this excessively brave young man?"

She put aside her embroidery and looked Harry over from head to foot. "It will not be easy. You have good skin, though. Do you shave?"

"Of course I do!" Harry rubbed his chin. "Shaved this morning, and already got bristles."

"Your beard grows in lightly, then. With a coating of rice powder, that should be no problem. Let me feel your hair." He leaned over and she fingered a curl beside his ear. "Soft. Nice color too. By November it will be a decent length. Short curls are not in style these days, but I don't expect you'll want to wear a wig."

"Bloody right I don't."

"Mind your language, young man. If you are to masquerade as a lady, *bloody* is hereby purged from your vocabulary."

"Sorry." He scuffed his feet on the carpet.

All too familiar with Harry's vocabulary, Ash foresaw a great deal of purging in the months ahead. "What about a wardrobe, Nora? He is slender, but not precisely shaped to wear a dress."

"He will be, once he's strapped into a corset."

"Oh God," Harry moaned.

"If we pad him on the buttocks and where his breasts need to be, he'll do fine."

"Oh God."

"The new fashions allow us to conceal a multitude of sins under ruffles and lace, thank heavens. We'd not get away with this in the days of dampened muslins and Grecian gowns. Have you hair on your chest, young man? If so, you will need to shave it. And your fore-arms, I daresay, along with the backs of your hands."

"Holy shit!"

Glenys dissolved in laughter. On the sofa, Geoff was doubled over, his hand plastered to his mouth. Only years of rigid self-control kept Ash from joining them.

Harry swung around. "You said nobody would make fun of me, Glennie!"

"I c-can't help it," she sputtered. "It's funny."

"Not to me!" He turned to Ash. "Would *you* shave your chest, m'lord?"

Holy shit, Ash thought, firmly on Harry's side. "Not without a compelling reason."

"Guess I have one." Harry sniffed. "But if everybody keeps laughing at me . . ."

Glenys put her hands on her hips. "Oh, laugh *with* us, gudgeon. Pretend it's a lark. And think how jolly it will be to humbug all the London lords and ladies."

"Easy for you to say. You get to be a girl, and you already are."

"The first time I met her," Ash pointed out, "she was pretending to be a boy. I failed to see through her dis-guise."

"It was dark," Harry said incontrovertibly.

Ash hid a smile. "You don't have to do this, what-ever threats your sister has wielded. It won't work unless you put your heart into it and permit Lady Nora to guide you. If it helps, I'd not have asked unless I thought you sharp-witted enough to deceive the *ton*."

Harry's face brightened, and Ash's heart sank.

He'll do this for me, he thought. He'll do it because I flattered him, even though I meant what I said about his cleverness. He'll do it to earn my respect, which he already has. How dare I play this out, at the expense of these gallant children?

Dimly, he heard the end of Harry's question to Nora.

". . . shave whatever you like, because it will all grow back when we are finished, right? So, what else?"

"Walk around the room," Nora instructed. As he obeyed, arms swinging, she sighed. "This will never do. Try again, with small steps."

Teeth gritted in concentration, Harry minced from the door to the bay window. "How's that?"

"Hopeless. You walk like a man when you aren't thinking about it, and like a fop when you are. Even your sister can scarcely manage a feminine stride, although by Novem—"

"I have an idea," Glenys interrupted. "What if he limps? Harry could have a lame foot, like Lord Byron. Did you ever meet him, Lady Nora? One of the senior girls at Miss Pipcock's saw him once, and said he was clubfooted."

"Oh God. I have to be a *gammy* woman?"

"That's not a bad idea, Miss Shea," Ash said.

She glowed at his approval. "What's more, with a lame foot you won't be asked to dance, Harry."

He went white.

"Too bad, though. I'd like to see you waltzing with a moonstruck swain."

"Enough, Miss Shea!" Ash poured a glass of wine and handed it to Harry. "You have earned this, sir. Not only will you be spared dancing lessons, but you'll have an excuse to carry a cane. A sword cane," he added meaningfully.

"Which will require more fencing lessons," Killain noted. "No point carrying a sword cane if you can't use it to advantage."

Eyes bright, Harry practiced limping around the salon.

"We'll work on it," Nora said after a while. "If he's

forced to lean on a cane, at least one of his arms won't be waving about. One last thing, young man. We'll need to rouge your cheekbones and lips."

"Oh God."

"You have the most difficult task of all," Ash said quietly. "In return for your best effort, Harry, whether we see this plan through or not, you may ask anything you want of me."

"Like in the game with the croquet balls?"

"No. Not like that. This time the stakes are life and death. Play well, and I will give you anything in my power to offer." He looked at Glenys. "I cannot make you the same promise, Miss Shea, but you will be well provided for."

She blushed and nodded, and he knew she understood what he meant. No more kisses. Nothing that required him to do what could only hurt her.

"If we are all agreed," Nora said briskly, "pass us the lists so we can get started. November seems a long time away, but it will be here before we blink."

23

Glenys perched on the window seat in Harry's room at Chatsworth, her nose pressed against the glass. Because the window overlooked the front entrance, she had an excellent view of the carriages pulling over the stone bridge and stopping just below her to disgorge their passengers.

Evan and Jane Cordell, the only relatives invited to the betrothal ball, were expected for dinner beforehand and would remain overnight. She wanted an advance look, to take their measure, but no one matching their description had yet arrived.

Harry sat in front of the dressing table, shaving. He cleared his throat. "Uh, Glennie, I got a problem."

"What else is new?" she inquired absently.

"This is serious. After lunch, Lord Mumblethorpe asked me to stroll with him in the garden. *Stroll*, would you believe?"

"Did you?"

"Are you queer in the attic?" Harry put down his

razor. "Told him I had the headache, but he wouldn't let up. Said he'd sit with me tonight at the ball."

"He's probably just being nice." A coach drew up, and she watched the liveried footman scurry to open the door and let down the steps.

"What if he likes me, Glennie? How do I get rid of him? What do you do when a man is after you?"

An elderly woman descended the carriage, followed by an even more decrepit gentleman. She sighed. "How would I know, Harry? No man has ever been *after* me."

"Guess not." He turned back to the mirror. "Draw him off, will you? Damned if I'll flirt with the bloody oaf."

"I am betrothed, gudgeon. How would it look if I made moon-eyes to Lord What's-his-name?"

"Mumblethorpe. And you ain't really betrothed."

To be sure. But sometimes it felt so real, with Ash playing his role to perfection. Whenever they were in company with the duke, he hovered at her side, all attention, touching her arm or even holding her hand as if he couldn't bear to be separated from her.

It was purely a charade, of course. When they were alone, or with the other conspirators in their plot, he kept his distance.

They had been at Chatsworth for two days while the new staff became familiar with the estate and their duties. Ash and Killain, preoccupied with security arrangements, left the Duke of Devonshire to entertain the ladies.

Glenys thought him charming. Nearly as tall as Ash, with blue eyes and a sweet smile, his grace put her immediately at ease. With transparent pride he showed her the treasures in his great house, which was larger than most villages she'd ever seen. That morning, he had displayed for her a model of the "new Chatsworth." Major reconstruction would begin while he was in Italy, and he was terribly excited about it.

Often he put her in mind of a child playing with a vastly expensive toy.

Arm in arm they strolled through the galleries, the enormous private chapel, and the extensive library. Ash had helped him arrange the purchase of several collections, the duke informed her, pointing out two First Folios of Shakespeare's works.

Overwhelmed and certain her mouth was hanging open nine minutes of every ten, she nearly forgot the crucial business at hand when she was with the duke. But tonight all their careful plans would be put to the test.

Forty guests were invited to dinner, and another hundred to the ball. Except for Evan and Jane Cordell, none were on Killain's list of suspects. This was a trial run for the staff and, primarily, a chance for Harry and Glenys to practice company manners.

Since they had passed muster with the Duke of Devonshire, Glenys had no fear of being twigged as an imposter. A few guests had arrived in time for luncheon, including Harry's hopeful suitor, and Lady Nora said afterward that the Sheas made an excellent impression. All was well, so far.

The ball would be a greater challenge, but she was looking forward to it. Her own plans for the evening centered on Ash's cousins. She had resolved to latch on to them, fire up her instincts, and learn everything she possibly could about the man who would soon inherit the title if Ash was killed. And about the heir's wife, who might be playing Lady Macbeth in a murder plot.

A loud grunt startled her. She glanced over to see Harry, wearing silk stockings, lacy pantalettes, and a chemise, clutching at the bedpost with both hands. His maid, perspiration on her brow, struggled to lace him into an oddly shaped corset.

Glenys had seen the results, amazingly effective when

he was fully dressed, but had never watched the actual process of transforming her brother into Miss Harriet. The corset, padded at the top to give him a bosom and at the bottom to give him hips and a rounded derriere, was tightly nipped in at the waist. He swore under his breath as the maid yanked at the laces, one foot propped against the side of the bed for leverage.

Glenys erupted into laughter, which drew a furious glare from Harry.

"Devil take it, Glennie! This is bad enough without you chortling like a hyena. Go put on your own corset. We gotta be ready in half an hour."

"I never wear a corset," she said with one last look out the window. Still no sign of Jane and Evan. "Don't tell Lady Nora, though. She hasn't noticed."

"Laugh at me one more time and I'll spill the beans. Damned if I won't."

She flashed him an insulting hand signal on her way out.

Glenys contemplated her reflection in the mirror, rather pleased at what she saw. Her ball dress of pale green gauze over a white slip was cut low over her shoulders and deep at the back. They were her best features, her shoulders and back, and Lady Nora made sure her gowns were styled to show them off.

Ash had given her an emerald choker to wear, and a matching bracelet was secured over her elbow-length white kid glove. There were earbobs too, which had required her to have her lobes pierced before leaving Ravenrook. She had never owned a single piece of jewelry in her life. When he told her the emerald set was hers to keep, she nearly wept with pleasure. Of course, she fully intended to give it back.

But the gift had reminded her of the stickpin she'd

chosen for him the day Charlie was killed, and she went immediately to her room to retrieve it. When she gave it to him, Ash seemed delighted with her simple offering. Even touched, although it was worth a fraction of what he must have paid for the emeralds.

He never wore it, though. At the formal dinners where she and Harry rehearsed proper manners, she waited in vain for it to appear on his cravat.

Prudence, responding to a scratch at the door, admitted Lord Killain and Harry. Her brother wore a canary-yellow gown with long mutton sleeves, a high neckline, and lots of lace. With a touch of rouge at lips and cheeks, his soft hair curling around his ears and neck, he made a strikingly attractive young woman.

"Lord Mumblethorpe will positively swoon when he sees you," she whispered as Killain led them down the Great Staircase.

Harry thwacked her on the ankle with his cane.

When they came into the glittering salon, a hush fell over the room. All eyes lifted to the doorway, and Glenys felt like the center of an archery target. Politely, the guests resumed their conversations, but they continued to regard her with surreptitious glances.

Dazzled by the gleaming chandeliers and brighter company, she froze in place. How could she meet these people? What would she say to them? Glenys Shea did not belong here.

Killain's hand pressed against her waist. "Come, my dear."

Stumbling slightly, she moved into the room, a smile carved on her face. She forgot to look for Jane and Evan. Forgot everything but staying erect. Dear God, where was Ash?

Then he was directly in front of her, bowing, taking

her gloved hand, and lifting it to his lips. Her vision cleared.

Her heart stopped.

In all her twenty-one years, she had never seen anything so splendid as the Earl of Ravensby in full evening dress. Against the black and white of his stockings, kneebreeches and tailed coat, the white-on-white embroidered waistcoat and whiter cravat, his eyes glowed like gray-green flames. And at his neck she saw the stickpin she had given him.

Confidence flooded back. She curtseyed, holding his gaze with her own for an intimate moment before turning to greet the duke. Devonshire complimented her with obvious sincerity and beckoned to a servant, who offered her a glass of champagne.

Soon after, the guests began to filter in her direction to be introduced. Her confidence fled again. This was an elaborate dance, she realized, and they knew all the steps. Lady Nora had taught her to manage herself in a formal receiving line and how to behave at table, but nothing had prepared her for the intricacies of affairs like this one.

Ash stood on one side and Devonshire on the other, both of them enviably at ease. As they presented her to the Mayor of Sheffield, Lord and Lady Something, Mr. and Mrs. Something Else, Viscount Gridley or Grumley—she wasn't sure—and the rest, she smiled. She nodded, smiled, and murmured pleasantries. She smiled and sipped champagne. She smiled and smiled and smiled.

For a brief few seconds she was alone with Ash and the duke. "Relax," Ash whispered. "You are doing wonderfully."

"You lie through your teeth," she whispered back. "I am the veriest country bumpkin."

"On my honor, you have stolen their hearts. Now prepare yourself. Here come Evan and Jane."

A rod of iron suddenly appeared in her back. Passing her empty glass to the duke as though he were a footman, she regarded them with avid curiosity.

Evan, a stocky man just above her own height, seized Ash's extended hand and pumped it vigorously. "By the mass, it's good to see you again. Too long, I say. Too long."

He turned to Glenys as Ash murmured introductions and gave her a frank look of appraisal. Like a man deciding whether or not to buy a brood mare, she thought, examining him with equal calculation. She liked what she saw. Evan Cordell had open, friendly eyes, ruddy cheeks, and the bluff heartiness of a country squire content with himself and life in general.

Apparently she too passed inspection. "Ravensby is a lucky man, Miss Shea," he said, pressing her hand between his. "Pleased to meet you."

He acknowledged the duke with a belated bow and returned his attention to Glenys. "May I present m'wife? Jane, come meet our new cousin."

Jane had held back, behind her husband, fluttering pudgy hands as if ruffled to be in the exalted presence of an earl and a duke. Like Evan, she was short, slightly overweight, and dressed with no eye to good taste. Simpering a "So kind, your grace, to invite us," she curtseyed to Devonshire before focusing cold, hard eyes on Glenys.

A woman to be reckoned with, Glenys knew immediately. Sharp intelligence lay behind her addled conversation, which was frequently punctuated with nervous giggles.

When Ash inquired about her children, she rambled on until even the excruciatingly polite duke grew bored and wandered away. And all the while, her pale blue eyes stared at Glenys with barely concealed hatred.

Oh, yes, Jane wanted to be Countess Ravensby. She practically vibrated with ambition while her mouth spewed nonsense. And all the while, Evan regarded her proudly. He loves her, Glenys thought, astonished. Probably because she had given him three sons and two daughters. Farmers, and Evan was a farmer right down to his toenails, cherished fertile ground.

But was she able to mount the attacks on Ash? Direct the murder of his wife and the ambush that killed Charlie? Jane was surely capable of doing whatever it took to achieve her goal, but had she the funds to hire accomplices? A country squire's pin money wouldn't turn the trick.

Knowing she required more information, but certain Jane would be wary of her, Glenys slipped into the role of awestruck twit. Not unlike Jane's false persona, certainly, but the more effective for that reason. Jane would not imagine anyone else wily enough to carry it off.

"I long for children," Glenys divulged when Jane's monologue wound to a close. "If only Ashie and I are blessed as you and Evan have been. Will you mind very much if I quiz you later about . . . personal matters? My mother died before she explained, well, the essentials, and I've no one to ask. We are to be cousins, after all."

Jane regarded her with distaste before recovering her poise. "Of course, my dear."

Glenys batted her lashes. "Ah, I misspoke myself. Forgive me. I do not refer to matters between husband and wife. Ashie will know all about those. But he cannot be familiar with birthing. I shall ask you later, when it becomes necessary, about that. Meantime, I worry about fulfilling my duties as helpmeet. I want to take from him the burdens of managing the household and, most particularly, the finances. Ashie is writing a book. He should not be distracted with day-to-day affairs."

Jane's reply was cut off by the butler, who rang a silver bell to announce dinner. Evan immediately took her hand and hauled her toward the door, clearly looking forward to his meal.

Glenys watched her draw him aside with a sharp tug. Jane knew well they ranked very low in the order of precedence. Resentment flicked across her chubby face.

"Ashie?" Ravensby inquired with a raised brow.

"Never mind that. Jane is a witch and bears close scrutiny. I'll try to be alone with her, tonight if possible or tomorrow before she leaves. Do what you can to throw us together."

"Yes, ma'am. Any further instructions?"

Laughing, she shook her head. "I should concentrate on my manners, I suppose, so as not to disgrace you."

"No fear of that. But it will look odd if you spend the evening interrogating my cousins. This is your betrothal ball, Miss Shea. Do try and remember I am in the room."

As if she could forget him any moment of the day or night. He still haunted her dreams. She always awoke with the sheets twisted around her, clutching a pillow, her breasts and the place between her legs aching to be touched.

She was blushing hotly by the time they reached the elaborate dining room, where she was seated to the duke's left and across the table from Ash. She felt him looking at her through the long meal, and drank rather more wine than was good for her.

Fortunately, Lord Mumblethorpe, who was placed beside her, kept her busy answering questions about her lovely sister. He was a sweet, earnest young man. Torn between embarrassing him and the delights of promoting his courtship of Miss Harriet, she settled for making friends with him instead.

After dinner the gentlemen relaxed over port and cigars while the ladies went to their own chambers to make repairs. The ball guests would arrive within the hour. Glenys heard the orchestra tuning their instruments as she mounted the stairs, a bit woozy after all the wine she'd drunk.

Harry caught up with her in the passageway, breathing heavily. "What did you say to Lord Mumblethorpe?" he demanded. "I saw you talking at him all through dinner."

"Oh, I gave him the benefit of my wisdom. If he takes my advice, perhaps we can announce *two* betrothals at the ball."

Harry followed her into her room, sputtering with rage. "If you put any wrong ideas in his head, Glennie, I swear I'll tear you limb from limb."

She regarded him with a frown. "Speaking of limbs, why are you favoring your right foot? In the salon, it was your left."

He looked confused. "Was it? I can't never remember."

"You had *better* remember, lout. If I noticed, others will." Proceeding to the armoire, she searched the back reaches for one of her plainer gowns and tore off a small button. "Choose a bad leg and put this in your slipper as a reminder."

"It'll hurt."

"All the better. Which leg?"

"Left, I guess."

"Very well. I'll make sure your maid tapes a button in all your left shoes. Harry, the earl's life is at stake here. We can't afford any blunders."

His face grew solemn. "I know. Your life too, Glennie. Take care tonight."

The Duke of Devonshire led Glenys out for the opening minuet.

She had practiced for hours with Lord Killain and knew the steps, but private rehearsals had not prepared her to be the center of attention at a ball. She felt nervous and graceless, with sticks for legs and noodles for arms. Whenever the figure permitted, she clung to the duke's hand for support.

If he noticed, he gave no sign. He smiled into her eyes, told her he envied Ravensby, and before the long dance ended she had regathered most of her spirit.

"I quite understand why Ash is so fond of you," she said as Devonshire made a graceful bow and escorted her from the floor. "How very good you are to invite us here tonight and give us the use of your home in London."

"Not at all. When you are wed, I'll expect to see the both of you often. Ravensby is my closest friend, but he has played the hermit far too long. I'm delighted to see him happy. And because you have made him so, Miss Shea, there is nothing you cannot ask of me."

The offer was too good to refuse. "I wish Evan and Jane were not leaving tomorrow morning," she said earnestly. "They are Ash's nearest relations, and I'd hoped for more time to pursue our acquaintance. Could you possibly invite them to remain another night, your grace? In a small circle of family and friends, we can all relax and come to know each other."

"Certainly, Miss Shea. A capital idea. But come. I must hand you over to Ravensby and make the formal announcement. Then, as you waltz together, I'll speak with Mr. Cordell and his wife."

He led her to Ash, who stood near the stage where the conductor waited for a signal. When the duke mounted the stairs, the orchestra played a fanfare. Ash took her hand as all the guests turned to look at them.

The duke spoke quietly, as always, but in the hushed ballroom his words were clear. "My lords and ladies, ladies and gentlemen, I am honored to announce the betrothal of Ashton de Vesci Cordell, Lord Ravensby, to Miss Glenys Amelia Shea. May God smile upon their marriage and bless them with every joy."

Glenys saw Jane standing a few feet away, her small blue eyes glittering with unmistakable malice.

Ash turned to her then, and immediately she was lost in his beautiful eyes. As when she first saw them, they held her mesmerized. He led her to the center of the dance floor and put a firm hand at her waist. Dreamily, she placed her left hand on his shoulder and felt him lift her other hand as the waltz began to play.

They danced alone for a long time, circling the floor while the others looked on. She had never danced with him before. The lessons at Ravenrook were left to Killain, who always held her like a brother would hold his sister.

Ash held her like a lover. He gazed into her eyes, and smiled at her, and drew her close to his body as Killain had never done.

She couldn't help herself. She gave herself over to the fantasy, imagining they were truly in love and really to be married. He was playing a role, she knew—pretending for the guests who watched them. But for her the waltz was magical, and she let the dream carry her away to Caliban's island where the skies opened and dropped riches upon her.

"What are you thinking?" he asked as other dancers joined them on the floor.

"Oh, I'm counting the measures," she lied. "Trying not to trip over my big feet. What are *you* thinking?"

"That I never enjoyed dancing. Until now."

He must have regretted the confession because his arms grew rigid. "We'll set out for Ravenrook tomorrow afternoon, when the other houseguests have departed. Be ready to go."

She gave him a chipper smile. "Plans change, Lord Ravensby. I suggest *you* be ready for a surprise."

24

In defiance of Ravensby's strict orders, Glenys slipped out of the house the morning after the ball.

A servant had told her Mr. Cordell was gone to examine the sheep, and there were plenty of them about. Wrapped in her heavy wool cloak, she padded across the rolling lawns in search of Ash's heir. Eventually, she located him near the cascade that flowed from a hill overlooking the estate.

Evan was crouched in front of a bored-looking ewe, running his fingers through its fleece. "Excellent stock," he remarked when she came up beside him. "Quite different from my own southland breed, of course, but the wool is of superb quality."

"If you say so, sir. I know little of sheep."

"No reason you should, young lady. Men's work. And call me Evan, what?" He stood, wiping oily hands against his trousers. "I'm on my way to that flock by the river. Would you care to accompany me?"

"Yes, indeed. It will be a lovely day, once the

haze has burned off, and I've seen nothing of the grounds."

They strolled side by side, with Evan recounting the different varieties of sheep bred in England. Grateful for the heavy morning mist, which made them invisible to anyone more than a few yards away, she waited for an opportunity to break into his monologue.

"I am boring you, what? All this talk of farming and livestock."

"Not at all," she protested. "But I'm most interested in your own lands, and how they are managed. Is it a profitable venture, farming?"

"Depends on the weather and any number of unpredictables. Most years we turn a lively profit, but the land belongs to m'father, not me. I do everything, of course. He's not well, and hasn't taken an interest for years."

"I've heard Squire Matthew is ailing," she said sympathetically. "Lady Nora fears he may not live another winter."

"Likely not. We tend to him as best we can, but it's a wonder he's held on so long." Evan winked at her. "Our little secret, Miss Shea, but Jane was mighty fretful he'd stick his spoon in the wall before this do-up at Chatsworth. She wanted to come here something fierce. When he does breathe his last, we'll have the year of mourning ahead, y'know. No society tra-las, even to celebrate Ravensby's wedding."

Hang on, Matthew, she willed. I need Evan and Jane in London five weeks from now. Immediately regretting her selfish thoughts, she touched Evan's arm. "I expect you'll miss your father terribly."

"Oh, he's been gone in the head this past year or more. But he hurts, and has pitiful bedsores. I'll be relieved when he's in peace."

They came over a small hill, and Glenys heard the

rush of water just ahead. The river was narrow at this spot, barely eight feet across, the grass thick and lush along its banks. The sheep were taking full advantage, cropping placidly, scarcely noticing the arrival of two humans in their midst.

"The farm will be yours?" she ventured. "When Matthew dies, I mean. Or will it be divided between you and your brother?"

Evan gave her an astonished look. "Divided? Never. I've not seen the will, but Jane says all the land comes to me as firstborn son. A good thing too. Jervase would gamble it away in a fortnight."

"How awful. But surely there is some provision made for him?"

"As to that, I couldn't say. Jane takes care of business matters with m'father's solicitor. I've no head for ledgers and the like. One quarter of each year's profits are given me to buy more land, or more animals, or experiment with crops. The rest is . . . " He shrugged. "You must ask Jane. She controls the money."

"Indeed?" Glenys choked back her next question. She had already meddled too far in Evan's affairs. "Forgive me, cousin. I do not mean to pry. Ash tells me I must learn to govern my curiosity and my tongue. I always want to know everything, even if it's none of my business. He says that is a flaw in my character, and will earn me the disdain of friends and family."

"Never you mind about that. Ravensby was always punctilious to a fault, but we country folk love a dollop of gossip with our tea and scones. I don't mind a bit talking about the farm. When you come to visit, I'll show you every acre and you can question me to your heart's content."

She smiled at him, but he'd already turned away, more interested in the sheep than their conversation.

She watched him drop to his knees on the wet grass in front of a black-faced ewe, murmuring to her softly as he checked her fleece and bone structure.

Knowing he'd forgotten about her, Glenys headed back for the house before the alarm was sounded. If Ash discovered she had gone missing, all hell would break loose.

It would be worth it, a tongue-lashing from him or worse, because she had learned much of what she needed to know. Jane had access to a great deal of money, assuming the farm was profitable. Given Evan's dedication and obvious talent, it most certainly was.

But what of the solicitor? Did he have charge of the accounts, or could Jane siphon funds at will? Use them perhaps to hire the men who besieged Ash and murdered his wife?

Wringing information from Jane would not be easy, and the blatant approach she'd used with Evan would be ineffectual with his wife. But flattery might work, so long as she maintained her pose of bird-witted wigeon seeking advice from her wiser, more experienced cousin-to-be.

Glenys reentered the house through the kitchen, snatching a warm cinnamon roll from a tray and winking at the pastry cook. After a bath and a change of clothing, she'd corner Jane and begin her interrogation.

Hearing voices, she took care to avoid the public rooms and main passageways. It was still early, but the guests who'd stayed overnight would be taking their leave throughout the morning. She located a back stairway, used mostly by the servants, and made her way to the second floor where her room was located.

Free and clear, she was thinking just as her luck ran out.

Ash came up the main staircase before she could dart into her bedchamber. He paused for a moment, eyes narrowing as he took in the heavy cloak draped over her shoulders. Then he came at her with an expression on his face that backed her against the wall.

"G-Good mornin', Ash," she said around a mouthful of cinnamon roll.

He fingered her damp hair. "You've been outside."

She regarded him helplessly, a wad of pastry lodged in her throat.

When she began to choke, he turned her around and thumped her hard on the back. A lump of half-chewed roll hit the wallpaper and stuck there. She stared at it in dismay for the brief moment before he spun her again and seized her shoulders. Then he shook her until her teeth rattled.

"Have you lost your wits?" he roared. "What will it take to exact obedience from you? Shackles?"

Two doors opened and a pair of wide-eyed guests looked out to see what was going on.

"Bloody hell," Ash muttered. He seized her arm and steered her into her bedchamber, slamming the door behind him.

Prudence cowered against the armoire. The gown she'd been holding dropped to the carpet.

Ash pointed a finger at her. "Out!"

She fled.

By this time, Glenys had recovered a bit of her mettle. "How dare you shout at me? Bully me in the halls? What will everyone think?"

"I don't give a damn about them. You went outside alone, against my express orders. Anything might have happened to you."

Inches apart, they glowered at each other. Glenys raised her chin another notch. "Nothing did. I am here and perfectly fine. What's more, I wasn't alone."

A muscle ticked in his jaw, but some of the fire went

out of his eyes. "A small mercy, although I'll have the hide of the bodyguard who permitted you onto the grounds without my permission."

She backed away slowly, hoping he wouldn't notice she was putting distance between them. He would never raise a hand to her, of course, but she didn't relish the thought of another shaking. Even now she was astonished at that mild loss of self-control. A measure, she knew, of his rage. Or his fear for her.

She took a deep breath. "As to that, none of your men were aware I left the house. I wished to speak with Evan, who wished to inspect the sheep. We did so together, for a few minutes, and then I came directly back."

"Evan?" Ash hit the palm of his hand against his forehead. "One of the two people in this house we have some reason to suspect. You are daft. What if Evan is the killer? He might have put a knife in your heart."

Well, yes. Though her instincts told her Jane was the more likely villain, Evan could not be ruled out. Perhaps they were working together. In her eagerness to question him about his wife, she'd never considered that possibility.

"I was foolish and reckless," she admitted grudgingly. "But never in danger. I asked a footman if he knew where Evan could be found. Had I been murdered, Evan would have been the prime suspect. He'd surely wait for a better opportunity."

Ash gave her a look that blistered her cheeks. "Shall I assume Evan was aware you questioned that footman before leaving the house?"

She crushed the remains of the cinnamon roll in her hand. "Probably not. Very well, certainly not. Even so, no harm done. And in future, you have my word I'll not set a foot outside without your leave."

"Damn right you won't. Nor will you have the

chance. As of now, you are confined to this room. We are scheduled to depart after lunch, but you'll eat yours from a tray. The maid will pack your things. Be ready to go at two o'clock."

"Go? But we are staying another night. The duke said so."

"Ah, yes. I'd forgot that piece of Shea manipulation in the heat of dealing with your subsequent crimes. Hart informed me over breakfast that you'd arranged for a private family convention this evening, and that Jane was most pleased to accept his invitation. I was on my way to discuss your impertinence when we met in the hallway."

On surer ground, Glenys dug in her heels. "It was a good idea. At the dinner and the ball there was no opportunity for me to feel out Evan and Jane. I have good instincts about people. Even Killain says so. This afternoon and tonight I'll get more information from both of them than you've done in the last six years. You can bet on it."

He shook his head. "You really don't understand, do you? My fault, in part. I assumed you would place enough trust in my judgment to obey me, despite the fact you've yet to heed a single one of my instructions."

"And I've told you from the beginning, in plain language, that obedience is not in my nature." She fired a sharp look at him. "I *am* capable of listening to reason, but you never *explain* anything. It's always 'Do this, Glenys.' 'Don't do that, Glenys.' Is it any wonder I pay you no mind?"

"I wonder at it constantly. But I agree that I have failed to make clear what I thought should be obvious to you by now." He folded his arms. "Do you imagine, Miss Shea, that we travel anywhere without meticulous preparation? Without ordering, in advance, every precaution Killain and I can devise?"

"I know you make plans," she said uneasily, sensing she was about to hear something that would put her firmly in the wrong.

"We are scheduled to depart at two o'clock. Before dawn, the first group of men rode out to check the roads and ask questions at pubs and posthouses about strangers in the area. Soon after, other men left to inspect likely spots for an ambush. I'll not have a repeat of what happened to Charlie. By the time we leave here, there will be armed men all along the route, checking their watches."

He moved directly in front of her and gazed steadily into her eyes. "During the last few months, Killain timed the journey between Chatsworth and Ravenrook under various weather and road conditions. The guards know when we are to leave, and when we are expected to pass the spots where they are posted. If we fail to appear—"

"Oh."

"You begin to grasp the reasons why a sudden, secretive change in plans, like the one you engineered with Devonshire, cannot be tolerated. The chaos that ensues whenever Miss Glenys Shea takes the bit between her teeth."

She licked dry lips. "Y-Yes."

"At last, you listen to reason." He fixed her with a scornful look. "We depart as planned."

"Certainly. I'm sorry. I didn't know." In fact, she'd underestimated him. And that was the most stupid of all the things she'd done, because she admired Ash Cordell and respected him beyond any person she had ever met. "I should have trusted you. I will do so from now on, without question."

"Why do I doubt that?" he murmured. "Have your bath, Glenys. Pack your things. And while you do, think on this. The Duke of Devonshire has exerted himself for the both of us. He has offered us free run of Chatsworth and Devonshire House, and gone out of his way to be kind. How have you rewarded him?"

Ash shook a finger in her face. "He cannot withdraw the invitation to my cousins to stay another night at Chatsworth. When the other guests are on their way, he'll be left to entertain farmer Evan, who is bound to prattle about sheep and mangel-wurzel all through dinner and over port afterward. Even worse, the duke will be toadied to distraction by—" He paused for effect. "—*Jane.*"

"Oh dear." Glenys bowed her head in remorse.

"Humble now, are you?" Ash strode to the door. "A refreshing transformation."

"I am a worm. Will the duke change his mind about letting us use his house in London, do you think?"

"Not if I tell him I still want it. But I'm not at all sure that I do. I've a mind to call this off here and now, and you'll be treading thin ice even if I postpone the cancellation. With exceptionally good behavior, you may possibly earn another five weeks to convince me our plan should go ahead."

He looked back at her sternly. "Be assured, Miss Shea, that I shall require a great deal of convincing."

25

Glenys sat quietly in her room at Devonshire House, waiting for Ash. Those were his instructions, and for five weeks she had taken care to obey him in every regard.

Compliance with his wishes had got her all the way to London, although she'd yet to see a square inch of the city. They traveled from Ravenrook in closed carriages and were inside the gates of Devonshire House before she was permitted to look about. A high wall surrounded the enormous house and gardens, effectively shutting out the rest of the world.

For three days there was little to do but read and practice social skills with Lady Nora while the men secured the house and rehearsed the servants. But now everything was in place. Her elaborate ruse to snare the killer had come all the way from proposal to reality.

Within the hour the entire family would gather in the drawing room and she would meet, for the first time, Jervase Cordell and Wilfred Baslow. Tonight there was to be a ball, one of three planned during their stay in London.

She hugged herself, so excited she could scarcely remain on her chair. What was keeping Ash? This unnatural docility was near to driving her mad.

As if summoned, he knocked and opened the door.

She leapt to her feet, but he shook his head. "A few words before we go down, Glenys. Prudence, you may leave now."

The maid gathered her sewing and went to the adjoining parlor.

Ash clasped his hands behind his back. "Be warned, my dear. Hostility is practically visible in the drawing room, although little of it will be directed at you. Lady Nora dislikes her husband, as you know. And everyone dislikes Jane, except Evan."

"He loves her."

"A wonder, that. But you have already met Jane and know what to expect. As for Jervase, take no heed of his sarcasm. He has already begun to torment Harry, who is behaving admirably. Lady Nora is acting as a shield."

"I'll draw his fire, then. Harry won't put up with him for long."

"You stay out of his way. Jervase takes no prisoners. It amuses him to brew trouble wherever he goes."

She grinned. "Rather like me."

"You make trouble enough, certainly, but your intentions are good. Jervase likes to draw blood."

"Indeed? That makes him a prime suspect, wouldn't you say?"

"He has always been so. We've tracked his movements for years. But for all I'd like to cast him in the role of villain, we have pretty much ruled him out. Jervase was not in England when most of the attacks took place, and a flawless alibi carries more weight than a grating personality."

"Yes. Well, I can't wait to meet him. Shall we go?"

"One last thing, if you please. Do not call me *Ashie*."

Laughing, she took his arm. "Agreed. Jane will have to assume I've grown up a bit since we met at Chatsworth."

Ash led her to the drawing room, and she understood immediately what he'd meant by *hostility*. Any moment now the curtains would surely go up in flames.

Jane and Evan sat together on a sofa across from Lady Nora and Harry. Jane looked up when the door opened, her small eyes narrowing when she saw who had come in. Deliberately, she returned her attention to Evan, patting him on the hand with elaborate affection.

Geoff stood behind Harry's chair, keeping watch. Several footmen were aligned against the walls, and Fortesque directed the two underbutlers who poured tea and offered refreshments.

Glenys had thought her arrival would make a ripple in the water, at the very least. But except for that one flash of antagonism from Jane, everyone ignored her. A careful balance had been established, and the others seemed bent on preserving it. Even Harry spared her no more than a brief nod before returning to the conversation.

Shrugging, she looked around for the two men she hadn't met. Wilfred Baslow—it had to be him—was hunched on a chair in the corner, pawing through a heavy book. Gaunt and frail, with mussed hair and rumpled clothing, he seemed unaware there was anyone else in the room.

Shaking loose from Ash, she headed in Wilfred's direction. "Mr. Baslow?" she inquired, giving him her sunniest smile. "I'm pleased to make your acquaintance."

He glanced up, regarding her with an annoyed expression. Clearly, he did not wish to be disturbed.

"Glenys Shea," she explained. "Lord Ravensby's fiancée."

"Oh, yes." He struggled to his feet and produced an old-fashioned bow. "Pleased to meet you." Then he dropped back onto the chair, spread the book open on his lap, and continued reading.

"How charming," she murmured under her breath. No wonder Lady Nora wanted nothing to do with him. By her account, Wilfred Baslow cared for no one born after the twelfth century.

Ash was conversing with Lord Killain, so she went in search of Jervase Cordell. There were several bow windows in the enormous drawing room, and she spotted a tall, lean man relaxing on a bench at one of them. He observed her progress with a lazy smile.

When she drew near, he uncoiled himself, stretched broadly, and tilted his head. "The prospective bride, I presume. Ash has better taste than I'd imagined."

She curtseyed. "Thank you. I think."

"Oh, it was a compliment. There is intelligence in your eyes. He values intelligence above all things."

"A backhanded compliment, then. You must be Jervase."

He bowed. "The black sheep of the family, as I expect my cousin has told you. And I did not mean to slight your other attractions. They are considerable, to my astonishment."

She regarded him with cool, speculative appraisal, the same way he was looking at her. Ash had understated Jervase Cordell's caustic humor.

"I'll not ask you to list my *other attractions*," she said mildly, "or even inquire why you are astonished. But I *am* curious why you have chosen to be rude."

His ice-blue eyes widened for a moment. Then he laughed. "Cry peace, Miss Shea. Jane told me you were a chuckleheaded antidote, and I was witless enough to believe her. You took me aback. I did not expect a sharp mind, a forthright manner, and beauty in one slender package."

"Nor I an acid tongue suddenly dripping with honey. No wonder Ash spends so little time with his relations."

"Indeed, we are a sorry lot. Until Jane married into the family, I was the worst of the bunch. Now we vie for the dishonor, although she will defeat me in the end. No man can best a woman for wickedness if she is set to trounce him. Have you wrapped Lord Ravensby around your little finger, Miss Shea? I daresay my cousin is tied in knots by now."

"If love always ties a man in knots, yes. I prefer to think I've set him free."

Jervase brushed a swatch of pale blond hair from his forehead. "May that be true. Ash deserves better than he's had these last few years. I used to envy him, you know. But since he's been forced to hide out at Ravenrook, I can only be glad it is him and not me who is under siege."

"A lovely sentiment on your part."

"Oh, take no offense. I am ever concerned for my own welfare. Ash is quite right to dislike me, Miss Shea. In general, I don't much care for myself."

Ash claimed her then, before she had time to respond to that remarkable statement. She heard Jervase laughing softly as she moved away.

Ash allowed her a few minutes to converse with the others before drawing her out of the room. In the hallway, he paused.

"I trust you've had enough of my family for this afternoon, Glenys. I certainly have. And I allowed you to speak privately with Wilfred and Jervase, so doubtless you have satisfied your curiosity."

"I've made a beginning, at any rate. And to be perfectly frank, I think any one of them is capable of murder."

Ash raised a brow. "Even Wilfred?"

"He's very odd, you must admit." As Ash led her upstairs to her bedchamber, she gave more thought to the frail old man. "Well, perhaps not Wilfred. And certainly not his wife. But Jervase is a snake, and Jane is a predator to her pointy fingernails. Evan loves her, though. For her sake, I expect he would kill."

At the door, Ash lifted her hand and brushed his lips over her wrist. "Have a nap, my dear. Tonight you will meet a great number of potential suspects. And compared to a few of them, Jane and Jervase are a pair of cherubim."

By ten o'clock Devonshire House overflowed with guests.

Ash attached himself to Glenys and warned Geoff to stay close by. In this crush it would be easy for the killer to slide a stiletto between her ribs and melt back into the crowd.

He wished to hell he'd never agreed to this ball. To a single one of Glenys Shea's harebrained schemes.

At least a third of the men and women in this room despised him. Another third disliked him, to say the very least. Except for a few of his friends, only people with a motive to kill him had received invitations. He felt like a rabbit tossed into a pit of vipers.

Glenys, naturally, was enjoying herself. She sparkled at every compliment, sincere or not. She laughed at the weakest jokes. She made much of awkward young men and shy young ladies, drawing them into the conversations. He followed in her wake as she moved from group to group, feeling rather like a small boat towed by a ship under full sail.

Finally the orchestra began tuning up and the center

of the ballroom was cleared for dancing. As host, he was expected to lead out his betrothed for the opening minuet—another ordeal he'd been dreading. It must have been five years since he danced, except for that one waltz with Glenys at Chatsworth.

To his surprise, he was soon caught up in the music and the intricate, courtly figures. As the dance proceeded, he found himself wholly enchanted by the sorceress who partnered him.

Lovely and graceful in her ivory ball gown, Glenys danced as if she were making love.

Oh, she was proper enough to suit the tabbies. But her eyes held his so tenderly it was almost a physical embrace. Her smile spoke secrets, and he longed to ask what they were.

He thought of Greek temples and torchlight. Satin sheets and wine drizzled over her body. A private orgy, just the two of them, pagan and carnal . . .

"Ash?"

He realized the dance had ended. Glenys was tugging at his sleeve.

"Harry needs me," she whispered. "He just signaled from the chaperone's corner. Lord Mumblethorpe must be making a nuisance of himself, and I promised to come to the rescue."

"Take Geoff with you," he ordered, too late. She had already vanished into the throng of couples lining up for the next dance.

He started to follow her, but Lord Peasboro, one of his father's hunting cronies, stepped in his way. The man wished to reminisce, it seemed, about grouse season at Ravenrook. Ash listened politely, wanting all the while to shove the doddering ancient into a potted palm. Fortunately, he wasn't required to speak. Peasboro was deaf as a doorstop.

Just when Peasboro's rambling began to wind down, a loud voice cut across the room.

"You! Ravensby!"

The first notes of the country dance faded off. The dancers stumbled to a halt.

An elderly man with thick white hair and sharp black eyes forced his way through the crowd, wielding his cane like a club.

The Marquess of Quarles. Ash knew his son, too well.

"Don't think to run or have your guards send me away, Ravensby. You will hear me out!"

Ash bowed, slightly, and waited.

Space opened around him as everyone stepped back from the confrontation. Even Quarles kept his distance, leaning on his cane now, making sure his actions could not be interpreted as a challenge, although no one would expect Ash to duel with a man nearly twice his age.

But Quarles's voice was strong, echoing in the hush that had fallen over the ballroom. He held nothing back— none of the venom, or the agony, or the savage rage.

Ash scarcely heard the words and did not try. He had heard them before, or words much like them, from others. From his father.

Everything receded until he was standing alone in a cold dark place. All he could do was keep his back straight, his face without expression. Only his fingers, clenched against his palms, betrayed any emotion. He tried to loosen them and could not.

"You drove him from England," Quarles bellowed. "It was your lies sent my boy into exile. Five years since I set eyes on him. My only son, and now he's dead."

With effort, Ash held still. The Foreign Office had tracked Richard's every move, making sure Ash knew his whereabouts and what he was up to. Running guns to hill bandits, by last account. But news of his death had not been reported.

As Quarles raved on, about a common grave in Albania and no chance to hold his son again, Ash battled the unholy urge to tell him the truth.

But what purpose would it serve? Raw with pain, Quarles would not believe him. The others might, those who stood and watched and listened. But Ash could not defend himself at the cost of more pain to the father of a wayward son.

"You killed my boy! It's your fault he is dead."

It didn't seem possible, but the cave in which Ash stood grew even colder. Quarles believed in his son's integrity, despite overwhelming evidence to the contrary. Ash respected that. Admired the unconditional faith of a loving father.

Most of all, he longed for such trust from his own father, although it was far too late. Like Quarles's son, Milton Cordell was in his grave. There could never be reconciliation and a new beginning.

Death settled over him like a heavy cloak of black ice. He had killed Jack Shea. Quarles held him responsible for Richard's death. Two men incriminated by his investigations had put bullets to their heads. One of them was his father's best friend. There were others, he was sure, men whose lives were ruined and ended because he'd exposed them. Perhaps they had cursed him with their dying breaths.

He could barely draw air into his own lungs now. Sheer force of will kept him erect, although his legs seemed to be melting under him.

Then something warm forced itself into his clenched right fist. A shoulder pressed against his arm. The scent of jasmine reached his nostrils.

He didn't move or look at her. His gaze remained

fixed on the indistinct face of Quarles, wavering from the light just beyond.

But Glenys was there, with him, holding his hand even as Quarles continued to roar at him. At *them*. He was no longer alone in the cave.

She remained as motionless as he, but warmth stole from their clenched hands, up his arm, all the way through him. He found that he could breathe again.

Gradually the darkness around him became light. Quarles's mottled red face stood out against the pale faces of the onlookers surrounding him. Tears sparkled against the man's cheeks, and Ash felt his own eyes burning.

I'm sorry, he wanted to say. Sorry for your grief, but not for what I did to cause it. I had no choice.

Glenys's hand felt on fire. He sucked warmth and strength from her grip and remained silent.

"He was innocent," the old man insisted in a voice grown raspy. "Richard would never betray his country."

Ash continued to look back at him. Gradually the tirade dwindled. Ceased. Their eyes met. The silence in the crowded ballroom was the quiet of a tomb.

As their gazes held, Ash was sure the marquess knew. Quarles had fought as long as he could, but now, without a word spoken against his accusations, he was unable to evade the truth. Perhaps he had always known, in his heart.

For some reason, that was worse to Ash than listening to his denunciations.

Quarles's flushed face went pale. He staggered, and Geoff was there to take his arm. Bystanders parted as they made their way to the door.

Ash wanted to rush after them and assure the marquess none of it was true. But he could not. Instead he clung to Glenys's hand, hoping that Quarles had someone like her. Someone of his own.

As if sensing a cue, the orchestra began to play again, faltering at first but finding the rhythm as dancers moved back into place. It was a waltz this time. The conductor must have realized the lively reel, interrupted when Quarles appeared, would have been unsuitable.

Glenys squeezed his hand. "Will you dance with me, Ash?"

Not ready to look at her yet, he took her in his arms. They swept onto the floor, she staring at his face, he staring past her into his own darkness. Nothing was said between them, although others recaptured the spirit of the party.

Ash heard laughter and the clink of glasses. He heard music and the shuffle of feet against the parquet floor. Mostly he heard Quarles's voice, and now the words were clearer than before.

"You killed my son," the voice said. "It's your fault he is dead."

Fingers tightened on his shoulder. "Come outside, my lord."

Ash realized they had come to a stop near the French doors that led to the terrace. It was deserted. Apparently everyone had gone into the ballroom when the altercation began.

He followed Glenys to a marble railing overlooking a lantern-lit garden. Below, a fountain bubbled softly. Two night birds sang from a bare tree branch.

Ash leaned his hands against the cold marble and lifted his head to the sky. A slice of moon, with Venus nesting close by, shone back at him.

"Is it always like this?" she asked gently. "When you go into society, do they cut you? Attack you openly?"

He shrugged. "Early days, there was some . . . difficulty. Efforts to blackball me from the clubs, that sort of thing. Little came of it, beyond the unpleasantness.

One man called me out, but the seconds persuaded him to withdraw."

"I should think anyone making too public a display would be considered unpatriotic. After all, you were serving your country. But someone nursing a private hatred and seeking a furtive retribution, yes. That is easy to believe."

"Not Quarles, though."

"He can certainly be ruled out. But there must be a score of men in that ballroom who wish you dead. I see it in their eyes."

"I see it too. Most have been investigated, in cursory fashion, but it's impossible to track so many. We can barely keep up with my family." He took a deep breath. "Now we should go back inside, Glenys. It's not as if I didn't know what to expect. And I feel a coward, hiding out here."

"Hiding? You? It's perfectly clear you were hankering for a clandestine snuggle with your fiancée. People are looking at us out the window, Ash. Shall we convince them you find me irresistible?"

It wouldn't be a lie, he thought, turning to gaze at her moon-washed face. Her lips curved in a flirtatious smile. Her slanted eyes glowed with mischief and—did he imagine it?—a touch of longing. "Shall I kiss you, then?"

"Better *now,* if you please."

She meant to tease him out of his dark mood, he knew. Put on a show for the guests and make this sham betrothal appear a genuine love match. All very good reasons to kiss her, to be sure.

But he took her in his arms because he wanted to. He pressed his body against hers because he yearned to feel her close to him. And he kissed her, deeply and for a long time, because he couldn't help himself.

26

Ash tossed the engraved square of parchment paper onto the salon table. "What the devil put this into his head? We'll not go, certainly."

He glanced at the others. Killain was frowning. Glenys and Harry stared at the paper with huge round eyes.

Nora looked thoughtful. "You can scarcely refuse. His invitations are more in the nature of commands."

"Read it to us again," Glenys begged.

"You heard it the first time." Ash clasped his arms behind his back. "And spare me the wheedling, young lady. There is no chance in the world I will permit you to leave Devonshire House. Even to dine with the king."

"The king," she echoed reverently.

Exasperated, Ash stomped to the bay window and looked outside. A bodyguard, holding the leash of a large dog, was patrolling the garden wall. "His Majesty is poor company these days. Trust me, you would be sadly disappointed."

"Perhaps you find him tedious, but I will not. He is the King of England, for heaven's sake. I'll never have another chance to meet a king, Ash."

"You don't have this one. The answer is no."

"The invitation says it will be a small, private dinner," Nora pointed out. "Surely Carlton is secure enough."

"His Majesty's idea of small could well mean a hundred guests. As for security, if there is any, it will be focused on him."

"I'll have my sword cane," Harry put in. From his enthusiastic tone, he could barely wait for a chance to use it.

Ash just shook his head. After their many sacrifices on his behalf, he took no pleasure depriving Harry and Glenys of what they imagined would be a treat. But it was too dangerous, at least for Glenys. He worried for her every minute of every day and most of every night. How long since he'd slept more than an hour or two?

Killain appeared at his shoulder. "I think we must accept," he said, too softly for the others to hear. "You've more than enough enemies without antagonizing Georgie. And to his credit, he has been one of your greatest defenders. The two of us shall go, without the children. We'll tell the king they are ill."

Ash lifted a brow. "And who, pray tell, will break the news to Glenys?"

"Point taken." Killain propped a shoulder against the window frame. "How about this? No guest list will be made public, and only the five of us know about the invitation. Who is to guess where we are headed tomorrow night? Naturally we shall travel under heavy guard, but the destination can remain secret until we are on the road."

"Oh, hell," Ash muttered succinctly.

"That's my opinion, but what choice have we, really?

You know Prinny—I mean, the king. He takes offense at any perceived snub, and he wants to meet your bride. We had better let him."

"Why in blazes would he take the slightest interest in my affairs? I haven't seen him in years. Indeed, I'm surprised he even knows I'm in London."

"Have you forgot how gossip spreads in the city? Besides, I'd wager it's his mistress got wind you are staying at Devonshire House. She hopes to see her daughter married to the duke, and knows you are his closest friend. Lady Conyngham wants you there, which means the king wants you there, which means we have to show up."

"As if I had anything to say about Hart's selection of a wife. Lord, I wish Nora had been invited. When the ladies withdraw after dinner, it will be only Glenys and Harry."

"Precisely the situation we have been training Harry to deal with. He'll do fine."

"Amazing, isn't it, that no one has guessed? To be honest, I never thought he'd bring it off. But sometimes even I look at him and see a reasonably attractive young lady."

"He worked hard these last months. I'm proud of him."

"And I." Ash rubbed his forehead. "Very well, Geoff. We'll give the youngsters an evening with the king. Arm yourself to the teeth, though, and if anyone tries to search us, we take our leave."

As Ash had predicted, Glenys was disappointed with King George. His eyes were nearly invisible, small gray beads surrounded by puffy lids and swollen cheeks. His stomach hung to his knees. He wore an unpowdered wig, limped on gouty feet, and thumped his massive thigh with a chubby fist whenever he made a joke. He greeted her warmly, though, and held her hand longer than he should.

At dinner she had been given the place of honor to his right, but most of his attention was focused on his mistress. Through the interminable meal, where he ate enough for three people, he drank prodigious quantities of cherry brandy and touched Lady Conyngham's glass before every swallow. It seemed to be a ritual between them.

Only twenty people sat to table, including Count and Countess Lieven, the Esterhazys, and two of Lady Conyngham's daughters. While Ash made conversation with Sir William Knighton, Glenys smiled when the king addressed her and otherwise amused herself by observing him.

He seemed quite taken with his mistress, although he was well into his sixties and she would not see fifty again. Over sherry in the Crimson Drawing Room, Lady Lieven had remarked that Lady Conyngham was more a habit than an object of affection. Her husband always spent the night under the same roof, to avoid any appearance of loose behavior on the part of his wife or the king. Lord Conyngham tolerated much, including that bit of hypocrisy, for the well-paying posts that fell his way.

Lavish jewelry dangling from every plump appendage, Lady Conyngham must have been quite beautiful in her youth. She had a sweet, musical voice, and spoke tenderly to her lover. Mostly, she flattered him.

Glenys thought them both rather sweet.

"I've never been so bored in my life," Harry whispered as the ladies withdrew, leaving the men to their port and cigars. "And I need to pee."

"Shh!" Glenys looked around her. The salon, decorated with Chinese oddities and hung with yellow silk, was even more garish than what she'd already seen of

Carlton. King George, she decided, had no taste whatever. "We can't disappear now. It wouldn't be polite."

"Won't be polite if I wet m'drawers," he fired back.

Footmen handed out cups of coffee and offered trays of sweets while Harry squirmed on a violently red sofa.

Within minutes Glenys knew they wouldn't be missed. After a few halfhearted attempts to make bland conversation with them, the other women gathered into tight clutches. She didn't mind. They were all twice her age, knew each other well, and had nothing to say to a pair of strangers.

As fragments of gossip floated to her ears, she eavesdropped with blatant curiosity. They used bigger words, but otherwise these highly fashionable women sounded exactly like the girls at Miss Pipcock's School. People are all the same under the skin, she reflected. Even in the house of the king, they talked about clothes and who had said what about someone else.

Harry tugged at her arm. "I gotta go," he insisted. *"Now."*

"Oh, very well."

Lady Conyngham glanced up as they stood. Glenys smiled at her, and she nodded graciously, as if giving them permission to leave.

A footman, his powdered wig slightly askew, met them outside the door and led them down a long hall to the retiring room. Inside, Glenys turned her back as Harry scurried behind an ornate screen.

"Damned skirts," he complained. "Don't know how you females put up with 'em." He took a long time, and a foul odor engulfed the small room.

"I'll wait in the hall," she muttered, escaping into the dim passageway.

As she closed the door, a large hand slapped against her mouth. A beefy arm wrapped around her, pinning her arms to her sides. She struggled in the man's grip, but he was too strong.

Her heels skidded along the carpeted floor as he dragged her down the hall. One slipper came loose and was left behind.

His forefinger pressed against her nostrils, cutting off her air. She heard the click of a latch, and the slam as the door closed again. He had pulled her into a room. There was no light, or maybe there was and she couldn't see it.

Half conscious, she tried to kick at him and heard a gruff oath. Then he let go her mouth and arms, and both his hands closed around her throat. Her body dangled helplessly as he choked her.

I'm going to die now, she thought with amazing clarity. Oh, Ash, I'm sorry. Don't be sad for me. I only wish I could have helped. I tried—

And then she was on the floor.

Gasping for breath, she heard muffled sounds. A scream. Silence.

Two hands pushed at her shoulders, and Harry's voice wafted from a great distance. "Glennie! Say something. Are you all right? Please, Glennie. *Please.*"

With all her strength she managed to force a noise from her burning throat. "Ghhuuuuh."

"Thank God." Harry's arms closed around her, and she felt moisture on her cheek as he pressed his face to hers. He rocked her back and forth, shuddering as he wept. "The guv was right," he whimpered. "We should never have come here."

Her vision cleared, and in the light from the open doorway she saw a body curled next to her, its eyes staring vacantly in her direction. She pushed Harry away and vomited.

Finally, she sat up, aching all over. "What happened?" she asked in a whisper.

"He's dead," Harry told her, his voice shaking. "I stabbed him in the back. Let's get out of here, Glennie. Can you walk?"

"Y-Yes. Help me s-stand."

Harry supported her down the hall, one painful step at a time. When they reached a wider passageway, lit by gas lamps, a footman lifted himself from a bench where he was nearly dozing and sprang forward. Harry put Glenys behind him and raised the sword.

Unable to stand on her own, she dropped to her knees.

Moments later she was surrounded by people. And then she was in Ash's arms, her head on his shoulder as he carried her into a bright room.

She was scarcely aware of the light because her eyes refused to open. It was all she could do to breathe. Her throat hurt. A man had tried to kill her. Harry had killed him.

She wanted to sleep.

27

Glenys stared at the pale blue damask wall-covering, wishing that a hand would appear and inscribe on it the answer she so desperately needed.

Lounging in bed against a bank of pillows, she had spent the morning lining up every conceivable argument why the London plan must go forward. She'd compiled an impressive list of reasons, but they were the same reasons she had used at Ravenrook. Now, because of the attack at Carlton, they would carry no weight with Ash.

Prudence sat by the window, sewing basket at her feet, stitching quietly. Ash had given orders Glenys was never to be alone, nor was she permitted any visitors. Except for the doctor and her maid, she had seen no one since falling asleep in the king's drawing room.

She had no recollection of coming back to Devonshire House, or of anything at all until waking early this morning with a fiercely aching throat. She could swallow only water, which hurt going down, and her body felt like she'd been dragged by a horse. For all that, she had escaped lightly.

Ash would not agree, to be sure. And doubtless he considered their plan at an end—no discussion required.

How was she to change his mind?

When a knock sounded at the door, Glenys perked up. Ash would be best, but she wanted to see Harry too.

She lapsed back with a sigh. It was only Robin, followed by two footmen, all of them carrying enormous vases of flowers.

"From the king," Robin said with reverence in his voice.

"All of them? My heavens."

"These and more, Miss Shea. We'll bring them up directly."

After three more deliveries by the footmen, Glenys's room looked like a hothouse conservatory. There were flowers on the dressing table and stool, on every table and chair, on the windowsills and, from necessity, on the carpeted floor. A few bouquets bore cards from the Lievens, the Esterhazys, and other dinner guests, but most of them—including all the truly elaborate displays—were gifts from King George.

Their fragrance was nearly overwhelming. Prudence hastened to open the windows while Glenys looked around her in delight.

His Majesty had given her flowers. And with them, bless his extravagant heart, the answer she had been looking for.

Ravensby appeared an hour later, looking startled when she greeted him with a happy smile. He stood, braced for trouble, at the foot of the bed. "How do you feel, Glenys?"

"Perfectly fine," she croaked.

He frowned. "The doctor assures me there is no lasting damage, but he suggested you not speak for a day or two. I'll have paper and writing implements brought to you."

"I won't need them," she said, her voice a husky whisper. "Honestly. I know I sound awful, but that will soon pass. It certainly won't shut me up."

"I expect nothing would do that," he said coolly. "Nothing short of what almost happened last night."

Oh, dear. The Earl of Ravensby was on the verge of making a Pronouncement. To deflect him, she held out a hand. "Come sit beside me, Ash. That way I can whisper."

He looked around for a chair, but they'd all been converted to flower stands. Clearly displeased, he sat next to her waist and reached for the lapels of her satin bedjacket. "Let me see your throat."

His fingers brushed her collarbone as he gently pulled the fabric loose. Heat radiated from his body and from the strong hands that lingered on her shoulders as he stared at the marks on her neck.

"Sweet Christ," he murmured.

"When Prudence gave me a hand mirror to look, I had much the same reaction. But they are only bruises, and they'll soon fade. Meantime, she is adding a high lace collar to my gown for dinner tonight. I intend to set a new fashion."

"The party has been cancelled," he said sternly. "There's no use trying to talk me out of it, because we've already sent word to the guests. What's more—"

"I've been hard put not to bite my nails all morning," she interrupted. "There is so much I wish to know. Tell me what happened after I dozed off last night."

He opened his mouth, closed it again, and sent a harsh breath between his teeth. "You've a right to know, but I would prefer to wait until you are stronger. You should rest, young lady."

"I promise to try, *after* my questions are answered. All of them," she added mutinously.

He muttered something that sounded like "incorrigible," and must have realized he was still holding her shoulders because he let go in a singularly swift motion.

For a terrible few seconds, she thought he'd leave. From the look in his eyes, he was certainly considering it. But he folded his arms across his chest, told Prudence to have her lunch in the servant's kitchen, and fixed his gaze on the Devonshire crest carved on the headboard.

"The real footman was discovered in the mews, trussed, gagged, and stripped of his livery. He was hit on the head from behind and saw nothing. The man who attacked you is dead."

"Did anyone recognize him?"

"We assume he was a hired thug. Killain stayed at Carlton, to question the servants while we brought you home. No luck. A drawing was made of his face and taken to Bow Street. Runners will attempt to trace his identity and the places he frequented, in case he was seen making contact with whoever paid him. A slim possibility at best, but we will pursue every lead."

His expression hardened. "Only Lady Nora knew we would be at Carlton last night. She is now confined to her room, under guard."

"Oh, no, Ash! She could not—"

"Who else? Moreover, she went out yesterday afternoon, alone. To purchase art supplies, by her account, and she did in fact return with canvases and paint. But she took a hackney, so none of the staff can verify her story."

"I believe her," Glenys said immediately. "Come to think of it, her husband might have known about the king's invitation. Harry and I were talking about it in the library. We thought ourselves alone, but then Mr. Baslow came out from one of the bookcases. Some of them are like doors, you know. They open to vaults holding other books."

"Were you speaking loudly?"

"Well, Harry was. Mr. Baslow looked surprised to see us there. He mumbled a greeting in that absent-minded way he has and wandered off to a desk, carrying an armload of books. We left after that. You should go into that vault and have Harry say something from the place we were sitting. Find out if you can hear him."

"I will. But the panel may have been cracked open, in which case the sound would surely carry through. However, there is little reason to suspect Wilfred. He's not left Devonshire House since he arrived."

"Practically growing roots in the library," she agreed thoughtfully. "And it is difficult to imagine him acquainted with London thugs or the sort of places they can be found. Jervase would know, I'm certain. Where was he?"

"When we run him down, we'll question him. Killain located his mistress, and it seems Jervase spent the night with her. This morning, he left for a mill. She didn't know where."

"A mill? Why on earth would he go to a mill?"

His lips curved. "Mill is slang for a boxing match, my dear. They are generally held at posthouses in the country-side. Jervase was always partial to them. As for his activities yesterday, he stopped here briefly to change clothes and pick up a few items. Otherwise, we don't know how he spent the day. Evan and Jane were preparing to go out, so he rode along in the carriage and they dropped him near St. James's Street. He said he was headed for his club. Killain will find out which one and how long he stayed."

"Lord Killain has been very busy."

Ash pulled his gaze from the crest and looked directly at her. "Yes. He hasn't slept. And I can be of little help to him, since he has ordered me to remain in the house. I do so only because it gives him one less thing to worry about."

She nodded, fully in sympathy. The inactivity was harder on Ash than on her. "What of Evan and Jane's excursion?"

"They separated for about two hours, when Jane visited a mantua maker. The carriage stayed with Evan while he called at several shops. It will take time to verify each story, of course."

Time. Just what she most wanted. "How about the guests at Carlton?"

"None were involved in my war investigations, if that's what you mean. I have asked them to call here, separately, this evening and tomorrow. One or more may have known we were invited and mentioned it casually to someone else."

"Excellent," she said. Questioning them would give him something to do. "At least we know our plan is working. The villain understands he must strike soon or lose his last chance. He has made a try, improvised and inept though it was, and—"

"Not inept! My God, Glenys. You nearly died."

"My fault entirely. I should have stayed with Harry, but I went alone into the passageway. The man would not have attacked us both. You made provision for every contingency, Ash, except my stupidity. I'll not be so careless again."

"Nor will you have the opportunity. The *plan* has failed. It was always far too dangerous, and I was a fool to agree in the first place. When you are recovered, we return to Ravenrook."

"Not I," she said resolutely. The husky sounds coming from her throat did not begin to carry the force of her determination. "You cannot force me to leave, Ravensby. I am of age, and I make my own decisions."

He gave her a scorching look. "Not in these circumstances, Miss Shea. You have no money and nowhere to go. And if you think to seek refuge with Lady Nora, I'll see her thrown into Newgate first. I may do that anyway."

"Harry too? He'll stick with me, and he knows how to get by on the streets."

Ash regarded her as if she'd lost her senses. She looked at his hands, clenched into tight fists. Well, she'd expected a hostile reaction.

"However," she said, before he translated his fury into words, "I've no intention of camping in a doorway. Carlton is not so lovely as Devonshire House, but it will be infinitely more comfortable than the pavement. If you cast me out, sir, the king will take me in."

"Dear Lord," he muttered. "What will you think of next?"

"You doubt it?" She made a sweeping gesture at the room. "He sent me all these flowers."

"A matter of a moment, child. He gave an order to a servant."

"Because he feels guilty. I was his guest, attacked in his very own house. Believe me, a man will do almost anything when he feels guilty. Even take a young woman under his wing when she applies to him in desperation. I can be rather convincing, my lord earl, or haven't you learned that yet? I assure you, the king will be easier to deal with than you ever were."

Ash swiped his fingers through his hair.

"I haven't decided which story to give him," she continued pensively. "But he's clearly a romantic at heart, so likely I'll play on that. He already thinks you vastly in love with me, and I with you. He knows you to be honorable to a fault. Perhaps I'll tell him you mean to exile me in America, for my own protection."

"I do," Ash put in.

She ignored him. "But I don't wish to leave England.

I cannot bear to be an ocean away from you. And the villain will be surely be caught, if the king uses his considerable resources to help us chase him down. Something on that order, anyway. I'll refine my plea, but when I do, he will help me."

"Why in bloody hell would you think so?" Ash jabbed a finger at her. "He is the King of England, goosecap. I am an obscure peer, and you are nobody."

"Thank you very much."

He flushed. "I *mean,* he will not exert himself for either of us. He's an old man. He can't even mount a horse without a launching ramp. At most he'll pat you on the cheek and wish you well."

"That is your opinion. For all he's a king, I don't think he has ever felt important or useful. I have good instincts—even Killain says so—and I can bring him around. Care to put a wager on my success or failure before you head north without me?"

With an oath that would have astonished Harry or her soldier father, Ash jumped up and stalked the edges of the room. And then he astonished *her,* by taking a swipe at a vase on the windowsill.

The vase remained intact as it landed on the plush carpet, but water spilled out and flowers scattered at his feet. He kept moving, crushing more than one white rose under his boot.

"Well?" she demanded.

"You actually expect me to go on as if nothing happened?" he shot back.

"In fact, yes. The killer has realized he must finish the job here in London. There will never be a better time to catch him. And I am the one who almost died last night. If *I'm* willing to continue, why aren't you?"

From the corner, he turned and met her gaze. "I don't want you hurt, Glenys. Not again."

Hot coals seemed to be lodged in her throat. Her voice had given out. "Ash," she whispered, sure he could not hear her. She beckoned him forward, and was surprised when he came. At her gesture, he sat beside her again. She put a hand on his knee.

He watched her closely, reading her lips because little sound escaped her mouth. "I will do whatever I must, whatever it takes. I'll not give up until I know you are safe. Let us see this through, please."

For a long time he only looked at her.

Did it require a hammer to his skull to bring him around? She had all but enlisted the King of England on her side, for heaven's sake, and still this obstinate man refused to yield.

"As you will, witch." Leaning over, he brushed her cheek with his lips. "We proceed. With tighter security, mind you. I'll not let you out of this house, even for the Second Coming. And in another nine days, it's over. Agreed?"

I love you, she wanted to say. "Agreed," she said. "On the tenth day, you can send me to Madagascar if you wish."

"An excellent idea. I expect you'd directly make yourself queen of the local cannibals."

She grinned. "If it's any comfort, sir, the villain will almost certainly go for you now. I'll be three deep in bodyguards."

"At the least. You will also be excessively cautious and strictly obedient. Beginning immediately, for you promised to rest when your questions were answered."

"I'm sure there are more," she began, "such as what happens next, and when can I—"

He lifted a hand. "Glenys, enough. I'll check on you again in a few hours."

When he was gone, she hugged herself with relief and elation. It had worked, her nonsense about throwing herself at King George's feet. Well, for all she knew,

His Majesty might have responded just as he ought. But she was just as glad not to be putting him to the test.

Pestilential female, Ash reflected on his way downstairs.

Glenys had hauled out the heavy artillery, and he'd surrendered with scarcely a fight. Worse, he couldn't even remember how she brought him down. Something about the king, as if Georgie gave a rat's arse what became of Glenys Shea or Ash Cordell.

Big Charlie must have felt like this after the shrapnel hit him at Waterloo.

And yet, how could he argue for retreat when a slender girl, the marks of a killing attack on her throat, challenged him to go forward? Her courage had compelled him to match it, like the arrogant male he was.

In honor, he'd no choice but to hustle her to safety. But what, he wondered, had *become* of his honor? Around the time he first met Glenys, it was left behind in the dust. And whenever he thought to go back and retrieve it, she led him somewhere else.

Whereupon he followed her like a puppy.

Dear God.

As he passed the morning room, he glanced through the open door and saw Harry leaning against the bow window, his head bowed. The slim body, in a lavender dress with a bright purple sash, was a portrait of dejection.

Geoff should handle this, he decided. Major Lord Killain had dealt with young subalterns after a bloody battle and knew what to say.

Ash located Fortescue, ordered him to send a maid to sit with Glenys, and found himself headed back to the morning room.

Harry had not moved.

Stepping inside, Ash quietly closed the door and

went to the window. Harry straightened, but did not lift his head.

They stood together in silence for a few minutes. Ash knew what the boy was feeling. He had felt much the same way when he killed Jack Shea. And it remained, the gnawing pain, after all these months. He wanted to spare Harry that regret, but had no idea what to say to him.

Harry let out a ragged breath. "I had to stop him, didn't I? He was killing Glennie."

"You did the only thing you could, Harry. And you would do it again."

"Y-Yes. But why is it so hard, sir? I don't understand why it's so hard."

Ash wrapped his arm across Harry's shoulders. "Killing ought not to be easy. No decent man should take it lightly, even when protecting his own life or another's. We would else be savages."

"*He* was a savage. But I'm still sorry."

"It will pass," Ash said, lying because he had to.

"The worst part is that everyone keeps telling me I'm a hero. And I wanted to be, you know. All the time I was practicing with the sword and the gun, I kept imagining how it would be to save Glennie, or you. I even prayed for the chance."

He wiped his brow with the back of his gloved hand. "I thought it would make me important. But my prayer came true, and now I wish it hadn't."

"The fact is," Ash said quietly, "you *are* a hero. You trained hard to be ready if you were needed. You acted with intelligence and speed. You saved your sister's life. But the bravest thing you will do, I believe, is come to terms with it now. Although it cannot help, you have my gratitude, Harry Shea. And my respect."

Wide hazel eyes, shimmering with tears, turned to him. "Really, sir?"

"Really." Ash squeezed his shoulder and let him go. "Glenys is sleeping now, but later you may speak with her. When you do, I expect this attack of remorse will dissipate substantially."

"Wish you'd talk in plain words," Harry muttered.

Ash chuckled. "You'll feel better."

"Maybe. But the whole thing still scares me. It were a near-run thing, y'know. If Glennie hadn't dropped her shoe, I'd have figured she went back to the other ladies. And if she wasn't wearing white shoes, I might not have seen it at all. I just barely heard a noise when I passed the room where he took her. Damned close, it was."

Too damned close, Ash agreed silently.

"And all for nothing," Harry said, downcast again. "Now you'll call it off, and Glennie will have almost died for no reason."

"You underestimate her," Ash observed dryly. "I had every intention of whisking you both to Ravenrook, but she cast some diabolical spell over me. We proceed as planned."

"Cor! That's the best news I've heard since we got started." Then Harry gave him a look of sympathy. "I know how you must've felt, though. You gets your mind made up, and next thing you know, she's changed it. I never wanted to dress up like a girl, but here I am."

"And a good thing too, young man."

"She was right," Harry agreed peevishly. "Usually is. But don't tell her I said so."

"Trust me, there is no danger of that."

Harry's eyes were brighter, and he looked more himself, but Ash knew from experience what happened when a man was left alone to brood. Harry needed company and something to distract him.

But what? Except for the servants, only Evan, Jane, Wilfred, and Nora were in the house. They remained suspects in his own mind, all of them, although Geoff had narrowed his choices to Nora. In any case, Harry should be kept away from them for the time being.

Glenys was asleep, or ought to be.

That left . . . him.

He glanced at Harry's smooth cheek, and at his trembling lower lip. The black mood was coming over him again.

No stranger to that mood, Ash decided even his own poor companionship would be an improvement. "Come sit with me," he said, casting about for something to talk about.

Harry shuffled to a chair and dropped down with a sigh, forgetting to keep his knees together. Ash noticed he wasn't using the cane. Probably he never wanted to see it again, although he had no choice in the matter. If the masquerade were to continue, Miss Harriet must carry the weapon. Later, Ash would tell him so.

Meantime, what? Ash pulled up a chair, straddled it, and folded his arms across the back. Harry's hands drooped between his knees. As he looked at them, Ash got an idea. "I've noticed you and Glenys signaling each other with your hands. Is this a secret language of some kind?"

Harry looked up. "Shoulda figured you'd catch on."

"Only that you were doing it. I haven't deciphered the code. But it might be useful for me to learn a few basics. What if I need to communicate with you, or Glenys, without anyone knowing?"

"I could teach you," Harry said. "The easy things, anyhow. Glennie and I have been practicing for months, so we can almost talk without words. Want to try?"

"I do," Ash affirmed. "Now, if you don't mind."

Sitting up straight, an eager look on his face, Harry peeled off his kid gloves. "We'll start with the signal for *danger*."

28

A week later, time had all but run out.

And so had every ounce of Glenys's self-restraint. With only three days to go before Ash whisked the Sheas back to Ravenrock, or clapped them on a ship for America, something had to be done.

The idea came to her at dinner that evening, between the lobster bisque and the roast capon. Then she had to endure endless courses of tasteless food before escaping to the salon, where she set about planting her seeds. As befitted her perfectly brilliant plan, they swiftly took root.

Of course, when Ash found out what she'd done, she might be safer in the middle of the Atlantic Ocean without a boat.

Prudence chattered away as she slipped a muslin night rail over Glenys's head, about the handsome footman who'd sat to tea with her in the servants' quarters. Then, still talking, she poured water in the basin and set out a bar of soap and a towel.

Glenys bit her tongue to keep from telling the maid to shut the devil up.

She was never alone, never left in peace. Prudence slept on a truckle bed in a corner of the bedchamber. The door to Harry's adjoining room was kept open at night, and he snored. Some nights he set the windows rattling.

"I'd wager that footman is off duty by now," Glenys said, picking up a book from the side table. "Since I plan to read for several hours, why don't you go see? Have a glass of hot milk and gossip with the others in the kitchen."

"I dunno, Miss Shea. The earl wouldn't like it."

"But he's gone to bed and need never know. Harry is next door, and there are guards all up and down the passageway. I'll be perfectly safe."

Prudence looked tempted, but she shook her head. "No, miss. It's my job to stay with you."

"And I want you *out* of here!" After a shocked moment, Glenys gentled her voice. "Go, please. If I don't have a bit of privacy, I think I shall scream."

Flushing hotly, the maid left without another word.

Glenys sat cross-legged in front of the fire, exasperated with herself. It had been an inexcusable display of temper, directed at a kindhearted girl who deserved better. It was also the least of her crimes that evening.

By now, although it was the middle of the night, gossip was filtering through the great houses of London. The women she'd chosen were known as the Town Criers, and they would probably outdo themselves with this particularly juicy morsel of scandal.

Action, at long last.

Since the attack at Carlton, nothing of consequence had occurred. For two days Ash confined her in her room and invited no one to the house while the bruises on her neck turned from purple to mottled yellow.

After that came a small family dinner, and selected guests were admitted for afternoon calls. The king had surprised them all by appearing to make certain his "sweet Miss Shea" was recovered from her ordeal. He brought her a gift—a miniature of himself that must have been painted thirty years ago. She promised to treasure it always.

It was a measure of her state of mind that the king's visit ranked as inconsequential. He had served his purpose and was on the point of becoming a nuisance. The only thing that mattered was catching the villain, which required him to strike again within a few days. To her growing frustration, Ash was doing everything in his power to prevent that.

She'd won his promise to stay the course, but he was merely counting the hours until they could leave London with her person intact. The guard around her had tripled, and few outsiders were permitted within the walls of Devonshire House.

That night, only because she had begged and wheedled for two days, fifty guests sat to dinner. Predictably and politely, with expressions of concern for her health, Ash had shooed them out before the evening was half done.

But *not* before she cozed with the Town Criers in the drawing room over a tray of coffee and sweets. While Ash took port with the gentlemen, she set herself to fan the dying flames of her plot.

If what she told the ladies failed to rouse the murdering beast, nothing would. This last, desperate try had to work. It just *had* to.

She stared into the fire, Harry's snores grating at her ears. In all fairness, she thought, she should tell Ash what she'd done. Too late now for him to snuff the rumors, and he was bound to hear them tomorrow morning.

Standing, she gathered her courage. His fury was certain as sunrise, and she had never been one to put off the inevitable. Better to get it over with, and all the better if she was seen entering his bedchamber at midnight.

In the armoire, she found a pair of slippers and a robe. After pausing long enough to run a brush through her hair and murmur a prayer for fortitude, she stepped into the passageway.

Robin jumped to his feet from the stool beside her door, his face wreathed with concern.

She gave him a bright smile. "If Prudence returns before I do, tell her I'm with Lord Ravensby."

His jaw dropped. She patted him on the arm and sped past two other guards to the bedchamber at the end of the long corridor.

"He's expecting me," she told John Fletcher, who regarded her with the same slack-jawed expression as Robin. Before he could stop her, she opened the door and scooted inside.

Ash was sitting by the fire, a thick book open on his lap. It fell to the floor as he stood and whirled to face her. "What the devil—"

Glenys slammed the door in John's face, rather sure she'd clipped him on the nose. "*Not* the devil," she said. "It's only me."

Ash looked like he'd rather Mephistopheles had come to call. "Have you lost your wits, Miss Shea?" Then he frowned. "Has something happened?"

"In fact, yes, but do relax. I've not been attacked again, or anything of the kind. But I need to speak with you on a matter of some importance, and it could not wait until morning."

"In that case, you should have—"

"Ash, spare me the ritual lecture about proper behavior. I do know better than to be here, but here I am. Have you any brandy?"

With a loud sigh, he went to a side table set with decanters of liquor and glasses. As he poured, brandy sloshed onto the table.

He had removed his shoes, and wore a forest-green brocade dressing gown over his trousers and shirt. She watched his every move, noting the set shoulders, clenched jaw, and wrinkled brow. Of a certain, she was in for a fight.

Even so, Ash was unfailingly courteous. He gestured her to a chair beside the fire and handed her a glass of brandy. He had poured one for himself too. It dangled from his hand as he stood in front of her, one arm draped over the mantelpiece. "Well?"

She took a long sip of brandy for courage, and another for endurance. What the hell? She emptied the glass. He regarded her with a stunned expression.

She grinned. "Tonight, I informed the Waller sisters and Lady Rotherham that you and I are long since married, by Special License." He swore loudly, but she plowed ahead. "I said an early wedding became essential when we learned that I am carrying your child."

The glass dropped from his hand and shattered on the hearth.

"I rather thought you'd be surprised." To her own surprise, she was enjoying herself. But she always did, the rare times she managed to break through his rigid composure.

"You are insane," he muttered. "Deranged. Mad as a March hare."

"Redundant, my lord. And inaccurate. I knew exactly what I was doing and why. If you offer me another helping of brandy, I'll explain it to you."

Circling the splinters of glass at his feet, he snatched the snifter from her hand and returned to the sideboard. "This had better be good, young woman. Bloody hell, what am I saying? There is no conceivable justification for what you have done."

She decided to face him standing up. When he turned around, she was directly in front of him. "This is Wednesday night. Well, Thursday morning, to be more precise." She took the glass of brandy. "On Saturday, it will all be over unless the villain makes another move. I merely provided him an incentive."

"And ruined yourself."

She ignored that. "The pot had to be stirred. He can't afford to wait now that I'm pregnant with your heir, assuming the inheritance is even a factor. Should the murderer care nothing about it, I'm in no more danger than I ever was."

"Oh, but you are," he said between his teeth. "I'm within a heartbeat of wringing your throat."

"I trust the real villain will entertain equally murderous notions. Indeed, I am counting on him to act rashly, without time to cover his tracks. An impromptu strike will make it easier for us to catch him. And really, Ash, what have we to lose at this point?"

He was silent for a long time. Then he gazed directly into her eyes. His own were molten green and smoke. "You," he said softly. "You."

She lowered her head. His anger she could deal with, but not his pain.

Always he protected her, because of who he was. *What* he was. She had never dared to take it personally, or imagine he cared for her more than he would another female who stumbled into his life. Ash Cordell would put himself between any woman and danger.

She felt the glass being removed from her hand, and a moment later his arms wrapped around her, so tightly she couldn't breathe.

"I won't let you be hurt again," he said against her throat. "I would sooner die."

His lips pressed against her neck, warm and moist. They moved up, to her chin, across her cheek. "Stop me," he whispered at the corner of her mouth. "By God, you drive me beyond all reason, Glenys. *Stop* me."

Whatever for? she thought vaguely, opening her mouth, welcoming his kiss. When he tried to pull back, she dug her nails into his scalp and urged him on.

Their tongues met. His hands cradled her bottom and lifted her against him. He moved his hips the way his tongue moved, and she answered his silent, demanding call with her own.

In a heap, they collapsed onto the thick rug. She pushed aside his robe and tugged his shirt loose from his breeches. He drew away her robe, lifted her night rail over her head, and pressed his lips between her breasts.

"Stop me," he implored again. "Glenys. Please."

She kneaded his back and kissed him more deeply.

Without letting her go, he came to his feet. She nestled in his arms while he threw back the covers, and then he lowered her onto his bed. She lay there, wide-eyed and breathless, while he stripped off his pants and shirt.

His magnificent body was just as she remembered it from the night she looked at him through the pool house window.

Except for one detail.

One enormous, pulsating, mind-boggling detail.

"Oh my," she said, reaching to touch it. When she did, it grew, impossibly, larger. She wrapped her hand around it and could not put fingers to thumb.

He groaned, moving his hips, his head thrown back.

Oh yes. He likes this. She pressed harder.

"Sweet heavens, Glenys!" He gripped her wrist and forced her to release him. "Wait."

"Whatever you say, but—"

Suddenly he was on top of her, and whatever she'd meant to ask him was lost in his kiss. He covered her entirely, his hands moving over her ardently as he plied her mouth with his tongue. His hot, heavy manhood pressed between her legs and he rubbed himself against her.

A thousand sensations scrambled for her attention. The scratch of his legs against her. His large hands, neither gentle nor hurting as they kneaded her breasts and then her buttocks. His damp hair against her forehead, the bristles on his chin against her cheek as he reached deeper into her mouth with his kisses.

When he lifted her knees and moved closer, probing, a deep ache reached out from her. Her hands reached out too, clutching his hips, drawing him in. She wanted. Wanted. Wanted.

Then he was inside her, swiftly and deeply. Pain flashed by like a shooting star and was gone. She felt only great joy, and a profound certainty they were meant to be joined like this, flesh to flesh. As he moved in her, gasping with every stroke, she held him and loved him and gave all of herself into his keeping.

Years too soon, he pulled out of her body and knelt back, holding her with one hand when she tried to sit up. He made a soft sound, deep in his throat.

She plucked at his arm. "Ash?"

With a deep, audible breath, he stretched beside her and drew her into his arms. His chin rested on the top of her head.

His pulse thudded against her ear. She put her hand over his heart. Like a galloping horse, she thought, wondering if she'd pleased him despite her inexperience. She hoped so, to make up for the trouble she was all too experienced at giving him.

If she asked, he would tell her yes because he was a gentleman. Perhaps he'd tell her that anyway, from sheer good manners. But he didn't seem inclined to talk. Well, she too could be polite. Harnessing the questions that galloped in her mind the way his heart raced in his chest, she waited.

After a long time, he threw his legs over the side of the bed, put his elbows on his knees, and buried his face in his hands. Then he spoke two words in a shaky voice.

To her absolute horror, they were "I'm sorry."

Of all the things in the universe, that was the last thing she wanted to hear. The unsettled feelings roiling through her body centered in a hard knot of shocked rage. Kneeling up behind him, she pounded a fist against his slumped shoulder. "How *dare* you be sorry? I will *not* hear that from you! Take it back."

"It's no more than the truth. I cannot take it back, any more than I can undo what I just did. Or any more than I could keep myself from doing it."

"*Stop* that!" She hit him again, as hard as she could. Then she scrambled off the bed and knelt at his feet. "Look at me, you wretched man." With both hands she knocked his elbows off his knees.

Startled, he met her gaze with unblinking eyes. Disconsolate eyes.

"Dammit, Ash, there were *two* of us on that bed. At least one of us wanted to be there. I'm not in the least sorry. To the contrary, it was the best choice I ever made, and it *was* a choice. My decision as much as yours, or more so, because you would have stopped if I asked you to. I, on the other hand, would not have *let* you stop if you'd tried."

He exhaled slowly. "That's because you are infatuated, Glenys. And you are an undisciplined young woman with no experience of the world who cannot wait to try everything, regardless of the consequences. It was my duty to protect you from yourself."

"Balderdash!" Was ever a man so mule-headed as this one? Some part of him was rooted in the Middle Ages. "Who gave *you* the right to protect me? Not I, sir. My life is my own, and I'll do with it what I will. And my body is my own. *That* I freely gave you, and shall again if you should want it."

"Dear Lord."

With a murmur of disgust, she stood and went in search of her clothes. "Clearly there is no reasoning with you in this state. But I must say that I'm vastly disappointed."

"I daresay."

She cast him a scorching look. "Instead of holding each other and being happy together, we are having a row. That is *your* fault. Your only fault, by the way, but it puts me out of all patience with you."

She found her nightgown on the other side of the bed and drew it on. "This should be a wonderful night, and you have ruined it. Well, not altogether," she added honestly. "Only from the moment you said that you were sorry. Before that, it was heavenly."

"For me. You, my girl, have no idea what you are talking about."

"Oh, do shut up, Ash." Where the devil was her robe? One knee on the bed, she fumbled among the twisted blankets and sheets. Then she froze, staring in dismay at a large red stain. "Holy hollyhocks," she muttered. She'd bled all over the bottom sheet. This was a disaster.

"Get off!" she ordered, pushing at Ash's naked

rump. He lurched from the bed and she began flinging the covers to the floor, barely aware of him gazing at her in astonishment.

"What in blazes are you doing?"

"Hiding the evidence. Or I shall, when I get this sheet off." It was tucked firmly all around the mattress. She circled the bed, clawing at it with both hands.

"Whatever for?" he asked in a bewildered voice. "Bleeding is perfectly natural the first time. The maids will clean it up in the morning."

"I'm supposed to be *pregnant,* you dolt. The maids are loyal, but they're bound to gossip. If word gets to our murderer, he'll know I was lying about the marriage and the child."

"Good."

She swung around. "How so? He will also know a part of that lie may have become a truth. If I weren't pregnant before, I could well be now."

And what a lovely thought! Ash's child taking life in her body. She savored the private vision as she finished stripping the bed.

Her robe was discovered near the headboard, and she put it on before gathering the offending sheet into a ball. Then she had a mental image of herself striding down the hall, past John Fletcher, Robin, and two other guards, holding a bloody sheet in her arms.

That would never do. She glanced over at Ash, who was busy putting on his own robe. He looked somewhat dazed, as if he'd been hit on the head with a croquet mallet. Dear Lord, how she loved him.

She nearly told him so, but he'd had more than enough surprises for one night. She was burden enough to him, without adding love to the weight he bore. It wasn't as if he could marry her, after all. She was a soldier's brat. No fit wife for an earl, as Harry had reminded her. She'd always known that in her heart, but it didn't stop her from loving him.

Nothing could stop her from loving him.

He thought her infatuated, and that would have to do. Women recovered from infatuation. When, inevitably, she said goodbye to him for the last time, she would pretend her recovery complete. She'd be very convincing, to make sure he never worried about her.

Meantime, what was she to do about this blasted sheet?

She shook it out and found two corners. "Ash, come here, please. Help me fold this."

Muttering to himself, he picked up the other ends and they managed to compress the fabric into a tight square. She stuffed it under her night rail, at her waist, and tied the sash of her robe securely to hold it in place.

Gazing down at the prominent bulge under her breasts, she chuckled on her way to the door. "It seems I'm even more pregnant than I thought, Lord Ravensby. From all appearances, the birth of your heir is imminent."

29

Ash rushed after her, but Glenys beat him to the door and closed it behind her.

He put his forehead against the paneled wood, arms limp at his sides. Then once, twice, three times, he hit his head against the door. Not hard enough, since it failed to knock any sense into him, but the sound caught John Fletcher's attention.

"Any problem, m'lord?" he asked, knocking from his side.

Reckoned conservatively, only several thousand. "No, John. I was careless." He aimed himself at the brandy decanter. Careless. Stupid. Frantic. Altogether berserk.

In a few blazing minutes he had surrendered the last of his principles, what few were left to him. One by one, in the six months he'd known her, Glenys had plucked the others away.

With his cooperation, to be sure. From the beginning she set him dancing to her tune. And he'd danced all the faster because the alternative—putting her out of his reach—had been insupportable.

He poured brandy into a glass and swirled it around, making a belated act of confession to himself.

He'd yielded to her outrageous demands because he couldn't bear to lose her. And all the while, he convinced himself he was being noble by hiding in his study instead of seeking her company.

Like Odysseus, he tied himself to the mast and heard the Siren call, but he omitted to sail on. Instead, entranced by her song, he ordered the ship to keep circling.

He kept Glenys at Ravenrook. He brought her to London. Even when she was nearly murdered—for his sake, hell confound it—he permitted her to carry on with her masquerade.

And tonight, when she swept in, all full of herself because she had joyously leaped from fry pan to fire, he took her virtue.

Looking at the glass in his hand, he was surprised to find it empty. He drank without thought, the way he'd done everything else.

God, he had been furious with her. Angrier than he'd ever been in his life. And Glenys—rackety female that she was—smugly boasted of her outrageous gamble with death. Already married to him and months pregnant, for pity's sake. She might as well have pinned a target on her back.

He refilled the glass and glanced outside. It had begun to snow, and puffy flakes floated in the shafts of light from the house windows. Cold, directionless souls they were—doomed the moment they hit ground. He willed them to stay aloft.

The sun would burn them up regardless. Dawn would incinerate him too, for there was no question what must happen next. Even a man without honor could rouse himself to decency when there was not the slightest choice.

Meantime, he had the rest of this night to gnaw on his regrets. And, to his eternal shame, he regretted most his failure to abandon the last shreds of honor months ago.

So long as he was going to ruin Glenys at the end, why had they not become lovers at Ravenrook? She wanted to. He wanted to. But he self-righteously preserved her innocence, only to snatch it in a swift, scorching act of passion that left her without pleasure. Without her virginity. And with nothing to compensate her for its loss—not even a memory to cherish.

All she took with her was that bloody damned *sheet*.

Cursing himself every way he knew how, he went to the writing table and sat for a moment, head between his hands. Futile now to worry over what could not be changed. Glenys had taught him that piece of wisdom.

Logic. Discipline. Calm. He summoned his muses and gradually they filtered back. There were plans to be made. He should begin now, while Glenys was sleeping. When she woke up, everything must be in place.

As he sharpened a pen, he decided to begin with lists. Another of her lessons, the value of making lists. When he was sure no detail had been overlooked, he would write the necessary letters and set his plan in motion.

It was damnably hard to think, with the feel of her still on his body and the fragrance of her in his nostrils. As he worked, he imagined her just behind him, reading over his shoulder.

He'd put his first list safely in the drawer and was compiling assignments for Geoff when the door burst open.

Glenys looked even more pregnant than when she left, and she was giggling.

John Fletcher stood behind her, eyebrows raised in a question. Ash dismissed him with a wave of his pen. With the other hand he shoved the papers under the blotter. "What in creation are you doing here again?"

Untying her sash with a flourish, Glenys delivered a rolled-up bundle of linen. It landed on her bare toes. "Voilà!" she exclaimed. "My firstborn bedsheet."

Ash watched her, stupefied.

"Do you know," she said thoughtfully, "it looks exactly like you. All wrapped up and starchy and white as a—" She shrugged. "Pardon the cliché, but there's no help for it. White as a sheet."

He staggered to his feet. "What foolishness is this?"

"We cannot leave your bed in disorder, sir. I have merely brought a replacement, and you ought to be offering your congratulations. Disposing of the soiled item and replacing it with a relatively clean one has not been easy."

He didn't want to know. But from the eager look on her face, she clearly wanted him to ask. He leaned his lands on the table, resigned to his fate. "Just how did you accomplish this Herculean feat, Miss Shea?"

She rewarded him with a glowing smile. "Miss Harriet, poor thing, began her courses unexpectedly. The other sheet is on her bed. This one used to be."

"Dear Lord." His lips began to twitch. Hercules himself wouldn't have dared such a thing. "Harry is none too pleased, I expect."

"When I left, he was curled on the floor, wrapped in his blanket and swearing up a storm. He'll not go near that bed again."

"His maid knows the truth about him," Ash pointed out.

"Oh, she is delighted to be part of the scheme. Tomorrow, she'll complain of the mess to the other servants when Wilfred, Jervase, Evan, or Jane are in the vicinity. I said we hoped to dispel any suspicions that Harry is not a female."

"That should do it. But how did you account for the blood without giving yourself away?"

She made a face. "Never mind. They are satisfied with my explanation. Well, *she* is. I'm sure Harry guessed the truth."

Ash went cold. "If so, he has every right to call me out."

"A duel at dawn, to avenge my honor? Rubbish. In this matter, he has far better sense than you, my lord." She picked up the sheet and crossed to the bed. "Shall we repair the damage?"

She meant the bedcovers, certainly, but a shaft of pain cut through him. The true damage could never be mended.

At her direction, he took a position across from her and helped lay out the sheet. It barely reached over the sides.

She pulled it off again. "I should have realized. Your bed is larger than Harry's, of course. We'll put the other sheet on the bottom and leave this one mussed on top. I doubt the maid will notice." A minute later she had finished tucking in her share and came around to check his work. "I gather you've never had occasion to make up a bed, sir."

"No," he replied, unaccountably embarrassed.

"Earls do not, I suppose." She pulled loose the mess he'd created and quickly produced smooth, neat folds. "Quite professional, don't you think? If all else fails, I shall hire out as a chambermaid."

Every one of her jests sliced into him, although he

knew she didn't mean to be sarcastic. From her high spirits, it seemed she had consigned what happened an hour ago to a distant corner of her mind. She had reacted to her father's death the same way, he recalled.

Glenys never looked back. What was over, was over. She faced the consequences, dealt with them in her own incomprehensible way, and moved on.

Or so he thought, until she sat on the bed and patted a spot next to her. "We must talk, Ash."

Damn and blast. He lowered himself beside her, resting his hands on his knees. "I'm sure you are right, although there seems precious little to say."

"I can think of a great many things. To begin with, why did you tell me you were sorry?"

"By all that's holy, Glenys!"

"Well, I never said you would enjoy this. But when you reply, do pass over the nonsense about my virginity. The whole concept is vastly overrated, don't you agree? Young women are preserved in woeful ignorance until they find themselves in bed with husbands chosen by their parents. The tiniest hint they've been compromised beforehand, however untrue, dashes all their hopes and dreams. Who invented these rules? The same coxcomb who invented chastity belts, I suppose."

"A man wishes to know his children are his own," Ash said stiffly.

"Then a man ought to wed a woman he trusts." She clicked her tongue. "Let us not debate this now. Aside from the dubious notion that I have been *ruined,* why else were you sorry?"

"If you must know, I cannot help but regret my failure to deal with you as a gentleman must deal with a lady." Could he have said that more awkwardly?

She rolled her eyes. "Oh dear. *Honor* rears its head again. It always does, with you. And here I am, poor fool, jubilant because you forgot honor for just a while and dealt with me as a man deals with a woman. Altogether a different thing, yes?"

"Not . . . necessarily." Where was the Spanish Inquisition when he needed it? Better the rack than an interrogation by Glenys Shea. *"Penes te arbitrum huius rei est,"* he mumbled.

"Claptrap, I'm sure, whatever it means. And cowardly of you to resort to Latin, Ash. For shame."

His cheeks burned. "It slipped out. 'The decision of the question rests with you.'"

"A refreshing change," she said, putting a hand on his wrist. "And a slippery evasion. I understand more than you give me credit for, and I'm not referring to Latin. You see, I know about the urgency."

He swallowed, hard.

"I felt it too, Ash. The same uncontrollable force came over me, and all else went away. Honor, virginity, consequences, even curiosity. I was damnably curious about what was going to happen, but when it did, I forgot everything except how much I wanted you."

He stared at her hand, at the faint blue lines against her pale smooth skin, at the slight throbbing as blood pulsed through her veins. He'd felt all that. Exactly that. He'd forgot everything except how much he wanted her.

"Before, it was only a theory," she said. "But now I truly understand why you keep a mistress. Yes, I know about that too."

The rack. He was on it and she was turning the screws. "Past history, Glenys."

"Oh, you needn't apologize. I am assured all wealthy men have mistresses. The others go to street fairs."

Street fairs? "Who filled your head with this twaddle? Never mind. It must have been Nora."

"Don't lay yet another crime at her door. I've pieced together dibs and dabs from many sources, most of them unreliable. You've no idea how frustrating it is, wanting to know when all the world is determined you shall not. Even now, when I ask you direct questions, you refuse to answer."

"Not . . . refuse. Dammit, Glenys, I'm no good with words unless they're in books. I was . . . I *am* sorry for dishonoring you. I realize, as you do not, that virginity is important for a young unmarried woman. It's the way of the world. And too, I am sorry for betraying a code of honor I've tried to live by until just recently. But that is my concern, not yours."

He picked up her hand and pressed it to his lips. "What is most difficult to explain will remain unsaid, because there are no words."

"Ash, an hour ago you were inside my body. I welcomed you there. After such intimacy, how can you withhold *words* from me? They exist, imperfectly, like all other words we use to express ourselves. Do the best you can. I *need* to understand."

She would not let go. Were all women like this? He was blisteringly aware how few women he'd ever spoken with, beyond the merest pleasantries. Not his wife, certainly. Nor the few women he'd taken to his bed. They did not come there to talk.

But this was Glenys, a creature unlike any he'd ever met. And after what she had done for him, and what he had done to her, he owed her anything she asked. At the least, he would try to explain.

He couldn't look at her, though. He cradled her hand between both of his and addressed her fingertips. "Your first experience with a man should have brought you pleasure, my dear. They all should, to be sure, but especially the first. Perhaps not a purely sexual pleasure, though, for I understand that is difficult for a virgin."

He took a deep breath. "You see, I too have picked up dibs and dabs from unreliable sources. My experience is greater than yours, but less than you seem to imagine. I do know that I took no care of you. You call it urgency. I call it madness. I also know what you missed, because I had from you greater delight than ever before. From me, you had nothing at all."

When she was silent, he mustered the courage to look into her eyes. They gazed back at him, confused.

"How can you say that?" she asked in a reedy voice. "You are mistaken. Nothing in all my life has ever been so wonderful."

Sweet, foolish girl. He longed to hug her. More than that. Show her. Lead her to feel what her clever mind groped to understand. But that would be yet another betrayal of honor.

And suddenly he didn't care. In a few hours, she would be gone from his life forever. Between now and then was time out of time, a brief space between pain and pain where he could love her.

If she wanted him to.

He put his hands on her shoulders. "Perhaps I *can* explain, Glenys, but not with words. If you truly wish me to try, stay the night with me. Otherwise, go back to your room now. *In te omnia sunt.* Everything depends on you."

"*Fiat,*" she murmured, wrapping her arms around him. "Be it done, Ash. Above all things, I want you."

He drew her to her feet, meaning to remove her robe and nightgown. But she brushed his hands aside, loosened the sash at his waist, and ran her palms over his shoulders and down his chest.

"You are so beautiful," she said. "I love to look at

you. It makes me go tingly all over." Then she smiled. "Forgive me. It's the curiosity again. I'll try not to analyze what is happening, but oh, how I love to look at you."

He thought he'd melt in a puddle at her feet. "May I look at you too?"

She wrinkled her nose. "If you insist, but I cannot think why. God made you splendid and me from spare parts. They all work, my arms and legs and such, but the overall effect cannot be pleasing. No flummery, Ash. I've seen myself in a mirror."

"Not through my eyes," he said softly.

He applied himself to her robe and night rail. When she was naked, he set her back and looked at her for a long time. "Exquisite, Glenys. Whoever told you otherwise?"

A blush crept over her, from toes to forehead.

With a smile, he shrugged out of his robe. "Your turn, then."

She licked her lips, examining him with unconcealed fascination. "May I touch you?"

"You may do whatever takes your fancy. Unless I stop you," he amended hastily. "If I do, it's because this time there is to be no *urgency*. This time, we shall make every moment last forever."

"Mmmmm. That sounds wonderful." She stepped forward and put her hands on his wrists. Then she stroked her fingers up his arms, tracing the curves of his muscles. "You are exceedingly strong. And hairier than Harry." A gurgle of laughter escaped her lips. "How silly of me."

More earnestly, she continued her exploration of his body. He held still, consumed from the inside out, repressing the flames with all his might as her hands wandered over his shoulders. She moved around him then, and he felt her fingertips on his back, and waist, and buttocks.

"I think," he said in a choked voice, "you had better stop now." Turning, he swept her into his arms and lowered her to the bed. Her eyes, wide and unafraid, gazed at him with longing.

He took a moment to regather control, and remembered to pick up a towel from the dressing table. Then he lay beside her, propping himself on one elbow.

"Now I will touch you, Glenys. Everywhere."

She shivered as he began to caress her arms the way she'd done to him, and her neck, and the sweet curve of her ear. He pushed the hair back from her face, massaging her scalp gently.

"Kiss me," she whispered.

"Soon."

He stroked her collarbone with his forefinger, and the valley between her small, perfect breasts. He moved down, slowly, to her waist and navel. Under his finger her hips began to move restlessly. So passionate she was. So eager.

When he returned to her breasts, she made a little noise of pleasure. He touched the soft side of one breast, just above her ribs, and moved his finger slowly around and up, until it brushed her nipple.

"Ashhhh."

"Do you like that?" He devoted even more attention to her other breast, still with one finger. Then he bent his head and replaced the finger with his tongue.

Her hand caught at his neck, pulling him closer.

"Patience," he murmured. Then he took her in his mouth and suckled. Her sighs became groans of pleasure.

His hand strayed over her belly, to her flanks, as he

loved her breast with his mouth and tongue. He caressed her sleek buttocks, molding them in his hand.

She was writhing under him now, holding his shoulders with both hands. His fingers drifted to the silky flesh of her thighs and moved upward.

When he touched the curly hair between her legs, she let out a tiny cry, opening her knees. Demanding more. Wanting it immediately.

As did he. But he forced himself to take his time, letting her feel, inch by inch, his approach to the center of her need.

His finger slipped between the twin folds of swollen flesh, slick and moist with desire. He raised up to look at her. Her head was thrown back on the pillow, her eyes squeezed shut as she gave herself over to the sensations he roused in her body.

Never had he seen anything more beautiful than Glenys in the throes of female passion. It staggered him, her open, unbounded sensuality.

He sought her tight opening and heard her moan as he slid his finger inside her. She closed her legs around his hand, twisting her hips, reaching for the completion her body knew to crave.

"Not yet," he told her, still watching her face. "Slowly, Glenys. Relax and feel me."

She tried to obey. Her knees fell open and he moved his finger in her, deeper with every stroke.

"Kiss me now," he said, sliding one hand behind her neck and lifting her slightly. Her mouth welcomed him, her tongue licking around his as his finger penetrated and withdrew, in and out, a leisurely, compelling rhythm he matched with his tongue.

Aware his control was near to shattering, he put his thumb against her bud and pressed it once, twice, and again, a silent promise.

Finally he broke the kiss, long enough to kneel between her legs, his finger still buried in her. "Now, Glenys?"

"Oh yes," she said breathlessly. "Please."

He kissed her, gently this time, and put one hand on her breast. Withdrawing the other from her body, he guided himself to her entrance and held there for a moment. "Remember. Slowly. Let yourself feel everything. Me going into you. Us, joined together."

"Slowly," she echoed. "But hurry."

Ah, he wanted to. He burned for release. He could have it, swiftly, and she'd be there to meet him. Her nails dug into his back. Any moment now and the urgency would send them up in flames.

But he went inside her little by little, groaning as she closed around him until he could reach no farther. Gathering her into his arms, he began to move his hips. She did too, in small circles, wringing the last ounce of control away. He gave himself up to her passion, plunging harder and harder, lifting her so that he rubbed against her nub with every stroke.

Then she shuddered, and convulsed, and he held still as the pleasure flooded through her body. "Ohhhh," she sighed. "Ohhhh."

When she quieted, savoring the last throbbing pleasure, he pulled away and reached for the towel.

"Ash?" A limp hand settled on his arm. "What are you doing?"

"Shhh." He swallowed his groan of release and stretched out beside her. Immediately, she curled against his chest. He closed his arms around her.

"I understand now," she said. "And you were right, Ash. There are no words."

"None."

She nuzzled his throat. "I think my bones have melted."

"Mine too."

"Is it always like this? My body wants to go to sleep, but that's the very last thing *I* want to do."

"Tonight, Glenys, you must do whatever your heart desires. Sleep. Even talk, if you must."

"All these choices, and me limp as a dishrag. May we do it again—what we just did?"

"Yes. Or something like. Not immediately, though, unless you are set on it. If so, I'll do my best."

"Ah. Maybe I'll sleep then, for a few minutes. Promise to wake me up very soon?"

"I promise."

He wasn't sure she heard him. Her hand, the one that had been stroking his chest, went still. Her soft breath, rhythmic and even, warmed his neck.

His eyes drifted shut. I promised to wake her up, he told himself. I musn't go to sleep.

When she nudged him awake and pressed her lips to his, the fire had burned to coals in the hearth. The room was cold. He'd forgot to cover them with blankets.

She moved over his body, on top of him, liquid smoke on his flesh. "Love me again," she whispered, licking at his ear. "I am fire to your ice, Ash Cordell. Love me again."

He did.

30

The gray, drizzly afternoon might have been specially ordered to reflect her mood.

Glenys gazed listlessly at the wintry hedgerows, their skeletal twigs trembling in the wind. Killain and three bodyguards rode outside the coach, muffled in heavy greatcoats. Harry sat across from her, fiddling with his cane.

Lord Killain had promised him a chance to shed his dress for trousers when next they stopped, which lifted his mood briefly. But Glenys had refused to answer her brother's persistent questions, and finally told him to leave her the devil alone. Since then he'd maintained a sullen silence.

His feelings were hurt, but she could not bear to speak to him. She was still finding it difficult to breathe. Tight bands had wrapped themselves around her chest and throat six hours ago, not loosing their grip as the day wore on.

Ash was sending them to America after all.

That morning she had awakened in her own bed

with no remembrance of how she came to be there. Deliciously aching from the long night of passion, she soaked in a hot bath while Prudence bustled about, laying out a heavy chemise, long-sleeved woolen dress, and halfboots for her to wear. Still distracted and dreamy, she put them on without a second thought.

Had she wondered at their unsuitability for Devonshire House, she might have been prepared when Ash summoned her. Instead, she floated into the parlor expecting a warm kiss from the man she loved.

A stranger met her, steely-eyed and rigid as a block of ice. Not Ash, but Lord Ravensby . . . more stern and forbidding than she'd ever seen him, even when he thought her a hired assassin. He held up a hand to keep her from advancing too close.

And then he issued orders, clicking them off one by one from a list in his hand. His voice was a hammer on a cold anvil. Lord Killain would escort the Sheas to Newhaven and a ship scheduled to sail on the midnight tide. She was to speak to no one before leaving. He had prepared instructions how to proceed when they landed in Boston Harbor.

There were words about bank drafts, letters of introduction, luggage being packed . . . words and words and words. She heard none of them after a while. Her heart pounded too loudly. Tight bands closed around her chest. Tears burned her eyes. She fought them for a time, but they spilled over, scorching her cheeks and lips.

In a haze of pain, she realized the earl had stopped speaking. She wiped her sleeve across her eyes and sought him in the dim room. He wavered, like a ghost, somewhere near the window.

"Wh-Why?" she asked in a strangled voice.

"Did you fail to attend me? No questions, Miss Shea, for I have no answers you'll wish to hear. I do only what I should have done long since. You and Harry will be well cared for."

"And what of you?"

"Christ! You never listen. I am giving you all that I can—a place to go, a secure income, a new life in America. Make of it what you will. If nothing else, think of your brother. He needs you, and I do not."

That rocked her on her heels. "Even if you put your child in me last night?"

"There won't be a child, Glenys. Even in the madness that gripped me, I took precautions." His voice gentled, marginally. "You are hurting now, and I am sorry for it. But you'll quickly rebound. You always do. It is one of the qualities I most admire in you, along with your courage."

He made a wide circle around her as he went to the door and opened it. Killain was there, waiting to take her in his charge. He had shuffled her away before she could throw herself at Ash's feet and beg him to keep her.

Now, she replayed their last meeting over and over in her mind, searching for one crumb of hope, the tiniest indication he meant to contact her again. A hint that he even wanted to. There was nothing.

He had cut her off like a dead flower from a rosebush. He thought to plant her in a new place, imagining she would bloom again, but she was unable to conceive of a future without him.

She didn't try.

More compelling than her misery was the certainty he intended to force a confrontation with the murderer, whatever the risk. The man who made love to her with unmistakable ardor, only to cast her away within a few hours, did so with benighted reasons of his own.

He meant to remove her from harm's way and put himself there, alone. Make an end, once and for all, to years of torment and exile.

He had been cruel, only to make her despise him. He wanted her to forget him. Idiot. As if she could. As if, once past his searing rejection, she wouldn't put two and two together.

She still hurt, awfully, but she understood. The devil of it was, she couldn't stop him. Nor could she help him. He'd made sure of that.

Even so, she roused herself at the next posthouse and ate a hearty meal while Harry changed clothes. If an opportunity presented itself, she was determined to be ready. What sort of opportunity, she had no idea, but damned if she'd sail off to Boston and forget about Ash Cordell.

Something would come up. It always did.

When Geoff ushered Glenys from the parlor, Ash collapsed on a chair with his head buried between his hands. Pain knifed through his skull.

The headache had gripped him hours ago, when he carried the sleeping Glenys to her room and kissed her goodbye. And because there were too many plans to make, too much business to handle, he couldn't fend off the pain with brandy or laudanum.

Nor could he let it stop him now. Soon, Glenys and Harry would be on their way to the coast. He'd wait until they were beyond reach before speaking to Jervase, Wilfred, Evan, and Jane.

Had he covered everything? With a shaking hand he drew out his lists and went over them again.

He'd sent a man to examine shipping schedules and chosen an unlikely vessel from a small port. Geoff would pay whatever it took to see Glenys and Harry aboard. The Sheas were resourceful and would have no trouble locating his friends in Boston. Lord Heston already knew they might arrive at any time.

Ash had provided a large amount of cash for inci-
dentals, and a relative fortune to be claimed when they
submitted papers to the bank.

His solicitor would be here shortly. For all his precautions, there was a remote chance he'd put a child in
Glenys. Bloody damned maniac, yielding at the last
moment to a temptation he'd resisted for months!

No help for it now. He couldn't even bring himself to
regret their night together. Thirty-four years he had been
alive, and for only those few hours had he been truly
happy.

Now, curse his black soul, Glenys would pay for it.
Today he would amend his will to leave her most of his
money and all the properties not entailed. Money and
safety. He had nothing else to give.

He ran down the list, reassuring himself the smallest
details had been dealt with. Nearly all concerned the
Sheas. He wasn't certain of his own plans, beyond
telling his family the wedding would not take place.

Perhaps he'd go to his estate in Sussex and see to the
tenants. Or he might remain in London, although with
the Little Season drawing to a close almost everyone
would be leaving the city.

Whatever he decided to do, he'd give the murderer
every opportunity to get at him. Glenys, fearless and fool-
hardy, had made herself a target. To his infinite shame,
he had permitted it. Now he would expose himself to the
killer, as she had done, without fear of the consequences.

With care, and luck, he would come out alive.

Two hours later he bid his solicitor farewell and went
to the library to speak with Wilfred Baslow. The man
scarcely attended him, more interested in the dusty tome
he was reading than news the wedding had been called off.

"Must I leave right away?" he asked, wiping his thick
spectacles. "Fascinating, this. An account of King Alfred's

navy. I've already begun an article for the Historical Society."

"I'll close the house in a few days," Ash told him. "Finish up by Monday and be on your way."

"Plenty of time, plenty of time. Sorry about your bride. Why did you say she left?"

"Ugly rumors," Ash repeated impatiently. "Not a word of truth in them, but she cried off and headed east. For France, I believe. No matter now."

"Just so." Wilfred picked up his magnifying glass. "I am seeking details about the Christmas attack at Chippenham. Perchance you have the information I require in your library at Ravenrook. Going back, are you? But of course you are. No point staying in London now, what?"

Rather sure Wilfred wouldn't hear him if he denied it, Ash left in search of Evan.

His heir was finally located in the mews, cross-legged on a mound of hay, rollicking with a litter of puppies. The placid bitch kept watch from a corner of the stall.

Ash crouched beside Evan, and a pair of wet noses immediately began sniffing at his knees. He picked up a squirming puppy and stroked it as he told his cousin about the cancelled wedding.

"I say!" Evan regarded him with sorrowful brown eyes. "She just up and left you, because the old tabbies were gossiping? Bad form, Ash. I wouldn't have thought it of her. Nice girl, Glenys. Smitten with you, I'd have wagered."

"I think she cared for me, but before now she led a sheltered life. It was all too much for her to deal with. Sooner or later she'd have been eaten alive by the high sticklers."

Evan sighed. "I can imagine how she must have felt. God knows I wouldn't hold up past a week as Earl of Ravensby. Wish she'd stayed the course and got a son by you, though. I'd breathe a lot easier if you had another heir. And it would get Jane off my back."

Setting the puppy aside, Ash came to his feet. "Where is Jane, by the way? I should inform her of the change in plans."

"Last I knew, she was still in bed. Maybe the breakfast room by now? Anyway, tell her we'll leave for the farm tomorrow morning. You won't want us hanging about here, although I expect she'll be none too anxious to go. Likes London, Jane does. Don't understand it myself. Dreary place. No room to move about."

Ash nodded and unclasped a puppy who'd developed a fondness for his boot. He was on his way out when Evan spoke again.

"I'm truly sorry, Ash. You ought to be happy, the way I am."

Any man who could be happy married to Jane was either a saint or a lunatic, Ash reflected as he went looking for her in the breakfast room.

She was there, working her way through a large plate of eggs, bacon, sausage, mushrooms, and fried bread. And, as he'd expected, she was not displeased to hear his bride had fled. Jane made all the correct noises of sympathy, between bites, but her sharp eyes glittered in triumph. Once again she stood next in line to be Lady Ravensby.

Almost before he'd finished his story, she pushed herself from the table. "I must do a bit of shopping before Evan drags me home," she said, taking two caramel rolls with her as she headed for the door. "It's not often we get to London, you know. Pardon me, but I cannot think you wish company now."

Ash stared at the remains of her breakfast. How kind of dear cousin Jane to let him lick his wounds in private.

What a family.

He'd put Jervase for last, never eager to cross verbal swords with the man. Jervase had slept the last few nights at Devonshire House, probably because his latest mistress refused to welcome him back. Spooked, no doubt, after being questioned about her lover's comings and goings.

In general Jervase slept till well past noon. But he had gone out, a footman said, only a few minutes ago. He gave the hackney driver an address on St. James's Street.

One of the clubs, Ash decided. His head had become a whole separate being, all made up of spikes digging into nerve ends. It required massive concentration to stay erect as he stumbled to his bedchamber. But when he saw the bed, he could not bear to lay himself on it. The memories were too fresh—Glenys in his arms, he inside her body, loving her.

He took a pillow and went to the sitting room next door, stretching out on the carpet for a few hours of sleep. Later, when Geoff returned, he'd figure what next to do.

The *Western Wind* had seen better days, most of them in the previous century. It was small enough to tie up at Newhaven's lone dock, where cargo was still being loaded, and Glenys began to hope there'd be no room for two last-minute passengers.

Evidently there was. Killain strode across the gangplank to where she waited on the wharf, beckoning his men to carry the luggage aboard. "It won't be a comfortable voyage, I'm afraid. The accommodations are meager, but clean enough, and the captain knows what he's about. You sail in two hours."

"Can we eat first?" Harry asked. "There's a pub down the street."

"Please shut up, Harry." Glenys took Killain's arm and drew him aside. "What is Ash planning to do? You *must* tell me. I am worried for him."

"With reason. When the ship is gone, I'll return immediately to London."

"Don't wait," she urged. "Start back now."

He gave her a quelling look. "And leave you and Harry to scarper? I think not, my dear. Ash would have my head if I failed to see you aboard when the ship goes out."

"I will be. I promise. You have my solemn word that Harry and I will leave Newhaven with that ship in two hours. We'll go on board now and stay there. You can even station a man on the dock to make sure that we do. But go back, please. Be there to stop Ash from doing something hopelessly dangerous."

He searched her face, clearly wanting to believe her but not at all sure she could be trusted. "Your word, Glenys? You won't under any circumstances head for London instead of Boston?"

"I swear I'll not return to London. I will sail with the ship. What more can I say?" She gave him her most earnest expression. "Your place is with Ash, not hanging about here to no purpose."

With a nod, Killain ushered her and a loudly protesting Harry to the captain and made introductions. Then he gave Glenys a swift hug, shook Harry's hand, and told them both to behave.

Having made a decision, he was anxious to be on his way. From the railing Glenys watched him gather his men, post one on the dock, and swing into the saddle. Moments later, three riders and the carriage were gone.

"I say, Glennie!" Harry plucked at her sleeve. "What was all that about? I'm bloody hungry."

"Too bad. We have work to do. Make some friends, Harry, and quickly. A local pilot will guide the ship out of this harbor, and he'll have to come back to shore. That means a small boat, and I intend to be on it."

In the amber lantern light, Harry's face looked like an astonished orange. "You wouldn't dare!"

"Of course I would. You can go on to Boston or

come with me, but I'm not leaving England. Except for a few minutes, because I promised to be on the ship when it sails. I didn't promise to *stay* on it."

"The captain won't let us, you ninny. He was paid to take us to America."

"And will be bribed, if necessary, to leave us behind. What's more, he won't have to feed us on the trip, and considering your appetite, that will save him a fortune. I shall also inform him I get violently seasick, even in a bathtub, and stay that way until I'm on solid land again. Mark my words, he'll be only too glad to bid us farewell." She paused. "You did say *us?*"

"'Course I did. Can't leave you to get in trouble by yourself. So, what do I do?"

"As I said, choose one of the sailors about your own age and make friends. Ask him questions and concentrate on the pilot. You're not stupid, Harry. Figure out what we need to know and bring me the answers. Oh, and find someone who is familiar with the town. We'll need to hire horses. I'm going to the cabin and select the few items we can carry with us. Just before we sail, I'll speak to the captain." She clapped her hands together. "Get moving!"

Two hours later the *Western Wind* pulled away from the dock. Glenys waved at Killain's man, who waved back. He watched a few minutes longer, and then went to where his horse was tethered. When he was out of sight, she joined Harry beside the rope ladder that would take them down to the pilot's small boat.

The captain had cooperated fully, after she insisted he retain the outrageous fee Killain paid him. He'd been none too comfortable having a young, unchaperoned female aboard, and was pleased to keep the money and rid himself of her.

Harry had done extremely well. The sailor he befriended was brother to the harbor pilot, who had precious little work in this backwater port. For a few guineas Walter Smithins agreed to ferry them ashore and help secure transportation out of Newhaven.

"I cannot go with you to London," she told Harry as they waited. "Unfortunately, Killain was clever enough to secure my promise. Nothing was said about Ravenrook, though. Mr. Smithins will escort me to Brighton, and from there I'll take a public coach. Then I'll hire a post chaise at Derby or Sheffield—wherever I wind up. I've plenty of money."

"You ain't going all that way by yourself, Glennie. I won't have it."

"Rubbish. If I left you to make the decisions, we'd be stuck on this ship all the way to America. And on the first ship headed back, because I'd not have stayed there. I am for Ravenrook, alone. You will go to London and tell Ravensby and Killain what we've done."

"Oh God."

"By far the most difficult task, I agree. But you are up to it. Have you a weapon?"

"A small pistol. Killain gave it me, so I could protect you on the ship. And this." He lifted the sword cane.

She took it from his hand. "If you don't mind, I'll take the cane with me. How do you get the sword part out?"

He showed her, with a dramatic flourish that startled Mr. Smithins as he came up behind them.

"Ready to go down, young missy? We gotta move fast now. They're loftin' full sail."

"Aye aye, sir."

A few minutes later, settled in the tiny boat with Harry, Mr. Smithins, and a burly man to pull the oars, she watched the *Western Wind* disappear around the promontory, on its way to America without her.

31

At a run-down pub on the outskirts of Buxton, money changed hands.

"You know what to do. Wait on the road, however long it takes. Sooner or later, he'll come by. Then bring him to me. Barry, give them directions to the cave."

A rough map was shoved across the ale-streaked table.

"What if 'e puts up a fight?"

"Kill him, if you must, and bring me the body. I'd rather secure him alive, but it's not essential. My employer won't care."

"'E won't be alone. We needs more men."

"Unfortunate. There aren't any more. But I understand he sent Killain and a squad of bodyguards to God knows where, so you may have a clear shot at him. If you're badly outnumbered, give it up and we'll try something else."

"This is your hunt. Why ain't you comin' with us?"

There was a deep sigh. "It seems I will be forced to do so, as you've not one functioning brain among the four of you. Barry, go on to the cave and set the charges. And make sure there is no possible exit. I intend to see him dead before closing him inside, but Ravensby has more lives than a cat. We'll take no chances."

The man named Barry stumbled away, head bowed.

"I don't trust 'im. 'E don't like this business."

"No, but he's in too deep to go back. With a murder charge already hanging over him, another cannot make a difference. He'll do what he's told or he'll swing. Now, gentlemen, one more drink for the road?"

"She's on the way to R-Ravenrook," Harry stammered. "I couldn't stop her."

Ash leaned back in his chair and closed his eyes. He should have known Glenys would find a way to thwart him, and Geoff, and three bodyguards, and her own brother. The ship's captain too, and the pilot. All of them men, blindly underestimating one slender, iron-willed female.

"Why Ravenrook?"

"Promised Lord Killain she wouldn't come back to London, same way she swore to be on the ship when it sailed. Glennie never lied, sir."

"If you believe that, you have not grasped the nature of truth. She has been a deceitful, prevaricating little witch. Killain should have seen through her ruse, but he was hell-bent to take me under his wing again and not thinking clearly." Ash came to his feet. "You are burned to coals, Harry. Go to bed."

"You aren't mad at me?"

"In fact, I'm wholly in sympathy with you. We are, all of us, putty in her hands. You did the best you could. Indeed, you made excellent time from Newhaven to London. Killain arrived little more than an hour ago."

Harry grinned. "I hired a new horse at every post-house. Figured you'd want to know right away what Glennie was up to."

"Yes. Thank you. Now get some sleep. Tomorrow you can follow me to Ravenrook, along with Killain. He too is exhausted and in his bed. I'll leave instructions for you both."

When Harry was gone, Ash rang for the butler and issued a spate of orders. Then he went upstairs to change clothes.

He'd make better time on horseback, he decided. Like Harry, he could hire a fresh mount whenever nec-essary. John Fletcher and Robin would travel with him.

He gave brief thought to his family, so carefully gath-ered in London for a scheme that failed to pay off. Evan and Jane had left that morning—on their way home, he presumed. Jervase had never returned from his club, but that was hardly unusual. If he came upon a woman, and he generally did, he'd prefer to spend the night with her. Wilfred Baslow was puttering around the library as of an hour ago, and Nora remained impris-oned in her room.

None of them would know he'd taken off for Ravenrook. None could possibly know Glenys was on her way there.

Even so, murky visions of disaster played in his head as he began the long journey north. A sense of dread gripped him. He felt it to the marrow in his bones.

He was going to be too late.

Glenys relaxed on the squabs of the post chaise, savor-ing the privacy and a chance to stretch out. The long trip from Brighton in public conveyances had worn her to the socket.

She'd arrived in Sheffield more than thirty hours after leaving the ship, lucky to find a coach for hire at the post-house. No driver could be had before morning, however, so she made do with a young man riding as postilion. He had grown up in the High Peaks and knew the roads, even the one leading to Ravenrook. She hoped he spoke the truth, because she had no idea how to get there.

Ash would follow her, she was nearly certain, once Harry told him where she'd gone. That meant he'd be safe at Ravenrook again, not pursuing some wild scheme of his own to catch the murderer. What he would say to her when he arrived was too ghastly to think about.

Better to sleep and gather strength for the confrontation than worry about it. Wrapping her cloak around her, feet resting on a box of hot bricks the landlord provided for an extra guinea, she closed her eyes.

"Wake up, sir! Someone's comin'."

Uncoiling himself from a nest of dried grasses, the tall man stood and drew out his pistol. "Go down a bit, Dawber, behind that tree. Pelsom, get ready to take hold of the horses. Willows, you stay with me. How many guards?"

"None," he wheezed, out of breath from his run. "No driver either. One man, on the right leader horse. Shutters drawn, so I couldn't see no passengers."

"It might be a ruse. Men hidden inside, like the Trojan horse."

"Dunno about fancy nags. Looked to be a hired coach."

"We'll soon find out." Concealing himself behind a large outcropping of stone, he watched the road. The sound of horses and the rattle of the wheels could be heard before the dim light cast by the lanterns became visible. Just before the coach drew even with him, he stepped out and fired his gun in the air.

The shot sent the horses into a frenzy, but Dawber and Pelsom were there to control them. Dawber threw the postilion to the ground and planted a foot on his back.

Gun pointed at the carriage door, he waited.

A moment later the door opened and Glenys Shea jumped out, a heavy cloak draped over her shoulders.

He couldn't see her hands. "Drop whatever you are holding," he ordered, "and remove the cape."

A cane hit the dirt, followed by her cloak. She held out her arms.

"Now step away from the door, slowly."

Again she obeyed, in silence.

Moving past her, gun aimed inside the carriage, he checked to make sure there were no other passengers.

Suddenly she was on his back, clawing at his eyes. With a yowl, he tried to throw her off. She clung to his waist with her legs, scratching his face, pulling his hair, screeching like a banshee.

He brought his arm back and caught her in the ribs with his elbow. To no effect. She held on, pounding his nose with a clenched fist. Blood streamed from his nostrils.

Then she was plucked away, taking a fistful of his hair with her. Dizzy from pain, he swung around to see her struggling in Willows's arms.

"Bitch!" He slapped her as hard as he could, and when she swore at him, he hit her again.

Her knees buckled and she slumped to the ground. He kicked her.

Willows put a hand on his arm. "You want her alive or dead, sir?"

The hot rage burned down, and he became aware of

the prize he'd captured. Not so good as Ravensby, but the earl never traveled without guards. Men would have died, and he might have been one of them.

Now, for the price of a scratched face and a bloody nose, he had the perfect bait to draw Ravensby into a carefully arranged ambush. He drew out his handkerchief and pressed it to his nostrils, nudging the girl with the toe of his boot.

She lifted a defiant chin. "Bastard! Devil's spawn!"

"A clever bastard, though," he said easily. "And I'd as soon have the devil on my side when I'm out to kill a man. Where is Ravensby, by the way?"

"Out of your reach. He has no intention of coming back to Ravenrook. I grabbed a last chance to steal what I could from the house."

"A lovely tale, my dear. I could almost believe you, if only for the fact you are on this road unprotected. Not like the earl to send you here without bodyguards. But I rather think you've taken the bit between your teeth, for reasons that do not concern me. I have you now, and he will try to get you back."

"Not likely. He called off the wedding and threw me out because I'm pregnant. The child isn't his. Ravensby wouldn't trade sixpence for me now."

He tilted his head, regarding her with a touch of admiration. A superb liar, Glenys Shea. If he hadn't learned so much about her, the chit might have convinced even a practiced deceiver like himself.

"What about the coach and the postilion?" Willows asked, clearly impatient to get off the road before they were discovered.

"Kill the boy. No bullets. Hit him on the head and put him back on the horse. Then have Pelsom drive the coach to some obscure place where it won't be found for a while and send it over a cliff."

He tossed the girl onto his saddle and swung up behind her. "I will tie and gag you," he warned, "if you make the slightest nuisance of yourself."

Followed by Willows and Dawber, he set out for the cave where William Barry waited. After dropping her off, he would post letters, one to Ravenrook and the other to London. Ravensby would come for her. He was sure of it.

Then he'd spring the trap.

A solemn-faced footman, one of the few servants remaining at Ravenrook, ran outside to take the horses when Ash, Robin, and John Fletcher arrived.

Jumping down from the saddle, Ash handed over the reins. "Where is Miss Shea?"

The boy looked puzzled. "Not here, m'lord. Weren't expecting you neither."

Not here. Dear God. The sense of foreboding, oppressive since he left London, clouded his vision. Alarms sounded in his aching head.

He regathered his wits. He'd traveled at a breakneck pace, and Glenys might well be a few hours behind him. Harry said she planned to use public transportation. She could be anywhere. At a posthouse, waiting to make connections. Slogging along a muddy road. Anywhere.

"Robin, John, get some sleep. I may need to send you out again in a few hours."

"A letter came for you this morning," the footman said. "It's on a tray in the vestibule. Marked 'Read at once.'"

On a run, Ash sped into the house and tore open the sealed letter.

"I have Glenys Shea," it read. "Come alone and

unarmed to Winnats Pass just after sunset. You will be watched all along the way. At the slightest indication of trouble, I will slit her throat."

His hand went limp. The paper fluttered to the carpet.

Blood drummed in his ears. He took a deep breath and then another, forcing himself to concentrate.

He would go, of course. Follow instructions. He looked over his shoulder to the long-case clock. After sunset, the note said. At this time of year, dusk fell early, around four. One o'clock now. Two hours from here to Winnats Pass.

He picked up the letter and went to his study, where he scribbled instructions for Killain. Geoff was likely to arrive at Ravenrook before morning. Too late to be of help, but just as well. Geoff would try to stop him from going in alone.

A maid appeared at the open door, asking if he wished a bath or a meal. "A pitcher of hot water in my room," he said, "and something to eat. Within a few minutes, please. See to it the best horse in the stable is saddled and ready at two o'clock."

When she was gone, Ash looked at the image of his face Charlie had carved from the block of granite. It sat on the mantelpiece, staring back at him.

Charlie, Ellen, and Jack Shea, all dead because of the man who now threatened to slit Glenys's throat. It was a man's handwriting on that letter. He didn't recognize it. Disguised, no doubt. The killer would not leave anything that could be traced to him.

Nor would he leave Glenys alive, once Ash Cordell walked into his snare. It was a fool's errand, the ride to Winnats Pass. For all he knew, she was already dead.

Ash went to his bedchamber, washed his face, and changed out of his sweaty clothes. He ate the bread, cold meat, and cheese left by the maid. It went down hard, but he managed to swallow it. He would need the strength.

Forty-five minutes later he put on his greatcoat, left the killer's letter and his instructions for Killain on the tray in the vestibule, and mounted a bay gelding tethered near the front door.

"When Lord Killain gets here," he told the footman, "make sure he sees my note immediately." Then, without a backward look, he set out for a confrontation that had been brewing for years.

It will be a relief, Ash told himself as he neared Winnats Pass, just to get it over with.

He'd come around the long way instead of riding through Castleton, where he was apt to be noticed. The killer hadn't specified a route. Shadows closed in as he passed the church, pub, and scattered cottages in the tiny village of Edale. Long before he reached the thrusting peaks that marked Winnats Pass, he was shrouded in darkness.

A sliver of moon peeked out now and again from the scudding clouds overhead. The bay picked its way along the narrow, winding road. Ash heard only the sound of hoofbeats, his own harsh breath, and the cry of ravens circling overhead. They rode the last currents of warm air rising from the hills, one final dance before calling it a night.

He'd come to a gorge where he could reach out and touch rock on both sides of him when a loud voice shattered the silence.

"Stand down!"

Dismounting, he stepped away from the horse and lifted his arms. Moments later a gun was pressed at his heart. Another man was behind him. Hands ran over his body, checking him for weapons.

Three men in all, he realized when another took charge of the horse. When they were satisfied he'd come unarmed, they led him along the road for a time and then turned onto a narrow track. It wound through rock-strewn gullies, forcing them to go single file. Always, there was a gun hard against his back and a man ahead of him.

Twice they turned off in a different direction. Wherever they were taking him, the place was deeply concealed within the hills. No-Man's-Land, the miners called it. Centuries ago the Romans had plumbed its depths for lead. Long since, the last remnants of ore in this area had been dug out and the mines abandoned.

The man in front struck a flint and lifted a torch. The light cast eerie shadows over the rocky crevasses as they plunged ever more deeply into the hills. Then he crouched and made a sharp turn to the right. The light disappeared.

Ash felt a hard blow at his shoulder.

"On your knees, milord. The tunnel is low about a hundred yards."

Entering the shaft, Ash saw the torch ahead of him. There was space enough to walk, bent over, but he'd been ordered to crawl. So he did, aware of the man at his heels. After a time he saw a brighter light where the tunnel opened to a large cavern the shape of an egg. On the opposite side was the entrance to another tunnel, high enough for a man to walk upright.

He took that in, before the man behind him gave him a hard push. Propelled forward into the cavern, he landed with his face against wet stone. A booted foot pressed against his neck.

"Welcome to my kingdom," said a familiar voice. "My kingdom, and your grave."

32

Jervase.

Goddamn. He should have known. In his heart he *had* known, despite all evidence to the contrary. But he failed, when it mattered most, to heed his instincts.

"You are wondering if I really have Glenys in my clutches." The voice was silky now. Jervase meant to enjoy this. "The answer is yes. When I let you up, you'll see her. Still alive too, though not for long. I rather liked the chit, until she tried to scratch my eyes out."

Good for her, Ash thought as the boot pressed harder against his neck.

"Are you attending me, cuz? I want you to slither on your belly to the wall which is directly in front of you. Then you may turn around and sit up. Forgive me for taking every precaution, but you've put me to a great deal of trouble over the years. Besides, it gives me pleasure to see the Earl of Ravensby brought low."

Ash obeyed. When he reached the wall, not far from the entrance to the other tunnel, he sat up with his back against hard, wet stone. Across from him, about ten yards away, Glenys lay crumpled in a heap.

"Drugged," Jervase explained. "Only a bit. Tiresome baggage. Kept kicking and clawing and wouldn't shut up. It was laudanum or tie and gag her."

"Bastard."

"Oh, worse than that, I'm afraid. You're a damned hard man to kill, cuz. You should have made it easier. At the least, you ought not have married. I've little partiality for slaughtering females, but you keep leaving me no choice."

"Dear God. This is about the bloody inheritance?"

"What else? Oh, not that patch of rocks and weeds I'll acquire when you've cocked up your toes. No, I am, as always, a mere hireling. Devonshire was never so demanding as my other employer, but neither did he pay so well for delivery of statues as Wilfred does for murder."

Ash leaned his head against the damp stone wall. Wilfred Baslow. Useless old Wilfred Baslow, rutting around among his books while he orchestrated one killing after another. Incredible. "Do you know why it is he wants me dead?"

"Never much cared. It has something to do with barrows on that piece of land he'll inherit. He's got the notion there's a tomb or the like under one of them. Pretty convinced of it, actually, since he's paid out most of his fortune trying to eliminate the major obstacle. That being you, of course."

And any woman who might be carrying his heir. First Ellen, now Glenys.

Nora had often spoken, with disdain, of Wilfred's obsession. His hunger to unearth a treasure from the past. It seemed no more than a scholar's pet crotchet, a harmless fantasy. They had all misjudged him.

"You have been after me for six years," Ash said. "I wonder he failed to hire someone more proficient."

Jervase laughed. "Indeed, I was the veriest amateur when we began. What's more, I've little taste for killing and less for exerting myself. But who else had he to call on, living as he does in the backwaters of Suffolk? I needed the money, had occasional access to your person, and am not burdened with a conscience. He chose well enough, as I will prove tonight. Which reminds me . . . "

He came up to Ash and held out his hand. "I require your signet ring, as proof I've done the deed. It's unlikely your body will be found anytime this century."

Ash twisted the ring from his finger and dropped it at Jervase's feet.

Their gazes caught and held. For a moment Ash was sure Jervase would hit him. He wanted him to. If Jervase got that close, he'd grab his arm and bash his head against the wall.

But Jervase kicked the ring in the direction of a guard and told him to pick it up. "Past time you stopped underestimating me, cuz. And remember, I can make this easy for you, or excessively painful. I'm even willing to dose you with laudanum before pulling the trigger."

"Thank you. I much prefer to look you in the eye."

"Not unexpected. The true aristocrat declines a blindfold, does he not, to show how very superior he is? But I daresay you'll bleed as red as any commoner, Lord Ravensby. As will your bride, although she is, of course, common as dirt." He gestured to Glenys. "Before you say or do anything else to annoy me, I suggest you consider how she is to die. On a whim, I might give her to these men before putting a bullet in her head."

Ash heard Jervase laugh through the roaring in his ears. Burn in hell, he willed. Burn in hell.

And so the bastard would, but not before killing

Glenys. Ash took his warning seriously. At the slightest insult, Jervase would hand her over to be raped. And force him to watch.

Jervase craved admiration. Acknowledgment of his brilliance by the cousin he'd always envied. He wanted to bring Lord Ravensby to his knees.

But not too easily, Ash was certain. Christ, if it would help Glenys, he'd be licking the man's boots at this very moment.

That would please Jervase, but not enough. He would recognize the gesture for what it was—a bending of the knees but not the will. He demanded genuine respect, or whatever Ash could muster that would pass for it. A grudging respect too. If it came without a struggle, he'd not believe it.

On a whim, he'd said. The slightest false step and . . .

Ash closed his eyes, but the vision of Glenys under the pounding bodies of those four louts writhed in his head. Anything but that.

Keep him talking, he thought. Let him boast. And don't be impressed right away. Force him to convince you before giving him what he wants.

"The ring," he said, "might persuade Wilfred you have dispatched me. But the authorities will demand greater proof, and until I am declared legally dead, he inherits nothing. Without a body, that could take years."

"Just so. And his problem, not mine." Jervase accepted the ring passed to him by the largest of the thugs and slipped it in his pocket. "I doubt Wilfred will think of that right away. He's quite mad, you know. And by the time he does, I'll be well on my way with a fat bonus in my pocket for killing you, along with funds to mount a search for your pregnant wife."

Ash, genuinely puzzled, rubbed his forehead. A search? "Glenys carries no child. That was a rumor."

"I thought it might be. You are too damned honorable to bed her out of wedlock. Or were you indeed married by Special License?"

"No."

"Too bad. But even if you are lying, it matters not. I'll inform Wilfred otherwise, and assure him the chit carries a legitimate heir. You sent her into hiding when word got out. He heard the rumors and will believe me. He is nearly bled dry, I fear, but I'll take what money he has left and vanish. Brazil, perhaps."

"Not far enough. When the three of us disappear at the same time, you will be the prime suspect. Killain will track you down."

"He can try. And if he succeeds, cuz, you'll never know about it. Quite soon, your role in this farce will be done with. I only wonder you've no interest in how we got to this point. In your place, I'd be vastly curious."

The devil you would, Ash thought savagely. A man expecting to die within a few minutes doesn't give a damn about the particulars. He's at his last prayers, or looking for a way out.

Gritting his teeth, he said what Jervase wanted to hear. "I grant you've been clever enough. Hell, you fooled me, Killain, Bow Street, and a score of hired investigators. What's more, you were our first choice. Of all possible candidates, we devoted the most effort to tracking your every move. And still you eluded detection."

Jervase looked pleased. "It wasn't so difficult. In the early days, you thought yourself the victim of an accident. A misfired shot at a hunting party, or food poisoning."

"So I did. But how did you handle the poisonings? You were never invited to my home in London."

"I noticed. Paltry stuff, the attempts to get at you with poison, but Wilfred required some indication I was about my job. In fact, we nearly succeeded. Twice the doctors despaired of you. I supplied the poison, of course, and gave strict instructions how to use it. But the chits never got it right."

"You bribed the maids?"

"No point wasting money. I seduced three of them, at different times, and paid them a trifle." He pulled a flask from his pocket. "That was before you got strict about who you hired. Later, when I knew anyone on your staff would turn me in, I sought a better way to get at you."

"With a gun."

"Have you forgot? I started out by shooting at you. Once in Hyde Park, and another time when you wandered off by yourself at Oatlands while the others were hunting. Only winged you, though." He took a swig from the flask. "Couldn't shoot worth a damn back then, but I've improved. Picked off that giant of a bodyguard with one bullet."

Bile rose in Ash's throat. "*You* killed Charlie? But how? You were on your way to Italy."

"Ah. I was also in Scotland when Ellen went over that cliff, and abroad when most of the attacks on you took place. A wonderment."

Ash could barely force himself to look at the smirking face, the narrow eyes, the strut as Jervase circled the cave to draw everyone's attention to himself. He wanted even the thugs to admire him.

They had spread out, one on either side of the entrance, another beside Glenys, and the fourth crouched by himself against the wall. He looked unhappy.

Ash took note of that. Not an ally, but clearly troubled. Now and again he glanced at the sleeping girl, as if distressed by the thought of killing her.

Jervase looked a bit offended when Ash failed to respond. "You aren't curious how I did it? Managed to be two places at the same time?"

Ash shrugged. "My imminent death is a sliver more compelling, but yes, I am confounded."

"And I admit to a stroke of luck." Jervase took another drink from his flask and wiped his lips. "Or, it may be the devil watches out for his own. While in Scotland, I chanced on a man who looks enough like me to be a twin, except at very close range. He was poor, and poorer still when I took what little he owned at a game of cards."

"A double." Ash whistled between his teeth. "That never occurred to us."

"He was remarkably cooperative. I used him sparingly, of course, and never allowed him in contact with anyone who knew me. But he did well enough, traveling with forged papers and the like. When I killed your wife, with the help of several hired ruffians, the young man was closeted at an inn in the Highlands, pretending to be ill. Your investigators followed up, I know. They spoke to the physician, the landlord, and most of the villagers."

"And reported that Jervase Cordell barely survived a mysterious sickness," Ash said. "He had a high fever, and was bled."

"Ah, that cost me. A slight touch of the poisons I fed to you, but he agreed to swallow them on the assurance I needed him alive. Getting rid of Ellen was only the first step, you understand. Then you went to ground at Ravenrook. Unsporting, cuz."

Ash nodded absently. From the corner of his eye, while Jervase was speaking, he had seen Glenys move. Only her hand, slightly, but she'd begun to shake off the laudanum-induced sleep.

Not now, he begged silently. Hold still.

He swung his attention to Jervase, who regarded him with overbright eyes. Opium, he thought. Hoped. Opium mixed with the liquor in that flask.

"It was your double boarded the ship in Liverpool?"

When Jervase nodded, Ash made a gesture of respect. "I put two men on you, good men, and you gulled them."

"Nothing to it. When I arrived at the inn near the docks, he was already there. Disguised, naturally, and in company with one of these gentlemen. Your men saw me drinking in the taproom most of the evening. Later, in my bedchamber, we switched identities. Willows here supported my double to the ship. He kept his head down and stumbled to conceal differences in the way we walk. Meantime, wearing the disguise, I took my leave through the back door."

"Impressive. Too bad you weren't on my side, Jervase. I'd have paid you better than Wilfred. Or did you relish the idea of killing me?"

"In fact, no. Oh, I've always longed to knock you down a peg or two. But murder? Took me a while to get used to it, you being my cousin and all. But I'm deep in blood now, and tonight's work will be no more bothersome than snuffing a candle."

He drained the flask and returned it to his pocket. "Best to get on about it, since I want to be well away before dawn. Dawber, retrieve the horses and bring them to the entrance. Barry, I assume the charges are set and ready to fire?"

Jervase was all business now. As he inspected bore holes at the narrow entrance to the cavern, Ash looked at Glenys from the corner of his eye.

She hadn't changed positions, but her left hand moved slightly. Wiping his forehead to conceal his eyes, Ash looked more closely. It was one of Harry's signals. *All's well,* she said.

Hardly. But she meant only that she was awake and alert. He saw her eyes flicker open and close again; she would observe him through her lashes, he realized. *Be ready,* he signed back.

Ready for what, he'd no idea. But they would make a

fight of it, somehow. He pretended to be nervous, mauling his hair with shaking fingers, rocking back and forth on his hips. That would please Jervase, and cover the signs he made to Glenys.

As he rocked, he noticed pebbles scattered near the cave wall. He lifted a knee and draped one arm across it, signing Glenys to run when he shouted.

Where? she asked.

Deeper into the cave, he wanted to say, but he didn't know how. *Back. Inside. Understand?*

After a moment—*yes.* One finger pointed briefly to the tunnel at his right.

Good girl. He rested his free arm on the ground beside his hip. Still moving his body, hoping it looked to be an indication of fear, he began to gather a handful of pebbles. Risking one more glance, he saw that Glenys lay still as death.

Jervase had finished his examination of the gunpowder charges. He drew a pistol from his coat pocket and took up a position in the center of the cavern. "Our revels now are ended, cuz. Which of you will be first? Better the girl, yes? She is sleeping and won't know what hit her. Otherwise, my first shot will rouse her. You see, I intend to be kind."

Ash prepared himself to move. "D-Don't make me watch you kill her," he said in a breaking voice. "Start with me."

"If you insist." Jervase took a step forward and leveled the gun.

"Wait!" Ash lifted his chin. "For God's sake, let me die on my feet like a man."

Frowning, Jervase glanced over his shoulder as if making sure the men were there to back him up. Then he shrugged. "Very well. You were ever the aristocrat, Ash. No harm letting you play that role to the end, I suppose. Stand, but do it slowly."

Muttering a prayer, sincere but meant to convince Jervase he'd resigned himself to death, Ash struggled to his knees and planted one foot against the wall behind him.

Then, with a roar, he launched himself at Jervase and hurled the pebbles at his face.

The gun went off, ricocheting from the wall as he threw Jervase to the ground. Two men rushed for him.

At his right he saw Glenys on her feet. She had grabbed a lantern and dashed it against one of the men. With a howl, he fell back, the sleeve of his shirt on fire.

Ash propelled himself at the other man, catching him with a blow to the stomach. "Go!" he shouted to Glenys. She fled past him as Jervase rolled over and came to his hands and knees. He raised the gun, and Ash dove for the tunnel.

A searing pain cut across his ribs, but he kept moving, aware of Glenys just ahead of him. Within seconds the passage was dark as ink. He put a hand against the wall to guide him and plunged ahead, nearly overrunning her with his longer stride.

"I'll lead," he said, moving to the front. "Hold on to my coat. They'll be after us soon, with lanterns."

Wasting no breath on a reply, she seized a handful of cloth and kept to the swift pace he set. Several minutes later the tunnel split. Tossing a mental coin, Ash took the right branch.

Behind him, panting, Glenys held on. They splashed through pools of water, sometimes ankle deep. Once, he tripped over a knob of limestone and dropped to his knees. Glenys landed on his back. And then they were moving again, blindly, ducking whenever the ceiling lowered.

Barely in time, he caught himself from running directly into a solid wall of stone. He felt up and down, on either side and straight ahead.

Dead end.

33

Glenys bent over, gulping mouthfuls of thin air. "Shall we go back?"

"No point," Ash whispered after a moment. "They'll come for us or they won't. And if they do, we'd only run into them. Most likely they'll give up before advancing this far."

She didn't think so, and knew he didn't either. "At least we tried."

"Yes." He pulled her against him, her back against his chest. "Keep still."

In the stark blackness every sound was magnified. She became aware of water dripping from overhead, and the tiny splashes when it met rock or shallow pools. She put a hand against the wall. It was cold and clammy. Rivulets streamed between her fingers. This is my tomb, she thought. This dark hole inside a mountain.

Her knees buckled, and Ash crossed his arms over her breasts, holding her upright. He felt more solid than the rock. Dizzy from the long run and the laudanum, she leaned against him, absorbing his strength.

In silence they waited an eternity, or so it seemed to her. She was nearly sure the men had given up the search. And then she caught a glimmer of light reflected from the water-streaked wall. Listening hard, she heard the unmistakable sound of boots splashing through puddles, now and again hitting solid stone.

They had been found.

Ash pushed her behind him and put a hand on her head, pressing her into a crouch. The light grew brighter. It reached out, across the other side of the passageway and around the cul de sac as the man lifted his lantern. Then it fell on them.

The man stopped moving. She felt Ash tense, and knew he was preparing himself for a last fight.

The light moved away. "Nothin' here," the man grumbled. "Must've gone down the other tunnel."

Moments later they were again shrouded in darkness. Glenys stood, and felt Ash turn, and then she was enveloped in his arms. "What happened?" she murmured against his lapel. "I thought he saw us."

"He did. But he was alone, and is probably on his way for reinforcements. Stay here. I'm going after him."

"Not without me."

Ash swore under his breath and headed back the way they'd come. She followed, clinging to the hem of his coat.

After a long time, she heard voices. Ash swept her against the wall with one arm and they both held still.

". . . and no sign of 'em."

The same voice, she realized. The man who'd found them.

"Damn." That was Jervase. "Are you sure there is no way out of this cave, either direction?"

"Walked as far as I could walk yesterday, just like

you told me. If there's a shaft left, even a mite of one for ventilation, I never came on it."

Jervase made a noise she couldn't decipher.

"I been careful, sir. Ravensby saw m'face. If they escape, I'm for the hangman."

"Indeed. Fetch Willows and let's get out of here. We'll set off the gunpowder, close off the only exit, and then I'll pay you. Evidently they prefer a slow death to a bullet in the head. So be it."

There was more noise as the man shouted for Willows. The echo clanged in her head.

"Go back," Ash whispered. "Now."

Moving by inches, cautiously, she felt her way along the tunnel. A few minutes later she stopped and waited. Dear God she was cold, and wet all over as the dripping water seeped through her dress. She thought briefly of the cloak left behind on the road when she was abducted. Ah well. Nothing would keep her warm and dry here.

A slow death, Jervase said. Ought they have let him—

She bit her lip. The mere idea was unworthy of her. Shameful. There had to be a way to stay alive, and Ash would find it.

After a long time, she heard a tiny noise—the sloshing of water. She pressed herself against the wall and froze. A hand touched her shoulder. Ash. She threw herself into his arms.

"They're gone," he murmured at her ear. "In a few minutes there will be an explosion. Hold tight and don't be afraid."

"Why didn't that man tell Jervase where we were?"

"I don't know. He was nervous from the beginning. I noticed it when we were in the cavern. He's the one who set the gunpowder, and probably the one who told Jervase about this cave. I expect he's a local miner, in over his head, having an attack of conscience."

"But he said there was no way out of here."

"Certainly there is. He was lying."

So was Ash, she knew. He had said that to bolster her spirits. And if there was, in fact, a way out, they might never find it. She felt cold lips brush her cheek before he set her back. Then she heard the rustle of cloth.

"You are a block of ice, my girl. Put this on." After some fumbling, he stuffed her arms into his riding coat. It was wet, but warm from his body. He drew the lapels across her breasts. "We may as well head for the other tunnel. Hold on to my shirt."

At least they'd had some practice making their way together, unable to see where they were going. The last time was a vast open space with bogs on either side. Now they were closed in, and she was truly frightened. It was like a coffin, this tunnel. Without Ash, she'd die of sheer terror.

Finally they came to where the tunnels branched. Ash led her a little way into the second passage and stopped. "From now on," he said, "we move slowly and feel along the walls. You take the right side. A ventilation shaft could be at knee level or below. Let me keep a little ahead of you, and make sure you feel solid rock before you put all your weight on either foot."

Reluctantly, she let go of his hand and fumbled along the slick wet stone to her right. They had gone only a short way when a blast of noise, almost like a living thing, roared through the tunnel. Shortly after, the walls and ground shuddered.

The entrance to the cave was now blocked.

Ash touched her arm. "Keep moving."

She did, feeling up and down the wall until her back ached from bending and raising. It was hard to breathe, and grew more difficult as they penetrated deeper into the cave.

And always she feared another dead end . . . a place where the miners had given up, decided to abandon the shaft, gone elsewhere in search of lead. No one had been here for centuries, she knew. Even the constant streams of water could not account for the smooth stone under her fingers if the mine had been recently worked.

For some reason, she didn't know why, neither of them spoke. Only the dripping water and their footsteps broke the silence. At least an hour passed, maybe two, before Ash flung out an arm. He was a bit ahead of her, and his hand caught her on the chest.

"Stay there," he ordered, his voice harsh.

She leaned against the wall, tuning to him, listening for the noises as he moved. This is what it is like to be blind, she realized. Not the barest flicker of light. Only sound, mysterious and unreadable. She thought he had gone to his knees, but could not be sure. There was a faint rustle of clothing, a scratching as if he were crawling forward, and then the splash of water.

"A pool," he said. "Deeper than I can reach with my arm. It could be a shaft, Glenys. One that filled with so much water it couldn't be pumped out."

She dropped to hands and knees and felt her way to his side. "What does that mean?"

"I'm not sure. Possibly another dead end, in which case we'll go back to the entrance and try to dig ourselves out. But first I'll see if there's a tunnel on the other side. This might be only a large depression where water has gathered. You wait here."

"No. I want to come with you."

"Dammit, there's no point us both getting wet."

"I'm soaked to the skin already, and I can swim."

"Fine. If I come upon an extension of this tunnel, I'll call back to you."

More sounds, as he pulled off his boots. She knew that

because one of them landed on her knuckles. Then she heard him cut into the water. He paddled to his right, slapping his hand against the wall as he went. The opening of the tunnel, if it continued at all, could be anywhere.

She sat back on her heels, praying for strength. Her greatest fear was that she'd slow him down. On his own, Ash would have a much better chance of escaping, but he'd never leave her behind. "Make me strong, Lord," she begged.

From a great distance, she heard a voice. At first, she imagined it was God.

"I found the passage," Ash called. He was directly opposite her, but not close. "The pool is about a hundred yards across. Can you make it on your own? Tell me the truth. Easy enough to come back for you."

"Stay. And keep talking so I know where you are." She peeled off Ash's coat and her halfboots and lowered herself into the water. It was even colder than the pool at Ravenrook. Immediately she began to swim, following the sound of his voice.

At first she made swift progress, but soon her muscles started to cramp. Every few yards she was forced to stop, treading water as she massaged her calf or shoulder or thigh. It seemed she had been in the water for hours, although Ash sounded little closer than when she'd begun.

"Glenys? Are you all right?"

"Yes," she called. "Just a bit slow."

She resumed swimming again, varying her strokes, her whole body shrieking with pain.

Then something touched her arm and she screamed.

"Stop thrashing," Ash said from beside her. "Turn on your back and float."

"I th-thought you were a monster," she gurgled as he

wrapped an arm across her chest and began towing her through the water.

"Shut up and breathe," he ordered.

A minute later he helped her locate the edge of the pool with her hands. She held on as he lifted himself out, seized her under the arms, and hauled her up.

She fell immediately to hands and knees, retching uncontrollably. Even when there was nothing in her stomach, she couldn't stop.

After a long time, she knelt back, hiccoughing. Ash lowered himself next to her and wiped her face and lips with a wet handkerchief.

"Thank you," she murmured. "I'm s-sorry."

"It was the laudanum," he said gently. "And I should not have let you try to swim by yourself. Come. You'll feel better after a drink of water."

"Is it safe?"

He turned her around until she could reach the pool. "Absolutely. It's been filtered through a mile of limestone."

It tasted sour to her, but that was because of the vomiting. "At least we won't die of thirst."

"Nor anything else," he said firmly. "At least, not in this cave. Are you able to stand?"

"I think so." She found his extended hand and he tugged her against his chest.

"Your muscles are cramped," he said, feeling her shoulders. "Hang on and I'll work the knots out."

She clung to him as his hard fingers kneaded her aching arms and shoulders and back. Then he went to his knees and applied himself to her thighs and calves. One by one he lifted her bare, frozen feet and massaged them to life again.

She drifted, mindless, as he worked. Blood surged back into her limbs. They burned like fire, but even the pain felt wonderful. She made a little cry of protest when he stopped.

"You mustn't go to sleep, Glenys. We have to keep moving. Take my hand and come along." He led her a short way down the tunnel. "Hop up and down if you start feeling drowsy."

She let go and tried a few steps without his support. "I'll be fine. Shall I feel along the left side or the right?"

After a pause he said, "The right. But we'll switch now and again." His fingers tangled in her hair and he planted a kiss on her nose. "Brave girl. Don't give up now. The man was trying to give us a clue, I think, when he said he'd walked as far as he could walk without finding an exit. The way out must be on this side of the pool."

"He also said something about a ventilation shaft being *left*," she said thoughtfully. "I thought he meant *left over* from the old days, but it might have been another clue."

"Possibly. We'll try both sides, though. The shaft might even be overhead, although I doubt it. We are pretty deep in the mountain now."

Rather sure they had reached the center of the earth, she began feeling along the wall and heard Ash doing the same. As before, they kept silent, hoarding their strength. Three times the tunnel widened into grottoes, smaller than the one where Jervase had taken them, but they soon located another passage and continued on.

The shaft wound like a snake through the mountain, and at one point they were forced to crawl for several hundred yards. Then they emerged into another grotto, larger than the other three.

"Wait here," Ash told her, "while I make sure there isn't a shaft or another deep pool."

She concentrated on the sounds of his movements, forcing herself not to hear the steady dripping of water all around them. She had begun to hate that sound. She loathed the opaque darkness with all her heart. From now on, she would always keep a candle lit when she went to bed.

Ash's arm settled on her shoulder. "The tunnel continues across the way, but we'll stay here for a while. There has got to be a source of air not far ahead. Otherwise, the miners couldn't have opened up this section."

"It might be a natural formation," she said.

"Yes. I'd hoped you wouldn't think of that. Still, we've been searching too long, repeating the same patterns. We're apt to grow careless."

"Believe me, I won't miss a hole in the rock."

"You might, if it's grown over with mineral deposits or partly caved in. One hour and we'll go on."

"Have you any idea what time it is?"

He pulled out his watch and shattered the crystal against the wall. "One-thirty, or that's where the hands point now. They must have stopped when I went into the pool about two hours ago, so make it three-thirty. By the time we come near the exit, the sun will be up. That will help."

The sun. Would she ever see it again? Ash sounded so confident, but that was for her sake. Did he really believe they'd escape this hellish cave? She didn't ask him, because he would say only what she needed to hear.

"Although we are resting," he said, "we must not stop moving. If we fall asleep, we are as good as dead. So, Miss Shea, will you grant me the honor of the next waltz?"

For a moment, lost in her own gloomy contemplations, she failed to understand.

"Are you cutting me?" he chided. "Think on it before

you do. There are few partners at this rather exclusive ball."

Rallying, she curtseyed even though he couldn't see it. "I shall be honored to waltz with you, Lord Ravensby. Of a certain, you are the handsomest man in the room."

With a laugh, he took her in his arms. "We must dance slowly, lest the stalagmites trip us up."

"Our hostess has a perverse notion of decor," she remarked as they began to move, almost in place. "And I cannot approve the orchestra. It puts me in mind of a leaky faucet."

"Perhaps you could hum a tune, to drown it out."

"La, sir, no one has ever wished to hear me sing. And for good reason, I must add. How about you?"

"Only if you are partial to the howling of a demented wolf. Since neither of us has a gift for music, we'll talk instead. And I suggest you warm your feet by standing on mine."

Embarrassed, she stumbled and felt his hand tighten at her waist. "My feet are somewhat large, I'm afraid."

"Mine are larger. Up you go."

Of a sudden, she was standing on the tops of his feet. To hold her there, he had let go her hand and wrapped both arms around her back. It was natural for her to hold him in the same way. Her chin rested on his shoulder, and against her cheek she felt the pulse of blood at his throat.

Nestled in the warmth of his body, rocked in the cradle of his arms, she felt her mind slipping into a delicious dream.

He pinched her arm. "Talk to me, Glenys. You must stay alert. Tell me about Miss Pipcock's School."

She shot awake. "G-Good heavens. That would put us both to sleep. My life there was tedium relieved by occasional boredom. Dull dull dull."

"But you were there for most of your life, and I want to hear about it. Digress at will, but keep talking."

He was right, of course. If she fell asleep, she'd not wake for days. Maybe never, if they didn't find a way out of this hole. So she talked and talked, and when she faltered, he asked questions and she talked some more. After a while he knew all there was to tell about her years at the school, so she spoke of her mother. To her horror, she heard herself tell him about her grandparents, and how they refused to acknowledge her existence.

He asked more questions then, but she had the presence of mind to fend them off.

"It seems I am not the only one cursed with pernicious relatives," he said finally. "You needn't say any more. And your voice is becoming scratchy. Does your throat hurt?"

It did, probably because of all the retching. "Yes, and you have heard the story of my life. It's your turn now."

His muscles went taut. "I am certain Killain has already told you everything there is to know about me."

"Of course he has not. He is loyal and discreet, although I admit to quizzing him incessantly."

"I daresay. And he'd not have been able to resist you."

"You would be surprised," she said with a chuckle. "Be fair, my lord. Tell as much about yourself as I have told you about me."

He began dancing with her again, slowly. "You are, I believe, one-and-twenty. I am thirty-four. At your age I was still at Cambridge, so I'll give you stories of my own time at school. And I assure you, they are more humdrum than your tales of Miss Pipcock and your students."

"In that case, I shall bid you good night. Actually, I

am all but asleep already. The laudanum, you know. It will require a lively story to keep me awake."

He made a grumbling sound, which she suspected was an oath. "And it is nearly time to resume our search. But in honor, since you spoke freely to me, I'll allow you three questions. Ask what you will, and I'll reply as best I can. I'm not good with words, though."

Nor anxious to talk about yourself, she thought, sifting through the questions she'd wanted to ask him for a long time. Only three, and she had hundreds of things she longed to know about him. Thousands.

34

Ash prepared himself for her interrogation, consoling himself that it could not be so onerous as the last one. The night they made love.

Only five nights ago. A lifetime ago. He drew her closer, remembering how she had felt in his arms. The splendor of her unbounded passion.

Now he could practically hear the wheels turning in her head as she devised the questions most likely to wring from him stories he didn't want to tell. "Ten minutes and we resume the search," he reminded her, wishing, too late, that he'd said five minutes. Or three.

"Very well. I'll start with something simple. When we escape, and you've tracked down Jervase and Wilfred, will you continue to live at Ravenrook or go to London?"

That was harmless enough. He breathed easier. "Neither, in fact. The family seat is located in Sussex, and I'll return there."

"Will you finish your book?"

"I expect so, eventually. Perhaps in my old age, if I am permitted to have one."

She laughed. "Oh, you'll dodder into your nineties, still scribbling away in Latin. Jane will be so disappointed."

"It grieves me to let her down, certainly. But come, Miss Shea. Your third question, so we can move on."

"Second, by my count. What were—"

"It seems you are somewhat deficient in mathematics, my dear. You asked where I will live, and if I plan to finish the book. That is two questions, by standard arithmetic."

"Oh, infamous!" She stomped her foot on his, to no effect because his feet were numb as rocks. Then, to his surprise, she put one cold hand against his neck, gently, and touched his chin with her thumb. "I wish above all things to know about your wife," she said.

He caught his breath. Not that. Dear God, he couldn't tell her about Ellen.

"Have you ever spoken of her, to anyone?" Glenys asked into the tense silence.

Never. It would be the most profound violation of honor he could imagine. Ellen couldn't help what she was. In her way, as God created her, she had been perfect. The most beautiful woman he ever saw. Gentle. Sweet-natured. Generous. Loving.

In the way a kitten was loving, or a child.

He could not explain. Glenys had no right to ask. But the memories exploded in his head as if a volcano had erupted. What he'd kept buried spewed from his hard heart and rose like molten rock to his tongue. He clenched his teeth. He would not let it out.

"You must tell me," Glenys said softly. "Her death changed everything. It ended all your hopes. She carried your child. You had everything a man could want, and Jervase took it from you. Don't grieve alone, Ash. Not any longer. The pain is worse when you keep it to yourself."

He meant to set her away, off his feet, from his arms. Instead he drew her closer. He knew, distantly, that his fingers were digging into her back. He thought he must be hurting her.

But her hand brushed the damp hair from his forehead, stroked down his cheek, and lingered there.

"It wasn't like that," he managed to say. "I can't describe how it was. It's too complicated."

"Then tell me how you feel. One word only. Choose a word that describes how you feel."

"Guilty," he said in a rush. And even as he uttered the word, the sense of release stunned him. He felt guilty. He always had, for not loving Ellen when she lived. For not missing her when she died. Oh dear God. His eyes burned. Oh dear God.

"No more," he whispered.

Glenys stepped away, off his feet. "Say it, Ash. For your own sake. If you do not, the time will never come again."

He swayed. She was right. For years he'd wanted, desperately, to tell someone.

Often he wished he were Catholic, like Geoff, so he could confide his sin to a priest in the confessional. Bare his soul, accept penance, and free himself of the guilt. But he had never believed that telling another person would help. God already knew, after all. Ash Cordell knew. Ellen was dead, and would not have understood in any case. Who else mattered?

Glenys lowered one hand to his chest, directly over his heart, and he knew the answer.

"Ellen had the mind of a child," he said tonelessly. "She couldn't help it, of course. Something went wrong.

I don't know what. She never grew, mentally, beyond nine or ten years old. Her family taught her, carefully, how to go on in society. She smiled, always, and knew to speak of pleasant things. Most of the young women I'd met did exactly the same. One would have to be with her privately to discern how she really was, and we were never alone together. A conspiracy, I expect, between her family and my father. They arranged the marriage."

"Would you have refused, had you known?"

"To be sure. Another man, one more tolerant and less demanding, would have suited her better. Been patient, as I was not. She liked having me at her side, when she visited tenants or sat by the fire, embroidering. But I was so damned uncomfortable. I had nothing to say to her, and dreaded being alone with her. It was a relief when the parish ladies came to visit, so I could make my escape."

"All this was in your head, Ash. I warrant she never knew what you were thinking."

"Who knows? She may have sensed it. I did try, but I hated each day more than the last. And I wanted children. She did too. Ellen loved children and they adored her. But she could not endure physical intimacy, and failed to understand the connection between lovemaking and giving birth. On this point, after several months, I overruled her. Luckily, she conceived right away."

Glenys was silent, although her fingers curled against his chest.

Bedding Ellen had been an ordeal for them both. She lay still and unresponsive. He was as gentle as he knew how to be. But it always seemed as if he were ravishing her.

"Did I do wrong?" he asked. "Her mother spoke to her and explained what was to happen and why. She said Ellen would welcome me to her bed. And when she didn't send me away, as she'd done on our wedding night, I thought . . ."

"Good heavens," Glenys chided softly. "Any other man would be congratulating himself for his restraint. If there is guilt to be apportioned for this mismatch, all of it belongs to your father. Were he alive, I'd take a horsewhip to him."

He had no doubt of that. "The earl was . . . offended by my war investigations. He sought to cut me off from polite society, so I could not further shame the family. Marriage to Ellen was the surest way to achieve that. She was happy in the country, among familiar faces, and I could neither take her to London nor leave her behind."

"Well." Glenys put both hands on his shoulders. "Well," she said again. "I suspect the only way to rid you of this mutton-headed guilt is a thwap upside the head. But now is scarcely the time."

"Don't you understand? I saw to it she carried a child, and for that reason she was murdered."

"Murdered by Jervase and Wilfred, not you. Holy hollyhocks, Ash. What is Latin for 'dicked in the nob'?"

Ah, Glenys, he thought. You transform my guilt to self-indulgence by making fun of me. And the devilish thing is, I have indeed played the fool.

"Bad enough you've picked up English cant from your brother, my dear. I'll not expand your unacceptable vocabulary into another language. Let us go on now. We've a ventilation shaft to find."

"And are past due for a bit of luck, wouldn't you say?"

He took her hand and led her to the tunnel. "*I would say, Virtutis fortuna comes.*"

She laughed, a sparkling sound in the gloom. "Was that your way of telling me to be virtuous?

"Not at all. It means 'Fortune is the companion of valor.' And since you have valor enough for the both of us, we are overdue for vastly good fortune."

"Oh." She squeezed his hand. "Thank you."

"You are also a baggage, young lady. Now, to work. Take the right side."

Another hour passed with none of the good fortune Glenys deserved. The tunnel twisted and turned, sometimes so narrow they were forced to walk single file. Once it branched, and by silent agreement they went to the left.

There were two more small grottoes, the second awash in water up to their thighs. After making sure of the path, Ash led her across. The water was also deep in the tunnel on the other side, sometimes to their knees.

His fingers and feet grew even more numb. The wound in his side, where the bullet had creased him, throbbed painfully. It couldn't close while he kept moving and stretching, and he felt blood streaming from it, warmer than the cold water that dripped incessantly from the limestone above them.

Glenys never complained or suggested they rest. He was aware of her beside him, a little to the rear, examining every inch of wall with her fingers. Occasionally she paused long enough to cup a handful of water and swallow it. Then she quickly caught up.

Intrepid child. No, he corrected. Valiant woman.

After a long time, he sensed the ground had begun to slope upward. Ever so slightly, though, and he couldn't be sure. With little feeling in his legs, disoriented as he was from exhaustion and loss of blood, the sensation could be no more than wishful thinking. But the level of the water continued to fall, and soon there were only shallow puddles under his feet.

He called a halt. Glenys fell into his open arms with

relief, and he set her back to rub her icy fingers and icier feet.

"I expect you wish Killain were here with you instead of me," she said between chattering teeth. "You wouldn't have to give him these massages."

"Nor would I have danced with him. And so far, that waltz has been the high point of our holiday in the Derbyshire caves."

"N-Next time, sir, please may we go to the seashore?"

He chuckled. "Agreed. Ready to continue the search?"

She turned again to the wall, choosing the left side. "A change of scenery, if you don't mind."

Glenys remembered what Lord Killain had told her about forced marches over hostile territory. The soldiers plodded blindly ahead, moving by sheer force of will until their bodies separated from their minds. Had they thought of what they were enduring, they could not have kept going.

I'd make a damned good soldier, she decided, ignoring the pain in her swollen, blistered hands. If there is another war, God forbid, I'll take the king's shilling. Better than returning to Miss Pipcock's School, at any rate, and I much prefer the company of men.

Especially this man. Ash Cordell. When the mountain closed around her and sucked her breath from her lungs, his ineffable calm held the demons away. She fed from his strength and drew air from his quiet confidence. Found the will to keep moving.

The tunnel had lowered again, and soon she was forced to bend double at the waist. It was harder on Ash, several inches taller than she, but his pace never slowed.

She began to make a list of the first things she'd do

when they escaped. Hot bath. Sleep. Hot meal. Sleep. Hot fire, and she'd sleep in front of it. But before all that, Ash would go after Jervase, and she would go with him. Maybe he'd take a carriage, and she could sleep on the way.

The tunnel grew larger, and she was able to stand again. It didn't matter much, since she had to bend in order to check for an opening near the floor. And when she found one, she'd moved past it by several yards before realizing what had happened.

"Ash!" She dropped to hands and knees, scuttling backward until she found the opening again. Instantly he was beside her, and she directed his hand to the empty space.

It was small, crusted at top and bottom with deposits of lime. But she could crawl inside, if she kept her head down. It would be a tighter fit for Ash, perhaps impossible with his wide shoulders, but only one of them had to get out and find help. With men and equipment, the debris at the front entrance could be removed.

"Ventilation shaft," he said. "It must be blocked at the other end. The air is no fresher here."

"Maybe only dirt and pebbles. I'll go see."

"Glenys—"

"I'm smaller."

"Yes. But how am I to know if you get in trouble? We'll both go."

"Not a good idea. You rest. If this doesn't work out, you can take the next shaft. Sound carries in the caves, so if I shout, you'll hear me."

"Not good enough. Remember Ariadne? Take off your dress."

She understood immediately and stripped down to her chemise. Ash began ripping the skirt at the hem, creating an ever-lengthening band of fabric. Sometimes it split, and he tied the ends in knots. As he fed the material to her, she wrapped it in a tight ball.

"This may not be long enough," he said. "If you run out, signal me and I'll come in behind you. Give five sharp tugs, pause, and five more. Got it?"

"Aye, sir."

"On your way, then." He gave her a last, swift hug. "Don't take chances, love. And for God's sake, don't get stuck."

Glenys headed into the narrow channel, on fire with hope. Burning hotter because he had called her "love."

It was casual. Meaningless. She knew that.

Or the word had escaped the guard he maintained over his feelings. In the excitement, perhaps he had spoken a truth without realizing it.

Later she'd consider the implications, if there were any. Right now it was all she could do to crawl ahead.

Her bare knees fell, always, on jutting lumps of limestone. Sometimes she had to slither on her belly for several yards. Ash would be torn to pieces if he tried to come through. Men must have been smaller in Roman days, when the shaft was carved out. Centuries of dripping water had created a barrier of stalagmites and stalactites, some of them sharp as needles.

She unwound her ball of fabric as she went, praying it would not run out. It grew smaller and smaller. She smelled blood, and knew it came from her hands and knees. Oh please, God, she begged. Oh please.

Her forehead struck rock.

35

Ash felt the tugs on the line wrapped around his hand. Five. Pause. Five.

He plunged into the narrow shaft.

There were places he was sure he'd not be able to pass, but he managed to wriggle through them. Limestone shredded his hands and knees and shoulders. He thought it must be tearing off his hair. And he shuffled ahead, refusing to think about Glenys in trouble.

She had only run out of their makeshift rope. When he caught up with her, they would continue together.

"Glenys," he called, so breathless the sound must not have reached her. But he heard a reply, or imagined he did, and moved all the faster.

Her voice came again, more clearly. "Ash! I see light!"

He stopped for a moment, heart pounding. *Light.*

Minutes later he was close enough to sense her just ahead of him. But he couldn't see her. If there was an opening to the outside, it must be small indeed. The channel had heightened, though, enough that he could crawl without bumping his head. Soon he'd made his way to the end.

"Look!" She moved aside, and he discerned the barest speck of light. "There must have been a landslide. I've been pushing at the rocks, but they won't move."

"The devil they won't! Let me in front of you." He lay flat. "Slide back over me."

She put her feet atop him and slithered over his body. Then he moved forward and began shoving at the rocks. Sure enough, they refused to budge.

He would do better, he decided, to use the greater strength in his legs. It required several minutes of twisting and squirming in the narrow shaft, but finally he sat with the soles of his bare feet pressed against the stones. "Glenys, put your back to mine for leverage."

She was able to make the turn more easily, and he felt her slender shoulders pressed against his. "Dig in and hang on," he advised. With all his power he pushed at the rocks. Nothing. He pushed again, and again, and again.

"Rest," she said.

He obeyed, and started up once more. The stones were too heavy, and he too weak after the long ordeal in the cave. But there was no choice, so he rested and pushed, rested and pushed.

And felt the slightest movement. Only a little, but the speck of light was a slice wider. The stale air seared his lungs as he breathed heavily and pushed again.

He could see the sky.

Only the tiniest hint of blue, and a sliver of sunlight. But after hours of blackness, the light dazzled his eyes. His head swam. "Almost there," he remembered to tell Glenys. "Hold tight."

With a last mighty kick, one heavy stone rolled away.

Light flooded the narrow shaft. He leaned against Glenys and felt her fingers cover his right hand.

"You did it," she murmured.

"We," he panted. "*We.* But we're not out yet."

The other rocks moved more easily, those that moved at all. Two refused to give way. Glenys would be able to worm her way through, but he was too large.

"Move back," he told her. "I'll stretch out again so you can get to the opening."

She made her way over his chest, past his legs, and squeezed through the narrow portal. He heard a jubilant cry.

Glenys was safe. All of a sudden, every muscle in his body went limp. He lay on the jutting spines, a bed of limestone nails, and gave thanks. She would send help. Someone would come for him. Meantime, with the sunlight pouring in, warm on his feet, he could sleep.

Glenys pinched his toe. "I'll dig from this side," she said. "One of the rocks is tangled up in some roots. Be ready to kick again when I tell you."

He should have known she'd not desist until they were both free. Glenys could give a mule lessons in obstinacy. He sat up, grinning. She would probably say the same about him. Through the small opening he watched her face, screwed up with concentration as she dug out the roots with a sharp-edged stone.

Dear God but she was beautiful.

He'd always thought her so, in a way that did not correspond to usual standards of beauty. No portrait could capture her elusive charm. But she shone.

Like the sun, she wrested life from earth and water. Hope from a man who had forgot how to laugh, until she reminded him how good it felt.

"Kick!" she ordered.

He scrunched forward, planted his feet on the rock, and pushed.

She went back to work with her stone shovel, lower lip clenched between her teeth. He looked at her with affection. With love.

"Try again," she told him.

He did, and this time the rock fell away.

Feet first, he propelled himself out of the cave.

Glenys threw herself on top of him, laughing joyously. He wrapped his arms around her, laughing too. And then he kissed her, long and hard.

"Oh my," she murmured when he released her. "Don't be too hard on Jervase when you find him. I'd gladly crawl through his damned cave again for another kiss like that one."

"If you are angling for kisses," he said huskily, "I prefer your game with the croquet balls."

"As you wish." She gave him a radiant smile. "Either way, I seem to wind up in cold water."

"Up, my girl." He struggled to his feet and lifted her by her elbows. "We still have a long way to go."

"Do you know where we are?"

He made a complete turn, surveying the landscape, and pointed to a high crest. "That is Mam Tor. You'd have seen it from the other side when you were in Castleton. We'll head in that direction and then circle toward Edale. One of my men has family there. Better if no one sees us, Glenys. For one thing, I'd rather Jervase not get wind we are alive. For another, you are all but naked."

She glanced down at the thin, water-soaked chemise adhering to her flesh like paint. It reached only to mid-thigh and concealed nothing. "Oh dear," she said.

"Exactly." He peeled off his shirt. "Wear this."

Ignoring the shirt he held out, her eyes focused on a spot under his left arm. "You are bleeding! What happened?"

"It's nothing. A scratch. I hurt all over, and so do you. Put this on and let's find some help."

He struck out in the direction of the one landmark he recognized.

Glenys darted back to the cave and retrieved her ball of fabric, tearing with her teeth to free it from the length that reached deep into the tunnel. Then she put on Ash's shirt. Sodden and blood-streaked, it failed to cover her nakedness to any effect, but she was more concerned about his wound.

Hurrying to catch up with him, she grappled his arm. "Wait. Just for a moment. Please."

He held still long enough for her to wrap the bandage around his chest. Then he moved on, without a word, and she knew he was conserving every ounce of strength. Blood caked and dried on his shoulders under the weak November sun. It hurt just to look at him.

But they were alive. Free. Soon, Ash could go wherever he wanted and do whatever he chose, without fear of a bullet cutting him down. She remembered to offer a prayer of thanks.

As her limbs began to thaw, she felt the sharp rocks on the path cut into her feet. Who would have imagined that pain could feel so good? Pain, sunlight, and the call of birds in her ears. *Anything* but cold and dark and dripping water!

They had gone barely a mile when Ash stopped and pushed her behind him. On tiptoe, Glenys peered over his shoulder. A horse picked its way down the rocky

slope of a hill across from where they stood. As it came
to the narrow track, the rider raised his arms to show
that his hands were empty.

She recognized the man who had followed them to
the dead end in the cave. The man who had not
betrayed them to Jervase. She felt Ash relax, slightly.

"Wait here," he said. "I mean it, Glenys." He strode
toward the rider, who dismounted and came forward,
leading the horse.

She followed, of course. It never occurred to her not
to go with him. And she wanted to hear what they said
to one another.

"Milord." The man stopped, head lowered. His face
blazed scarlet in the morning light.

"Where are the others?" Ash demanded harshly.

"T-Two of 'em went home to Buxton. As for the gentlem'n and Willows, I dunno. They never said."

"Did you see which direction they took?"

"East, sort of. Inter the hills. Not wantin' anybody to
see 'em, I trow." He reached into his pocket.

Ash's muscles bunched for a leap, but the man
pulled out something small. He opened his hand, and
she saw the glint of gold coins.

"This is what he paid me, sir. I canna keep it.
Brought it to you."

"Blood money." Ash shook his head when the man
tried to give him the coins. "Put them in the poor box at
your church, if you have a church."

"I do, sir. We go Sundays, me an' m'wife and children. Got seven. Thing is, the mine where I worked
shut down. Been hard for them, me with no job 'cept
now and again. Then, last spring, the gentlem'n came
by a pub where I was drinkin' and said he needed
some'un to show him the caves. Said he was an
explorer. So I hired on."

He stared at the coins, his face shadowed with misery. "I was with 'im when he shot the big man. Didn't know he were gonna do it. Said he carried a rifle 'cause he liked to hunt and mebbe we'd see a stag. After, he told me I'd be hung lessen I kept m'mouth shut."

"That did not," Ash said in a lethal voice, "prevent you from taking up with him again for this latest *exploration*."

"Swore he'd turn me in to the constable, secret-like, if I didn't help. I wuz scared, m'lord. For m'children."

"Who would be pleased, no doubt, to claim a murderer as their father. What is your name and where do you live?"

At first Glenys thought he wouldn't answer. But he pulled himself straighter and lifted his bearded chin. "William Barry, of Little Hucklow."

"I once encountered another man who couldn't find work," Ash said coldly. "He thought to rob me in order to provide for his children. I shot him."

Barry closed his eyes. "I unnerstand, sir."

"Do you?" Ash glanced over his shoulder at Glenys.

She stared back, confused and infuriated. The man had saved their lives, for heaven's sake! But Ash was angry too, and she bit her lip to keep from interfering.

He turned again to William Barry. "Why did you come here? Planning to dig us out?"

"No, m'lord. I'd not have done that. But I hoped you'd come upon the shaft. And if you did, you was bound to find me sooner or later. Guess I'd rather it be sooner."

"You would have left us there to die?"

Barry nodded wretchedly.

"You might have lied. I might even have believed you."

"I canna think so, sir."

Ash barked a short laugh. "Dear God. An honest coward."

"There's men lookin' for you, m'lord, over by to Winnats Pass. You better take m'horse." He held out the reins.

"I also require your coat, for the young lady."

After the first glance, Barry had carefully avoided looking at her. He stripped off his rough woolen coat and handed it to Ash.

"Go home, William Barry, and reflect on your crimes. Speak to no one of this matter. Not a word. I have unfinished business with my cousin, but when that is done with, I'll see to finding you a job."

"M'lord?"

"You heard me. Now get out of here before I change my mind."

In spite of the warning, Barry held still another moment, kicking at a stone with his boot. "I'm sorry, sir. For the man that was killed, and what happened to you and the young lady." Then he turned, head bowed, and moved slowly away.

Glenys looked at his broad back, remembering her thin, sickly father. Reflecting on the desperation that drove both men to crime, and the weakness of character that oiled their paths. Good and evil, all mushed together again. The final accounting on Judgment Day was going to be a major challenge, even for God.

Ash tossed her the coat and she stuffed her arms into the scratchy sleeves, which reached well beyond her fingertips.

His expression was grim. She thought it best to keep quiet until he calmed a bit. In the past, when she'd seen him angry, he was cold and aloof and forbidding. This rage was different. He looked like a man who wanted to hit someone. Jervase.

But Jervase wasn't here, so he'd nearly struck out at William Barry. She had seen the tightly clenched fists

and the stiff shoulders. Had she been standing in front
of him, she would have seen what Barry saw—eyes
blazing with murderous intent.

Being Ash, though, he had controlled himself. And
chosen the path of mercy, although it must have galled
him to do so.

He swung into the saddle and held out his hands.
She went to him, and he lifted her across his thighs.
One arm around her waist and the other holding the
reins, he chucked the sluggish horse into a canter.

36

Ash leaned his head against the pillow that Glenys had tossed into the carriage. Wilfred Baslow lived in north Suffolk, near a town named West Coney. A hundred fifty miles from Ravenrook. He intended to travel straight through, stopping only to change horses.

There was no guarantee Wilfred would be there when he arrived, of course. Or that Jervase was also on the way to West Coney. The two conspirators might have planned to rendezvous in London, or just about anywhere in England.

But his instincts clamored for Suffolk. He'd have set out directly from Winnats Pass, on horseback, but Geoff overruled him. The men who'd been searching the area needed fresh mounts. Glenys required an escort back to Ravenrook. And there were plans to be made.

Geoff was right, as usual.

He hadn't been thinking clearly. After six years of hell, with the end blessedly in sight, he must take care. One rash blunder could put Jervase beyond his reach.

He agreed to return home, but only long enough to coordinate an organized search.

Within an hour of arriving, he'd dispatched men to London—one for Bow Street to set Runners after Jervase, another to Devonshire House in case Wilfred hadn't left. The servants Geoff had trained, most of them former soldiers, would fan out to check ships departing from the major port cities.

The magistrates in Derby and Sheffield had been alerted. Men were asking questions in the small towns of north Derbyshire, because Jervase would not travel far without a drink. Three men were on their way to Buxton, where two of his accomplices resided. A search was mounted for the post chaise Glenys had hired and the body of the luckless postilion. The boy's family must be found and notified.

When Ash satisfied himself that nothing more could be done, he submitted to the tight-lipped Mrs. Beagle. She cleaned his wounds, dabbed them with basilicum ointment, and wrapped a clean bandage around the gaping slice under his arm.

Over Geoff's continuing objections, he refused to wait at Ravenrook while other men pursued the chase. That meant he was forced to deal with Glenys, who claimed her right to be in at the finish. He was equally determined to leave her behind. They were both exhausted and out of temper, and it had been an ugly scene.

Even now he could not be sure he'd won. When had he ever given Glenys an order and been obeyed? When did Glenys listen to *anyone?* She had promised Geoff to stay on the ship until it sailed, and then arranged for the pilot's boat to take her off in the harbor.

Devious, conniving, impossible female.

He made her give her word she'd not leave Ravenrook until he returned. He said that if he met up with Jervase in person, which wasn't likely, fear for her safety would put him at risk. To his surprise, that argument seemed to convince her. She touched his cheek, looked into his eyes, and pledged to wait for him to come back. If her vow concealed a trap, he'd not detected it.

Ash returned his thoughts to Jervase as the carriage rocked and swayed on the back-country road. Three of Geoff's best men were scouting ahead, calling in at pubs and posthouses. Jervase was smart enough to stay off the main roads, so they focused on obscure byways.

Ash had studied a map and chosen his route with care. He put himself in Jervase's place, imagining what he would do if he'd just killed two people, had to meet up with the man who would pay him, and then escape the country.

Geoff and four other bodyguards escorted the coach. Harry rode with them. There was nothing more to consider, Ash decided as his eyes closed. Soon it would be dark. God, he was tired.

Someone was shaking him. "Ash!" a voice said. "Wake up."

He forced his eyelids apart and gazed blankly at Geoff. The coach had stopped, he realized. Geoff's shoulders were white.

"Merton located the man you described, the one traveling with Jervase. He's drinking in a taproom about three miles from here."

At that, Ash shot fully awake. "And Jervase?"

"Not sure. Merton didn't want to spook the man by asking questions, so he came directly here."

Ash put on his hat, gathered the folds of his heavy woolen greatcoat around him, and jumped down from the coach. It had begun to snow, which explained

Geoff's white shoulders. Six men on horseback circled near him, waiting for orders. He looked at Harry's face. The boy's long lashes were clumped with ice, but his mouth curved in an eager smile.

Harry, scenting a fight, wanted desperately to be part of it. So much for commandeering his horse, which Ash had planned to do.

In the warm light of the coach lanterns, the snow was a drizzle of gold. He beckoned to Merton, who described the exterior of the ramshackle inn. He'd gone no farther than the taproom, where three locals swigged ale and talked with the proprietor. Jervase's man sat at a corner table, alone.

"Pretty much foxed," Merton reported. "Won't give us any trouble."

"Good work. I'd let you get warm in the carriage, but we'll need you to show the way." Ash turned to John Fletcher. "You stay with the coach, John. I require your horse."

He directed the driver to keep to the road and proceed slowly. "With luck, we'll rejoin you about the time you arrive at the inn. When you've gone three miles, find a place to pull out of sight and wait for us."

Ash rode side by side with Merton, quizzing him for more details. Geoff, Harry, and three other men followed. Despite the snow, he felt almost on fire. Jervase was at the pubhouse. He could smell it.

When they came near the Ploughman's Inn, he gathered everyone in a copse of oaks fifty yards from the entrance. "Brady and Yarrow, go inside and escort our friend here with a minimum of disturbance. Unless you spot Jervase. In that case, have a drink, make some noise about getting home, and leave."

Five minutes later, they returned with Jervase's accomplice in tow. Ash recognized the man named

Willows. So drunk he could barely stand, Willows dropped to his knees when the men let him go. Then, with effort, he lifted his head and caught sight of Ash.

"Bloody shit!"

"Seen a ghost?" Ash inquired mildly. "I hope it sobered you enough to answer a few questions. Where is Jervase?"

Willows blubbered incoherently.

Ash grabbed him by his greasy hair. "I remember you, gallows-bait. You tried to bury me alive. You helped my cousin brutalize an innocent woman. But I don't give a damn what becomes of you, so long as you lead me to Jervase Cordell. Tell me where he is and you might live another hour or two."

"Upstairs. B-Bedroom."

"Alone?"

"Last I saw him. Might've p-pulled in a wench. Usually does."

"Has the room a window overlooking the front of the inn?"

That question befuddled the man. "Dunno. Don't think so. Saw a river, a little one, from his window."

Ash let him go. Jervase must have a room at the rear and would not see them approach. "Merton, keep company with our friend. The rest of you, come with me."

He strode purposefully into the taproom, sent one man to guard the rear exit, left another to watch the front, and approached the landlord. Once a sovereign had crossed his palm, the landlord was heartily willing to point out the room Jervase had taken for the night.

"I don't want no trouble," he muttered from the stairwell. "Run an honest place, I do."

"If there is trouble, you will be well paid to clean up after it," Ash assured him. "Is the door locked?"

"No keys here, sir."

Geoff came up beside Ash. "How do you want to handle this?"

"Alone. Jervase is mine."

"But—"

"Wait outside, Geoff, in the passageway. I have my pistol. You will leave this to me."

Grumbling under his breath, Geoff moved to the other side of the bedchamber door and signaled Harry to take up a position opposite him.

Ash stood for a moment, gathering his concentration. Then he raised the latch, flung the door open, and stepped inside.

At the sudden noise, Jervase lifted up from the pillows. He was sitting against the headboard of a narrow bed, puffing on a pipe. The sweet scent of opium permeated the small, squalid room. An empty wine bottle was overturned on a side table next to him.

He peered at Ash from dilated eyes. "By God! You're supposed to be dead."

Ash closed the door. "But as you once told me," he said softly, "I am damnably hard to kill."

"So you are. I don't suppose you've come here by yourself?"

"Not this time. There are men in the hallway and at all exits. It's over, Jervase."

"Damn." He drew deeply from his pipe. "I'd have liked to best you, cuz. The devil knows I tried. But *chi non fa, non fall.* 'He who does nothing makes no mistakes.'"

"A lesson I too have recently learned. A young woman taught me. And because you hired a man to strangle her at Carlton, and because you drugged her with laudanum and threatened to have her raped, and because you shut her in a cave to die, I will stand directly in front of you when you are hanged. I'll look you in the eyes when you take your last breath."

Jervase waved a languid hand through the drifts of opium smoke. "Ah, but I'll *not* hang. I am a gentleman, or was. And you are the quintessential gentleman, Ash, honorable to your fingertips. You won't begrudge me a proper departure from this vale of tears. I require leave to put a gun to my head, and you will grant it."

"Think again, animal."

"Oh, but consider the disgrace. A Cordell dragged before the courts. Testimony from your bit of muslin. I'll put out that you bedded her in London, and doubtless at Ravenrook too. Lovely gossip." Jervase set his pipe on the side table. "As if your reputation could bear yet another scandal. If you are ever again to hold your head high, we end this now."

Jervase swung his legs over the side of the bed. As he did, Ash lifted his right arm.

When Jervase came to his feet, unsteadily, he held a pistol in his hand. "You ought to know by now I sleep with a gun at my waist. Well, maybe you did not. All my whores know it, though. The pistol holds two shots, as you probably recall from our sojourn in the cave. The second is for me, because I'll not swing while cits suck on oranges and laugh. The first—need I say?—is for you."

He raised the gun and sighted down the barrel. "Goodbye, cuz. I'll see you in hell."

Ash flicked his wrist and the pistol dropped from the sling into his hand. Without a qualm, he put a bullet in Jervase's heart.

His cousin's shot hit the ceiling. Jervase fell back on the bed and slid onto the floor, blood streaming from his mouth.

Ash didn't bother to look at him again.

An hour later, again settled in the carriage, Ash cleaned and reloaded his pistol.

Willows had verified Jervase's plan to meet with a gentleman in Suffolk. Geoff sent him off with Merton, who would turn him over to the nearest constable and report the incident at the Ploughman's Inn.

Next was the mastermind—the obsessed historian willing to put any number of people in their graves so he could dig up a buried treasure.

Slowed by the light snowfall, they arrived midmorning at Wilfred Baslow's small country house. It was much in need of repair. Only two servants lived there, an aging housekeeper-cook and her husband. Intimidated by the swarm of men who appeared at the door, the Geesoms were quick to give Ash free run of the place.

He wandered through the dusty rooms on the lower floor, every one of them lined with books. There were stacks of books on the worn carpets, chairs, window seats, and tables. He imagined Wilfred huddled among them, oblivious to his comfort as he pursued his quest for immortality.

Locating the room used as a study, Ash began to thumb through the books and papers piled on the enormous desk. It was impossible to tell what Wilfred had been working on. There were articles, penned in his crabbed writing, destined for historical journals. Letters to and from his many correspondents. Notes about a Roman villa uncovered in Hertfordshore. Nothing at all about barrows and buried riches, but he would not leave clues lying about in plain view.

Geoff appeared at the door, carrying a tray. "Mrs. Geesom made up pots of tea for the men. There's no food in the house, and Wilfred hasn't paid her wages the last six months."

"I'm not surprised. All the money was sucked from him by Jervase. Find out the location of the nearest pub and send the others to have a meal. Wilfred may not arrive today, and he'll be no threat if he does. Go with them, if you wish."

"Not a chance. Unless I miss my guess, Harry won't go either. He was smart enough to pack sandwiches and cold chicken in his saddlebags. Says there's enough to share with you."

Ash chuckled. Harry never went anywhere without a supply of food, although he remained slender as a wand. "I've no taste for a meal, but thank him. Make yourselves comfortable and let me know the minute you spot Wilfred."

When Geoff was gone, Ash sipped at his tea and continued rummaging through his uncle's papers. In a drawer, concealed under a false bottom, he located a map of the area where the barrows were located. They weren't marked, but Wilfred had drawn, with care, an outline of the territory he was to inherit. It was northeast of Ipswich, along the Deben River and estuary, in Sutton Parish.

Ash had never been there and was unaware his family owned the land until his father willed it away from him. Or nearly so, because it was currently held in trust for his son. Ash had no control of it, or he'd gladly have sold the parcel to Wilfred. Even given it to him, for Nora's sake.

He returned the map to its hiding place and closed the drawer. So far as he was concerned, whatever was buried on that land could stay buried another thousand years. Too many people had died in Wilfred's attempt to claim it, and too much of his own life had gone virtually to waste.

One day his son would own that bit of Sutton Parish. When he came of age, the trust would expire and he could do with the land as he wished. At some point, Ash knew, he'd have to decide whether or not to tell him about Wilfred's buried treasure—if it even existed. And if he ever had a son.

Late in the afternoon, Harry woke him from a heavy

sleep. Head resting on his folded arms, he had been dreaming he was buried in a cold dark cave.

"He's here!" Harry said exultantly. "Lord Killain is bringing him inside."

Ash sat up and combed his fingers through his hair. "I want to be alone with him. You and Killain wait somewhere out of earshot."

Looking disappointed, Harry withdrew. A minute later Wilfred Baslow appeared in the doorway. Geoff stood behind him. At Ash's nod, he stepped back and shut the door, closing the two men in the study.

Wilfred seemed infinitely older than the last time Ash had seen him, only days ago. Older, weary, and resigned. But when the man lifted his eyes, Ash saw the glint of madness Jervase had spoken of and wondered why he'd never recognized it before. Wilfred rarely looked directly at anyone, though. He always seemed part of the furniture, frail and musty as the worn books he read even when in company.

With obvious effort Wilfred pulled himself straighter, one hand planted against the wall for support. "What now, nephew? Will you kill me yourself? I presume that is why we are alone here."

"I'd like to," Ash confessed. "But no. I have a few questions before we turn you over to the magistrate. Sit down if you wish."

Wilfred stumbled to a chair, carefully placed the books on the floor, and lowered himself with a groan. "I expected to meet Jervase here, and that encounter would have been only a trifle less unpleasant than this one is apt to be. I've no money left to pay him with, and rather thought he would be angry enough to dispatch me. Have you come upon him?"

"Yes. He's dead."

"I'm not sorry to hear it. Loathsome fellow, Jervase."

"As are you." Ash tapped one finger on the desk. "Was Nora involved in your plot?"

Wilfred gave him an astonished glance. "Of course not. She despises me."

"I have misjudged her, then. She knew about the dinner at Carlton, where Glenys was attacked, so I assumed—"

"You were wrong. I overheard a conversation in the library, between your fiancée and her sister, and relayed the information to Jervase. He hired someone. It cost me the last of my ready funds, that misbegotten endeavor."

"It nearly cost Glenys her life!" Ash forced himself to stay on his chair behind the desk. He could not beat an old man, however much he longed to see pieces of him strewn across the floor.

"Nice girl," Wilfred observed. "She was kind to me. But really, everyone dies sooner or later. Some things are more important than the lives of an insignificant young woman and an aristocrat who has already antagonized half of society. I speak of *history*, Ashton."

"You speak of greed. Of your ambition to become a part of history by discovering a token from the past."

Wilfred's eyes shifted. "I'll not tell you where it is. Or *what* it is. If I am not permitted to uncover it, you will not." His fingers clawed into the arms of his chair. "The secret will die with me."

"I don't want your bloody treasure, uncle. Take your secrets to the grave and be damned."

Wilfred stared at nothing, his eyes vacant. "Since I was a boy, I dreamed of finding something important. I've spent fifty years searching records, following clues. Married Nora to finance excavations. All for nothing, until I chanced on the greatest discovery in England. Only to find that my own brother-in-law held title to the land where it was buried. And he wouldn't give it to me, or sell it. He always despised me. Said I was too bookish. Not a real man."

Ash had heard that same lecture often enough. His father sometimes compared him to Wilfred. Once, in a rage, he said his wife must have bedded his brother-in-law. How else to explain why Ash turned out like that useless stick instead of a true-blooded Cordell male?

Wilfred lurched to his feet and began pacing the room. "Then you got in trouble with him, for your war investigations, and I put a flea in his ear. Told him to will the land away from you. I think he did it just to shut me up. But he didn't do it right. I wouldn't get it if you had a son. Not right."

In his agitation, Wilfred kicked over a stack of books. "When he told me about the trust, I knew the only solution was to see you dead. I expect you know the rest."

"Most of it. You hired Jervase to do the dirty work, and he has bled you dry ever since. Now it's finished." Ash stood. "I know you are tired from the trip north, but I've no wish to remain here. You may ride in my coach, under guard, to Derby. The magistrate will determine the proper jurisdiction for your trial."

Wilfred held out his arms. "No trial. Let me die here, with honor."

"You lived without it, uncle. And frankly, I doubt you've the mettle to put a gun to your head. Nor will I give you a weapon."

"Not a gun. Poison. I have some, in my luggage. Prussic acid." He laughed harshly. "I was going to use it on Nora at Devonshire House. Needed the rest of the family fortune, the part she controls, to pay Jervase and see to the excavations when I inherited the land. But you enclosed her in her room after the fiasco at Carlton. I couldn't get to her."

Ash whistled softly between his teeth. Wilfred had

planned to kill Nora! Dear God. Only his own misguided suspicions had kept her safe. A lucky mistake on his part. But she would be caught up in the aftermath of her husband's crimes, for all she had never lived with him. She'd be called to give evidence at a trial. Her position in society was bound to suffer.

He rubbed the back of his neck. Bloody hell. He didn't want to play judge and jury in this matter. Killing Jervase had been self-defense. He had no choice then, although he was privately glad to have been the instrument of the bastard's demise. Perhaps his conscience would trouble him later, but he rather expected not.

"Let me take the poison," Wilfred begged. "It will be so much simpler for everyone."

And that, Ash knew, was without question. He had to think of Nora, and Glenys, and the others. A long trial, with the inevitable publicity and gossip, would drag this out for months.

He looked at Wilfred's sunken face and blank eyes. Sometimes, it was better to walk away.

So many years he had spent tracking the killers. And when he faced them at last, Jervase and Wilfred, the encounters were so very brief. What was there to say, after all? His throat felt scalded with words, but they turned to soot before they reached his tongue.

Glenys would tell him not to waste another moment on a past that could not be changed. She would turn him around and point him to the future.

He went to the door. "I will search your bags for weapons, uncle, before bringing them here. Then I'll leave you alone for one hour. Do what you must. If you are alive when I return, we head out for Derby."

37

Glenys rattled around the house, irritated because the snow kept her indoors and furious with herself for permitting Ash to leave without her.

Not that he gave her the slightest choice in the matter. And she had been so awfully tired. When he was gone, she crawled into bed and slept the clock around.

She spent the next two days prowling through his library, looking for an erudite book to impress him with her taste in reading. And one interesting enough to distract her. It was heavy going, what with so many of the tomes written in foreign languages. She wondered if the man ever read a book for pleasure.

And she worried about him constantly. Until Wilfred and Jervase were in custody, Ash could fall victim to a lucky shot. Or spend more years tracking them down, because he would never rest until they were brought to justice.

Were it left to her, she'd put a knife through their black, shriveled hearts.

Glancing out the window, she saw that it had finally stopped snowing. A pale winter sun lit the sky. Glenys returned *An Account of Greek Rites and Customs* to the shelf and sped upstairs for halfboots, gloves, and cloak.

The air, bitingly cold, nipped at her cheeks and ears and nose as she crossed the wide lawn. Ankle deep in snow, she skirted the frozen lake and headed for the hill where Papa and Charlie lay under a mantle of white.

"No flowers today," she told Charlie, patting the stone cross that marked his grave. "Hullo, Papa. I hope you are watching out for Ash." She brushed snow from his headstone and read the simple words Charlie had carved there. JOHN SHEA. YOU WERE LOVED.

"It's nearly over," she promised. "When Ash comes home, all will be well. Then you can truly rest."

Sunlight glistened on the snowy fields. The stark, leafless trees sparkled under a glaze of ice. Glenys lifted her cloak and began to whirl in circles, dipping and swaying, discharging her pent-up energy in a giddy waltz.

She thought of her dance with Ash in the cave, their feet numb in the arctic water as they warmed each other with their bodies. Laughed together. Teased one another. In the darkness, they had created light.

Breathless, she staggered to a dizzy halt, clutching Papa's headstone for balance. She thought she saw him then, Ash, striding up the hill toward her. The capes on his greatcoat fluttered in the breeze.

Shielding her eyes against the glare of sunlight on snow, she looked again. He was still there, closer now, moving steadily in her direction. He lifted a hand and waved.

"Ash!" She pelted down the hill and flung herself into his open arms. He held her, rocking her back and forth as she blubbered into his neckcloth. "You're really here. What happened? Is it over? Are you hurt?"

He detached one arm, lifted her chin with his finger, and kissed her soundly. Then he set her back and gazed warmly into her eyes. "I am here and perfectly fine, if a bit repellent after four days of travel in these clothes. And yes—it is over."

"Oh, heavens. You must be exhausted." She took him by the hand and hauled him toward the house. "I'll see you have a bath, and food, and a fire. A good sleep too, but first you must tell me everything. I know I should let you rest first, but I cannot."

Laughing, he took her arm in his. "Slow down, imp. I stopped at the house only long enough to find out where you'd gone. No doubt you are impatient to hear the end of the story, and so you shall. Every last detail. You have earned the right to know even the parts I'd prefer to withhold."

By the time they reached the house, he had dutifully recounted his meetings with Jervase and Wilfred, and the outcome of both.

"I'm *glad* they're dead!" she declared when he was finished. "I only wish I'd been the one to make sure of it."

"Bloodthirsty wench. But I'll not pretend I'm sorry to escape the thorns of two scandalous trials, followed by two public hangings. There will be legalities and turmoil enough, and gossip too, but we'll come off lightly."

Fortescue took their coats and gloves when they stepped inside. Ash requested a fire and a meal in the salon. "Something simple and quick," he added. "Right now I could eat stewed thistles. Glenys, will you join me?"

"Yes, indeed. I'm exceptionally partial to thistles."

"I'll join you in a few minutes. First, there is something I must attend to in my study."

She trailed behind him, unwilling to let him out of her sight. Even with four days' growth of beard and shadows under his eyes, he was the most beautiful thing she had ever seen.

Tired as he was, a heavy burden had been lifted from his shoulders. He walked with a lighter step. His eyes glowed with new purpose. He had reclaimed his life.

"I might have known," he said when she followed him into the study. "Have a seat, then, while I write a letter to Nora. She should hear the news from me. And she has been imprisoned in her room at Devonshire House for nearly two weeks. Will she forgive me, do you think?"

"Of course. You are a man. She expects you to behave like an idiot."

"Ah. I needn't wait for her to rake me over the coals. You will do it for her."

She chuckled. "Write the letter, Ash. And don't be too humble. She won't believe you've gone meek and apologetic overnight. Will you tell her Wilfred planned to murder her at Devonshire House?"

"Certainly not."

When he'd dispatched the letter with a footman, Ash led her into the salon. A fired blazed in the hearth and two wing chairs were angled in front of it. On a low table was spread enough food for six people. Beside one of the chairs was a smaller table with wine and brandy.

Ash peeled off his rumpled coat, waistcoat, and cravat. "Do you mind? I've a shameless desire to be comfortable."

Glenys waved a hand. So far as she was concerned, he could remove all his clothes. She rather wished he would.

He dove into the food, eating with habitual good manners although he didn't pause to make polite conversation. Only once, as he poured a fresh cup of coffee, did he answer two of the several hundred questions burning on her tongue. "Killain is still in Suffolk, dealing with the authorities. I expect him here within a day or two. Harry is upstairs. Fast asleep by now."

As he continued eating, Glenys nibbled at the edges of a ham-and-cheese sandwich. She ought to be rejoicing because Ash was safe. Free to make a new life for himself. And she was. Truly. Six months ago, an hour ago, she would have insisted that his happiness was the only thing in the world she cared about. It would have been the truth.

But what was to become of her now? Selfish creature, to fret about her own fate as if it mattered. Ash would make sure she need never worry about money. With Jervase and Wilfred dead, there was no reason to hide herself in America. Wherever she went and whatever she did, it would be far better than the life she had faced before meeting him.

And no life at all, now that she *had* met him. Now that she loved him. Oh damn.

She had an idea, though. It had simmered in her mind ever since she came upon *An Account of Greek Rites and Customs* in his library. What she read, what Lady Nora had told her, and what Ash had taught her, all came together in a sudden blaze of awareness.

It couldn't last, her prospective career. But while it did, it would be heavenly. And when it was over, she'd resign herself to the barren years ahead. Perhaps Lady Nora would teach her to paint.

Ash wiped his lips with a napkin and glanced at her. "You haven't eaten, Glenys."

"I had a large meal at lunch." She went to the bellpull, and servants quickly appeared to remove the tray. When they were gone, she tugged an ottoman in front of Ash's chair. "Put your feet up and relax."

With a sigh of pleasure, he crossed his ankles and leaned his head against the padded chair. "I'm certain you are brimming over with questions, my dear. Fire away."

She took a poker and jabbed it at the flaming logs. Sparks shot over the flagstone hearth. Where to begin?

"Harry rode back with me in the carriage," Ash said. "We discussed his future. He wishes to breed and train horses."

"That's a step up. Last time I spoke with him, he wanted to be an ostler."

"So he told me. I said he could aspire higher than stablehand if he agreed to more schooling with a tutor. Harry continues to speak like an urchin from the streets unless he minds himself carefully. If he behaves, I'll see him apprenticed to a trainer. Eventually I'll give him responsibility for a piece of land and money enough to buy mares and a stallion. It will be a good investment on my part. I expect Harry to breed the finest horses in England."

She set the poker against the fireplace. "It's what he's always dreamed of."

"He seemed pleased," Ash agreed. "Then he fell asleep and dreamed of God knows what. Your brother snores up a storm, Glenys."

"Do tell." She sat on the ottoman. He started to move his legs, to give her more room, but she put a hand on his knee. "And what of me, Ash? What will you do with me?"

His eyes glowed like green fire. "Whatever will make you happy, if it is within my power. What do *you* dream of, Glenys Shea?"

"Oh, that the heavens will open and shower riches

upon me. Sometimes, I dream even more fanciful whimsies. But we must be practical, I suppose. And as it happens, I do know precisely what I want."

His eyes narrowed. "Why do I fear you've devised yet another outrageous scheme?"

"Because I have. You read me all too well these days, which is most annoying. I cannot slip anything past you."

"If only that were true," he said with a dramatic groan. "Am I meant to guess, or will you tell me what you have in mind?"

"Oh, aye." Her fingers tightened on his knee. "I want to be your mistress."

He sat forward as if the chair had gone on fire. "I beg your pardon?"

"You heard me. Naturally you are shocked, but that will pass."

"You never fail to shock me," he muttered, subsiding again when she directed him with a wave of her fingers to lean back.

"I've reasoned it out, you will be pleased to know, according to strict rules of logic. Well, I'm not sure what those are, but I've reasons good enough. You require a wife of good breeding, and when you marry again, it must be to a woman you love. Such a paragon will not be easy to find. It will take time."

"Not at all. I—"

"Please. I'm not accustomed to being logical, and I'll lose my train of thought if you interrupt me. Now, where was I?"

"Wife. Long time to find one."

"Thank you. While you conduct the search, there will be the inescapable urgency. Bound to happen, for all your best intentions. And I'll not have you hanging about street fairs. You require a mistress."

Ash poured himself a drink.

"Ordinarily, I'd not consider myself a likely candidate. I've no beauty, and you already know I am inexperienced. But I learn quickly. And I'll not be expensive."

He choked on a swallow of wine.

"Really I won't. In fact, if I didn't require a place to live, I'd ask nothing at all." She poked a finger at his thigh. "I am a veritable bargain, Ash. Did you know that the courtesans in ancient Greece charged a fortune? The good ones, anyway. There was one, in Corinth, who demanded ten thousand drachmas from Demosthenes for one night. *One night!* Can you imagine?"

"I can't imagine how you came to know that."

"I read about her in one of your books. I expect she was exceedingly beautiful and knew all the ways to please a man. For that matter, I've no idea what a drachma is worth. In any case, if I put my mind to it, I can be a good mistress to you."

He lifted a brow. "Men do not choose mistresses for their minds."

"Smart men do," she countered immediately. "Besides, I recall a night when you wanted my body, such as it is. I cannot grow large breasts or change my face to something Raphael would want to paint, but I can please you. You will teach me how."

"Gladly." He set his glass on the table. "As you will teach me to please you."

Her heart jumped to her throat. He meant to have her. And without the argument she'd expected. "I will be everything you want me to be," she promised.

"I hope you mean that." He held out his arms. "Come here, Glenys."

With joy, she climbed onto his lap. He took her face between his hands. His eyes held her transfixed.

"I want you to be my wife," he said.

For a moment the room went dark. Her head swam. Then she managed to check the "Yes" forming on her lips and realized what he was doing. She ought to have foreseen it. Ash Cordell, bless his heart, could not do otherwise. And for his sake, she had no choice but to stop him. "I see," she said. "It's the honor thing."

"I beg your pardon?"

"You know. The gentleman's code. 'I spent all night with her in a cave, so now I must do the honorable thing and marry her.' That sort of balderdash."

"Not to put too fine a point on it, but what exactly does a young woman who lived most of her life at Miss Pipcock's School know about the gentleman's code?"

"I know *you*. Everything an honorable gentleman aspires to be, you are."

"Hardly. Or have you forgot a certain night at Devonshire House? A gentleman does not debauch a virgin, even if he is betrothed to her. And our betrothal was, at the time, a humbug."

"I shall never forget a single instant of that night, as well you know. Perhaps you violated the code, but under duress, since I practically ravished you. And it was, for you, a brief and reckless fall from grace. The very next morning you were back in usual fettle, all starch and decorum."

"What we did," he informed her mildly, "was not very different from what I'd been fantasizing about doing with you for months. The reality was better, of course."

"Truly? Oh my. I wonder if your fantasies were anything like mine." She felt herself blushing. "They were rather explicit, except for the parts I didn't know about."

"One day I'll expect you to tell me precisely what

you thought would occur. For some reason, it fascinates me. But now, shall we return to my question and your response?"

"It was no," she said after a moment.

"Ah. I hoped I had misheard you. But clarify, if you will. Do you refuse because you do not wish to marry me, or is this some misguided attempt to protect me from the consequences of my honor? Alleged honor," he corrected. "To my mind, I abandoned honor the day we met. Or perhaps it was sanity I left behind. God knows you have twisted me beyond all recognition. Led me to do things no gentleman would ever agree to."

"Which only proves I am no fit wife for you, Lord Ravensby. But you must admit I'd make an ideal mistress. I suit your ungentlemanly moods. I can fill the odd hours between proper social engagements. Mind you, I'll take myself off once you are wed. You are a man who will keep his marriage vows, and I'd not come between you and your wife. But in the meantime—"

"There *is* no meantime, infernal woman. You have delusions of being noble, to protect me from being falsely honorable. For once in my life, I don't give a bloody damn about propriety, honor, or anything at all but you and me. You more than me. Speak from your heart, Glenys. Do you *wish* to marry me?"

Once again she crunched a loud yes between her teeth. Why must he make this so difficult? "Good heavens, Ash, I'm not a complete moron. What female would *not* wish to be your wife? But you will find someone more suitable when our adventure together has faded from memory. A real lady, not a soldier's brat. She will fall in love with you as I did, and make you happier than I could ever do."

He looked absurdly pleased. A beautiful smile curved his lips.

Yes, my lord, you are off the hook, she told him silently. And at the moment, I am the most honorable person I've ever known. More even than you, because I am letting you go free when I could have you.

He picked up both her hands and gazed steadily into her eyes. "The devil of it is, Glenys Shea, only you have ever made me happy. You are the only one I trust to keep me that way. That is selfish, I concede, but we top-lofty aristocrats are accustomed to getting what we want. And I want a great many things from you. It was you who taught me to make lists, so here is mine."

He lifted her right hand to his lips and kissed it. "I want to take you everyplace you've ever dreamed of going and show you everything you've ever longed to see. I want to make love with you when the urgency strikes either one of us, day or night, wherever we may be. Well, perhaps not in public, although I rely on you to prevent a serious indiscretion. I cannot trust myself, as I have already proven."

He kissed her other hand. "I want to have children with you. A great many, if you don't mind. I want to see the universe through your eyes instead of my own. My eyes are blind, I have learned, to the beauty you discover everywhere. I want you to tease me, and teach me to laugh at myself. What else? Oh yes. I want you to read poetry to me in front of a fireplace, naked."

"Ash!"

"What's more, I want you to stand in a church and promise to obey me. After that, I want to watch you break that vow every time I tell you to do something without discussing it with you first. But I don't want that so very much, so feel free to obey me if it pleases you."

"W-Wait a minute. I have to promise to *obey* you?"

"It's one of the vows, yes."

"You are jesting."

He shook his head.

"Of all the things! I had no idea. But then, I've never been to a wedding. What happens when you give me an order I don't wish to follow, and I give you an order which goes against your command? When our orders contradict one another, which one of us breaks the vow?"

He took a moment to puzzle that out. Then he grinned. "I lost you for a moment, sweetheart. Permit me to add an item to my list. I want you to learn a bit of syllogistic reasoning. As for conflicting vows, it will not be a problem. Only the wife promises to obey."

"Holy hollyhocks!" She scowled at him. "A man wrote these vows, I presume?"

"No doubt. But don't let that trifling promise stop you from wedding me. We'll both know you don't mean it, and so will God. Neither He nor I would dare hold you to the impossible."

Her heart was turning great somersaults in her chest. Ash truly did want to marry her. The Earl of Ravensby and Glenys Shea, married.

No. She must be dreaming. He was wielding syllogistic reasoning against her, or something of the kind. She loved this man. She must on no account permit him to make such a sacrifice for the sake of his aristocratic honor. Or even for her sake. *Especially* for her sake.

"Is this because I helped you free yourself of Jervase and Wilfred Baslow? You owe me nothing for that, Ash. I wanted to help, more than I've ever wanted anything."

He put his hands on her shoulders and gave her a gentle shaking. "Have done with these absurd objections and heed me. I speak to you from my heart. Marry me, Glenys. Please, marry me."

She brushed a fall of hair from his eyes. Her hand lingered on his forehead, and then stroked down his cheek. Across his lips. "You have said what you want, Ash. You have not said what I must hear."

His wonderful eyes clouded for a moment and then grew bright again. "Oh. Of course. Forgive me. But I have never said the words before, unless I did so to my mother when I was a child. They do not come easily, you see. They are too new, and vastly unfamiliar. Never doubt I mean them, though. I love you, Glenys Shea." He kissed her deeply and whispered the words again into her mouth. "I love you."

"I almost believe it," she said when he set her back, searching her face for a decision. As if he could doubt that she would follow him again into the bowels of the earth. Fly with him to the moon if he took wing.

"Ah," he murmured. "You'll not trust me until I tell you in Latin. Is that it?"

She smiled.

He put one of her hands against his chest, over his heart, and brought the other to his lips. "Believe me now, *deliciae meae. Te amo.*"

Epilogue

Palma, Majorca, 1827

"*Papa, why do those men* have holes in their hair?"

Ash clamped a hand over his son's mouth and gazed helplessly at Glenys, who had her own hands full of a squirming two-year-old. Melanie, flirtatious and willful, fancied someone in the pew behind her.

The procession of brown-robed men, each holding a candle and tonsured in the way of Franciscan friars, moved slowly down the center aisle. When Geoff came even with their pew, he winked at his young namesake and brushed Melanie's hair fondly before continuing to the altar.

Today, Lord Killain would take his final vows, putting aside title and wealth for poverty, chastity, and obedience. The liquid sound of Gregorian chant filled the stone church. A sweet fragrance, of incense and flowers, wafted over the congregation.

As the service proceeded, Melanie began to squeal. When Glenys tried to hush her, the squeal became a loud wail of protest. Two small feet thumped against the wooden pew.

"I'll take her outside," Elaine whispered.

Gratefully, Glenys handed the child to Harry's wife and returned her attention to the altar. The rites were mysterious to her, but lovely. When Geoff spoke the solemn vows, she heard joy in his voice. Profound joy and a great peace, as though a wearisome journey had come to an end, freeing him to begin the adventure he'd longed for all his life. Tears gathered in her eyes.

She glanced at Ash and saw him blink away tears of his own. He hugged their son to his side. Harry looked over his shoulder from the front pew and smiled at her. Next to him, Lady Nora pulled out a handkerchief.

Thank you, Lord, she prayed silently. All is well now. We are so very happy. Thank you.

After the service, Geoff—Brother Lawrence, Glenys reminded herself—led them on a tour of the monastery gardens. The summer sun poured down like hot butter.

"How can you bear that scratchy robe?" she asked, untying the ribbons of her bonnet.

He laughed. "I like it well enough on winter nights when we sing Matins and Lauds. For the rest, it's by way of penance, I suppose. And I've sins aplenty to atone for. But come. There's an arbor just ahead, with shade and a fountain."

Ash, with Melanie asleep in his arms, walked with Elaine and Nora. Four-year-old Geoffrey, who had spotted a lizard, was in wild pursuit down a gravel path.

Glenys frowned. "Where is Harry?"

Ash and Brother Lawrence exchanged glances. Immediately suspicious, she planted herself in front of them with her hands on her hips. Ever since leaving

England, she'd been certain Ash and Harry were conspiring together. They spent too much time in private conversation, and sprang apart with guilty smiles whenever she appeared.

"What is going on, gentlemen? And no trumpery. You mustn't tell lies in a monastery."

"A surprise," Brother Lawrence ventured after a moment. "Look, here's the fountain. Why don't you sit on one of the benches, Glenys?"

Purple bougainvillea climbed white trestles and spilled over the grotto, providing shade from the glaring sun. A statue of St. Francis stood in the center of a marble fountain. In one hand the saint held a dish of water. Two birds were enjoying a cool bath.

"I think not," she said firmly. "What sort of surprise—Oh!"

Harry came into view, escorting an elderly woman. Her back was straight as a pikestaff and she stared straight ahead, never looking at Glenys.

Ash passed Melanie to Brother Lawrence and came to stand beside her. "Your grandmother, my love. Lady Esther Haversham."

It might have begun to snow, so cold she felt all of a sudden. "How *could* you, Ash?"

"It was Harry sought her out, soon after his wedding. Elaine encouraged him to reconcile with his family, or make the attempt. Now it's your turn."

"I won't speak to her. Take me away from here."

He wrapped an arm around her waist. "Lord Haversham died two years ago, and their only son was killed in the war. Lady Esther has no one, Glenys. Only her grandchildren, lost to her until Harry made a brave trip into Northumberland."

"*Lost?*" Glenys stamped her foot. "That old witch disowned her daughter. She wanted nothing to do with me or Harry. She paid for my schooling on the condition I never contact her again."

"Yes." He brushed a kiss on her cheek. "She is stubborn, rather like you. If you must, send her to the devil. But do it face-to-face. You were never a coward, Lady Ravensby. Your grandmother is tough as leather and can take whatever you hand out. Better a harsh clearing of the air than lingering bitterness, don't you think?"

"I think you and I will be clearing some air later this evening," Glenys said between her teeth.

Harry seated Lady Esther on a wooden bench and led his wife away. Melanie had got hold of the cord dangling from Brother Lawrence's waist and was chewing on it. To distract her, he mumbled something about newborn kittens in the stables. Nora followed in his wake.

"I'd better find our son," Ash said, "before he demolishes the monastery."

Within a minute Glenys was alone. Or nearly so. Her grandmother sat rigidly on the bench a few yards away.

"Oh, damn," she muttered. But what choice did she have? It was a long way from Northumberland to Majorca. If Lady Esther had come this far to meet her, she could walk a few steps into the arbor.

Lady Esther's voice exploded like a cannon shot. "You hate me, I daresay."

Startled, Glenys jumped a good two inches back.

"You've every right, of course. Don't think I'm here to change your mind. Harry told me you've sworn never to speak with me, and you need not do so."

Glenys might have spoken, but not a single word came to her tongue. In her bed at Miss Pipcock's School she'd often imagined a confrontation with her mother's parents. She told them, eloquently, that they were lower than reptiles for casting off their daughter because she'd fallen in love with a soldier.

Now she was speechless.

"In spite of my crimes," Lady Esther continued in a flat voice, "I wished to see you before I die. I do not expect your forgiveness. I only hope you will permit me to make the acquaintance of my great-grandchildren. Lord Ravensby said it must be your decision."

Against her will, Glenys moved closer. For all Lady Esther's stiff posture and cold demeanor, her lips trembled.

This isn't fair, she thought sourly. I don't want to be nice to her. She doesn't deserve anything from me. Because of her, Harry spent years on the streets of Liverpool. A wonder he lived to . . . to bring her here. To make his peace with her.

Oh Lord. Harry is so much more generous than I am. I want to scratch her eyes out.

She scuffed her foot against the ground. "We named our daughter Melanie, after *your* daughter."

"The child I threw away. I am a terrible old woman, as well you know. I deserve every bit of the acid in my throat and the nightmares that torment my sleep. Above all, the loneliness. I brought it upon myself, and Haversham was equally foolish. Our home became a prison for Melanie. We tried to mold her into an image of ourselves—austere and proud. She wanted to laugh and be happy, but we would not permit it. We drove her away."

Glenys fisted her hands. "She loved my father. John Shea was far more to her than a means of escaping you."

"Perhaps." Lady Esther cleared her throat. "I never thought so, until I met Harry. No one of pure north-country aristocratic blood would have survived what he endured. We are too inbred, you see. The wealthy families of Northumberland intermarried for centuries and watered us down to the likes of your grandfather and me.

Even Melanie lacked the courage to break away until she met her soldier. It took John Shea to produce a man of Harry's quality and a woman of your spirit. You'll not believe this, but I respect him now. And Harry, and you."

Lady Esther sat, impossibly, even straighter on the bench. "Will you allow me to meet young Geoffrey and Melanie?"

Damn. How could she do otherwise? The impossible old woman was her grandmother. Except for Harry and the children, her only living blood relative. She sighed. "Look you, Lady Esther. The men are trying to hide behind that tree."

"Terrified, I expect, that they'll have to pick up the pieces if we come to blows."

"It's tempting to worry them a bit longer, but you'll be wanting to hold Melanie in your arms. I only hope Geoffrey hasn't caught that lizard. If you hug him, be warned. It may be in his pocket."

She beckoned to Ash, who made it to her side in record time when he saw her smiling. "Lady Esther wishes to see the children," she said. "But it's awfully warm out here, even in the shade."

Brother Lawrence spoke up. "Nora and Elaine are in the parlor. It's a trifle cooler, and there is lemonade."

Harry assisted Lady Esther to her feet and they followed Brother Lawrence. As they moved away, Glenys saw Harry make a finger sign behind his back. *Thank you,* he said.

She turned to Ash and pulled him into the arbor. "What a devious man you are, bringing us together on holy ground. You knew I dare not turn her away."

"I didn't think you'd wish to, once you calmed down a bit."

"Well, you were right on all counts," she said

grumpily. "I've never stopped thinking about my mother's parents and wondering what became of them."

"A loose end, and a painful one. Often, I thought of suggesting you write to them, and should have done so before your grandfather died. Now he'll never know you forgave him."

"Of course he will. Souls continue on, somewhere. Somehow." She took his hand. "Shall we join the others?"

"We had better. I shudder to think what your son is up to by now."

"Why is he always *my* son when he gets into trouble?"

As they walked, Glenys nibbled at her lower lip and wrestled with her conscience. Finally she tugged Ash to a halt. "Shall we ask Lady Esther to come home with us? I'm sure she'd like to be at Ravenscourt when Elaine delivers her next great-grandchild."

"She is welcome, to be sure, for as long as you'd like her to stay. Perhaps until February, or have I miscalculated?"

She blinked. "How did you know?"

"I live with you, beloved. I sleep with you. I know the rhythms of your body." He grinned. "And I could scarcely mistake the fact you've lost your breakfast the last three weeks."

"The doctor says January or February. Are you pleased?"

"Oh, indeed. I'm even prepared to endure the needles of jealousy when you forget I exist. You always do, especially the last few months. Then you scream for hours, and I die a thousand deaths until the babe pops out. After that I cannot make love to you for weeks and weeks." He arched a brow. "Remind me why I want these brats, my dear."

"Because you adore them. Still, we should make more time together, just the two of us. You are my life, Ash Cordell."

"And you are mine. But we cannot be alone if you insist on bringing company wherever we go."

He put a hand against the slight swelling at her waist. "Hello in there, little one. I must warn you straightaway that your mother is a scamp. But you are bound to love her, almost as much as I do. Welcome to our family."

Author's Notes

Wilfred Baslow's treasure was, in fact, concealed under the largest of the barrows near the estuary of the River Deben in Sutton Parish.

The burial mounds were first recorded on maps in 1601. Dr. John Dee, an alchemist and court astrologer during the reign of Queen Elizabeth, may have been commissioned by Her Majesty to dig them up in search of riches. While there is no record that he followed through, there are certainly hints of early interest in the site.

The smaller barrows were plundered long before Wilfred took up his fictional quest, and robbers nearly broke through to the real treasure. Ten feet down and inches above their goal, the shaft caved in. The mound was then abandoned, and it remained unexplored for centuries.

In 1938, Mrs. Edith Pretty, owner of the estate, decided to excavate the two largest barrows. A year later the Sutton Hoo Ship Burial was finally uncovered. Scholars think it may have been the grave of Raedwald, King of the East Angles, who died around 625. The Anglo-Saxon treasure was presented by Mrs. Pretty to the British Museum.

When I saw the splendid collection, years ago, it seized my imagination. And when I went looking for a motive powerful enough to drive a gentle, scholarly man to murder, the treasure of Sutton Hoo came to mind. I revisited the exhibit in 1995, before heading north for Derbyshire.

At once remote and desolate, beautiful and terrifying, the High Peaks were an ideal setting for the reclusive Earl of Ravensby. I wandered the boggy moors and explored the dark wet caves. I climbed to the ruins of Peveril Castle (Sir Walter Scott misspelled Peverel in his novel, *Peveril of the Peak,* and the mistake is now "official"). I even bought a pendant, made of Blue John, for my charm bracelet.

For two days I roamed Chatsworth, mouth agape and breathless with wonder. The sixth Duke of Devonshire (Hart), who never married, left a splendid legacy indeed.

My last night in the Peaks, I slept at the Snake Inn.

Engravings show that it looks much like it did in 1822, when opened for business by John Longden, the first proprietor. Well, I expect he hadn't installed "Jungle World," a tacky indoor playground, nor was the exterior painted white with green trim. But the Snake Inn still stands alone on the turnpike road, now A57, and Kinder Scout looms above, shrouded in mist.

A primitive version of croquet (*paille maille*) was played as early as the fourteenth century. By the time of Charles II the game was so popular that what is now Pall Mall in London was originally a croquet court. The name "Pall Mall" derives from *palla mallens,* Latin for ball and mallet. Over the years, the rules grew more complex.

Interest fairly died out in the eighteenth century, but resurged in force about 1840 when wooden sets were manufactured by the thousands. The Victorians had a passion for croquet.

Meantime, it had been played continually on the Continent and, most particularly, in Ireland. For purposes of my story, I've assumed the game was enjoyed in 1822 England by those who learned it on their travels abroad.

If you play backyard croquet, know the game is a bit different in England. "Wickets" are called "hoops" there. The Brits use only six hoops, as opposed to our nine wickets, and trace a different route on their way to victory.

Whatever the exact rules in 1822, I'm sure Glenys found ways of exploiting them to harass her brother.

LYNN KERSTAN
P.O. BOX 182301
CORONADO, CA 92178-2301
E-MAIL:l.kerstan @ genie.com

Let HarperMonogram Sweep You Away!

Chances Are by Robin Lee Hatcher

Over 3 million copies of Hatcher's books in print. Her young daughter's illness forces traveling actress Faith Butler to take a job at the Jagged R Ranch working for Drake Rutledge. Passions rise when the beautiful thespian is drawn to her rugged employer and the forbidden pleasure of his touch.

Mystic Moon by Patricia Simpson

"One of the premier writers of supernatural romance."—Romantic Times. A brush with death changes Carter Greyson's life and irrevocably links him to an endangered Indian tribe. Dr. Arielle Scott, who is intrigued by the mysterious Carter, shares this destiny—a destiny that will lead them both to the magic of lasting love.

Just a Miracle by Zita Christian

When dashing Jake Darrow brings his medicine show to Coventry, Montana, pharmacist Brenna McAuley wants nothing to do with him. But it's only a matter of time before Brenna discovers that romance is just what the doctor ordered.

Raven's Bride by Lynn Kerstan

When Glenys Shea robbed the reclusive Earl of Ravensby, she never expected to steal his heart instead of his gold. Now the earl's prisoner, the charming thief must prove her innocence—and her love.

And in case you missed last month's selections . . .

Once a Knight by Christina Dodd

Golden Heart and RITA Award–winning Author. Though slightly rusty, once great knight Sir David Radcliffe agrees to protect Lady Alisoun for a price. His mercenary heart betrayed by passion, Sir David proves to his lady that he is still a master of love—and his sword is as swift as ever.

Timberline by **Deborah Bedford**

Held captive in her mountain cabin by escaped convict Ben Pershall, Rebecca Woodburn realizes that the man's need for love mirrors her own. Even though Ben has taken her hostage, he ultimately sets her soul free.

Conor's Way by **Laura Lee Guhrke**

Desperate to save her plantation after the Civil War, beautiful Olivia Maitland takes in Irish ex-boxer Conor Branigan in exchange for help. Cynical Conor has no place for romance in his life, until the strong-willed belle shows him that the love of a lifetime is worth fighting for.

Lord of Misrule by **Stephanie Maynard**

Golden Heart Award Winner. Posing as a thief to avenge the destruction of her noble family, Catrienne Lyly must match wits with Nicholas D'Avenant, Queen Elizabeth's most mysterious agent. But Cat's bold ruse cannot protect her from the ecstasy of Nicholas's touch.